To Firoozeh & family

hope you enjoy it.

Faris Nejad

Faris Nejad is a sociologist and a political scientist, who has lived, studied and worked in the birth place of three of the richest civilizations of the ancient world. He was born and raised in Persia (Iran). At an early age his inquisitive mind took him to the foot hills of Mount Everest in India to attend school. This was followed with his residence in Athens where he studied in the filed of social sciences. He lived and worked in both coasts of the United States obtaining a Masters degree in political and social sciences.

His professional career includes working for human rights organizations in Athens, New York, San Francisco and London.

He is a regular contributor to Greek and international media writing on political and social issues as well as creating sketches relating to current events in Greece.

Currently, Faris lives in his small animal and fruit farm opposite Mount Pelion near the quaint port city of Volos in central Greece.

www.FarisNotes.com

The Curse of the Ancient Greeks

Faris Nejad

authorHOUSE®

AuthorHouse™ UK
1663 Liberty Drive
Bloomington, IN 47403 USA
www.authorhouse.co.uk
Phone: 0800.197.4150

Published by AuthorHouse 05/09/2016

ISBN: 978-1-5049-9888-8 (sc)
ISBN: 978-1-5049-9889-5 (hc)
ISBN: 978-1-5049-9887-1 (e)

Print information available on the last page.

I dedicate this work to Greek youth who all deserve
much more than what we have left for them.

Many thanks to the family members of the real characters in the novel who shared with me memories of such intimate and dramatic moments in their lives.

My thanks also go to all the beautiful people who have helped me make this work possible in the last three years. I must also thank scores of friends and associates who assisted me and agreed for me to interview them at a professional level on topics relating to their work.

Chapter 1

IT ALL STARTED at that Easter lunch. Maybe it began even before then, but that is as far back as I can remember. It seemed the whole world was there: a whole chessboard of uncles, aunts, cousins, grandparents, and people to whom I was somehow related. The most lasting image, though, was the scary-looking lamb with a skewer piercing its entire body and skull before emerging out of its mouth. It looked like it had swallowed a spear but was still alive! Above the hot charcoal, it revolved steadily, its eyes staring at me with every turn. The men were arguing over the speed at which it was supposed to turn, a fuss which continued every Easter throughout my childhood.

That year I was trying hard to help. All the girls were assisting their mums with the preparations, but for some reason I was not allowed to help.

'Panayoti, you are a boy. Go and play with the boys,' is what I was told every time I went to my mum. At my last effort she shouted, "If you really want to help, go find your sister and tell her Mummy needs her in the kitchen." That Easter was the day that I became a big boy.

My grandfather asked me to help turn the lamb on the spit. Inviting me into his arms, he pretended that the spit was too heavy for him and that he needed my strength. I was at the far end of the skewer, keeping as much distance from the lamb as possible. I took a wide detour around its length to get to my granddad and positioned myself on his lap in such a way that the lamb's eyes could not inspect me at every turn. As I struggled to turn the L-shaped handle of the skewer on my own, my granddad's strong hands clasped mine, squeezing tightly. The lamb started turning magically! It was turning under my control.

'See how strong you are? I am not doing anything, just holding your hands,' said my granddad in his thick, husky voice. He downed his drink, a full glass, in one swallow.

Was it really just me turning the beast, I asked myself? I did not want to take my eyes off the lamb's skull, but for a few seconds I dared to close them, pretending my granddad's hands were not holding mine. I squeezed the handle tightly in my hands, exaggerating my struggle to turn it, aware that a whole audience had gathered around the fire to admire me. Someone shouted towards the women and girls, who were preparing the table, 'Look, Panos is turning the lamb on his own.' Some women dashed towards the fire, shouting, 'Bravo, bravo, Panos.'

One of my aunts shouted: 'Now all you have to learn is to eat it! Look at you, skin and bones – that is what you are, skin and bones.'

'He will eat, he will eat,' confirmed my granddad, refilling his glass and taking a long sip.

A man joined the crowd. I thought he was coming to praise me. Instead he refilled Granddad's glass, genteelly poked the lamb, licked his finger, and walked away, saying: 'It needs more.'

Sitting at the table, I felt so special. Like a victorious warrior I wore a steady grin, staring at the lamb. Piles of the roast were mounded on my plate. Everyone was looking at me. It was my hunt, and I was feeding them all!

'Now eat, eat,' shouted my grandmother. I contemplated my plate briefly and then picked up the largest piece of meat. Opening my jaws as wide as I could, I took massive bites with all my force. Until that day, I had not liked meat. I am not sure if I liked it on that Easter day either, but I stood on my chair and ate like a hungry wolf, putting barbarism into it just for the show. I had forgotten my fear of the lamb's head and my fear of Granddad telling everyone the truth. Taking just one bite out of each piece, I reached for the main tray containing the biggest chunks. Nodding her head in appreciation, my mother shouted, 'He is hungry! He did the entire job himself. He deserves it all. Eat, my son, eat.' No one stopped me.

That afternoon, it was the beast that had the last laugh. Unexpectedly, I threw up. Whilst my mother and the other women were clearing the plates and the stray dogs were holding their own feast around the table, I sat away from the bones, watching the kids play in the garden, holding in my hands a big, empty bowl, just in case! The sun baked my body, and the afternoon breeze gathered from the sea, hitting me in the face. The smell of the sea was unmistakable, but mixed with it was the sour taste of vomit. Suddenly, I felt a chill. I looked around. Nothing had changed. I could hear the kids playing and laughing in the background, but it was getting darker. I squinted up to see that something had blocked the sun completely – a shape like a man's head. My stomach was turning. I dropped the bowl on the sand, took a short breath, and then screamed at the top of my voice. The shape moved closer, and the bright sun's rays filled the space again.

'Don't worry. Don't be scared. It is Granddad,' a voice said. He hugged me. 'What is wrong?'

I tried to pull myself together, embarrassed to have been scared of the shadow of my granddad. I wiped away my tears and said, 'Sun … sun in my eyes.'

My grandfather gently covered my eyes with his hands and said, 'Now nothing will bother you anymore. I am here.'

I could not see anything, but I could feel the warmth of his hands covering my face. It was a comforting feeling of being protected, cared for, and loved, and the lashing sun was not bothering me anymore.

'Granddad,' I whispered.

'Yes, Panos, I am here,' he replied.

'You saw it. I did the lamb. I turned it, me, on my own, on my own,' I repeated.

He reassured me, 'Yes, yes, little Panayoti, you did it on your own. You are so good. You are strong. Come now. Come with me. I want to show you something.'

I got up without hesitation. He was holding an empty glass in one hand, and with his other hand he grabbed mine and started walking towards the big table. When we reached the table he picked up a big bottle and filled his glass.

'To your health,' he shouted, looking at me. He drank the whole glass in one go and then started pulling me away. One of my cousins, who was helping the women clean up, saw us leaving and ran towards us, shouting, 'Where are you going? Can I come?' Granddad stopped and turned towards her.

'Darling, stay here with your mum. I will be back soon, and then we can play.'

My cousin was not happy. 'But I want to come with you. Where are you going?'

'I am going somewhere with Panos. This is for men, for boys. I will come back and then take you.'

My cousin did not want to be left behind. She flounced back to the table, picked up her cleaning cloth, and threw it on the ground. She sat on a chair, hugging her knees and sulking. I could feel her watching us as we walked away. My aunt shouted at her, 'Get your shoes off the chair! If you don't want to help, at least don't make a bigger mess!'

I did not feel well. I was still sick, scared, and exhausted, but I felt happy that I was the big boy and walking with Granddad. We passed some olive trees near the beach, the kind that I wanted to climb, and headed on towards a gentle slope. We entered an olive grove, passing a couple of derelict stone houses with broken windows. I quickly looked away, not wanting to see any ghosts in the darkness. The slope started getting steeper as the pathway turned away from the sea.

We were moving up a hill and gradually losing sight of the sea. I looked back and saw the ghost houses still looking at us from afar. I turned around. All I could see was trees.

'How far is it, Granddad?' I asked breathlessly. He turned towards me and picked me up without saying anything. The path had ended, and the climb was getting steeper. Granddad kept taking longer steps. We were heading towards the hilltop. He was out of breath too – I could hear it. He walked and walked for a long, long time. Eventually he stopped, put me down, and said, 'We are almost there, but I want you to walk the rest of the way yourself.' I started walking again.

'Do you see all these olive trees, Panos?' he said proudly, pointing his finger all around. 'My father planted them many years ago, when I was small like you. Do you see that village?'

As I turned around he continued, 'That is where my father was born. Come on now, let's walk.'

We continued until we reached a flat area with a gentle slope that seemed to go nowhere. There was no hilltop. It looked like the slope was leading up to the sky. My granddad suddenly put his hand on my chest and stopped me.

'Okay, now I want you to close your eyes' He covered my eyes with his hand and said, 'Keep walking.'

I trusted him and kept inching forward until he stopped me again.

'Okay now, are you okay? Now, give me your hand.' Still covering my eyes, he grabbed my arm with his other hand.

'Now, I want you to see this.' He uncovered my eyes, and the sun blinded me. Tears came to my eyes, and everything was a blur. Gradually I worked out what I was seeing. It was the sky, only the sky in front of us. From the top to the bottom, it was all sky, no end. I got scared.

'Are we in the sky, Granddad?' I asked fearfully.

'No, darling, we are on a cliff. Look down and you can see the sea at the bottom,' he said, holding my arm tightly. I looked down and could see the water at the foot of the cliff. We were really high up. With both hands I reached up to my granddad, begging him to pick me up in his arms.

'Look, Panos, look. You see the sky? Below it is the sea. Can you see?' He picked me up. Pointing his finger towards the horizon, he said, 'There is the sea, and then right up there is where the sky starts.'

'Granddad, Granddad, I only see blue. I don't see where the sea is. I don't see where the sky is.'

Pointing his finger down he said: 'Do you see that big rock? Do you see it, that big rock that looks like a monk? That is where the sea is. A monk is a religious man whose best friend is God.'

'Why did he go into the sea? Why did he turn into stone? Was he not a good monk? Granddad, let's go back to Mum,' I cried.

'Okay, okay, let me just tell you one thing.'

He put me down, knelt on the ground, and spread his arms wide open, as if trying to stop me from running away. He looked intently into my eyes and said: 'Panos, you may not like this now, but when you are grown up you will love this hill. This is where your granddad's dad worked. This is the most beautiful place, the best place, in all of Greece.'

'Can we go back down now?' I asked with tears rolling down my cheeks.

He ignored my pleas and continued: 'I am giving this land to you, all of it. All the trees, the view, the flowers, all of it. There used to be a tower here many years ago. Did you know there were pirates back then, and someone had to be here all the time to watch out for them attacking from the sea?'

I pushed my granddad aside to get a better view of the sea. He held my attention and continued, 'You are from here, and when you grow up you will know how blessed you are for being Greek. Here you can do so much. Here you will bring up your own kids. Here is the centre of the world, chosen by the gods and even pirates.'

'Pirates? Pirates were here?' I asked, interrupting him.

He stood up. I was so close to him that I could not see his face anymore, and then he said more, something about the birthplace of things. I could not understand him anymore. It was something about gods and their love for me, or maybe us – about Greece, using names of some people I didn't know. He told me Greece was where democracy was born. I remember that very well, very well indeed. As a toddler, I grew up thinking that Democracy must have been one of my aunts who had been born on top of that hill and that she was not at the table because the pirates had stolen her. It wasn't until years later that I realized that is not exactly what had happened.

'Did they bury treasure?' I asked excitedly. He looked down at me with a smile.

'Did they hide any treasure? Well, yes, all pirates leave treasures in places like this. Here they left a big treasure, but I don't know where it is. Come on now, we have to go. We will ask your uncle when we see him.'

He led me down the hill, walking quickly, passing the trees. I was happy to be going back to Mum to tell her all about the pirates and was almost running to keep up. But every few steps, I stopped and looked back, feeling as though I had left something behind. I could still see the hilltop, a small pile of rocks visible near the summit. The treasure could be under those rocks, I thought, maybe buried under a tree or in a cave, a hidden cave that no one had seen. My granddad walked on ahead. I looked back one more time and scanned the scenery. Going down the mountain looked different; the colours of the trees kept changing. The leaves glistened in the bright sun. A sea breeze stirred, and the orchard glittered.

'Your mum is waiting for you,' shouted Granddad. I rushed on to catch him up, keen to tell Mum all about it. She had never let me come so far up into the trees. I decided to make a painting for her to show what I had seen. But what colour were the trees? The path seemed much steeper than it had on the way up. Going up had taken a long time, but going down was faster. I held firmly onto Granddad's hand, only letting go as Mum came into view. I ran towards her, tripped, and fell. I didn't cry. She scooped me up, and from the safety of her arms I turned my head back towards the hill. Granddad was still struggling down. Behind him were only trees. I could not see the hilltop, just the silver leaves. 'Where have you been? Do you want something to eat?' she whispered in my ear.

Throughout the years my mother did not change her ways. A while ago the teachers were on strike and I had to drop off my daughter, Elpida.

'Why didn't you tell me before so I could make a nice meal for little Elpida? You know I am planting some trees today. I have workers coming, and I won't have enough time for the poor child,' she complained at the door. My mum loves to have Elpida over so she can feed her, but she doesn't understand that when teachers go on strike they don't announce it in advance.

'This time it was decided at eight forty-five, after I had dropped her off at the school,' I pleaded. 'If one of the granddads at the school had not called me to let me know there was no school, I don't know what would have happened.'

It is probably better that the teachers go on strike unannounced. Otherwise Mum would make a lot of food and then try to make Elpida feel guilty for not eating it all.

'She is just skin and bones! Look at her!' she reminded me, launching into her favourite war story about the lack of food when she was young. I must have heard that story about twice a month since I was eight. I had no time for arguments; I had to rush off to work.

On my way I drove past the school and was amazed to see so many grandparents picking up the kids. In the good years, before the recession, it was big, expensive, off-road four-by-fours that traversed the narrow road to drop the kids off in front of the school gate. It seemed as though the parents lingered in the narrow road for as long as possible to make sure everyone saw their cars. Some had only driven a couple of hundred meters from home to get stuck in the alley. Nowadays, hardly anyone could afford the taxes and the gas for those huge cars, and some had been repossessed by banks. The cheap option now was to use grandparents' feet to walk the kids to school. This option often came with a bonus – a freshly baked cheese pie from Grandma for lunch. People hardly used the nearby sandwich shop to stock up the kids with lunch anymore.

I ended up being late for work. Many of my colleagues had decided to go on strike on that day, and the office was almost empty. I started phoning the local farmers. Success came at the first call – the cotton farmer was home and happy to talk to me. I went back to my car and off to the country! Although the job had been getting me down lately, I cherished leaving the town and heading to the countryside. It felt like my big escape, albeit a temporary one. The other factor that kept me going was the thought that, as opposed to most other people, at least I still had a job.

My thoughts were interrupted by the ringing of my mobile phone. It was the bank. The usual routine questions began. Full name? Tax number? Date of birth? Sometimes I wished I wasn't the one they were calling. Would it help if I said the account owner was dead?

'Sir,' said the voice on the line, 'this call is to inform you that you are well behind with the mortgage payments on your house.'

This was just to inform me? How often do they need to inform me? Every day? Sometimes several times a day? Always another unfamiliar bank clerk was on the line.

'Hello? Hello, sir, are you there?' yelled the voice.

'Yes, I am,' I replied hesitantly. It took a couple of promises of small payments to satisfy the bank clerk.

Were they trying to scare me by proving to me that I was just one and they were so many, that I couldn't hide? I knew that if I didn't make any payments my file would get handed over to more powerful personnel. Could they kick me out of my house? What would happen if they repossessed all the houses that owed money?

Suddenly, I felt a strange pain in my chest, as though I were lying on my back and a heavy person were sitting on me. Then, as quickly as it came, it went away. I had been getting these chest pains more frequently. Could it have anything to do with the air pollution? Ever since they raised taxes on heating oil, most people had changed to firewood to keep warm, resulting in more smoke and pollution. Sometimes I could barely breathe.

'I don't believe it! Damn!' I shouted aloud. I had just passed my exit from the highway to the country road, which I took to avoid paying highway tolls. The toll on this section was really high, €3.20 each way plus €6 for petrol. There went half of my salary for the trip. No wonder the road ahead was so empty.

I was only forty meters past the exit. I made up my mind to go back. I reversed to the exit, aiming for a gap between the oncoming trucks who were also avoiding the toll. After a few attempts I was safely on my way, following narrow country roads through the villages. The trucks were having difficulty negotiating the winding roads and village centres. On several occasions parked cars blocked the route. Progress was slow because of cracks and potholes in the pavement, probably caused by the same heavy trucks, but we were a determined queue. Every narrow road, every hole in the tarmac, and every traffic jam made me more determined. The trip took longer than if I had taken the highway, but it was a satisfying feeling to be able to cheat the system and not pay the extravagant road tolls.

The final obstacle before reaching the farmer's house was a large tractor almost blocking the entire narrow village road. The farmer was standing next to his barn, waiting to greet me.

'Over here, over here!' When I raised my hand to greet him, I felt my chest drop down to my stomach. I tried to ignore it. 'Is your farm here, in the centre of the village?' I asked.

Before he had a chance to answer, my phone rang again. It had better not be from the bank; I'd had enough of them. I answered the phone. 'Hello?'

'Hello, is this Mr –'

I interrupted. 'Are you calling from the bank?'

'No, from the mobile phone company,' he answered.

'I can't talk now. Can you …'

This time the caller interrupted me. 'I am just calling to let you know your service is scheduled to be cut off tomorrow due to non-payment. You can make a payment today at any of our shops.'

'Okay, okay. Thank you, I will,' I said and hung up.

'Where were we? Oh yeah, is this your farm, in the centre of the village?'

'No, only my barn and the house. This is where I keep the tractor, my tools and all the junk, and a room in the attic for when my old lady nags too much!' He laughed.

I looked inside the barn and could see all the junk: some old, rusted tools covered with grease and his tractor, an old, rusty pile of metal with at least two punctured tires.

How about some ouzo?' asked the farmer.

'Ouzo? What are you celebrating?'

'I am always celebrating. You know, like you, I am a Greek. When I am happy I dance, and when I am sad I dance harder. Come on! Come, have something with me,' he replied.

'No, no. I have a long drive back. Let's start …'

He ignored me, turned towards the house, and shouted, 'Woman? Woman, bring some ouzo.'

Before I had a chance to refuse, he asked, 'Did you come on the toll road? Did you pay anything, or did you take the old road?'

'I used the old one. Why pay toll charges when you can come via the country road?'

'Bravo, good for you! You are not stupid.' He grinned and then continued, 'These days there is no money. Nobody has money, just enough to feed the children and the women. If there is anything more, they shouldn't know. You know, it is good you came today. Tomorrow we are blocking all the roads with our tractors. That will show them.'

'Them' supposedly referred to the politicians, but I dared not ask because I didn't know where the conversation would lead. I had to ask a set of questions, take a couple of pictures, and then go back to the office. Taking pictures would be a good way to relax him, a perfect ice-breaking strategy.

'Can I take some pictures of the barn, of you, and of the tractor?'

'Go, go, take any pictures you want. I've got to go find the woman. Where in hell has she gone?' He wandered off, mumbling.

The tractor looked much worse close up. It would make a good picture for my article for the newspaper, a perfect illustration of the state of the economy! A tool of production for the nation now lay abandoned in the corner of a large barn full of junk. Papers were scattered over his makeshift loft-office desk. There were piles of files on the office chairs, and everything was covered with a thick layer of dust.

As I was contemplating whether there would be any use taking some pictures of the office or not, I heard the farmer shout, 'Come on down! Your ouzo is getting cold!' followed by bellowing laughter.

'Do you use this office anymore?' I shouted.

'Use it for what? There are no more grants for any goddamn thing. Come down.'

I made my way down the old, wobbly staircase. 'And the tractor, do you still use it?'

'Yes. How do you think I am going to block the roads tomorrow?' he replied.

'Are you towing it to the highway tomorrow?' I asked.

A small table had been laid out with drinks, feta cheese, and some olives.

'What are you talking about, that tractor?' He asked, pointing at the old tractor. 'I haven't used that for years. My tractor is outside on the road.'

I was confused and a bit disappointed. I was hoping that he was not talking about the huge, spotless, brand-new tractor on the road. A picture of that tractor would be completely inappropriate for my article.

'Go out and take a picture of my big tractor on the road. Show them how everything is wasted when they cut our farm subsidies. I can't even sell it now, maybe just for scrap metal,' he said, handing me a small glass of ouzo.

'Why don't you bring it in and park it here so it stays new?' I asked.

'It doesn't fit. The road is so fucking narrow, and they expect us to work like this.'

He sipped his drink, shaking his head in disappointment, and continued, 'The tractor is too big. I really wanted a smaller one but with more power. You wouldn't believe what I had to go through to get the stupid grant. At the time, they only gave grants for big farms. I missed out on the small farm grants. To get the grant for the big ones I had to show my cousin's farm. His is the next farm. All that for nothing! Now I have the tractor, and I can't afford the petrol to run it. It doesn't fit in my barn, and it is not worth growing anything without subsidies. You can't imagine what some of us farmers go through. Write it, write it in your paper! At least maybe they can give me my money back for the tractor and take it away. They can take the old one too, which was even better. I am sick and tired of this life. You know what to tell them? Tell them …'

I interrupted him. There were parts of his story which I could use for the article, but there was clearly no use asking my formal questions.

'What do you farm now?' I asked in a desperate attempt to find some good material for the article. He put his ouzo down on the table, grabbed my hand, and pulled me outside towards his house, pointing to a small vegetable patch in the front yard.

'In this country now, this is the only thing worth farming: vegetables, for the family.' He walked to a plant, broke off what looked like a cauliflower bud, and forced it into my mouth, waiting for me to chew before continuing.

'Hey? Good? I planted this. It has to be good. You see my house? I am selling everything – the tractor, the house, the garden with the cauliflowers, the lettuces, and the farm, maybe together with my cousin's farm. You see the slope, over there?' he said, pointing his finger towards some fields far away. 'Over there, the silver sparkling olive trees – not the ones across, not the green ones. They belong to a cousin in Canada. I just take care of it for him,' he explained.

'Are they a different variety?' I asked.

'No, same shit,' he replied.

'Why are they a different colour?' I asked, genuinely interested.

'Heah, you town people know nothing,' he said with a grin. 'It's the wind. Have you ever seen an olive leaf? It's green on one side and different on the other side. What is it? Silver? Green? The colour, I don't care – it's a lot of work.'

'Do you pick them and sell the oil for him?' I asked.

'He doesn't want the oil. I have Albanians. I pay them something, and they do it.'

'What, they sell the oil?'

'They pick the olives and put them in sacks for the olive press. What do they know about selling? We use some oil ourselves, eat some of the olives, and give some away. I even give some to the

Albanians. They have to eat too. They have all our jobs, and we have got to feed them on top of it.'

'Did you get any subsidies for the land?' I asked.

'What subsidies? Not worth it. Come here, I want to show you something,' he said, walking towards the house. 'Look. You see this? You see the house? I am selling everything. In all of Greece you won't find this – the view and the air. Why are you smiling? You don't believe me?'

'It's not that,' I explained. 'You mentioned the air, and I have a bit of a pain in my chest. I think it is from the chimney smoke.'

He continued, 'Olive bark is best for firewood. You can burn tons of it, and nothing happens – no smoke, little smoke, you know? Look, come here next to me. You see the olive trees? Follow that line and come down. You see the pole? You see the grape vine and then the electric meter? Turn around and look at the barn. Forty years of work thrown away. I am selling it all – everything except the wife!'

He roared with laughter, almost choked, coughed, and then became serious, looking me in the eyes. 'Not the wife. She wouldn't know what to do without me.' For a moment he stayed silent. Then he roared with laughter again.

'What if they reintroduce the subsidies? Will you farm again?' I was hoping to hear something positive – some determination, some interest, some loyalty.

'They ate up all the money, the politicians and their mafia gangs. There is no more money. Even if there is, they pay it per ton of cotton, not by the size of the land. What if it doesn't rain one year and we have no cotton? Who pays for that? No, no sir, I'd have to be out of my fucking mind to farm again.' There was anger in his eyes.

'So, why are you blocking the roads tomorrow?' I asked.

'So they know I won't farm again, so they know they will starve now. All our money went to their banks in Germany and that other place, what is it? Switzerland? They stole it. Let them use it and feed themselves now. I am happy with my tomatoes.'

The little sense that I could make of him at the beginning was gradually disappearing as I was forced to sip more and more ouzo.

The time had come for me to leave. I was not used to afternoon drinks, and my feet had started feeling heavy. It was a struggle to leave, but I finally managed. On the way out I was even more careful not to scratch his five-star tractor. He would probably want it to stand out amongst tens of other tractors the next morning when he was going to demonstrate. I successfully manoeuvred around the tractor. Then I stopped, got out of my car, and came face-to-face with the giant tractor, its great tires each almost as big as my car. I took a picture. I knew I wasn't going to use it in the paper; neither was I going to advertise for him to sell it. Why did I take the picture? Maybe I was drunk; I usually get very philosophical after a bit of alcohol. The tractor symbolized something for me: something about our new world, something about our joys and fears, something about our past and our future, something about the economy and politics, something about that village. It symbolized something about Greece! An expensive tool made to produce had been hibernating for so long and was now coming back into use, not for production but to block roads, to look vicious and stop the flow of any movement. It was a flower bud, too big for its own jar even before blossoming, and now its roots were cracking the jar to drain out the little hope of moisture. It was a plant gone wild! A flower bud with the promise of beauty had been cheating us all out of our hopes and dreams and was now preparing to gift us with its ugliest hidden talent: obstruction – obstruction to movement, obstruction to reaching out, obstruction to our freedom, obstruction to making sense of what was happening around us.

Standing in the middle of the narrow road facing the stubbornly motionless tractor, I heard a voice from my high school years. It's only a plant, Panos, a freaking tree. If you work it you get olives. If you don't you get a pair of testicles. Back then I was staring at an ancient olive tree next to a motorway. That plant had not gone wild. It was the most patient of plants, with so much character and confidence that it could melt an iron bar. We were on a high school excursion near Athens. The voice was the voice of Stavros, my eccentric classmate. We had been on a visit to a museum with artefacts from ancient Greece and to see the ancient tree. Stavros was fine at the museum – maybe he made a couple of stupid comments – but when we reached the tree he started acting silly. I stood under the ancient olive tree's shade, thinking and visualizing the glory of Greece in ancient times. Plato had sat under that tree all those years ago. Here was the cradle of Western civilization – logic, philosophy, democracy – and there was Stavros talking about testicles. When he saw that he had offended me, the bastard liked it even more and went on and on. Ever since that day, he had made fun of me and nicknamed me 'Platoli', little Plato.

Lost in thought, I had lost track of time. I had to rush back to my mum's before she turned Elpida into a balloon. Contrary to what Mum always said, Elpida was actually somewhat overweight. I contemplated driving down the national road but changed my mind at the last minute. The country road was jammed with large cargo trucks, with cars trying to overtake at every opportunity. I made two attempts to pass a articulated tow truck without success. Little did I know that I would have to spend a full hour behind that same truck. An accident had happened further along the road, at approximately the same spot where, two nights previously, another accident had claimed the lives of four people. The spot was much more dangerous at night because half the lights were turned off to save electricity. After that deadly accident my colleague at the newspaper got a letter from a reader saying that turning off every other light was too dangerous; as soon as your eyes get used to the light, there is darkness, and then your eyes have to readjust when the next random light is on. The reader said it would be better if they turned off all the lights. The letter was never published.

When we did get through, seeing the car wreckage made me nervous and extra cautious for the remainder of the journey. Maybe if it weren't for the heavy road tolls, the accident would not have happened.

As I was nearing my mum's home, once again I became stuck behind a large truck. The smell of hot tarmac rose from its cargo. As we approached the traffic lights it came to an abrupt stop. Luckily, my cautious driving paid off, and I came to a smooth stop right behind it, avoiding some hot tar that had spilled onto the road. I manoeuvred my car around the hot tarmac, noting that all the cars behind me were doing the same. I was safely out.

The scene of accident was still fresh in my mind. What could we do? Complain and complain? Ask for better roads? Ask for more traffic lights and for better policing? Who wanted that? Everything got done after an accident – the police came to fix the road or put in an extra traffic light. It was their job. An idea suddenly came to mind. I would call the police myself and try to prevent an accident! I reached for my mobile phone and called the police. A very attentive but calm man answered the phone and told me that I had called the wrong number. He gave me the phone number of the municipal police. I called the number immediately, and after a few rings an old lady answered.

'Hello, emergency,' she said.

I explained, 'I am calling to report the spill of some hot tar at a traffic light.' There was silence.

'It is a dangerous spot. Somebody may have an accident on a motorbike or something … it is slippery,' I continued:

'Has there been an accident?'

'No,' I answered.

'You have to call the police,' she said.

'I called the police, and they gave me your number. Aren't you the municipal police?' I asked.

'Is there a lot?'

'A lot of what?' I asked.

She seemed a bit annoyed and asked again. 'A lot of tar?'

'No, not really, but …' I was interrupted.

'Who are you?' she asked.

'I am just a driver. I was …'

I was interrupted again. 'The driver of the truck?'

'No.'

'Look, have you called before?' she asked.

'No.'

'You should have called this morning,' she said politely. 'We are closing. There is no one here now. Could you call tomorrow?'

'Yes, yes, I will call first thing in the morning,' I said as I hung up. Maybe if I told her I was a newspaper columnist I would get a better result. Never mind; at least I had done my bit. I was feeling exhausted.

I was just in time to pick up my daughter. As I pulled into my mum's alley, my heart dropped. I saw a police car in front of her house. What had happened? Were they okay? Trying to be calm, I slowly parked my car behind the police car and then rushed in. The police were talking to my mum in the garden just outside her entrance door. Beside them was my daughter, holding something that looked like a pie. She was okay. The policeman's gun was hanging in its holster exactly at the height of Elpida's head. Elpida was staring at the gun with fascination.

'What is going on? What happened?' I asked frantically.

'Nothing. One of our wonderful neighbours has reported us to the police over the trees,' said my mum sarcastically.

'Are you her son?' asked the policeman.

'Yes, I am. What is wrong with planting trees?' I asked, surprised.

'It is not the trees. Your mum is making big holes in her garden. How do I know it is for trees? It could be for a swimming pool. These things happen when you have bad neighbours.'

'So why are you here?' I asked.

The policeman seemed annoyed with the whole ordeal.

'We have to check when we get a complaint from the neighbourhood. You must have done something wrong to upset them because ...'

My mum interrupted the policeman. 'It wasn't us. It was another neighbour They were playing loud music at two in the morning.'

'Okay, okay, lady. I am not here for that call. I am here for these holes for the trees,' said the policeman coldly. 'I must go now, but I may come back if there are any other calls. If you are only planting trees you are okay.'

Elpida suddenly jumped out in front of the policeman. 'Can I see your gun?'

The policeman gently pulled out his gun. 'I can get it out and show it to you, but you can't touch it.' More and more people were appearing on their balconies to see what was going on. Unexpectedly, with her fingertip, Elpida touched the gun.

The policeman laughed loudly. As he put the gun back in its case, he told Elpida, 'Normally I should arrest you for that, but if you finish your pie, I will let you off this time.' He got into his car and left.

'That was cool!' said Elpida with a mouth full of pie. My heart had still not settled down. Maybe it was seeing the police car or maybe it was the accident, but something was wrong. I wasn't breathing properly. My mum had gone inside. She looked very upset – pale and trembling, sitting on her couch.

'Can you light my fire?' she asked.

I spent the next half hour trying to ignite her wet, freshly cut wood. I didn't dare complain. The last time I did she shouted, 'I can't afford heating oil! Next time you buy the wood since you are such a know-it-all!'

Before I could say anything she said: 'The wood is there, and I don't want to hear about it.'

'What have I done wrong, Mum? Why are you upset with me?' I asked.

'You are the one who defends all these idiots – the police, the politicians, the system. I bet you wouldn't write about this in your paper! Look what they did to Maria! The poor woman was kicked out of her job. If she had an ounce of brain she would have kept her mouth shut and would still have a job."

'But my mum has brain,' shouted Elpida.

'What does Maria's job have to do with police coming to you about your trees?' I asked.

'It is all the same shit, the same shitty system,' she replied.

I had never heard my mum talk like that, especially in front of the kids. Noting her frustration I decided to defuse the situation, but

I could not find any words. A few sparks in the fireplace turned to full-grown flames.

'The fire ... the fire is finally lit. Let's go, Elpida, let's go.'

I said good-bye to my mum and left.

Chapter 2

MARIA WAS ALREADY home, and it was not long before she managed to take away all the relief I had felt by leaving my nagging mum behind just a few minutes earlier. I had come from one frustrated woman to another one. It was just like that morning and just like what I was going to face the next day: frustrated people! From the frustrated farmer to the frustrated taxi driver and the frustrated factory worker, the list went on. It even included my boss, who had been unhappy with my work lately.

Somehow whatever I did these days wasn't good enough for him. I was supposed to illustrate the people's frustration with the crisis and reflect their pain in a constructive way. But how could I put logic into what happened with the farmer today? How could I justify his demand for more grants and subsidies in an unbiased way? How could I write an article in favour of the farmer? After all, he was the one with the fancy tractor, and he was the one who was going to block my road tomorrow. He was the one …

'I am talking to you! Have you gone deaf?' shouted Maria.

I gathered myself and said: 'Hello, how was your day? How are you?'

'I just told you how my day was!' she replied. 'Didn't you hear? Where did you go? Elpida, come here. Let mummy see you. What happened at school?'

'No school, Mum. I went to Grandma again,' answered Elpida.

'What is wrong with these teachers? Another strike? At least they are getting paid, and they have a job. They work eight to nine months per year, get paid for fourteen months, and are still complaining,' said Maria.

'It is good, Mum!' said Elpida with a smile. 'I don't like school. I like strikes!'

'They don't get paid for fourteen months anymore,' I tried to explain. 'That was before. It has all been cut now. There are no more bonuses.'

'It went on for too long, and they didn't even do the job right. All the money we had to spend on Costa's private night school just to get him to university! That's why they do it, so they get extra jobs.'

'That's illegal! They can't work for the system and then work privately,' I explained.

Elpida tugged on Maria's skirt, trying to get her attention. 'I touched a policeman's gun, Mum.'

'It is not the teachers who are at fault. It is the system,' I stressed.

'Who is the system, Panos?' she replied. 'Tell me. Who is the system? Is it them? Is it you? Is it me? You can't hide behind the system anymore. You made it.'

'Me, I made the system? If I made …'

Elpida, shouting, excitedly interrupted me. 'I got a policeman's gun, and I shot the policeman, Mum. I shot him.'

'Okay, okay, Elpida. We are talking now. Wait a minute,' said Maria, turning her attention back to me. 'Even if you have not made the system, it is your responsibility to check it once in a while. Everything is not like this bulky clock taking up all the room in the house, looking old and sophisticated.'

'The clock?' I asked with surprise. 'What does the clock have to do with anything?'

'The clock doesn't need checking every day, and if it works with electricity, like this beast, you don't need to wind it up or replace the batteries,' she explained.

'What does a gift from my granddad have to do with our lives?' I asked desperately.

'It has been made to take care of itself, like everything else in your life and like everything else in this country,' she answered.

'So what is wrong with that?' I asked.

'It would be good if it all worked,' she answered.

'It does! Look, it is working,' I stressed.

She looked at me with disgust. 'I am not talking about the clock.'

I glared back. 'What are we talking about here?'

Elpida rumbled on. 'Dad saw me. He was there. Police came to Grandma. She was going to be arrested. The neighbours called the police. She was doing something bad. The policeman gave me his gun. Dad was there. He was doing nothing. Grandma shouted at Dad afterwards.'

'What happened?' asked Maria.

'We left Grandma with all the bad neighbours as soon as the fire was lit,' explained Elpida. She turned to me. 'Dad, will the policeman go back to Grandma?'

'Is your mum building something illegal again?' asked Maria.

'No,' I explained. 'She is planting some trees, so she dug some holes to plant them in. You know the neighbours; they're like hungry vultures with nothing better to do. They sit on their balconies and stick their noses into everyone's business.'

Maria replied sarcastically, 'Oh yeah? I thought it was the foreigners, but now it is the neighbours. Yesterday it was the teachers, tomorrow it is the butchers, and then it is the turn of the politicians. Make up your mind, Panos. We are running out of options. Was it ever your cousin's fault?'

'Leave my cousin out of this!' I protested.

'Why should I leave your cousin out?' she continued.

'My cousin is dead. He did what he did because that was necessary back then. I don't say anything about your dad retiring from the public sector at the age of forty-nine, so why should you criticise my cousin for being a unionist? Who was going to defend the rights of the factory workers?'

'There are no factories left in Greece to have any workers, so whose rights are you defending now?' said Maria, her voice raised.

I jabbed at the air with my index finger and shouted back, 'That is why the unionists are fighting in a different way for the country.'

'The unionists are doing the same thing they did fifty years ago,' said Maria, 'fighting for themselves, and asking for more and more. Who said anything about Greece? Go ask your unionist old classmate and see what is going on!'

I looked at her with a bit of surprise and asked, 'What do you know about politics? Since when are you interested?'

'Since I stopped reading your articles!' She grinned, paused, and then continued, 'If you write one about your unionist old classmate I will read it. It would be interesting to see how much bullshit you can write to please the readers!'

'I am an independent journalist. I don't take sides, but I happen to like the guy. He always stood up for other people's rights. He was the most selfless person I have met, and today he is still the same. He is now the defender of the working class.'

'Write that in your article. Your boss will like it. Also write something blaming the Germans and the French. Maybe it was one of your mum's Albanian neighbours who called the police? Write about them. Let's boycott them from tomorrow and not let their kids go to school. Wait a minute … the schools are on strike anyway, so no need to bother.'

I just hated it when she got sarcastic like this. There was no reasoning with her. She became worse after she was made redundant from the town hall. I was saved by a plastic gun pointing at me. I quickly grabbed the gun and pulled Elpida towards myself.

'Hey, you should ask if you want to touch my gun,' corrected Elpida.

'May I touch your gun, please, officer?' I asked her.

'No,' she replied. 'I am going to arrest your mother for the trees.'

The phone rang. It was my son Costa saying that he could not come home that night because the buses were on strike and he had no taxi money. He would sleep over at a friend's house. Maria and I did not talk for the rest of the night. She really needs to get a job. That was the only thing that would calm her down. She had become too anti-establishment, and I couldn't open my mouth and talk about anything without her jumping down my throat. I needed another drink and investigated what was left in the drinks cabinet. In the first years of our marriage I would sit down on the couch and she would bring me a drink. That was when she had a job. Tonight I would have to get my own. There was no wine and no beer! There were eight bottles left in the cabinet we called the bar. Five bottles were gifts from our aunts or people like that – sweet, disgusting liqueurs from unripe walnuts and sour cherries and homemade concoctions loaded with sugar. The remaining three consisted of an empty bottle of cheap whiskey from a discount store, a full bottle of something unspecified that I had tried before but didn't like, and a bottle of some kind of raki. We must have got it from an island trip sometime back in the good old days when we could afford to go to an island. This bottle had sat in the cabinet as a souvenir for years! We always used to keep something better around to drink in emergencies like tonight. The label had almost completely faded away, like the memory of the trip. It was open but almost full. I decided to have another go at it, just in case it surprised me and tasted better than I remembered. At first it burnt my tongue. Then there was a sugar attack, and my tongue stuck to the roof of my mouth. Was it getting better? No. My tongue still raged. Acquiring a taste comes with practice, and on this occasion, for the benefit of the evening, I tried to push myself a bit harder. It worked! There was nothing like an old good recession to clean out the cupboards. The aunts would all be proud of me.

I hadn't even finished my first drink before I thought of calling Costa again. I knew he was with a friend, but I had this sudden urge to call him and tell him about the farmer. Costa had always wanted to be a farmer, but – and this is an important fact I can't skip – since Maria's grandfather was a famous successful medical doctor, we had agreed that Costa should take the same steps his great-grandfather had taken. If we had saved all the money we spent on his private night classes to get him into the medical college for all these years, we could have opened up his own business.

I can't complain, really. Almost everyone I know has sent their kids to private night classes in order for them to catch up. Ironically, even if we had saved up the money and opened up a business for him, with the recession, his business would be closing now. I took another sip of the dreadful raki and then picked up the phone.

'Hi, Dad, what's happening?' said Costa as he answered the phone.

'Nothing, nothing, I was just ...'

He interrupted me. 'You know I am at a friend's. How come you are calling?' he asked.

I was struggling to find a reason for my call. I wasn't worried about him, and I couldn't exactly tell him that I called because I had met a farmer like he wanted to become. Telling him that I had a bit to drink and I thought of him was also out of the question.

'Dad, what's up? I've got to go,' he said hurriedly.

Stumbling on my words, I pushed to find something that I needed his help in. It had to be something real, some practical matter that he knew better than me.

'Dad, Dad,' he shouted.

'I, I am ... I am looking for an old friend, an old classmate. I was wondering if you could tell me what to do.'

'Your friend is not here, Dad,' he said sarcastically, followed by laughter from someone near his phone.

'I was thinking – was wondering if you could find him on the computer, on the Internet,' I explained.

'Just go on the Internet and Google his name. You remember his name, right? Just Google it. He might be on Facebook. You aren't, are you?' he asked.

I was not. Did I need to be to find him? I didn't really want to ask that question. I didn't know what response it would bring. Instead of answering him I just said: 'Never mind, fine, I will find him. Take care. See you tomorrow, okay?'

'I don't know, Dad. Maybe.'

After saying good-bye I went to Google and typed 'Stavros Papadopoulos'. Hundreds of pages came up. I found lawyers, accountants, and even football club owners. None of them seemed to be the Stavros that I knew. That night I gave up searching and even contemplated why I was searching to find him. As a kid, I didn't even like him very much. He was so odd and always challenged any stance I had. He made fun of me for supporting my football club and in history classes. He even made fun of me for holding the national flag at the school's Greek independence march. His voice still rang in my ear from the day that our history teacher told us about the accident with Plato's tree. A bus had run over the tree and had cut it in half. When he saw most of the class upset over the damage to the tree, still sitting on his chair and hiding behind a classmate, he said loudly: 'Let's choose another tree, can't we?'

I don't remember what the teacher said to him exactly, but it really shut him up. It was something like, 'We can't just choose what we want to believe in. We can't change our parents. We can't choose a new Parthenon, a new history, a new nation.' After that Stavros mumbled something from his seat, and then some kids started giggling. Unfortunately, that wasn't the end of his sly, cynical comments; he went on for years to come. These comments had washed away with time and had disappeared from my memory decades ago, but for some reason they had recently come back to me. Having lost hope of finding Stavros, I started looking around different sites on the Internet for a few minutes. Then, completely exhausted from the day, I walked to our bedroom. Maria was already in bed under the covers with her back towards my side. She hadn't even said good night. The distance, the coldness, was completely obvious. Things were really getting to her. I turned back out, quietly closed the door, and went to sleep on the couch.

'Potatoes' and 'police' both start with 'P', but in my country today, they have a much deeper connection than just that. This is what I learned on my way to work the following day. The streets were filled with armed policemen. I was not aware of any political rallies scheduled that day. Perhaps it was about an unannounced visit by a hated politician? Which one, though? They were all hated! I attempted to roll down my window and ask an officer but was quickly moved on. Curiosity does not just kill cats. I stopped next to a policeman and got out of the car, but before I had a chance he shouted: 'Get in your car, get in and move.'

'I am a journalist. I want to know what's happening,' I said with little hope of getting any straight answers.

'Potatoes! They are giving away potatoes at the central square,' said the policeman, pointing me to the car. That didn't really answer my question about the presence of police, but I was not going to try my luck again and ask too many questions. I got in the car. As I started driving, a sudden chill took over my entire body. My eyes stared forward in a straight line, as if I were looking not at the road but deep into the horizon. I was seeing images of drought-stricken African countries where food relief had to always be accompanied by crowd control forces. It couldn't have been! I had to see it for myself. I abandoned my car on the pavement of a side street and decided to walk to the centre to see it with my own eyes. As I got closer to the central square, I noticed a stronger presence of the police with heavier weapons. A thick smoke was rising up the square. The smoke was stronger near the ground, but it seemed to dissolve into the thick, already smoky air above the city. A police car suddenly rushed from an alleyway, and an elderly woman tripped over some rubbish next to a taxi with dark tinted glass. The driver got out to help her. As she regained her balance she asked the driver, 'What is going on? What is all the fuss about?'

As soon as the taxi driver realised the old woman was all right he started laughing and answered, 'They are giving out free potatoes to the Greeks, only Greeks.'

'What is burning? Are they cooking them too?' asked the old lady.

The driver answered quickly: 'If you are Greek you might even get some cheese filling as well.'

The old woman ignored the taxi driver and headed towards the square. The taxi driver, still smiling, turned to me and said: 'You see? We Greeks are so rich that even our poverty is comical.'

I smiled back and continued walking. Cops surrounded the square, but at the centre I could see perhaps only about fifteen to twenty people queuing up –a major anti-climax! There was, however, at least a demonstration. On the other side of the square there were about five hundred people chanting slogans.

'Nazis out of parliament, down with fascism.'

There was some rubbish being thrown around, including empty bottles and cans, and something that looked like an old mattress was set on fire. As I got closer to the potato queue I finally recognized the flags of the new far-right-wing party. Before I knew it I found myself at the end of the queue, ushered by a young man in complete black. There were a lot of them, maybe about twenty people all in black organizing the charitable event. Another young man turned towards me and said, 'Get your identification ready. You need a Greek identity card for the potatoes.'

'I, I ... didn't want potatoes. Just looking. Well done, this is good!' I said with a broken voice. Then the young man came closer to me and handed me a leaflet. I started walking opposite to the demonstration into another narrow alley. The leaflet had the names of the party's newly elected members to the parliament. This was the very first time the party had made such an achievement. At the bottom it said, 'No foreigners, charity for Greeks only.'

At first I thought, why not? Everyone can do something to help. All political parties donate strategically to gain support. But as I was walking back towards the car and looking at the cops, I thought, this must be the only country in the world where you need police protection to donate potatoes. How much per kilo were these potatoes costing the Greek public to be distributed? Was it really worth it? Was this help or just a political statement? My anti-climax at the square turned into a dramatic shock when I turned over the leaflet to read that the German neo-Nazi party had been invited for a visit to Greece by their Greek counterpart. I felt a cold sweat on the back of my neck and started walking faster, taking longer steps. I squeezed the leaflet in the palm of my hand as hard as I could and started rushing towards a bin. I not only did not want to be seen with the leaflet but also didn't want anyone else to be able to read these words. Nazis invited to Greece! It was this ideology, the same thoughts, that some half a century ago had occupied my country and had slaughtered my people. Now we were inviting the offspring of the same ideology to our country?

I was determined to destroy the pamphlet ceremoniously. The big green dirty bin in front of me was too honourable a place to dispose of the leaflet. I looked back towards the square, my breath still heavy and panting. I could still see the rising smoke. Targeting the smoke column, I took slower but steadier steps. My lips moved, trying to catch up with my mind: 'I am Greek. I am proud; I won't let our enemies back in. I won't be bribed by a sack of potatoes even if I am starving. If I see a hungry mouth I will feed it, regardless of its nationality.'

My mind was focusing on one word, a Greek word: 'philoexenia'. Armed with so much passion, I marched towards the fascists, bearing in mind that I was parked illegally and could get a ticket that I could not afford to pay. I was also late for work, so this had to be quick. We Greeks had invented democracy. There was no room for the fascists in here in the parliament, even if they got enough votes! At first I thought of getting some potatoes and giving them out to the foreigners who had no Greek ID. Besides the fact that I had left my ID in the car, there were also no foreigners around. So I just walked to the fascists, pretending that I was going to join the potato queue at first, and then walked past, ignoring them completely. Their leaflet was still in my hand, tightly squeezed. I changed direction and walked straight to the demonstrators. The whole square was watching me, I thought. I was welcomed by the demonstrators. As I got closer to the demonstrators their chanting got louder and louder. It felt good at the time, but thinking about it now, I realize the louder noise was only because I was getting closer to them and not for me! I walked up to the source of the smoke and with both hands threw the fascists' leaflet in the centre of the burning mattress. Then I looked around to see the people who were watching me. Everyone seemed to be busy with their own thing, throwing rubbish, shouting, and screaming. I walked up to the shouting and noisy crowd. A strange feeling of belonging overtook me, a feeling that I had not felt before except at national football matches. Here was a crowd with something in common, something so fundamental: We all rejected what we were seeing. It was good, really good. It was so easy and natural to join in rejection.

'We boycott them, we stop them,' shouted the crowed. I hadn't felt completely at ease yet, but I already liked them. Then came my membership's first bonus: A new leaflet, brightly coloured. 'No to fascism, no to capitalism. Boycott all foreign products. Boycott all foreign markets. Don't buy German.' For a moment it felt like half a century ago. It felt as if we were still under German occupation. This was a Greek recession, and leaflets from both sides of the square were about Germans, one about German neo-Nazis and the other one about German supermarkets. I folded the leaflet and put it in my pocket. I started chanting anti-fascist slogans again. As a journalist I hardly ever got involved in demonstrations, but this was different. I shouted and shouted until my throat hurt and my voice started changing. I was still not satisfied! It wasn't enough. I felt helpless against my own anger. I had to do something, something more than this. Going back to plan A, I finally decided to get a sack of potatoes to give it to a foreigner, someone without a Greek ID. I double-checked my wallet. I had no ID card. Was I going all the way back to the car to get it? The answer was a clear yes! That was the least I could do for my beliefs, for my people, for my nation. I zigzagged my way through the demonstrators, the crowds, the police, and the uncollected rubbish. What had we done to this beautiful, precious land? We had inherited so much wealth, and now there was rubbish on our ground and so much rubbish in our heads.

Just before getting to the car, I saw the taxi driver again; he looked at me with a smirk and said, 'Have they run out of potatoes?' I just walked past him without answering. But if it wasn't the Germans, whose fault was it? As a journalist, if I didn't know it, who did? All these mouths were talking! Who had the answer? Who could tell me, in simple words, who was at fault? I needed someone who spoke my language, in easy terms, with words that everyone could understand. As I got close to the car, I saw from afar that my nightmare had come true. There were two tickets on my car, one on each side of the windshield.

I rushed over, disappointed and defused. How could it be? They wouldn't give me two tickets. When I finally got to the front of the car I was relieved to find that they were not tickets. They were both leaflets. 'Believe in us, vote for us', said the first leaflet, from a newly energized old political party. The second one was from a newly opened shop and said: 'We buy gold for cash.'

Greece had regressed from the priceless age of the dialogue of Socrates and Plato to the age of the leaflets. My nation had become the great producer of cheap leaflets, all printed on imported paper from China. Our youth, instead of being the flag holders of a patriotic and proud nation on the world stage, were busy competing with each other to find windshield space on parked cars before they would be repossessed by banks. My nation was bleeding, and even our own blood was betraying us, attracting more and more money-hungry and power-hungry sharks from every corner of our chaotic ocean. The sharks gathered to take advantage of our fears and our weakness at a feast in which we ourselves were both the guests of honour and the main course! I felt good when I finally produced my Greek ID card to get the potatoes. It was especially good that it wasn't on me in the first place; I had to go and get it from the car. I didn't just have it; I had worked for it. I used my identity card to take revenge, to turn their plan against them, to show them that I was the one who was Greek. I had a heart; I was brought up with love. I was more Greek than all of them. No matter how many Greek flags they were holding, the real Greece was me! But I still did not know what screwed up my nation. How I wanted someone or something to appear and show me just what had gone wrong with my people and with my nation. No one could imagine my secret plan when they looked at me struggling through the crowd with a big sack of potatoes. And as for the lefties, for them I had another plan. If there was any change in the car, I was going to go to a German supermarket to buy another sack of potatoes to give away. If I could, I would find German tourists and give it to them. But first I had to get to the car before I got a ticket, a real one. I didn't want to be seen with the sack on my shoulder, and hardly anyone noticed me sneaking away except an overfed German shepherd dog! This must have been the most German day of my life! I was being followed by a large German shepherd dragging his loose chain. Balancing the sack on my shoulder, I expected some resistance when I reached for his leash, but the dog was as calm as a pussycat.

That's it, I thought, that's it. Here is my last sign telling me who is at fault. Why didn't a Tibetan Spaniel show up? It must be the Germans. The dog probably got away from his home. Maybe he was lost or abandoned. We have always had stray dog problems in the cities. Recently, however, the problem is getting worse; many dogs or cats are abandoned on the road because people basically have other financial priorities. This dog wasn't abandoned, though. The long chain was a clear indication that it had got away from a home. Maybe it got scared and ran away from all the noise. There were several stray dogs around sniffing about. With the potato sack on my head, I pulled the dog to myself, holding tight to the chain, and went straight to the car. As soon as I opened the car, the dog went to the passenger seat and sat down. I was sure someone, somewhere, was desperately looking for the dog; it must have been loved. As I drove off a bunch of stray dogs chased the car, barking and trying to bite the tires. I finally got away. I was already late for work. What was I going to do with the dog? How could I find the owner? Short of advertising for it in our paper, I had no other option, but that would take too long. I had to find a place for the dog immediately. As I stopped at the traffic light, the dog started barking. I looked around; maybe the owner was in sight. But who? There were many people on the sidewalk. Next to us on the corner was a typical street kiosk. I had a brilliant idea: I could ask the kiosk owner if he knew the dog. These people know everything about the neighbourhoods in which they operated. I pulled halfway up the pedestrian road and put my hazard lights on, but my quest was in vain.

The kiosk owner raised his eyebrows and shoulders simultaneously and said, 'How should I know who the owner is? The street is full of dogs.'

'Yes, but this dog is owned by someone, someone from this area,' I explained.

'What do you want?' said the kiosk owner.

As I went to answer I heard a voice from behind me: 'Three packs of Marlboro Lights.'

I turned around and saw a man with a lit cigarette in his mouth. He was close enough to have burnt the back of my neck if I hadn't turned around in time. I didn't waste time and asked, 'Sorry, are you local? Do you know the owner of this dog?'

'No' said the man with some ash falling on his shirt. 'Why don't you call the town hall?'

'How would they know?' I asked.

After paying for his cigarettes and opening one of the new packs he said, 'I think they have a program, something European. Give them a call. I called and complained so much, they came and picked up a few of them.'

Not believing a word of the guy's consultation, I asked the kiosk owner if I could leave my phone number just in case the owner showed up. He reluctantly took the piece of paper with my phone number on it and threw it in a small box next to him. As I got back in the car I had to push the dog away from my seat back to the passenger seat. Time was running out with my job at stake. Maybe I should try calling the town hall, I thought. But how could there be a program without any advertising for it? If I, as a reporter, did not know about a program for stray or lost dogs, what would be the use of such a program? Hoping to be wrong about my assumptions and having been left without a choice, I finally called the town hall. It wasn't before a series of calls that I finally became aware of the pleasant truth. Indeed, there was a shelter. On my way towards the dog rescue home out of town, I had a sweet and pleasant feeling. The distance did not bother me; I had almost forgotten about being late for my job. I felt proud; I felt good about having been wrong in assuming that there were no serious establishments to rescue abandoned and lost animals in Greece. All the articles I had written about the negative effect of the stray animals on tourism had finally been answered.

As if all the problems that my country was facing today had to do with stray dogs, I pressed the gas pedal impatiently, waiting to see the rescue home with my own eyes. It did not matter to me anymore that the program had not been advertised. It did not matter to me whether the funding had come from Europe or elsewhere. The fact was that there was an organized effort to deal with the problem.

Out in the distance, near an abandoned quarry, I finally noticed a building. As I got closer I saw several packs of dogs surrounding the building. Many of them seemed to have a collar, but some did not. I was by the main gate when the dogs almost blocked my way in. The entrance door was shut.

Is this where they keep the dogs, out around the building? I asked myself. As I rang the doorbell, I heard tens of dogs barking from inside the building. A young man finally opened the door. He was talking, but I could not hear him because at this stage all the dogs were barking. I pointed to the dog in the car. He went towards the car, still saying something. What was going to be the fate of the dog? Would it be left outside, or was he one of the lucky ones going in? What was inside? As soon as I saw the man pulling the dog in, I stopped wondering about the details.

'Did you find him'? he shouted.

'Yes, I am sure the owner will come for it,' I answered.

'It is a German shepherd, pure breed, right?'

'I think so. If the owner doesn't show up, what happens?'

'Don't worry, he will. It is an expensive dog'

'Can I leave my number in case no one shows up'?

'Your number? What for? Oh, okay, come on in. Actually, don't bother. It's fine. I am sure the owner will come.'

Then he shut the door. I had done my job. I had found a safe place for the dog, and now it was time to go to my real job. Walking to my car, I was escorted by tens of loose dogs around the building, some trying to get into my car. I wondered what the establishment was doing about these dogs. Burning with multiple questions, I went back to the building with half of the dogs following me. I rang the doorbell, which ignited loud barking from all the dogs inside. I could hear iron bars, possibly from their cages shaking. The door opened, and the young man looked at me with a surprise.

'What is up?' he asked.

'Oh, I was just wondering, what will happen to these dogs? Why are they outside?'

'Oh, they are street dogs.'

'Street dogs?'

'Yes, we keep the good dogs inside so they don't get lost.'

'They get lost?'

'Yes, and sometimes stolen. Everyone needs a guard dog now.'

'They get stolen?'

'Sometimes.'

'How long have you been here?'

'Over a year now, why'?

'I had never heard of you.'

'Well, you've heard now. Next time call me before you come.'

'But, why don't you advertise?'

'Advertise? What for? We are not a business.'

'So people know.'

'We don't have a budget for advertising. If there is any money left from our spaying funds, we use it for other expenses. We have enough problems without everyone knowing we are here, can't you see?'

'Yes, I can. Do you also spay dogs?'

'Whenever there is a budget for it, but it is only for street dogs, not yours. Why? Do you have a dog to spay? I can arrange it. It will cost a bit, but not as much as going private.'

'No, I was just wondering. So you only spay dogs if you have a budget? Some kind of a quota?'

'Do you want your dog back?'

'No, why would I want the dog back?'

'I am new here. I don't know. All these things you ask – do I come to your house and ask you how many eggs you eat every week? I am not responsible for your dog. If you want it, take it.'

'It is not my dog.'

'So where is the problem?'

'Nothing, nothing. I just wanted to say, well, good luck with the dog.' I smiled. he forced himself to a cold smile and then shut the door.

Chapter 3

MY BOSS WAS sitting at my desk when I arrived. I started apologising for being late when he interrupted me.

'I know, I know. There were demonstrations in town. What have you done with the farmer? Do you have an article?'

'I will have it in a couple of hours,' I replied. 'I have the full interview.'

'Make sure you show how bad things are for them – victimise them, you understand? A lot of farmers read our paper and buy a lot of advertising,' he explained. 'We need to show how they are suffering and how they have been left behind by the system.'

'Advertising? Do the farmers advertise for their produce in our paper?' I asked, surprised.

'Not for their produce, for their real estate,' he replied. He walked off towards his office. Then he stopped, turned, and continued, 'Also for their trucks. They are selling their trucks. Each advert is a few euros for us, for your salary.'

'But who would buy trucks now?' I shouted after him as he disappeared into his office.

I sat down in my chair, and my colleague at the next desk said, 'Well, that is better for us. If nobody buys them then they keep advertising, which means more salary for you!' Then, as if he was in no mood to laugh at his own joke, he raised his eyebrows and stared at his computer screen. It was hard for me to embody the cause of the farmer. I needed a new inspiration, something more than the threat of losing my job.

It had been a long time since I had written anything the boss had liked. I think the last piece was when I interviewed my old classmate, Pavlos, the unionist. That was almost two months ago! They gave me a full page and published what I wrote. It was about workers' rights and the principles of defending our rights as employees and as citizens in general: the right to demonstrate, to hold strikes, and for paid holidays, sick pay, minimum wages, more holidays, long-distance commuting subsidies, bonuses for being on time, and office space for union assemblies. The list went on. We already had many of these rights, but everything sounded so good listed out in the paper.

I remember my old classmate almost dictating my article as it was to be printed. In one section Pavlos said he would rather die than submit to a factory demand that took away any rights from his colleagues and co-workers. 'Where you see injustice and abuse, you shouldn't think of details like the consequences of fighting for your rights. You fight because of your principles.'

The joke was that Pavlos was actually a staunch supporter of the conservative party. He had done well for himself. He already had one pension as a factory worker and also a full-time job at another factory as a unionist. His dream was to become a government industrial inspector. He lived in a big house with a lot of land in a popular suburb, as expected. I really admired him. I admire people who love what they do. They have principles, and in the end they make a good income from their work. During that interview he told me about his villa, his horses, his swimming pool, his indoor gymnasium, and more. He even invited me to stay at his guest suite.

His voice still ringing in my ear: 'Come over whenever you want to get away from the city. Bring your wife, come alone, bring someone else's wife – I don't care. Come and stay for a while. We'll chat about the good old days.'

'Shall I get you a coffee so you can wake up?' asked my colleague at the office.

'No, no. I am fine, thanks,' I said, realising that I had been daydreaming at my desk. 'I think I have decided to call the farmer again.'

I had to call the farmer again. I had no choice. I hadn't even completed a proper interview; I needed to find a climax for the article. At this time of day the farmer would be out somewhere, blocking the road. It would be like on-site reportage. The phone rang and rang with no answer.

He must be busy demonstrating, shouting, blocking the road, and organizing the other farmers. Maybe he was having difficulty moving his barely-used truck out of the alleyway. Maybe he was still at home!

I decided to call his home number. It rang and rang before his wife finally answered.

'Where is your husband? At the road block?'

'He is asleep.'

'Why? Something wrong with the new truck?' I asked.

'Which truck? We only have one truck. Where are you calling from?' she asked frantically. I tried to calm her down.

'From the newspaper. I am the one who is covering the strikes. I was at your house yesterday …'

'Okay, now I know,' she replied. 'No, he didn't go. No petrol! Nobody went. Petrol stations are on strike.'

One strike prevents another one? How is anything going to be done properly in this country? I wondered. Then I heard the farmer's voice in the background.'

'Who is it?'

'The reporter,' replied his wife.

'Give it to me. Let me talk to him,' demanded the farmer.

'Hello, hello, is that you? From the paper?'

'Yes, it is me.'

'Listen, write we will block the roads, all the roads, okay? I can get some petrol, but nobody else can. All petrol stations are shut. As soon as other farmers get some petrol, we will block them all, all the roads. You understand?'

'Yes, I do. But no, I don't. How come you can get petrol but nobody else?'

'My cousin, who is my neighbour – you didn't see him when you came over; he was at work – he has a petrol station on the main road.'

'I see.'

'When you finish writing, come here. We will have a drink. Bring the paper. I want to see it. I must go now. I am planting some olive trees these days. Get the wife to call me when you come.'

'You are planting trees? How come? I thought you said it is not worth planting anymore. What happened?'

'Look, I am a farmer. I love planting. That's what I do best. What do you expect me to do? If I don't farm I will die, and all of you die with me. Got to go now. You get to writing.' He hung up without giving me a chance to say good-bye.

I had felt completely drained of enthusiasm, but his last few words, about planting trees, gave me new life. However, I still had nothing to write about. I got up and walked around the half-empty office. I was looking for something exciting, something worth writing about. Maybe I could write about the Nazis, about the food they were giving only to Greeks. Maybe I could write about the comment that familiar-looking taxi driver made about our poverty. I went straight to my boss's office to ask him if I could write about the Greek Nazis inviting in the German ones.

'Just do your job!' he shouted as soon as he heard my suggestion. 'We are not here to give free coverage to anyone!'

I tried to reason. 'Free coverage? This is outrageous!'

'Your salary this month is going to be outrageous.'

'What salary? You have not paid me for a while now.'

'Well, it will stay that way if you don't watch it. You have not written anything good for a while either. Go sit down, have a cigarette, and get to work writing your assignment, nothing else!'

'But I have to go and see the farmer again.'

'I thought you had finished interviewing him.'

'I need to go again. He is doing something exciting now.'

'What?'

'He is planting trees.'

'He is a farmer. What did you expect him to do?'

'You will read it. I promise it will be good. Just let me do another job right now.'

'No Nazis. Interview someone else. I can't believe I have to feed you ideas like a school teacher. Why don't you interview Yorgos?'

'Yorgos? Which Yorgos? The guy who was here last year? Your business consultant?'

'He is not my business consultant; he is the paper's business consultant. If it weren't for him you wouldn't have a job now.'

'Why should I interview him? What is so interesting about him?'

'He is a business consultant; he knows everything that is worth knowing about any business. He has just lost a lot of money, I think in the stock market. Interview him. He will give a good insight into all the problems.'

'If he makes his living through consultancy, don't you think he would hesitate to show he is himself one of the losers?'

'That's where you come in as a reporter. I don't know, maybe he can stay anonymous.'

'I don't think so. Why would he give free advice and make himself look bad? He will just lie to me.'

'You won't know until you try.'

I left my boss's office and went straight to the phone to call Yorgos. I was very interested to find out if he would share his business failure with us.

'Hi, Yorgos. It is Panos from the newspaper. Do you have a few minutes for me to come and conduct an interview about the recession?'

'Why do you want to interview me? What do I know?'

'Nikos, my boss, tells me you have recently been unfortunate in your investments and have lost a lot of money.'

'Oh, that. No, Panos, that had nothing to do with the recession.'

'If not the recession then what? Did you just lose the money?'

'Yes, I did.'

'Where? In the street?'

'No, in the casinos'

'Okay, Yorgos, fine, you don't want to talk. Are you doing any more business training courses for us this year?'

'No, Niko doesn't want to spend any more money on staff. All the grants for staff development have dried up. I've got to go now.'

'Well, stop by the office for coffee if you are in the area.'

And this was my last attempt of the day to get something written down. As expected, the business consultant was in no mood to discuss his own business failure with anyone.

It was a long day, and I was relieved to be driving back home. Two more phone calls from banks demanding money soon changed my relief. The second one came as I picked up Costa. I tried to sound calm and polite.

'Yes, it is me. I can't really talk now. Yes, I will. In a couple of days ... I can't right now ... I know that. I can't really talk now. Okay, I will. I will tomorrow. Yes, yes, I know. I will. Okay, yes. Thank you.'

As I hung up Costa asked, 'Dad, do you have any money for tonight? It is St. Valentine's Day today, and I wanted to go out ... go eat out.'

I had forgotten all about St. Valentine. I hadn't arranged anything with Maria. She hadn't said anything. I should probably get something for her or take her out, but she knew the situation. She wouldn't be expecting anything. Maybe I would just get some flowers, something really small so she wouldn't shout at me for needlessly spending money.

'Dad, Dad, you are driving into the curb! Watch out!' screamed Costa. I straightened the wheel quickly.

'Yes, I am fine,' I said, falling into a deep silence. I stared straight into the horizon, driving fast but comfortably senseless. The truth finally caught up with me.

'Did you hear what I asked about St. Valentine's Day?' Costa asked impatiently.

I bought myself a few more seconds by checking the change box that I kept in the car for tolls. There were a few euros in it, but I didn't want to get them out and count them in front of Costa.

'Dad, will you answer me?' he shouted.

I finally answered, 'Do communists have St Valentine's Day? You say you are a communist. Isn't your mother one?'

'What the fuck?'

'Watch your mouth,' I said sternly. Then I continued. 'Look, things are hard, and I don't think you will enjoy going out anyway. Hardly anyone goes out nowadays. Do something for her, something symbolic. You don't have to spend money. Let's buy some flowers.'

'Flowers are for dead people. At my age we go out and hang out. If you like someone you hang out with them. You don't buy them flowers.' He continued sarcastically, 'That's what we communists do. We spend time with each other and don't waste our money on flowers!'

I ignored his comments. I could afford to for a few minutes. I was the one at the wheel. He was in my car, and so he had to listen to me. Anywhere else he would already have walked away, but here I could drive on and tell him what I thought was right. Here, things were under my control. The only problem was, I didn't really have anything to say.

Noticing my silence, he broke his silence in the same sarcastic voice and said, 'So what do you socialists do on Valentine's Day?'

'Just because one votes for a party doesn't mean one is a socialist,' I answered quickly.

There was a long silence, again broken by Costa. 'Okay, fine, I will buy her flowers this year. I will get the same thing you get Mum!'

I felt the weight of my misfortunes doubling for the day. My eyes, as if having a mind of their own, glanced at the change box again.

I had two accounts with debit cards. I could check to see what was in them. The problem with most accounts is that the minimum withdrawal is twenty euros. I didn't think I had more than fifteen, maximum eighteen euros in each. If only they were both in the same account, I would have been fine.

'What is the deal on the job front?' I asked Costa.

He looked at me, surprised, not expecting this question now. He remained silent for a moment and then said, 'What is the deal with the job front? Job behind.'

Ignoring his sarcasm I said, 'Communism is about work, factories, and sweat; it is not just about holding red flags and blocking roads.'

'I don't take my red flag to job interviews,' he answered without thinking.

'You take your tattoos,' I commented.

'My tattoos? You think that's why I don't get any jobs? Is that what you think?'

This was not the direction in which I wanted the conversation to go. It was time to show some care, a bit of encouragement, and some hope.

'Have you been to any restaurants, beach bars, any …'

He interrupted me. 'Yes, Dad. I don't fit in. I have been to all the hotels in the area. I have filled form after form.'

'But there is still a lot of tourism. There is nothing wrong there!' I said.

'Yes but none of them speaks ancient fucking Greek. If, instead of spending money on private schools for me to learn ancient Greek, you had sent me to learn Russian, I would have a job now. Maybe if they knew I wanted to become a doctor but didn't make it they would have some pity on me.'

There was obvious anger in his voice. Why couldn't I just have a normal conversation with this boy, just to resolve something together? Why did he respond with so much anger and sarcasm? What had I done wrong? Unfortunately my silence gave him more confidence.

'If you had let me become a farmer …'

I had to step in, somehow. This whole recession was ending up as my fault. I interrupted him by calling his name.

'Costa! Costa!'

When he stopped, I said, 'Listen to me, listen. Farmers aren't doing well either, and I sent you to private ancient Greek classes so that you could pass your high school and enter university.'

'You told me learning ancient Greek makes me smarter. You told me that is why the ancient Greeks became philosophers. You also told me the whole world learns ancient Greek.'

'What is wrong with ancient Greek?' I asked desperately. 'Is that why you think you can't get a job? Do you think the recession is because we learn ancient Greek in high school, because I paid for you to learn ancient Greek?'

'No, Dad, you are right. This whole recession is because of my tattoo!' he answered.

I thought a bit. I had to have a defiant answer, something profound, something to shut him up. I wasn't having anyone insult my roots, my foundations. This was the language of philosophy, medicine, poetry, literature, logic, and knowledge. This was the language with which we taught the world democracy.

'You only want to learn Russian because you are a communist, not because of tourism,' I said, shaking my head to confirm my own comment.

'And you use ideology whenever you need it for your own benefit. What language do you socialists want to learn? Broken Russian with an American imperialist accent, so you can fit in any hole?' he asked.

'What Russian? What Russia? They don't even exist!' I said.

'Dad, Russia is not communist anymore. Forget about communism. Do you know what they are? Where they are? They are in all our beach-front hotels, on our islands, and in our shops.'

I defended my argument. 'If they had no oil, they would be nothing now.'

'Yes, and if you had got your hotel permit for your land you would be everything now.'

I hung my head unwillingly. In a humble voice I said, 'The case is not yet closed.'

'Well, I can't wait for fifty years while you finish with the forester, the topographer, the architect, the neighbours, the coastal authorities, the environment officer, the archaeologist, the post man ...'

'You don't have to be sarcastic!' I interrupted.

'I can't wait fifty years for you to build a hotel so that you can have an in-house doctor for your American geriatric clients. That is how long it will take me to become a doctor. By the way, next time the archaeologist comes to survey the land, take me along. I speak fluent ancient Greek. If he speaks as well as me, that will make two of us on the planet.'

I kept silent. After a few seconds he calmly asked,

'Why have we parked on the side of the street? I thought we were looking for a flower shop.'

I started the car again, looking for words but somehow content that I couldn't find any. Driving was the best I could do at this stage.

'There is a flower shop at the end of this road,' said Costa.

I kept driving and wished for the road to be long. Costa suddenly broke the silence.

'Damn, it's shut. What time is it? Why is it shut on a day like this? Why?'

We were back to normal, as if we had had no conversation. Our target now was no longer finding a job, sorting out Greece, or anything else. The mission was to find a flower shop.

As we reached the shop we noticed the 'For Rent' sign on the wall. There was another sign on the window that said 'For Sale'. Costa decided to go and ask around to see if they had relocated to somewhere nearby. I found a double parking space and waited. Several yellow and white signs attracted my attention. They were all on a closed-down shop. One was from an estate agent saying 'For Sale'. Another one from the same agent said 'For Rent'. Under it a handwritten sign said 'For Rent and Sale' with a mobile number next to it, perhaps directly from the owner.

I looked up. A large banner above said 'Property Consultants Agency' in big yellow letters. The banner had the same logo as the stickers on the window. Obviously the agency had closed down and used its advertising material one last time, hoping to rent or sell the shop they used whilst going bust. This is what I call perseverance: putting your guts out to get what you want, being positive, and never giving up. Maybe if Greece had more people like this, we wouldn't be in this position now. These were the kind of people I needed for my articles, positive people with hope.

As I looked around the car to find a piece of paper to take down the agent's number, Costa got back in the car with a small paper bag.

'What is that? Can you tear me off a small piece of paper?' I asked.

'How small?'

'Come on,' I said. 'Can I have a small piece of paper?'

Costa ripped a tiny little strip of paper from the bag and handed it to me.

'Did it have to be so tiny? You just do these things to piss me off.'

'Dad, there is a recession. We can't waste things, remember, especially if we are communists.'

The paper was so small I had to use both sides to squeeze on all the information.

'It has been closed for months; the next one is down the road,' said Costa.

'What is that?' I asked, pointing at the bag.

'Nothing. I just got something from the fruit shop,' he replied.

'What is it?' I asked again.

He shrugged his shoulders and said, 'I bought a cauliflower. I had to buy something. I went in, and he got up, thinking I was a client. I just bought something, something symbolic. Remember? Symbolic?'

He sounded sarcastic. If he was going to be sarcastic, I could do better. I was in a worse mood! Once again, I opened my mouth and this came out. 'Oh, I thought you were going to cook for her since you have no money to go out.'

He was quick to answer. 'The reason I have no money, Dad, is because of you. I have no job. You know why? Because you planned for me to be a doctor. I wasn't good enough to be a doctor, so I am nothing now.'

'Who said you are nothing now?' I said desperately. 'You have your whole future ahead of you.'

'Here is the other flower shop,' he said, relieving me from the discussion that was torturing me.

'Shit. It's closed,' he said, getting out of the car and walking straight towards the closed flower shop, as if expecting some desperate shopkeeper to open the door for him. A few meters before the shop window he stopped, turned around, got back in the car, and said, 'And think of all the money you spent on private schools.'

'I sent you to private classes because you weren't going to your morning school.'

'I didn't go to school in the mornings because I had to study for the national university placement exams. I was too tired to go to school. And anyway, no classes were held. Most of the students were absent. It was the teacher and four walls with chairs. You didn't expect me to go to university by going to school, did you?'

'I didn't expect you to go to the university by just going to school?' I repeated.

'Dad, I didn't go to university in the end, remember?' he said.

'You didn't want to go anyway, so where is the problem'? I said. He glared at me as if my comment were not worth answering.

'Do you know where the next flower shop is?' he asked. Noticing my silence, he said, 'Public schools aren't for getting you to university. That's not what schools are for. Who gave you that bizarre idea?'

'Oh yes, I think the next one is near the cemetery. They should be open,' I said, feigning enthusiasm.

'You see? I told you flowers are only for dead people.'

'It is too far away. It will cost us more on petrol than the flowers.'

Costa had his head down, gazing at the bag he was holding. Without raising his head he said, 'You are right. She will understand. No one has any money. If she loves me she'd better get used to the fact that it's cauliflower for Valentine's Day this year.'

I didn't know what to say. There were several choices. Keep quiet? He was waiting for a pulse, anything to show I felt his pain. Make a joke? Too risky. Ignore him? Too uncaring. Agree with him and support the cauliflower escape? Too, well, too cauliflowery. My son, a part of me, was in pain. I had to acknowledge his pain. I had to feel the pressure on him, and for a moment I had to forget my personal trivial issues and concentrate hard on him.

'It will not always be like this,' I said, profoundly hoping to be interrupted. I paused and waited. Then I continued. 'Life is full of opportunities; all you have to do is grab them.'

'Opportunities like your land on the hill? The one you wanted to turn into a resort? Where did that go, Dad? You would have been better off planting, err, cauliflowers rather than trying to attract high-class tourists.'

'We had that, Mum and I. We had that to dream about, that's all. It went wrong, and we accept that. What is your idea?'

He took a long time to reply. It seemed like a deliberate delay, a hesitation. At first I thought he was convinced, apologetic, regretful of his approach, or maybe just looking for a sharp reply.

Then he stared at me, forcing me to take my eyes off the road. 'Are you sure?'

'Sure of what?' I asked.

'Are you sure you and Mum can take it? You have spent all your money on that land, every single drachma and euro.'

'And the rest for your education, for private tutoring,' I replied.

'Yes, and both your ideas are bankrupt. The land is wasted, and I am not much different,' he declared.

'How is the land wasted? It is still there!' I said without thinking. 'I mean, I don't agree that it is wasted, but the land – I will build there, I guarantee you. We have the court case in a few months, and I will get the permit.'

'What court?'

'I am working on it.'

'You have been saying this ever since I learnt to talk,' he said.

'If I don't get the permit I will get compensation,' I said, trying to hide the fact that I would dread such a possibility. Costa did not want to leave the subject alone.

'How are they going to compensate you for thirty years of your life?' he asked. 'How many years before I was born did you start this?'

I had to change the subject. 'When are you meeting your girlfriend?'

He ignored me. 'Let's say I open a business and it is successful. Then they come and put a big tax on it to punish me. At least if I were being punished for being late to school, it could be partly my fault. But why should I be punished for what your generation did to Greece? For what your generation did to socialism, to Europe? Your father left you a bit of land, and what did you do with it? Nothing.

Your generation even destroyed the land, the dream; they got ideas from our ancestors and threw them in the bin. What are you going to leave behind for me? You are going to leave behind some taxes on a property that you can't do shit on, and what else? Mistrust from all our neighbours in Europe! And what else? You are also going to leave me a lot of cholesterol, not just in your veins but also in mine. That's my inheritance. I can't help you cure yours because your hospitals are closed down, and you can't help me with mine because in the good days, when you were eating lamb chops on credit, you weren't worried about the damage to your body or about how the restaurant bill would be paid.'

I was listening intently, making sure not to say anything that would sound defensive or weak.

'Where are we going?' asked Costa. I was getting used to not knowing what to say, but not knowing where I was driving to was another thing.

'I am going home.'

'Look, you are driving right into the crowds. There is a demonstration ahead. Can't you see?'

'Oh, shit, we are never going to get out of here now. Are they your buddies?' I said.

'No, they are from the public sector, but I think we helped them organise it. There is our flag, back there. Do you see?'

'We might as well park the car and sit somewhere,' I suggested. 'Shall we have a beer? I have some change.'

I double-parked the car on a side road and bought two cans of beer from a nearby kiosk. We hadn't had a drink together since his first beer at seventeen.

As we got comfortable sitting on the kerb I asked, 'You are going to give the cauliflower to her, right? It makes sense. I think she will like it. You will be the only boy in town who gives a cauliflower to his girlfriend.'

'Just as well. If there were more people doing the same thing, we couldn't even afford that any more. It would raise the price of cauliflower,' he said thoughtfully. Then he turned to me and asked,

'So, what do you think is the cause of the recession? You are so involved. You should know!'

'Are you being sarcastic again?' I asked warily.

'Tell me. I want to know what you think!' he answered.

'Well, I think it has a lot to do with the Europeans, with the Germans. They kept giving away loans, and we borrowed,' I said, shrugging my shoulders.

'Why do you think we got the money? Isn't that because of capitalism? Didn't they force us?' he asked.

'I don't know about forcing us, but no one told us it would get like this. They should have given us some time. They can't support you by giving you money and then all of a sudden tell you to take care of yourself!' I said with confidence.

'What is that grin? You don't agree? You think it is all because of capitalism and the markets?' I asked.

Still smiling, Costa answered, 'No, I just remembered something, something from years ago when I was in the elementary school. Never mind!'

'I am glad my professional knowledge reminds you of your elementary school,' I said with some obvious pain.

'No,' said Costa. 'I just remember myself facing the wall at the corner of the principal's office. It was pathetic.'

'What had you done?' I asked. 'Had a fight? Broke something? What?'

'I was late for school, all planned,' he said with sadness in his voice.

'Late, at elementary school? Whose fault was that?' I asked.

'I was set up by you and Mum. For some reason you hadn't gone to work that day. Every day Mum used to call me to get ready, but on that day you decided to teach me to be responsible, without telling me anything. You just left me to be punished. You made it all my fault. It doesn't matter. You probably thought it was good for me, you know, to learn the hard way.'

His voice was sad. Another silence filled the car. I wasn't trying to remember the incident as much as I was trying, yet again, to find a way out. I waited and filled the gap with facial expressions, pretending that I was struggling to remember but couldn't. Then I finally said, 'You can't compare the fate of a nation with an elementary school child. This is an insult.'

Costa did not say anything, and that worried me. Then the storm after the calm hit. 'Yes, you are right! I think kids are very smart. They sense everything. They say what they mean. They don't take shit. They move and adapt all the time. They survive. They don't get hooked up to things. They try so hard to be independent even if they can't be. I didn't mean to insult them.'

His endless sarcasm was so unexpected, so out of place, and so uncalled for that I became angry with him. I had to tell him what his roots were and where he came from.

'Wait a minute. I am the journalist here. I am not having you lecture me about the country and the people. What do you know about the recession? How did it affect you? The only change it made in your life was that you now have to lock up your bike helmet! What do you know about Greece? What do you know about our history and what we have been through? This country has been through a lot more than you know. You still remember your elementary school punishment? Do you know what our nation has been through? Occupation and starvation. My mum did not have food to eat. They boiled grass to eat, plain grass. Did you know that?'

'Dad, I sold my bike last year. Don't you remember? I still have the helmet in my room. It was too old. The buyer didn't want it,' he said.

'So you want a new bike now, is that it? Can we say the recession is over once you have your bike and get back to normal life?'

'Dad, if you can turn everything back to normal, why don't you run for office?'

'I will think about it! Why not?'

'Dad, you can't even run a family. I mean, you can, but it is difficult now,' he back-pedalled.

'What do all these idiots in parliament have that I don't, ha?' I asked.

No response. Then he gave another grin.

'What are you smiling about now?' I asked.

'Nothing, nothing. What do you have that they don't?' He burst into laughter.

'Are you going to tell me what you are laughing about? Is this to do with your elementary school again? Or is it just the thought of me in parliament?'

'No, it just reminded me of a joke,' he explained. 'You know, when you said what do they have that you don't.'

'What joke? Is it political?' I asked.

'Well, no, not really. Actually, sort of,' he answered.

'Are you going to tell me?' I asked.

'Okay, there were two people, a couple – well, not a couple, an old man and an old woman in an old people's home. They met and decided that since they couldn't have full sex for medical reasons, every evening they would sit next to each other on the couch, and the woman would just hold the man – you know.'

'Yeah, I get it.' I said.

'They would sit there for half an hour, both happy, and then would take their medicine and go to bed separately.'

'What is so funny about this?' I asked, not finding any relevance to our conversation.

'Wait … So one night the old woman goes and waits at the couch. The old man does not show up. So she waits, and she waits. Finally he appears, very apologetic but with a big smile. "Where have you been?" asks the old lady. Then the old man tells her that he has found someone else in the old home called Rose. "Oh yeah?" says the old woman, "What does Rose have that I don't have?"

'Parkinson's! Parkinson's!' says the old man.'

He burst into laughter and made me laugh too.

'What does this have to do with the Greek parliament?' I asked.

'Old people?' he said. 'Sitting around and doing routine things? Moving without control? Never mind, you are a journalist. You won't get it. You are right. There is nothing they have that you don't have, right?'

There was another long, uncomfortable silence. There were still people gathering to follow the demonstration. We couldn't go yet. It was getting a bit chilly. I looked around to find a subject, something to talk about.

'So is that why you hate school?' I asked.

'What, Parkinson's?'

'No, silly! Because of that punishment. Is that the most vivid image left in your mind from school?'

'No, I have a few – too many, actually,' he replied. 'When you love someone or something you don't know exactly why, but when you hate something, there are too many reasons. You don't know which one is the main one.'

'Besides that, what has stuck in your mind from the elementary school?'

'What sticks in yours, Dad'?

'Oh, it is a guy called Stavros. I will tell you about him. First tell me yours.'

'One day the teacher was asking everyone what they wanted to become when they grew up. When it came to my turn I said retired. The teacher got really mad at me.'

'That is really funny! Why did he get mad?'

'Because he had said it the day before.'

'Where, in the classroom?'

'No, to another teacher. I was listening to them.'

'You were spying on them?' I asked.

'No. One day you were late picking me up ...'

'I knew this one was somehow my fault too!'

'No. It was the jacket's fault!'

'The jacket?' I asked with surprise.

'Yes. My teacher was waiting with a new young teacher. It was them and me. We were waiting for you.'

'I know. You said that.'

'Anyway, he was really annoyed. All of a sudden he decided to wait for you outside. As we were coming out they saw a jacket on the ground. The young teacher went to pick it up, and my teacher stopped him.'

'Why?'

'He started telling the new teacher that it wasn't their job to pick up the students' jackets. The young teacher bent down to pick up the jacket. My teacher wasn't having it. He said, "This is not what we are paid for. If you pick this jacket up now, they will expect us to do this every day."'

So the young teacher dropped the jacket on the floor, exactly where he had found it, and we all came outside. My teacher started talking about retirement. He said he couldn't wait; he was going to get it early or something. Then he told the young teacher he couldn't wait to stop working at the school and become retired. I just thought retirement was some kind of a job, some sort of a dream profession that one had to face misery and hardship to get. I didn't know. When I repeated his words next day in the classroom, he got mad at me. He probably thought I was making fun of him.'

'Was it your jacket?'

'No.'

'How come you remember this so well?'

'Before that day I wanted to become a teacher when I grew up.'

'You did?'

'Do you know what happened to the young teacher?'

'He lost his jacket?' I asked, trying to be funny.

'No. Stop it. You get silly whenever you have a drink.'

'How do you know?'

'After a beer, I can see you, even if you can't see me.'

'What happened to the young teacher?'

'He worked there for that year, and then he left. They said he became a priest.' He paused and stared out at the demonstration. 'Hey, do you know any jokes?'

'No, not really. In my work we write true stories. We don't make things up just because they are funny or interesting.'

'I thought this is what you old people did. Whenever you can't make sense of anything, you turn it into a joke. Instead of complaining or demonstrating you sit around and amuse each other with your own misery.'

'It is not misery. We Greeks are used to it, but we do make fun of people who have done it.'

'Have done what?'

'Who have caused it … the recession.'

'So, you know who has caused it?'

'Yes, we all do. No, it is not the imperialists. Well, it is them too, but …'

'Just tell me the joke, Dad. I think it will be easier.'

'Okay, okay. I will tell you one that has something to do with parliament, not like your joke.'

'Skip the introduction. I might get the punch line.'

'Well, a robber with a gun stops a man in a dark alley and says, "Give me all your money!" The man says, "Be careful. I am a member of parliament, and you will get into serious trouble." The robber thinks a bit and says, "Okay, give me all MY money then!"'

It was so good to hear Costa laugh with me at my joke, but I wasn't expecting the follow-up.

'Our jokes, you know, they can't both be true at the same time,' he said.

'Both true, you mean?'

'No, really, both our jokes – one masturbating, one robbing. They can't be doing both!'

'Why not? We have two hands!'

'But one brain.'

'In the case of parliament, no brain!' I said, laughing.

'Yet you vote for them. You see, that's what I mean,' said Costa.

'What?'

'Masturbating thieves? Do you find that logical?'

'Who is doing the masturbating?' I asked.

'I don't know. Maybe us, by voting for them. Maybe we should start by cleaning things up from the top, getting rid of them all.'

'From the top?' I asked.

Costa nodded in agreement. I continued. 'You know the saying, the fish always starts rotting from its head. We should get rid of the head.'

Costa started laughing again.

'What is up with you tonight? Don't tell me you remembered another joke.'

Costa started again. 'There was a man washing his car's number plate in the street. A neighbour came and asked, "Why are you only washing your number plate?" The man answered, "No, I am washing the whole thing. But when my car is covered with dirt, I don't start from the top. I start from the number plate, just to make sure it is my car."' We both burst into laughter.

'When you clean up your parliament, make sure it is yours first!' beamed Costa.

That conversation was the longest I'd had with Costa for years. He told me some heavy stuff, but it still felt good. If I'd had any money that day I would have given it to him as soon as I had picked him up, and then he would have probably listened to music on his mobile all the way back home. As soon as we got home he took a shower, changed, got some money from Maria, and went out with the cauliflower wrapped in some aluminium foil that he found in the recycling bin. That night he actually said a proper good-bye to me. And they say there is nothing good about a recession!

Chapter 4

EXPECTING TO HEAR no, I asked Maria if she wanted to eat out that night. Up till then I had heard of negatively loaded yes answers, but that was the night I met my first negatively loaded no answer.

'No', she said, and then she continued: 'If you really wanted to go out you would have arranged it before. What are we going to do with Elpida? Costa has gone out. Do you have any money?'

Under pressure again, I opened my mouth, and this came out: 'I guess we have no money because you just gave it to Costa.'

My comment was like a rock that just slipped through my hands on a hill and started rolling down without control. I could not pull it back! When it finally hit the bottom, this is what I heard: 'He is our son. He is going out with his girlfriend for a cheap meal on St. Valentine's Day. Shall we keep him in and go out to celebrate instead? Celebrate what? What? Our wonderful relationship? That we have a son that we can't afford?'

It was time to be a man. It was time for me to stand up and tell her that it was not my fault. I had to protect her and show her that it was not her fault either, I took a step towards her, our eyes fixated on each other. We hadn't looked at each other straight on for so long.

'I need a coffee. Do you want one?' she said calmly. Without answering I turned around and walked to the living room.

Then I heard her say: 'Your St. Valentine's Day dinner is the fish you didn't eat last night; it is still in the oven. If you don't eat it tonight, throw it in the bin. I don't want it to stink up the place.'

There was some red, syrupy drink left in a bottle. I did not want to go back to the kitchen to get a glass. I took a sip straight out of the bottle and laid on the uncomfortable couch, keeping the bottle next to me. The sweet drink was disgusting, whatever it was. Then I remember my son barging back in the house.

'Hi, Dad, are you okay? I forgot something.' Then he went to Maria in the kitchen.

'I don't have any more. Ask your dad,' shouted Maria.

I could hear Costa's footsteps coming closer and closer. I closed my eyes for a second and then noticed the sound of his footsteps fading away. The next time I opened my eyes he was in the corner of the room against the wall holding something in his hand. Then he just said good-bye and left the house.

With the bottle next to my head on the table, laying on the couch, I did not look good. I know because in a few weeks' time I saw my picture posted on Costa's Facebook. He had called the picture, 'My dad on Valentine'. I had another sip, balanced the bottle on the table with no difficulties, looked at the ceiling, and gradually fell asleep, completely unaware that my day had not ended yet.

There was some noise in the kitchen, but the sound was slowly fading. I closed my eyes completely but could still hear something, some plates or maybe cutlery. I had not eaten but was not hungry. I felt light, completely weightless! It felt as if I were moving above the ground. I was not gaining any height, though. Everything around me was moving up with me. Everything was somehow stuck to me.

On my right I felt an irritation. I naturally turned around. It was my boss, looking at me and watching my movements. I observed his silent, staring eyes, sneaky charm, and meaningless smiles. I was lifted more, high enough to see the water. I was next to a sea near an olive grove on the slopes of a hill. It all looked familiar. There were some ruins at the bottom of the grove. They did not look scary. Everything was green, too green, but there were no olives on the trees. It seemed that all was painted. The colour of the sea was an exaggerated blue. The trees had more leaves than possible; the ground was too soft to be real. I was right above the green trees, not flying; it was more like floating. In the distance something was moving, slowly moving up the hill. It was an old man. At first I did not recognize him because I had never seen my grandfather from above. He was pulling on something and talking. It was a kid. He passed a tree, and then he was a teenager. He was not being pulled anymore but still moving up. As they moved up, they faded away behind the silver olive trees, which were not green anymore.

Near the top of the hill, there were more noises and movements. I wanted to move too. I wanted to see more, but I was helplessly above everything, stuck to the summit, and had to wait for everything to come to me.

Halfway up the summit, next to one of the trees that was still green, the bow of a ship was appearing. It was followed by the stern. I am not sure if it was the tree leaves moving away or it was the ship moving out from behind the trees. It must be a pirate ship I thought, but as the full ship appeared, I could see no black flags on it.

The silver of the leaves was getting darker. Before I had a chance to look for its flag, the ship left. With its departure, the tree's colours changed again. This time the tree's bark became fiery. There was a lot of noise. There were people amongst the trees, too close to the burning bark. Bodies were rolling down the hill, some with half-burnt clothes, some red, and some blue. The ship appeared again, this time with a definite blue flag. There were also other flags around. Some flags were both green and silver, a poor camouflage attempt of the olive leaves, but I wasn't fooled. It is not just the colour that makes a leaf; it is the way it moves in the wind!

I turned to look for my granddad. By the time I looked back, the ship's flag had gone green. Every time I blinked it changed colour, sometimes blue, sometimes green. Just like the flag colours of the Greek political parties. I chose to look away, completely ignoring the ship. Right near the summit, as I concentrated on some rocks, a most peculiar structure appeared. Almost out of nowhere, it grew out of the ground. It grew taller and taller. I had to move away, but I was powerless. I waited desperately until I was kicked away by its force. It was a tower! A slim, dusty watch tower! I put my hands over my face to avoid the dust, and through my fingers I could still see the tower. It was ugly. It was funny. It was strange. It was not real. The tower wasn't round; it had four corners. The walls were made from brown mud and straws, but the four corners were made of sculpted white marble like the Parthenon.

A calm breeze rose from the sea, gradually gaining force. The silver olive tree branches started moving with the wind. Some leaves slowly turned green, but this time the green was natural, an olive tree green, and the only black was the abandoned ripe olives on the trees. Gradually the olive branches started growing faster and spreading around, covering all the flags. A sudden wind blew into all the leaves. An olive fell on the ground and made no noise. It had no colour, not even a shade. At first it began moving downhill towards the ship, which had also disappeared. The force of the wind was not allowing the olive to roll downhill. I could hear the wind; I could feel it against my entire body. Another hard gust blew, and the olive began moving uphill towards me and towards the tower, which had disappeared too. As the sun came out of the clouds, the wind stopped, and the olive reached the top. The wind had taken all the dust off the scenery. Bright sunlight had given new colours to everything. It brought warmth and happiness. I partially closed my eyes to be able to look at the reflection of the sun on the sea. The big rock in the bay in front of the hill had moved. It wasn't a stone anymore. I smiled and heard children's laughter. They were shouting and screaming. One of them had found an olive in the swimming pool and was running to show it to her parents, who were sunbathing by the pool. I smiled. The tower had turned into a beautiful hotel. I rubbed my eyes, but it was all real to me.

I closed them and opened them again. Maria was sitting on a chair looking at me. I was still lying on the couch. As soon as she realized I was awake, she took a deep breath and said: 'Panos, I am leaving you.'

I was still smiling. I sat up and shouted: 'I went there! I went to our land. The hotel is there, a big hotel, on a resort. There was even a swimming pool, a big one, right on the edge.' She was shaking as if she could not hear me, but she kept staring into my eyes.

I continued: 'It was there. You don't believe me, do you? It was all there. I wish you could see it too.'

She kept looking at me. I said, 'It will happen. I know we will do it.'

'Did you hear me? I think that is the best way, for all of us,' she said calmly.

I sat up on the couch, not having woken up completely. I said: 'It was beautiful, just beautiful.'

'You have been dreaming, like always. You have been dreaming,' she mumbled.

I was staring straight ahead into nothing. I dropped down my head, concentrating on the sofa bed's tapestry. It was really only then that I realised I had woken up. I calmly whispered: 'You were not there. You were not in my dream.'

Instead of coming to my rescue, sympathizing with me, helping me, or at least having some pity on me, Maria mercilessly whispered, 'I have never been in your dreams, never.'

Then she seemed to whisper to herself: 'They are all your dreams – the land, the hotel, everything.'

Whilst I was still analysing the tapestry patterns as if they mattered, she raised her voice slightly and continued: 'Don't act so surprised. You knew this was coming. You have known this for a long time.'

I went to open my mouth. She interrupted me and said: 'No more talks. No more arguments. That's enough. I have had enough.'

'But I will sort it out. It is just one guy, one stupid, stuck-up old freak, who is stopping everything. I will show them. I will, even if I have to become an archaeologist myself. Didn't you see? Didn't you see how I learnt everything about forestry and finally got our clearance? Do you not remember?'

I was waiting. Maybe I was hoping that as usual, as whenever we were talking about the resort, she would shout and tell me: 'Oh, you have told me this hundreds of times. That stupid hill in the middle of nowhere screwed us. It came between us. It drained us. You risked your family for it, your children. You risked me. Is there anyone we don't owe money to because of that wilderness? After all these years, you still need a tank to get to it, let alone build anything there.'

But instead, she said calmly: 'I am not leaving you because of that hill.'

Without looking angry, without being sarcastic, and without belittling me, she continued calmly, indifferently, and selfishly: 'I have lost half of my life to you and your dreams.'

Then she got up and left me on the couch on my own. If I could only go back to sleep, if I could only see the resort again, the palm trees, the jagged reflection of the garden lights in the pool, the …

'Wake up, wake up!' I heard.

It was daylight. I saw the ceiling, not a familiar ceiling. It was not my bedroom. I looked around and saw the kitchen. An empty chair stood next to me.

'Are you up? Are you up, Dad?' said the voice.

I slowly sat up and asked: 'What time is it?'

'It was eight thirty about half hour ago' said Costa.

Not making any sense of his answer, I looked at the clock myself. It said eight thirty sharp, I must have fallen asleep again on the couch. Not too late for work, though!

'Where is Mum?' I asked Costa.

'I don't know. I just got home about half an hour ago. They cut off the electricity again. They were there when I was coming in.'

Then as soon as he opened the fridge door, as if he had just realized something important, he shouted: 'Oh shit, my mobile has no battery left. I need to charge it. What am I going to do now?'

'I have paid them. What is wrong with these people?' I asked desperately.

'Can you sort it out soon? I need to write to my girlfriend before I lose her completely.'

'Where is Mum?' I asked again.

'Your cauliflower idea didn't work. She didn't like it,' he answered.

'What cauliflower idea? Where is Mum?' I asked again.

'When do you think you can get the electricity back? We have no Internet!'

'I don't know. I've got to go talk to these bastards. They put me on an instalment plan, forty euros a month,' I explained.

'Did you pay?' asked Costa, going to his room.

'Where are you going?' I asked.

'Did you pay?' asked Costa from the bedroom. Then he continued, 'I'm going to Grandma's. Her neighbour has Wi-Fi. I can get it from her veranda.'

'Where is Elpida?' I asked.

'She must be at school, where else?' he said as he walked out of his room with a rucksack.

I was still sitting on the coach, trying to piece together what had happened the night before, when Costa said: 'Here is a note from Mum. What is it? You guys don't talk? Did you buy her a cauliflower too?'

I got up, but before I could get to the note Costa read it aloud: 'I will come back after you are gone!'

'Gone where? What? What is she talking about?' I said, acting surprised.

'I don't know, Dad. Maybe she went to pay the electricity bill,' said Costa.

'I thought she was leaving, not me,' I said, keeping the same surprised look.

'I've got to go. It's Friday. I don't think you can manage to get juice before the weekend. Let me know if you need any help,' said Costa, and he left the house.

'Costa, Costa, is there a red note on the meter? It is an A5-sized red note. Take it off.' Hearing no reply, I shouted again: 'Take the red sticker off the meter. I don't want the neighbours to see it.'

Still no reply! 'Bastards! They cut you off for forty fucking euros on a Friday, and just to top it up they put a big red sign up saying, "Cut off for non-payment" for the whole world to see,' I explained loudly as if I were having a conversation with someone. I had to get it off before the neighbours saw it. I struggled up onto my feet. My whole body was stiff. I felt my heart beat, but it wasn't a beat. It was strong, like a knock.

'Costa, Costa, are you gone?' I said as I walked out towards the meter. There was one neighbour across coming out of his house. Somehow I had to position my body between him and the sign. I got there without him noticing me, but I was not tall enough to block his view of the notice. I tried reaching the note with my hand whilst standing on my toes to block the view. But as I struggled up, instead of going up, I was descending!

The next thing I remember is the heads of more than half a dozen people gathered around my head looking at me. Some of the faces I could recognize, but some were completely unfamiliar. I was lying on my back trying to look in between the heads to see if the electricity notice was still up. As soon as I found a gap to look through, a new head came into the picture and blocked my view completely.

'I am a nurse. Let me through. I am a nurse,' said the new head.

I tried to get up and get to the electricity meter, but I was physically and authoritatively stopped by the new person.

'Don't move, don't move at all. It is nothing. You will be all right. You have a small scratch on your head.'

I tried to get up again, and she shouted, 'I told you not to move. What do you want?'

I tried to open my eyes wider to make more sense of the surroundings, still trying to reach for the red notice.

'What do you want?' she shouted again whilst cleaning my forehead with a cloth, keeping my head down with her other hand.

I said with a broken voice: 'The ... the note ... the paper on ...'

'Calm down. Tell me, slowly, what do you want?'

Then she turned around and asked for a glass of water from the neighbours.

'I want Petridis. I want Mr Petridis, right now,' I said, begging.

'Who? Mr Petridis? Who is that? Is that your doctor?' asked the nurse.

'No, he is not, but I want to talk to him. I have to see him,' I answered.

The nurse opened my eyes with her finger and looked into my eyes. Then she put four of her fingers on my wrist, looking at her watch. After a bit she said, 'You are fine. It's nothing serious.'

She turned around to the crowd and asked for some room. Someone in the crowed asked if they should call for an ambulance. Then there were some noises. Some more people came to the yard from the street. Some who were in started leaving. I was still lying on my back, looking up at the buildings around. I could see all the balconies and laundry hanging off the bars. There were also people in the balconies looking out to see what was happening.

'Can I get up now? I am all right,' I said to the nurse.

She calmly answered. 'Yes, but move slowly. I will have to get you to a doctor. Do you have a car?'

As soon as I got up and was standing on my feet, most of the crowd left the yard.

'Are you sure you don't need anything?' asked one of the neighbours.

'He is fine. It must have just been an alarm call. I will take care of it,' she answered. Then she asked, 'Are you alone? Is your wife or your son home?'

'No, no. She is at work,' I answered quickly.

'Your son?'

'He left too.'

'Let's go have a glass of water and relax a bit. Then I will take you to a doctor.'

'A doctor? Is that necessary?' I asked, as we walked inside.

'We can go to your doctor if you want, Mr Petridis,' she explained.

'Why a doctor? I am fine. There's nothing wrong with me,' I stressed.

'Well, if you have a record, at least give him a call,' she demanded.

'Give who a call?' I asked.

'Your doctor, Mr Petridis,' she said with an annoyed voice.

'Doctor Petridis? He is not my doctor,' I said.

'Whose doctor is he then?' She asked.

'Nobody's doctor, nobody's,' I repeated.

'Who is he then?'

'He is ... he is my archaeologist. I mean, he is an archaeologist.'

'Are you fine? Mentally, do you feel okay? Come on, let's go. The clinics are open now. What time is it? Wait, your clock is wrong. Do you have a car? I will drive. It's best if you don't drive now.'

It did not take her long to persuade me to see a doctor for a check-up.

'How long have you been feeling ill?' she asked whilst driving.

'I had a dream, the most beautiful dream,' I said, looking at the ceiling of my car.

'Well, unfortunately you woke up. How long have you been feeling ill?' she asked again.

'Oh, not long. It came as a surprise,' I said.

'Do you smoke?' she asked.

'Yes, ever since the taxes went up on heating oil. All I've got to do now is to go on the balcony and breathe in.'

'Okay, calm down. Sit back and relax. You can't blame your health problems on the recession too.'

'They are chopping all the wood from the forests. Is that my fault too?' I asked.

'Is that why you had a heart attack?'

'I really appreciate what you are doing. You left your job, and now you are even driving me. I couldn't get a nurse like you even if I had ordered one in advance. Do you live in the neighbourhood? I have never seen you before,' I said, looking at her for a response.

Without any facial expressions and without saying anything, she kept her eyes on the road and continued driving. After a pause I continued: 'You know, I am a journalist. I am writing about the impacts of the recession on ordinary people. I would love to interview you, if you have time, as soon as I get on my feet again.'

Still she gave no response!

'Did you always want to become a nurse?' I asked, wanting to have a conversation going.

'Umm,' she said again without an expression.

So I continued: 'My son wanted to become a doctor, but he didn't have good grades.'

'Are you sure he always wanted to become a doctor? What does he do now?' she asked.

'Do you work at the hospital?' I asked.

'No, not anymore. I know a lot of people who wanted to become a doctor and ended up becoming a nurse. Not me. All my life I wanted to become a nurse, and instead I became unemployed. I lost my temporary job at the hospital a couple of months ago.'

'Oh, I am sorry. How did that happen? What do you do now?'

'I was temporary. I didn't know anyone, didn't go on strikes, and didn't get involved with the hospital politics. They told me I worked too much and took too many responsibilities,' she said with an angry voice.

'They kicked you out for that? Really? You know, that is how my wife lost her job in the public sector.'

She immediately said with a surprised look: 'I thought you said your wife was at work. Did she ...'

'She went out for a job interview. That's what I meant.'

'What, in the public sector again?' she asked.

'No. Well, she went out to – you know, she hates it now. Why didn't you complain? Didn't you try to keep your job?'

'You stupid idiot,' she shouted, blowing the horn at a cyclist who cut her off. Then she continued: 'Complain? Complain to whom, my boss? They kicked him out too.'

'Who kicked him out?' I asked.

'The unions, the health service unions. The hospital was in a mess. They got a new hospital head who wanted to sort things out a bit. All the doctors and the staff went on strike. They complained to the ministry, and finally –'

'Finally, what?' I asked.

'Nothing. They finally got their hospital back,' she said with a cold expression.

'Their hospital?' I asked, surprised. Then, hoping to hear something positive, I asked: 'What do you do now?'

'Nothing. I am in a program. I am supposed to work five hours a day for six months. I go to a health centre and sit and wait. Once in a while I do something, but mostly I sit around. Once I finish the six months, I might even get unemployment benefit.'

'Who pays for the program? Is it from the European Union?' I asked.

'Actually, I don't know. Is there any money from anywhere else?'

'Why don't you find something else, a full-time job, maybe at a private home care or something like that?'

'I have to rely on public transport for that.'

'Public transport is good, isn't it?' I stressed.

She looked at me briefly and then said: 'Yes, when they are not on strike they are okay. But I can't leave a sick person on his own and wait for the transport workers' unions to decide his fate.'

'Why not? They decide the fate of millions of tourists every year.'

'If the tourists don't like it, they can just leave. But the sick old man sitting in his home waiting for care can't just leave. He might die,' she said.

'Yes, but if the tourists leave we will all die,' I said, laughing aloud.

'Don't laugh at your own jokes. You might choke and have a heart attack,' she said with a smile.

'You know so much about people and society. Are you sure you only studied nursing?'

'Am I supposed to thank you for your compliments?' she said sarcastically.

'Really, why don't you find a job in the private sector? You can't afford to buy a car? Is that it?' I asked.

She made a sharp turn, came to a sudden stop at a red light, and said: 'No, because I can't get a driver's license!'

My mouth watered, and I felt my heart dropping onto my lap. I swallowed my saliva and calmly said: 'Well, if I don't have a heart attack from laughing at my own jokes, I will have one ...'

'I can drive, you see?' She interrupted me and then continued. 'By law, if I am to get a driver's license, I have to take full courses and pay all taxes for so many hours. It comes to about eight hundred euros with taxes. A basic car will cost me only two to three hundred euros.'

'You mean you can't just take the exam and pass? You have to register and take classes and pay taxes, even if you can drive?' I asked.

She came to another sudden stop. I continued: 'I mean, sort of drive!'

She laughed and said forcefully: 'Sit back and relax. Don't talk so much.'

I leaned my seat back and stretched my legs. This was followed with another sudden stop, which made a noise in the back. At first I thought a car behind had hit us. She looked at me and said: 'Here you go, that's better. Aren't you more comfortable now? Don't look at the road. Look up at the ceiling of the car. You see? Look at this stain, right there.'

'Okay, okay, you look at the road then. One of us must look at the road.'

I thought it best to do what she asked so she could concentrate on her driving. I looked up at the ceiling of the car and kept quiet, but that only lasted a few seconds. I then announced: 'You have a very strong character for a woman.'

This time without taking her eyes off the road she said calmly: 'Oh, thank you. I wish I could say the same about you.'

'What do you mean?' I asked immediately.

'What do you mean?' she asked back and then continued: 'Was that a compliment, a joke, a sexist remark, a flirtatious comment – what was it?'

I gathered myself and sat up, trying to back pedal. 'No, it's just that not many women get into a stranger's car and drive him around the town.'

She took her eyes off the road, looked at me, and said: 'I am not driving you around sightseeing. I am a nurse, with a job or without. You are sick, you need help, and we are going to the hospital. That is my duty.'

'You seem to be very dedicated to your work. I admire that,' I said.

'Why do you think they kicked me out of the hospital? That's why.'

'But you are going back there now, for me?' I said with concern.

'The hospital belongs to us, to all of us. They only work there,' she said with confidence.

I thought for a moment and said: 'But you can say that about the whole country – about every town hall, the electricity company, the public phone company, the railroad, the …'

'I thought you were going to relax!' she interrupted me.

I continued: 'We can claim it all back. It all belongs to us. How can we do that, though?'

'Hey, slow down. I am a nurse, not a politician. Besides, I am only a woman, and how would I know?' she said followed with laughter, which made me laugh too.

Then there was a long silence. At first I thought maybe I had offended her. Maybe it was better if I waited for her to talk. She was young and refreshing, full of energy. Maybe that was what was wrong in my life: I was surrounded by old people, people who had run out of ideas but still kept talking. I was surrounded by old men rooting in their own stale thoughts.

'So, when did you see the fascists?' she asked, interrupting my thoughts. All of a sudden she moved her hand up to her mouth and looked like she was choking.

'Are you okay? Maybe I should be taking you to the hospital,' I said. She opened her palm and put her hand in front of her mouth, looking like she was going to vomit.

She had turned white, but after a few visible stomach spasms she said: 'I am okay. It's nothing to worry about. What were you saying?'

'Nothing, you just said I went to the fascists. What fascists? How do you know I went to them? I just went to interview them, for my job!'

'It doesn't matter. We are all in the same boat. So what if you got a sack of potatoes from them?' she said with assurance.

I asked immediately: 'How do you know about the sack of potatoes?'

'It almost hit me on the back of my neck at the last red light; it is lying on the floor of the car in the back. I know their sacks.'

'How do you know? Did you get any?' I asked with a grin.

'You will know if my potatoes hit you on the back of your neck.'

I was again speechless. She was never going to believe I had got the potatoes to give away. I was struggling to answer. I thought it might even be better to say I got the potatoes to eat rather than to say something that made me look like a childish liar.

'Are you going to interview the potatoes too?' she asked, looking serious.

'I got them so I could give them to some Albanians, just to piss off the stupid fascists. I didn't want their plan to work. I hate them,' I said with exaggerated anger.

Again, there was a long silence. My explanation must have convinced her. Otherwise she would have come up with another smart comment. I was beginning to see why they had kicked her out of her job. She interrupted my thoughts: 'Okay, we are at the hospital. I've got to park somewhere. Here is a parking spot.'

She turned around to reverse into a car park, her eyes meeting the black sack of potatoes. As she was backing in she said: 'I thought you were a journalist. How come you don't know anything about people? Are you sure you have studied journalism?'

She executed a perfect parking job, pulled up the hand brake, turned to me, and said: 'Albanians don't accept handouts. The ones who do did not come all the way to Greece to beg. They are back in Albania. Those who came, came to work, and they have worked all these years.'

Then she got out of the car, handed me the keys, and started walking towards the hospital.

'Is there a parking fee?' I asked.

'No. Well, yes. Pay it if you want. The whole country is not working. I don't think anyone will give you a ticket.'

The parking ticket machine was too far away, and I didn't seem to have any change on me. She had gone ahead. She seemed upset with me.

I rushed up to her, and the only thing that came to my mind to say was: 'I am sorry. I didn't know you were an Albanian. Your Greek has no accent.'

She took a few longer steps. Then she slowed down and said: 'I told you, you know nothing about people. I am not an Albanian, but I have Albanian friends. I know them well, even though I am just a nurse. And you don't know them well because you can't interview their husbands. They are back in Albania working, sending money for their wife and kids in Greece, so that you don't need to give your potatoes to them.'

'You don't have to be sarcastic. I am not prejudiced. I don't want to interview Albanians. I have nothing to do with them,' I said in self-defence.

'I wasn't being sarcastic. How can you write articles about Greece's recession without mentioning the Albanians, who were the main labour force here in the good years? You should interview them. You should write about them, but they are not here. You wouldn't interview women, would you?' she said with a childish grin, raising her eyebrows.

I tried to catch up with her and said: 'Now you are being sarcastic!'

She looked back at me and said: 'Interviewing woman is at least better than interviewing potatoes, isn't it?'

Then she burst into laughter. She wasn't mad at me, I saw an opening. 'I really got those potatoes to give away, really. You should have seen me. It was ridiculous. Can you walk slower?'

She slowed down a bit and asked: 'What was ridiculous, the fascists? I am sure they were.'

'No, me.'

'That's what happens when you abuse things. They come back and haunt you. Potatoes are for eating, not to be used to make a statement or to enslave people's minds. We have done the same thing to our political parties, to our factories, to our schools, to our philosophy, to the money we borrowed to rebuild our nation, to our democracy, and to our self-respect. Now you do it to a sack of potatoes.'

'How can potatoes haunt us? I think you are getting a bit too heavy on that.'

'Well, your potatoes just hit me in the back. That was just a warning. Before you know it, if you can't find anyone to give them to, they will rot on the back seat and stink up your whole car.'

'There is a lot we can't control in this country. I don't think a sack of potatoes is one of them. As I was saying, I was there in the middle of the crowds carrying a sack, in the middle of two fanatical crowds, pulling on a German shepherd dog.'

'Is this all a part of the dream?' she asked.

'No, this is reality.'

'Did you ever wake up? You know, you remind me of Karayozi.'

'Really? People sometimes tell me I remind them of Mr Bean.'

'No, Mr Bean makes us laugh at him; Karayozi makes us laugh at ourselves.'

Then I saw another smile on her face. I had more room to prove myself, so I said: 'You should have seen me there in the middle of the crowd. I had the communists on one side and the fascists on the other side with a German shepherd following me. You see, wherever there are fascists there are Germans, too.'

Then it was my turn to burst out into laughter.

'That's a fascist thing to say,' she said without hesitation.

'I am just joking,' I responded quickly. Then continued walking and she said:

'I wish you and your generation would leave us alone, we don't need your hatred, we don't need your hang-ups, we don't need your past. A young Greek, a young German does not feel this way anymore, we want to look forward, you and your generation keep pulling us back.' She was walking fast; I tried to catch up with her and said:

'You did not suffer, you weren't around during the war, so you don't know, you don't understand.'

'Neither were you.' She said softly.

'Anyways, this is not about the past, the Germans owe us money today, they owe us compensation for their war crimes.'

'Are you trying to claim compensation for your father or for your children? I want to know what your generation has done for me. What are you going to do with the money you think you will get from the Germans? Buy another BMW, go shopping in London? Maybe a winter trip to the Bahamas? Or maybe just pay your electricity bill?'

'How do you know about the electricity?'

'Don't worry I throw away the red notice.'

'When?'

'I think you were looking for your archaeologist. What would you do with the money?'

'I, I would build factories for our youth to go and work.'

'This is what you were supposed to do with the money you got from Europe, to catch up with them and become productive.'

'My generation built factories too.' I responded.

'No, instead of building factories you built demanding factory workers who are now all unemployed.'

'I thought you would be a Communist, you know, people your age usually are,… they say if you are young and you are not a communist you have no heart and if you are old and still a communist you have no brain.'

'Cute, what is your age?' She asked.

'Why?'

'Heart, brain, you seem to have neither.'

'I don't even allow my son to talk to me this way.'

'Maybe that's why he is not the one taking you to the hospital.' She responded quickly.

'Where is all this anger coming from? Why are you mad at me, what have I done to you?'

'It makes me really angry when people from your generation do things for themselves and claim they have done it for us.'

'What is this us and them, you are our children we are all in it together.'

'What would you do if your son took your credit card and went out spending, wouldn't you get mad at him?'

'Yes. So what?'

'This is what you have done, you took your son's credit card and borrowed in his name, spent the money, didn't do anything for him and now he is stuck with the payment, he owes money for the rest of his life, he has no job and his dad is trying to find out whose fault it was, not to fix things but to have material for his article and then tell him how much he has sacrificed. Next thing you will be teaching him about ideology and morality.'

'Could you slow down, I am not well, remember. Fine, forget about communism, how come you are blaming the demanding factory workers, I thought you would be for their rights.'

'If there is one lesson that the world has learned from communism is the harms of monopolies. Your generation abolished private owned monopolies and gave it to the state and the unions. Monopolies are bad, mine or yours, it is against progress, it creates greed, it is unproductive, it is uncompetitive.'

'I thought you are a nurse how come you know so much about politics?'

'I thought you are a journalist how come...'

'I know, you asked that already, how come I don't know anything.'

'Actually I am glad you see the progress in me, a few moments ago I was just a woman and now I am a whole nurse.'

'Look I have all the answers for you but it is difficult for me to argue with you when I have got my life in your hands, you are taking me to the hospital.' She turned and looked at me and said:

'This is exactly how my generation feels about yours.'

'Look, you can't blame the recession on me, my age or the factory workers, even if they are over demanding, they have the right to protect themselves. This..., the recession, came more like a natural disaster, like the tsunami.'

'Except that the tsunami came without any warnings and after the Japanese finished burying their dead, or at least those they could find, the next thing they did was to rebuild their factories and start production. They didn't sit waiting to get compensated for the Hiroshima.'

'No matter how you look at it, they owe us money.'

'The Persians also owe us money for burning the Acropolis but why should you get it now? As a young Greek I don't trust you to get our money. Our grandparents suffered, they lived in the worst conditions, they died for us and now you want to get their blood money to cover up for the mess you have made of our nation? What have you done with their legacy? What have you done with all that they left for you? What...' I interrupted her:

'What have I done? I haven't done anything?'

'If you haven't done anything, then you shouldn't get paid anything either. For now just worry about your heart and don't worry about our generation, thanks.'

'All this because I joked about the fascists?'

'Yes, but the next thing you will joke about is that the whole recession is the fault of the Germans. And then you will say, of course jokingly, that I shouldn't buy potatoes from German supermarkets either,' she said, pacing faster.

'Well, if the whole thing is not their fault, some of it is,' I said with caution. 'But I wouldn't boycott the supermarkets. There are Greeks working in them, selling many Greek products. It is not their fault.'

By this time we were near the front door of the hospital. There was a large crowd in front of the gate. It looked like an emergency situation. What was going on? Was there an epidemic? As I got closer I noticed most protesters were wearing white. They were stopping people from going in. Hospital doctors, nurses, and staff were blocking people from going in. To this day I am not sure whether I was hallucinating or I actually saw a big white tractor in front of the hospital's gate blocking the way in.

'Emergencies to the left, only emergencies. The hospital is closed,' shouted a bearded man in white as soon as he saw us coming towards the main entrance. Without making it obvious, I edged towards the left side of the entrance. There was another door with people blocking it.

'Is this an emergency? I feel all right now,' I told the nurse.

'No, they do this often lately,' she said calmly.

'No, I mean, my condition. It is not an emergency, is it?' I asked again.

She looked at me with surprise and said: 'What do you expect, to be bleeding?'

A woman all of a sudden blocked our way and asked: 'Where are you going?'

'To the emergency room,' shouted the nurse.

We ended up waiting in the hospital for hours; she stayed with me all along. Every time I asked her if she knew anyone to help us jump the queues, she ignored my request.

Everything depended on the result of the tests: blood test, heartbeat test, cholesterol test, and so many other tests. I didn't know that there were so many tests you could have just to see what was wrong with your heart. The problem was, not all the tests were being conducted that day in the hospital, only the emergency ones. Some of my tests were not urgent. I guess that was good, but for non-urgent tests I needed to show proof of my medical insurance payments. I guess that was bad. I wondered what my cardiologist would say if I had all the tests. I also wondered who my cardiologist was.

'At least something is working in this country,' I said as I picked up the parking ticket from the windshield of the car.

'How much is it?' asked the nurse.

I was devastated but tried to seem cool. I took a harder look at the numbers. Then I wrinkled up the paper and threw it away. Looking less cool, I went and found it in the bushes, opened it up, and said, 'Sixty euros.'

Then I folded it and put it in my pocket.

'How come the hospital doesn't work but you can still get a parking ticket?' I asked. There was no response, so I asked again:

'What was the blockage about? Do you know? You used to work there, right?'

I had not got in the car yet. She looked at me and said: 'Don't worry. We don't know if it was a serious blockage. It could be anything. You will find out when you have all your tests.'

Confused with her answer, I asked: 'Why were they blocking the hospital entrance?'

'Oh, that blockage.' She laughed. 'Sorry, I thought you would be more concerned about your heart than the hospital. There are a couple of issues. I think the cantina used to belong to the hospital workers association, and they are privatizing it now.'

'The doctors? Are the doctors blocking the hospital entrance for a cantina?' I asked.

'No, I think the doctors are owed money, their salaries.'

'Why was there a big white tractor in the middle of the doctors?' I asked.

'What big white tractor? Are you hallucinating?'

'I am sure I saw a white tractor blocking the entrance,' I confirmed.

'Maybe I gave you too many aspirin. Have yourself checked. I've got to go now. Do you know if you can drive?'

'No, I am not well. I want you to stay. But actually, I am fine. You have done a lot. I don't need you; I will have to make up for this. Maybe you can come over for dinner one night. Will you?'

She looked deep into my eyes, as if she were judging me. She smiled innocently but with a bit of embarrassment. I think at one point she felt sorry for me. So I said: 'My wife is a good cook; we will make dinner for you.'

She smiled and walked away without looking back. Her last words were: 'Make sure you do your tests and stop dreaming.'

Then she walked off, completely unceremoniously. Instead of thanking her, instead of asking her if she needed a ride, instead of anything, I shouted: 'I have a twenty-two-year-old son, did I tell you?'

There was no answer. She was already too far away.

Would she ever come back? Would I ever see her again? There was something soothing about her, something besides the fact that she was a nurse. She was the most sophisticated simple girl I had ever seen. She argued with no fear and disagreed so comfortably. If I were young, around her age, I would fall in love with her instantly! She kept walking and gradually faded away behind the hospital crowds. As soon as I lost her image, I remembered I had to call Maria. She had to know what had happened to me. I reached for my phone. As soon as I went to call her, the phone rang.

Chapter 5

'No BANKS, GOD, please.' I wasn't going to answer. I didn't want to talk to anyone. I looked at the phone screen. The caller was unknown. I didn't answer. It rang and it rang. I finally had to answer to get rid of the caller.

'Hello, I can't talk now. Call later,' I said hurriedly and closed the phone. After a few seconds the phone rang again. It was unbelievable. I was standing on the corner of the street, trying to have a conversation with my wife, and all these idiots were calling me. Hopelessly, I looked at the screen. The screen said 'Maria'. The letters seemed larger than usual.

'Hello, hello, Maria? Where are you?'

'Panos, I have gone. Elpida is at the school. She is fine.'

Her voice was trembling. Without me saying anything she continued: 'I have moved temporarily to my mum's. I will stay there until you get your things and move out. I think it is the best thing for all of us.'

'Why? What has happened? I just fell asleep, that's all,' I said calmly.

'Panos, I will come over tonight, without Elpida, and we can talk.'

'Why didn't you talk last night?'

'You fell asleep.'

'Fine, come, come. Wait, not tonight. Tonight I am – no, don't come.'

'Panos, that is my house too. It is our kids' house. What are you saying? You don't want me to come so we can talk? Are you kicking me out?'

Under no circumstances did I want Maria to come to the house before I had sorted out the electricity. I had to stop her. All that came to my mind was to say: 'You are the one who moved out.'

A big silence followed. 'Are you there? Are you still there?' I asked frantically.

Maria had hung up. I closed the call and pressed her name as quickly as I could. She answered before even a single ring. The few seconds till I heard her voice took forever. I knew when we talked she might say things I did not want to hear. But at least I knew, now that she had answered, that I would have another chance. She was calm, and her voice was like an invitation to peace, to a new start, to reconciliation and hope. But it was not her voice. I listened closely.

It said: ' … emergency numbers.'

What are emergency numbers? I thought. Who was that? Why did she end the call?

I called again, this time making sure it was her number I was calling. I read her name letter by letter, pressed the number, and listened properly from the beginning.

'Your phone does not have enough credit to complete this call. You may only call emergency numbers,' said the pre-recorded message, and then it went dead again.

'Emergency? How can anything be more of an emergency than this?' I asked myself. I had to get to a phone and call her. I rushed to the car and looked in the change box. If I could just gather five euros, I could buy a new phone card. There were three euros in the car, and I had two euros in my pocket. I locked the car and started walking towards a mobile phone shop but stopped halfway and turned back to the car. I took my parking ticket out of my pocket carefully, unfolded it, and flattened it on the car, putting some pressure on the folded areas to make them less visible. Now that I needed it, I showed so much respect to the same piece of paper I had thrown away only a few minutes ago. Then I put the ticket under my windscreen wiper.

I was at the phone shop very quickly; I must have run all the way there. A long queue was awaiting me at the phone shop. At the end of the queue I felt nervous but happy that I was doing my best. I did not want to waste time, but what could I do whilst waiting? Oh, I could get my SIM card out and get ready for the new card. As I was trying to turn the phone off to open it, I realized I did not know Maria's number by heart. I had to get it from my phone before shutting it down. Searching in my pocket, I finally found a wrinkled, tiny scrap, but I could find no pen. Passing everyone in the queue, I reached the counter to grab a pen on the end of a string. Almost everyone in the queue started shouting at me for jumping the queue. As I lifted up the pen with a string attached to show that it was the pen I had come for and not for jumping the queue, the base of the pen at the other end of the string came off the desk and flew over the room falling exactly at my spot in the queue. Then the string pulled the pen from my hand which also became airborne and a moment later, after hitting the shop's window, landed near its base.

'That is my spot; I will bring the pen back when I get here.' I told the lady at the counter and walked back to my space. Away from the counter I had to sit on the floor to write Maria's number on the small paper, letting all newcomers pass in front of me. Finally, at the counter, after putting the pen and its base back, I asked for a new SIM card for my phone, complaining that my phone had been cut off.

'I am a journalist, you know. I work with this phone. You have cut me off without even telling me.'

'You are a journalist? How come you don't have a pen?' I looked at her angrily but did not say anything. I put down the five euros on the counter.

'What is your number? We don't cut people off for five euros. Let me check your account.'

'I don't want you to check my account; I need a new SIM card.'

'Why don't you just pay the bill for the old one instead of changing your number? You are a journalist. You need your number.'

'I know what I am doing. Please, just give me a new card.'

As soon as I got the new SIM, I rushed out to go to a more private place to make my phone call and entered the numbers from the piece of paper. It was working! The phone rang and rang, there was no answer. I closed and called again. After a few rings the phone was answered.

'Hello,' said a man's voice.

'Hello, who is this?' I asked.

'You are the one who called. Who are you?'

'I want Maria. Who are you?'

'I am an estate agent.'

'An estate agent? Is Maria there? Is she selling the house?'

'We don't have a Maria here. What do you want? Can I help you?'

'Ea, are you – wait a minute.' I pulled out the piece of paper with Maria's number on it. I turned it around and saw the estate agent's name.

'Are you an estate agent?'

'That's what I have been telling you all along, and really, there is no Maria here. Do you want me to tell her something if a Maria shows up?'

'No, I am sorry. I got your number for something, for –'

'Well, if it has anything to do with real estate, I am happy to help. Are you selling or buying?'

'No, I am – actually, I am calling for something else. I am a journalist. I wanted to interview you. Can I call some other time?'

'What is it about?'

'Oh, about the recession.'

'It is all dead. What is there to talk about? You are my first caller this week. Which paper?'

'Really, I need to go now.'

'Fine, as I said, you are the one who called. Good-bye.'

'Good-bye.'

'Wait, look, don't call. Forget it. I am in no mood to be interviewed. They have destroyed our business. They have screwed up the whole country. What is it that I know that you don't?'

'You will be anonymous. You can say what you want. I've got to go now.'

'Forget it. Good-bye.'

At least fifty cents had been wasted from the card because of this stupid mistake. The first thing I had to tell Maria when she answered was that I was low on credit and the phone might cut off. Four and a half euros goes a long way, but I wasn't sure how long she wanted to talk to me. She seemed to have a lot to say. This time I double-checked her number and dialled. It started ringing and ringing, but there was no answer. I closed the phone and rang again. I did not want to look desperate to talk to her, but I had no choice. The phone rang until it started beeping, and then it was cut off. I still had the phone to my ear, staring unconsciously at a pharmacy on the corner of the street. How uncaring and selfish of her! How dare she want to sort things out but not even answer my phone call. She was the one who had walked out, and now she was the one who didn't answer my calls. She could call me if she wanted; I wasn't going to chase her to her mum's house just to be nagged at. I closed the phone, put it in my pocket, and started walking to the pharmacy.

I got to the counter and asked: 'Sorry, I have a heart problem. Are aspirin good for the heart?'

'Please wait. I am serving this man now. I will be right with you,' said the lady at the counter, pointing at an old man in front of me. The man looked really annoyed and started mumbling something. I wasn't sure if I could hear the phone if Maria called. I gently pulled the phone from my pocket and put it in the side pocket on my shirt.

'I will pay you when they pay me. They will pay,' said the old man.

The pharmacist seemed to be losing patience and said to him: 'That's not the point. This is how it works now. It is not like the past. You now pay first. I give you a receipt, you give them the receipts, and then they will pay you. When? I don't know.'

'These tablets are for what? Cholesterol?'

'Yes, they reduce your cholesterol. But they only work if you take them regularly, not once in a while as you do now.'

'Why are they so expensive?'

'You have been taking them for years. How come you are asking this now?'

'I didn't have to pay for them. Why should I look at the price when I don't pay for something?'

'They are expensive because they are good. They really bring down your cholesterol.'

'They are even better now that I have to pay for them from my own pocket. After paying you I won't have any money left to eat well. That brings down my cholesterol.'

'Look, do you want them or not? I can't put it on your account anymore. I am going bankrupt. Take them now if you want. Tomorrow is Saturday. We are closed.'

'You are all mafia. You are with them. Do you know why you close on Saturdays and everyone else works? Because you have got us by the balls. You know we have to come to you anyway, so you decide in your mafia meetings to all take Saturdays off, screw the people. Whatever suits you! As long as you have the monopoly, why not?'

With these words, he walked out, and the lady at the counter, looking completely exhausted, raised her eyebrows to me to get my attention. 'Do you have aspirin? Do they help with the blood?'

She first moved her head in confirmation and then, continuing to communicate by body language, opened both hands in the air.

I continued: 'How much do I want? I don't know, one box? How big are the boxes? Are there different kinds?'

She finally broke her silence and said: 'They are all the same.' She kept looking at me impatiently, seeming completely bored with her job.

'I have a heart problem; it is not for a headache.'

She grabbed two boxes of tablets from behind the counter and put them next to me, saying, 'Is that why you have your mobile on your heart? It is not good for you, you know.'

At least she showed a bit of care. Trying to break the ice I said: 'I am waiting for a romantic phone call. That's why it is next to my heart.'

Without even a smile she said: 'Why don't you go to the hospital? The emergency ward is working.'

'Oh, I didn't know at first that they were on strike today. I spent most of the morning waiting there.'

'They are even closing our hospitals. What else do they want from us?' she said.

'Who? The doctors?' I asked.

'The doctors want their pay. What else are they going to do? It is the Germans, the French, the EU, TROIKA – all of them. I don't even know who they are, and I don't care. All day, instead of doing my job I have been a doctor, a nurse, a psychologist, a dentist, and a cardiologist, and it's not just today. People don't pay their national insurance and come to the pharmacy. They think I am a hospital here. All day I haven't –'

From being dead calm she had become very talkative. I interrupted her: 'I, I only want aspirin, nothing else. Just tell me …'

My phone started ringing. Without completing my sentence I answered the phone: 'Hello, hello?'

'Hello. Look, if I remain anonymous, I can do the interview. When can you come?' said a male voice on the other side of the line.

'Who are you? What interview?'

'I am the agent you called a few minutes ago. Aren't you the journalist?'

'Yes, I am. I am the journalist, but I will have to call you later.'

'Look, at first I didn't want to talk. But now, thinking about it, I have a lot to say. Are you really a journalist, or it is just a joke?'

'I am, I am a journalist. I will call you.' I closed the phone and put it in my shirt pocket. The pharmacist was waiting, staring at me in some state of numbness. Then she came closer and looked at me. She went back and got some cotton, sprayed it, and gave it to me. Then she got a large plaster and put it on the counter.

'What is this? I came here for an aspirin,' I asked with surprise.

'Your head, you've got some dried blood on your forehead. What kind of aspirin do you want? We have some domestic ones, and we also have Bayer.'

'Are they any different?' I asked her as I was cleaning my forehead.

'Here, let me put on the plaster.' She then leaned over the counter towards me, placed the large plaster on my head, and said: 'No, they're all the same. An aspirin is an aspirin. Here, get the Bayer. They are a bit more expensive, but they are better.'

Then she put the tablets in a small paper bag and produced a receipt. 'One euro eighty cents.'

I pulled out my wallet and then asked: 'One euro and eighty cents? Only? I must have some change.'

I started searching in my pockets, just then remembering that I had used up all my change for the phone card.

Noticing my frustration she calmly said: 'Don't worry. I have change.'

I knew exactly what to expect if I opened my wallet, but at that stage I had no choice but to go through with the act. With the show finished, I put the tablets on the counter and said: 'I must have some money in the car. I will come back.'

'Take your tablets. Don't worry; bring me the money later.'

I took the tablets and walked out with my dignity still intact. I was sure I could find some change under the car seats. Before I knew it, I was in the street walking fast towards my car. The problem was, I wasn't sure where I was going. I thought, should I go back to the hospital and try to get a check-up? That was surely my priority. Sorting out the electricity, so that Maria could come back? That one was also surely a priority. My work? I hadn't been paid for two months, but again I should go, even if I was late, just to show up. What was I going to do if I lost this job too? Maybe I could get some of my money now, yes, to pay the electricity. Then Maria could come back. My job was definitely the priority. I picked up the parking ticket, got in my car, and started driving to work. When passing the pharmacy I drove faster, just to make sure she didn't see me. I was in no mood to look for change. A euro and eighty cents was not going to make any difference in her life for a few days. I finally got to work and rushed up the stairs. The offices were empty, but the door was open. What had happened? Had we gone under? Through the glass partitions, I noticed a movement in my boss's office.

I barged into his office and said: 'I was at the hospital. I had an emergency. I am sorry.'

'Hospital? What hospital? I thought they are on strike today!'

'Yes, I know. That's why I am late; I was waiting at the hospital.'

'What is wrong with you? What is that on your forehead? You went to the hospital because of a scratch on your head? I thought for a second that you had dressed up for Carnival.'

'What carnival? I have a heart problem!'

'Your heart?'

'My heart is – I don't know, there is something wrong.'

'And you didn't know the doctors are blocking the hospital today? What is wrong with you? You are supposed to be a journalist, for God's sake.'

'Anyway, I am here now, back to work, right?'

'No.'

'What do you mean, no?'

'What did they say at the hospital?'

'They wouldn't let me in. I bought a box of aspirin. Really, I am sick.'

'Can I have one?'

'Of course, you can have as many as you want. They are the good ones, the German ones. They were expensive. Should I get you some water?'

'No, that's fine, just give me one.'

'Where is everybody? Can I start work now?'

'Journalists are on strike today too, Panos. Are you sure you are all right?'

'No, no, I knew. I just came to make sure you were okay.'

'How did you know I would be here?'

'Are you sure you don't need any water with that?'

'Are you coming tomorrow?' he asked.

'What is tomorrow? Another strike?'

He looked at me with surprise and asked: 'Well, tomorrow is an optional strike. You can strike if you want, but of course you don't get paid. When was the last time you went to your union meeting?'

'I go all the time. When was it? I think, yes, last week I went.'

'There was another one last night.'

'What, a strike?'

'No, a journalists' union meeting.'

'I wasn't feeling well last night.'

'Go home and get some rest. I don't know for how much longer we will have a job.'

'You mean we as in you or as in all of us?'

'Ever since you have become freelance, the quality of your work has dropped. When was the last time you wrote a worthy article?'

'Am I freelance?'

'Panos, it has been a year. You had a choice of redundancy or becoming freelance.'

'Oh that, yes. I know. It didn't change my salary though, right? I just lost my desk?'

'What do you want a desk for? News doesn't happen here. You've got to be out where things happen. Nothing happens in here! Is your wife working?'

'She is fine, thanks.'

'Is she working?'

'No, no, we are in a bad shape. I need some money, desperately. You owe me two months' salary.'

'Panos, you haven't done anything in the last two months, and I have given you all these leads. What happened to the girl who was barefoot in the Independence Day march? I called you when the march began, as soon as she was spotted. You said you went there, but I never saw an article. You know people would just eat that kind of thing up.'

'But ...'

'Wait, I am talking. Things are bad. People are tired of hearing what the politicians have to say. They are looking for relief, a story, something to show their misery, something or someone to blame.

A sexy schoolgirl in short skirt marching in front of the politicians completely barefoot as a sign of protest, walking with her sensitive young skin on the cold tarmac – do you have any idea what a sensation that would be on our front page?'

'But I was …'

'But what? You didn't go!'

'I was there. I got there as soon as I could, but there were too many cops, special forces. It wasn't like other Independence Day marches. People were not there celebrating. They were there protesting, and the cops would not allow anyone through.'

'So what did you do?'

'I followed her all the way to the end of the march and got through the police line.'

'And?'

'As soon as I got to her, her teacher – I don't know, I guess it was her teacher who was marching behind her – handed her a pair of high-heeled boots and shouted at her not to wear high heels to a march again.'

'What? That wasn't for protest? She just couldn't walk with them? And what did you do? Didn't you suggest it to her?'

'Suggest what? Her teacher was already telling her off.'

'Suggest to turn herself into a teenage hero. She had already walked all that way barefoot. She might as well have pretended that she had done it as a protest, for her country, for the fucking sake of Greece.'

'I should have suggested to her to protest?'

'You know, Panos, that's why you are now freelance. Sometimes you just don't have the vision. You've got to be creative and give people what they want to hear, what they want to read. You fuck up everywhere and then have the guts to come here and ask for money? There is no paper this weekend, no adverts, nothing. Maybe next Monday.'

'I need two hundred euros so I don't have to ask my mum.'

'What is it for?'

'Forget it.'

'No, here, I have a hundred. Take it,' he said, extending his arm towards me with a note in his hand.

I was already halfway out of his office, but I stopped, turned around, and took the note. It was a full, green, hundred-euro note. 'Panos, I want you to come up with a good article, you understand? When is the article you are working on going to be ready? What was it?'

'What, the farmer?'

'Yeah, that one,' he said with his arm still extended towards me as if he wanted to take the money back. I had the note in my hand and started fiddling with its velvety surface. Then I put it back on his desk and started walking out.

'Where are you going? Come here, take your money. I just asked you a question.'

I turned back, walked up to his desk, took the money again, and said: 'Ask me tomorrow. Today I am on strike, don't you know?'

I started walking out again, and he shouted: 'Panos, listen, I am here just cleaning up a bit. You didn't see me here today, right?'

'Right.'

'I don't want the bloody unions on my ass tomorrow.'

'Right.'

Securing the hundred-euro bill in the corner of my pocket, I started going down the steps. Suddenly, I noticed a man sitting on the last step near the entrance door. I quickly pulled out my hand from my pocket so that he would not notice I had anything valuable on me. What was he doing there? I looked back. It was too late to go back up again; he had already heard my footsteps. I hesitated and tried to assess the situation.

Without turning to me, he said: 'Don't worry, Panos. I already saw you going up. I am also breaking the strike.'

Then he turned and continued: 'I am also doing the same thing. What is that on your forehead? Have you been in an accident, or did the boss hit you for breaking the strike?'

The man was my colleague, a fellow journalist. Relieved from my unnecessary fear, but still panting, I checked to make sure the hundred-euro bill was still in my pocket and said: 'No, I just put it on for the carnival. It was a cheap option. What are you doing here? Why are you sitting on the steps?'

'The boss won't let me in. He is scared of the unions.'

'Will you get paid for today? Sitting here?'

'No, of course not. Everyone is on strike.'

'Why did you come, then?'

'Why did you come?' he returned my question.

'I, I came … I am on strike.'

He got up from the stair, looked at me, and asked: 'Why, Panos? Why are you on strike? What are you striking about?'

'Well, I am on … wait a minute, I asked first. What are you not on strike about?'

'You have always had this. You find people who are doing normal things, like going to work, more strange than those who are doing abnormal things. I am not on strike because I don't believe in this bullshit. They laid off the workers of the national TV, and we have to go on strike for them? I go on strike for them? Why? So they get their well-paid, cushy jobs back?'

'Oh, that. Yes, of course. That's what it has been all about?'

'You didn't know? What planet do you live on?'

'I wasn't well for a while, but today I am okay. I just think – they are, you know, they are our colleagues. They are journalists like us. We shouldn't let the government do what they want to them. We have to think about society, all of us, not just our own immediate benefits.'

He looked deep into my eyes, smiled, and said: 'Why didn't you go on strike when the paper laid off Olga? Why didn't you go on strike when the paper laid off Apostolis? His desk used to be next to yours. Didn't you notice him gone? Why didn't you go on strike for him?'

'I didn't go because nobody asked me to go on strike. Why didn't you?'

He paused to light a cigarette and then said: 'I didn't because the paper was looking for an excuse to lay me off too.'

'Same with me. I didn't want to be kicked out,' I said immediately.

There was a long, uncomfortable silence. It felt as if we both had a lot to say but that something was stopping us. I decided to break the stillness and asked:

'So, why are you here today? Is this just to prove a point? To whom?'

'It is wrong, Panos. It is wrong. Just because some of them are journalists too, that doesn't make the people at the state TV our colleagues. They have different salaries, different benefits, different contracts, different work load, different … they are from a different class. You know, when they go on strike, the government borrows money and pays them more or gives them more benefits. When I go on strike I lose my wages.'

'Not anymore. The government can't borrow anymore.'

'And that's why we are in this shit, all of us, us and them.'

'We are all employees. Our struggle is one. There is no us and them,' I said forcefully.

'I have more in common with a typist in a Bangladeshi newspaper than a journalist for state-run TV in Greece. They are public sector workers, public servants, servants who have become masters. Would they go on strike if our paper went bust tomorrow?'

'We can't afford to show our differences and split the society. Then they will just take advantage of us even more. We must stick together. That's what keeps our society strong.'

'Who, who are you talking about? Who are they? The Germans again?'

'Well, them too – the Germans, the Europeans, all of them.'

'Panos, I know you are not well, but stop hallucinating. You are back in the war era again. I am talking about this occupation, not the one during the war.'

'Which occupation?' I asked, surprised.

'We have all been taken hostage. The whole nation is under occupation!'

'By whom?'

'The public sector, the unions, and their politicians. This is a dictatorship, the dictatorship of the majority, an oligarchy.'

'Oligarchy is the dictatorship of a minority. The public sector now is not exactly a minority either.'

'I know. That's why it is even more dangerous. The oligarchs are now so many, with so many mouths to feed and so many benefits to consider, that they are bringing down the whole society. You know why nobody complains? Because we all have someone – a wife, a father, a cousin, a son – someone who is amongst the little dictators.'

'You can't call it an occupation. We can't occupy ourselves. And we do complain! Who said we don't?'

'No, Panos, we don't complain. We moan. The next time you are in a public office, try to complain about something. See what happens.' Another absolute silence took over.

'At least if you are not happy with things you can vote,' I said confidently.

'Vote for what?'

'Elections. We still have our democracy. We invented it and are still practicing it. What is wrong with that?'

'Who do I vote for? The same shit? How many years have we given to the blues and the greens? How many more years are we going to give them? We gave the dictators less time and they achieved more,' he shouted.

'What? Are you for the dictators now? There is not just blue and green, not the same shit. There are some old parties that are getting a new life. There are some new parties too. It is your choice. This is democracy.'

'Panos, the most dangerous parties are the new ones. They are the same old people without new ideas but with new colours. With the old parties at least we know when they are lying. Can't you see? We have the same supply of party leaders, members, and supporters. No new ones are produced. They don't import new people from abroad.'

'It is still a democracy,' I interrupted.

'Democracy was supposed to be voting for your most favoured ideology, your most favoured party, and your most favoured person.'

'So, what is it now?'

'Now in our elections we vote for the least hated, not the most favoured.'

'Why do you think people are voting for the new parties, then? They don't hate them.'

'We don't know we hate them yet. They haven't had a chance to prove themselves. It is for the same reason that all the candidates, instead of boasting about being experienced, boast about being new, completely fresh, with no experience. You know why, Panos? Because in our politics, being experienced automatically means you have made dirty connections. It means your hands are already muddy.'

'So what do you suggest? Are you saying we shouldn't have the right to choose because we don't know?'

'What is the point of choosing, just to say to everyone we have a democracy? All these new parties that want elections, what are they trying to do? This is not a crisis of democracy. We are not having political crisis. We are not having a philosophical crisis. It is an economic crisis.'

'So what do we do then? Shouldn't we look for a new path?'

'What new path? We know the path. Which one of these new parties or the old ones have come up with a new path for you?'

'You can't live without ideology,' I said confidently.

'You can't feed your kids ideology, Panos. This is the time that we give our ideologies a break, this is not the time to promote them.'

'We still need a leader to do this.'

'Is this how weak your democracy is? You need to have a new leader every time you run out of food? When a car runs out of gas, Panos, do you start looking for a new driver or a gas station?'

'What is our gas station?' I asked angrily. Suddenly the entrance door opened.

A man walked in. Surprised to see us in the corridor, he said: 'Oh good, you are working today.'

'No, we are on strike today. You need to come back tomorrow. No, the day after. I don't really know,' I explained.

'Is there anyone upstairs?' he asked.

'No. Is this urgent? What do you want?' I asked.

'I have the local tourist office. I came hoping to book some advertising for next weekend, if there is a paper.'

As soon as my colleague heard this he said: 'Here you go. Here is one gas station!'

The man immediately replied: 'No, I have a tourist office, not a gas station. Thank God for that. All the gas stations are closing down.'

'No, my colleague was referring to your job as a source of income for the nation.'

'For the nation? I can't feed my own kids. Are you waiting for me to feed the nation?'

'No, what we are trying to say is ...'

I was interrupted by the man. 'Let me tell you something. We tourist agents are alone, completely on our own, and everything is working against us.'

'Why are you alone? How about all the subsidies, how about all the support?' I asked.

'What support? They are talking about elections right before our season. Foreigners plan their summer holidays now. Who wants elections? I don't want democracy. I want tourists! All these faggots in the street shouting, blocking roads, shouting against Germans, the French, the politicians ...'

This time I interrupted him and said: 'What do you want, for people to shut up just for a piece of bread for you?'

My colleague entered the conversation. 'When was the last time anyone asked him what to do to bring more tourists in?'

'What does he know?' I replied. 'He has a little shop renting rooms and selling boat tickets.'

'Do you trust your local politician or him to make decisions on tourism?' asked my colleague.

The man answered: 'Look, I see a lot of foreigners. I don't know what these politicians do, but whatever they do, they are not helping the tourists. If it wasn't because of our beaches, our mountains, and our people, we would be all starving right now. Tourists don't come here for anything that the politicians do. They come because this is Greece, at least for a little longer! If it weren't for these people sitting in their offices in Athens making stupid decisions, making stupid new rules, we would have more tourists. More would come.'

'What do you want them to do, come and ask you how to run the country? Come and ask you where to build the airport?' I asked, not expecting to get an answer.

But the travel agent answered: 'Look, I don't know about where to build the airport, but I am sure I would choose a different name for it. Foreigners just can't say "Eleftherios Venizelos" that easily.'

'What did you want them to call it? "Club Sunshine", "Prince of the Mediterranean"?' I asked angrily.

Taking a step towards us, my colleague said: 'Foreigners come to Greece for the sun and the sand. They don't come here to learn about our politics and modern history. That is a large part of our income, except for the borrowings, of course. We should look at things from their eyes, not ours. Venizelos is our pride, our history. We don't have to fly into him to appreciate him.'

I was getting more and more annoyed, almost losing control. I shouted: 'If it was up to him, we would all become waiters, waiters for the foreigners. It is just not us.'

Then I raised my head up with my arm outstretched, looking across the hall, and shouted: 'Hey, you in the white shirt, you! Yes, you, grandson of Alexander the Great, the conqueror of the entire known world: Bring me an ashtray, and come and clean my table.'

'What does Alexander have to do with this?' asked my colleague. He continued: 'I would rather take an ashtray to a foreigner and make a living than go to my government and fill out forms asking for handouts. Our own governments, the people we voted for and pay, are turning us into beggars so that they can stay in power, look down on us, and tell us how to fill out forms. If Alexander the Great were alive, do you think he would fill in forms to get money? No, he would go and shove the five-hundred-euro bill up their wide asses.'

'Are you kidding? Are you expecting us to whore our country to attract tourists?' I said eagerly.

The door opened. A bearded young man dressed up as a priest walked in. We all turned to him. Was he dressed up for carnival? The door opened again. A girl with a short skirt and heavy makeup, dressed as a, well, maybe a prostitute, walked in. The young man dressed up as a priest turned around and held the door open for the girl. A priest holding the door for a prostitute? That confirmed to me that he was not a real priest. The girl bent down to kiss the hand of the priest, exposing almost her entire cleavage. The young man dressed as a priest went along with the act in full and let the girl kiss his hand.

'See, you should be careful shouting "whore" in public, Panos. You might have a real priest walk in next time,' my colleague said to me jokingly.

I replied: 'I meant it metaphorically. Anyone can be a whore. You don't need to dress up for it.'

The door opened again, and a familiar-looking man walked in. He went straight up to the girl and said: 'Can I help you, young lady?'

Then he turned to me and shouted. 'Hey, Panos, come on, come help the young lady. See what she wants.'

It was Pavlos, my old classmate, the union leader. I was excited to see him, but he was the last person I wanted to see now. What if he found out my boss was upstairs?

'Pavlos, what are you doing here? We are on strike today. There is no one here,' I said frantically.

He looked around the room and said: 'Yes, I can see, no one here. Where is Nikos?'

'Nikos, my boss? He is not here.'

'I just talked to him on the phone. He is here. You are the one who is never here. I thought you worked here,' he said sarcastically.

'I am usually out interviewing politicians, minsters – you know, that sort of people. I am a reporter. Nothing happens here. Why should I be here? I must be out where things actually do happen.'

'What would you like, madam?' Pavlos asked the girl for the second time.

'Father was first. He came before me,' said the girl.

'I think we came together,' said the man dressed as a priest. 'Why don't you go first.'

'No, I insist. I should have let you come first,' said the girl dressed as a prostitute.

Then Pavlos jumped almost in the middle of them and said, 'As long as you came together, especially simultaneously, I am sure you are both happy.'

This made everyone except the priest laugh. The travel agent, seeing the priest's silence and serious expression, tried to change the subject and said: 'Good morning, Father. Any luck with the excursion?'

'The excursion? Yes, I am going ahead with it. How do you know? Do you want to join us?'

The travel agent, looking pleased, said: 'I am the travel agent you came to last week for estimates, estimates for the excursion to Tinos. Are you going there?'

Pavlos, still standing in the middle of the room, turned completely red and said: 'I am sorry, Father; I didn't realize you were a real priest.'

After a long pause the priest glimpsed at the girl again and said: 'It doesn't matter, my son. In situations like this, sometimes I forget too.'

We all laughed, this time even harder than the last time. It was a welcomed laugh of relief.

'Father, Father, you haven't answered my question yet. Are you going to use our office?' asked the travel agent.

'I am still considering it. Times are hard. I have to choose the cheapest option. It is a religious excursion, anyway. It is not for fun.'

Then, looking at me, he said: 'Today I have come to put an advert. Are you open? Why are you down here?'

'An advert for what? For the religious excursion that I spent two days working on an estimate for?' asked the travel agent.

'I just want to put an advert in the personnel section,' said the girl.

'What is your name?' asked my colleague.

'What does it matter? Are you taking down the advert now, here in the corridor?' asked the girl.

'No, I just wanted to know if your name is easy to say. You sure look nice,' said my colleague.

'My colleague here thinks that we should go whoring the nation, to get the foreigners to give us a piece of bread,' I said.

'The politicians have already turned the whole nation into a whorehouse anyway,' the estate agent said.

'Please, please, there is a lady present,' said Pavlos.

'It's okay. I am used to it. But please, if you have to use professional working girls as an example for your political arguments, at least use the word "prostitute". There is a priest present.'

'Don't you mind me, my children. There are many mentions of whores and whoring in Christian literature. One of the earliest theologians, Saint Augustine, in his sermons on the Gospel of John, verse XIV, says, and I quote in common language so you understand, "How evil a thing it is to go whoring your beliefs, to give up your faith in God and instead chose earthly pleasures, to choose the love of the world and earthly corruption."'

There was a moment of silence; for some reason everyone was looking at the floor. Finally Pavlos said loudly: 'Amen.' Which was followed by everyone, including myself, saying, 'Amen.'

'Leave it to our politicians. They are capable of even whoring a whore,' said my colleague with confidence.

'How can you whore a whore? A whore is a whore already,' said the escort.

Without hesitation, my colleague responded: 'In September 2006, our politicians artificially grew the country's GPD by 25 per cent using the nation's and imported prostitutes by forcing them to issue receipts.'

The escort looked at Pavlos and asked: 'What did they gain by using prostitutes?'

Pavlos answered quietly, 'I will show you later. And if you are nice to me, I promise it will be more than 25 per cent.'

'You are terrible,' said the escort, stretching her arms towards her feet to squeeze her breasts. Both she and Pavlos started giggling.

'You remember, they asked you to issue those useless receipts?' my colleague asked the girl.

She gathered herself up and said after a pause: 'Yes, I do. I mean, not me personally. I am not a call girl. I am a professional escort. I have been told by some friends that some women I know still have the receipts.'

'In the Netherlands they add value to their prostitutes by creating a sex museum to attract more interest and more income for the nation. In my country they give receipts to the prostitutes and tell them they don't need to issue them,' said my colleague.

'What was the point of the receipts?' I asked my colleague.

'They were just to deceive the other European minsters. We told them it must be included in the Gross Domestic Product index as a business because it has official receipts.'

'And nobody complained? Nobody said anything?' I asked.

'Who would complain? Would you complain that your prostitute has receipts but she doesn't give them to you because you don't want them? Would you want a prostitute's receipt in your pocket when you go home to your wife for dinner?'

'Who, me? Why would I want a receipt? I mean, why would I go to a prostitute?' I asked.

My colleague continued: 'It was the good times back then. Everybody was happy. We got our next grants, financial aid, and new loans, all thanks to the surprising but necessary growth in our economy and our ingenious politicians.'

Looking at the escort, Pavlos said: 'And don't forget, also thanks to our beautiful – what did you call them?'

The escort answered: 'Working girls.'

Pavlos repeated: 'Working girls, yes. I love all working people.'

My colleague continued: 'When you turn to sex to boost your economy and abuse your prostitutes, your economic policies are loose, your finance minister is a pimp, your treasury department is a box with a padlock under the bed, and your whole nation becomes a whorehouse.'

'That's not enough. You still need a tough and hard-working madame you can trust,' said the escort.

'Which we don't have. Can you suggest anyone?' said my colleague.

'Call her in twenty, I mean twenty-five years. She is busy now,' said Pavlos, which made everyone including the escort laugh.

Then she said: 'Make it thirty. Look, you men are just obsessed with sex. Sorry, Father, I am talking to them. Do you not talk about anything else, just football and sex?'

'You are so smart. Tell them,' said Pavlos.

Then my colleague, as if he were the centre of attention, continued his lecture: 'The same politicians who lied and made up numbers risking the nation's reputation for their own sake so to stay in power are now making up numbers telling me how much tax I owe the government. Why should I believe them? Why should anyone believe them? They say they have to raise taxes for the sake of Greece. Which Greece? With me in it or out? The Greece that my children are growing up in or the Greece that only includes their party member gangs in the public sector and the fat cat tax evaders they allow to get away with murder? Am I paying more taxes so they can build better schools, make more jobs, make better roads, and get better health care? Or am I to pay more taxes so that they can deceive the Europeans again, stay in power, and keep their supporters, cousins and uncles in their jobs?'

'Are you guys open or not? Why are you gathered here in the corridor? What evil is this you impose on us? Who is the boss around here?' asked the priest.

'Why the rush, Father? Tinos is not going anywhere. God willing it will be there after the recession too,' sarcastically said the travel agent.

'I have work to do,' said the priest.

'Will you be going to Mykonos too, for a dip?' asked Pavlos.

The travel agent laughed loudly and said: 'No, Father is too busy in the recession. We all work during the week. The priests work on

Sundays. We all lose our jobs in the recession, but the priests work harder.'

'Yes, my son, there are too many hungry people,' confirmed the priest.

'And you love hungry people. They are easier to drag to church. The more hopeless, the better for you,' said the agent.

The priest had a long look at the agent and said: 'You seemed like a blessed Christian when I came to your office. You even said you would come to church the following Sunday. What happened? Why have you changed so much?'

'Why should I believe in you? What have you done for us? What have you done for the country with the recession?' said the travel agent.

Everyone in the corridor looked uncomfortable, and the priest responded: 'Your faith should not depend on worldly goods. Your faith must be deeper than that. The church is not here to rescue you from your material misery. The church does not get involved with politics. The church is here to help you get closer to the Lord in the next world, in the eternal one.'

My colleague suddenly decided to enter the conversation and said: 'And the sooner we die, the sooner we get to the almighty. That's another reason you like the recession and you don't do anything to help the people on this earth.'

'As I said, we are not here to get involved with politics. We have another mission,' said the priest.

My colleague answered: 'Why are you not political, Father? Which part of the holy verses don't you understand? If we have the excuse of not understanding the ancient text, you have no excuse for not understanding the common language. What is not political in the holy script? Why don't you talk when you see evil instead of burying your head in the sand, instead of revealing the corruption, instead of being more involved when there is misery. Instead of giving more, you just pray more, bring people to Tinos, and tell them their salvation is there?'

The priest looked around the room, cleared his throat, and said: 'We at the Orthodox Church do not view the world only in the obvious but misleading timeline visible to common men. We trust that our Lord, the creator, is above all the wisest and the most merciful. We, the insignificant, are all his blessed children. The Lord loves us all. Our history as men is short and trivial, and our current life is a very small part of this long chronological order. As a divine entity, the Orthodox Church's ultimate responsibility is to the holy trinity and not to the interim, diminutive, and earthly troubles of the mortal man. Of course, the church must do its utmost to help and care for every troubled man who requires earthly assistance. But the church must first concentrate on man's soul by assisting the children of God to be patient and enlighten the believers not only to trust but also to cherish the ways of the almighty and beg for forgiveness. It is God, and only God, who is the supreme provider.'

This time Pavlos cleared his throat as if wanting to give a long lecture. He drew everyone's attention to himself and said: 'Aaaaaaaaaaaaaamen.'

The priest looked away, seeming very agitated, as if he did not fit in his robe. He went towards the door. The door opened again. An old man walked in. Pavlos started whispering something in the young girl's ear.

'We are on strike. We are not here today,' I said immediately:

'I must be in the next issue of the paper, please,' said the old man.

'I am an escort, not a whore,' shouted the girl to Pavlos. The situation was getting out of hand. I had to take charge before it got worse. So I stepped up the stair, looked down at everyone, cleared my throat, and began an announcement.

Just then the door opened again. A man walked in, saw me on top of the stairs, and asked: 'Where is the advertising department?'

'Who are you? What are you selling?' I asked.

'I ... I rent boats, kayaks, and dinghies.'

'In this weather? You are hoping for locals to rent your boats?' asked Pavlos.

'No, I am selling my boats,' said the man, still standing by the door since he could not really fit in. Everyone in the room looked at him with surprise.

'Why are you selling your boats? Are they old?' asked Pavlos.

'No, I am closing. I'm bankrupt. I owe a lot of money to people,' said the man.

'People? You mean the banks, right?' asked the travel agent.

'Have faith, young man. God is great. It is winter now. Of course you have no work. God willing you will have a long, busy summer,' said the priest.

The man looked at the priest, paused a bit, and then started talking. 'It can't be long enough, Father. Every year they give me my license to use the beach at the beginning of the summer. Last year they gave it to me in the middle of the summer. Every year I have to make new applications, give them all my life history, have a health check-up for safety reasons, insure all my boats, insure my business, apply for renting part of the beach, and get every stamp from a dozen ministries. Then they wait all the way till summer to come and check my facilities. They come with their families so they can really try out the boats and make sure they are safe. Before I get the permit, I can be fined for doing my business.'

He stopped, but that was just to get some air. Then he continued: 'The business I am registered for, they fine me for doing it. Foreigners book their trips from the beginning of the year. They book their flights in advance. They book hotel rooms in advance. Last summer I started the applications for the license at the beginning of the year, like every year, but this year I had no license till the middle of August. It wasn't ready; that's all they told me. Do you know how many clients that I had made through the years came to me disappointed and said they would never come back to Greece? Do you know how many had sent money to book hotels and cancelled their trips because I couldn't operate? The hotel owners didn't have the deposits to return, and I ended up owing my clients their money. Their holidays were ruined. Some people work for fifty weeks and dream about coming to Greece for two weeks. That's why I am selling my boats to pay them back.'

'Okay, okay, are you here to sell your boats or collect money for a charity? Stop the stories. How much do you want for your boats?' asked Pavlos.

'Were you selling hotel rooms? You are not a travel agent,' asked the travel agent.

'I was just trying to help them make a package for themselves. What should I do, wait for the minister of tourism to help market the area?'

'Everyone stop. There's no need to talk so much. How much do you want for your plastic boats?' asked Pavlos.

'I have no price for them yet. I don't know. Well, I thought people would call and come and see them, and then, you know,' answered the boat guy.

'You can't sell something without a price! Come on, don't get all emotional about it. It is just a boat, a piece of plastic. Give me a good price and I'll buy it now. I have to see them first, right?'

I moved up one step, cleared my throat again, and announced: 'Listen, listen, lady and gentlemen, we are on strike. Please leave and come tom ... Another day.'

Then I felt a tap on my shoulder. I turned around. It was Nikos, my boss. He was standing above me, two stairs higher. He genteelly pushed me away then pointed at the old man and said: 'What do you want?'

'I have lost my dog. I want to put an announcement in the next issue.'

'Didn't you hear? The office is closed today,' said Pavlos.

'Why are you here then?' asked the priest.

Pavlos looked at the young girl and answered: 'I am a consultant with the paper; I bring articles and news, about the unions. The editor needs them for the paper. I have news about our struggle to keep the economy going to get some bread on the workers' table.'

'Can I put an announcement for my German shepherd today or not?' said the old man.

'Your dog, was it your dog? A German shepherd with a chain?' I asked.

'Yes,' he said excitedly, 'Where is it? Do you have it?'

'No, but don't worry. I took it to the dog rescue. They must be open now.'

'Dog rescue? What dog rescue?'

'There is a dog rescue. I will give you the address. You can go now. I didn't know about it either,' I said.

'They can't advertise for all the dog rescues. They have a small budget from the EU. If they advertised there wouldn't be any room for your dog. All the bloody dogs in the street would be in it,' said Pavlos.

'Can we put our ads in?' asked the escort.

'But we are closed,' I said.

'Come on, I am the one who is paying your salaries,' shouted the escort. Then, looking down at my trousers, she said: 'You have got a hundred-euro note sticking out of your pocket. That could be mine from the past adverts.'

'What? I have never seen you here before,' I replied quickly.

'That's because you are never here, you stupid. Give her the hundred back and you will see more of her,' said Pavlos,

'Just give me the address; I will get out of your way,' said the old man.

The door opened again. This time a very frustrated-looking man dressed up as a funeral director walked in.

Nikos asked, sounding sarcastic and still on top of the stairs: 'And how can we help you, sir?'

Before the man had a chance to answer, Nikos talked again: 'It's been years since you were here, but you do advertise in the other papers.'

'No,' said the man, 'I haven't advertised for a couple of years now. I can't afford it.'

'So you have heard about our recession discounts for estate agents?' asked Niko.

'No, actually. I am here because a guy from your paper called me for an interview, someone called Panos. I have called him three times since this morning, but he doesn't answer his phone.'

Looking surprised Nikos asked: 'He called you for an interview?'

'Well, at first he was looking for Maria. When I told him Maria was not there he said he wanted to interview me,' said the estate agent.

Nikos, getting even more confused, asked me: 'Maria? What was your wife doing with him?'

I frantically answered: 'No, not my wife, another Maria.'

The estate agent smiled and said: 'You must have many Marias. That's why you keep losing them and can't keep track of them.'

'I called you for an interview,' was the only thing I could say.

Like a child who has solved a difficult puzzle, Nikos turned around to me and said: 'Well done, Panos. Are you marketing for our advertising department?'

'Panos, Panos, tell me where my dog is,' said the old man.

The estate agent said: 'No, I told you I have no money to advertise.'

'So, what? You want free publicity?' asked Nikos.

'Hey, you are the one who called me,' said the agent with anger. Then he left, banging the door against himself.

'Are you crazy, Panos? I thought you interviewed politicians. What do you want to interview an estate agent for? What do they know that you don't? The guy doesn't even have a high school diploma,' said Pavlos.

'What is it you expect me to do? Shall I come another day, or are you working today?' asked the priest.

Two more people walked in. Niko had quick look at them and announced with a grin: 'Ladies and gentlemen.' He then looked at the call girl and said: 'Sorry, I mean lady and gentlemen. I have always said if we workers stick to our demands and are not fooled by the claims of recession of the slave runners in high offices, we will come out of these difficult times. Look at this, look how we are back on our feet. This is an ordinary paper.'

Then he looked at Nikos and said: 'Well, not just an ordinary paper, a fine paper, one of the best in the city. Look, look, people are coming nonstop. There is so much traffic, so much hope. All of us are alive because we were patient and did not give in. Here are the fruits or our hard work, sticking to our rights and not taking one step back ...'

Pavlos would have gone on if my colleague had not stopped him by saying: 'Wait a minute, when did you see the recession end? These people are here selling everything they have. They are not producing anything.'

Pavlos contemplated a bit. Then, looking at the people, he shouted: 'We have hope, don't we? How many people here have a product? How many are advertising for new opportunities? Which one of you builds and produces? How many of you?'

An uncomfortable silence filled the air. Then Pavlos looked at the call girl and said: 'Look, don't be shy. We all make something. This beautiful young lady here produces happiness. Who else? Don't you all make something, do something?'

One of the newcomers, like a school kid, raised his hand and said: 'Well, I produced something. That's why I am here, to advertise. I produce metal.'

'You produce metal? You have a factory? Where? I don't know you,' said Niko with surprise.

'Well, I kind of produce metal – not exactly.'

'Not exactly? How is that? What are you advertising?' I asked.

The man looked at Niko again and said: 'Well, I buy metal and sell it. Nowadays there are so many factories closing down, and they are low on cash. I buy their machinery, their doors and windows, bathroom pipes, whatever is metal, and then we sell them.'

'Factories are selling their bathroom pipes?' I asked.

'Well, most factories are about to be repossessed by the banks, and the banks don't really care about machinery or pipes. How would they know, anyway?'

Pavlos looked impatient, and so did almost everyone in the room. Nikos moved up one step and announced: 'Okay, those of you who want to advertise today, I am willing to make an exception. But we are supposed to be closed, so I can't give you any receipts.'

People started following him up. The old man was gone within seconds after I gave him the address of the dog rescue. Pavlos was still in the corridor and asked: 'Are you leaving, since you are on strike, or coming up to help your boss?'

'No, I've got to go. It was really nice seeing you,' I said.

'You must come and see me at my villa. You must come, come and stay around for a few days. I have a guest house. We will catch up with the old gossip. We will have fun.'

'Pavlos, you must be very busy now, with all the lay-offs, the strikes, and the factories closing down.'

'Don't worry, Panos. I am always busy, even if there are no factories left. Hey, by the way, do you really not know that chick? Does she advertise here often? Is she in the paper? What is she called?'

'I don't know. I am hardly ever here. I just know she has a pretty name, kind of sexy.'

'They all have. How else would they run a business if they didn't? Everyone must think of their business. They can't afford to be like you.'

'What? You don't like my name?'

'No, Panos, your name is fine, but ...'

'But?'

'Listen, my dear Panos, from experience I can advise that there are significant and sensitive particularities in each working circumstance that must be carefully considered.'

'What are you talking about?'

'No wonder he doesn't keep you around. You just turn business away. You could have waited for that old man to advertise first and then called him and told him about the dog. That way he would know the paper works. Everyone has to pay something to get what they want. How is the paper going to pay your salary if you keep turning business away like this? I've got to go up. See you soon. Call me.'

Nikos appeared on top of the stairs, shouting: 'Pavlos, Pavlos are you coming up or spending all day in the corridor? Come on up.'

The door opened again. A well-dressed, overweight woman walked in. Niko was halfway up the stairs.

'Yes, please, how can we help you?' shouted Nikos from the top of the stairs.

'I am the person who came last week for a report, remember?' said the woman.

'What report? Who are you?' asked Nikos.

'I am an activist, an ecologist,' she replied.

'Are you always that way or it is your weekend hobby?' asked Niko with a grin.

'What do you mean?' said the woman.

'Oh, I remember now. You came last week. You are trying to stop planning permission for a tourist resort up in …'

'Yes, you asked me to come some other time,' she replied.

'But we are closed today. We are on strike,' I said.

'Panos, why don't you just interview the lady? It is for a good cause,' said Pavlos.

He was followed by Nikos, who said: 'We can't go on strike. Can you not see, Panos? For one hour we stop working, and the whole country falls apart. Just talk to the lady, Panos. She is from your area.'

'My area?' I asked.

'I am not from there. I, my group, is also active there.'

'Where is my area?' I asked Nikos.

'Where you have your land, the hill you keep talking about. Just interview the lady,' said Nikos.

'Where? Upstairs is full of people,' I replied.

'I thought you were on strike today,' said the lady.

'Don't worry about it, madam. Panos will take care of it. Just do it in the corridor, Panos,' said Niko.

'In the corridor?' I asked.

'We are going upstairs, to see what we can do for the other lady who is waiting for us,' replied Niko.

In order to distract the ecologist, I quickly turned to her and said: 'Okay, let's do it.'

She looked at me with surprise and said: 'But you don't even have anything.'

'Have anything?'

'Yes, you have no pen and no paper. How are you going to interview me?'

'Wait till you see his pen,' I heard Niko say to Nikos quietly as they were going up the stairs, which made them both laugh.

'Do you have anything on you so I don't have to go upstairs again? I have a bad heart. I shouldn't really be here today. I only came to work today because we are on strike,' I said.

'You are not making any sense. Are you sure you are okay?'

'I am not the one being interviewed, you are. You are the one who should make sense,' I said. 'I don't really need to write anything down. So tell me, what are you active in? What do you do?'

'As I said, I am an ecologist. It is my job to make sure our beautiful country is not destroyed for short-term benefits – for the tourists, for the builders, big business, banks, all of them. I believe we have to preserve our country for the next generation.'

'Do you go to these parts of the country? Are you active locally?'

'Well, have you heard the saying: "Act locally, think globally"? It is sort of the reverse for us. We act globally and think locally because the locals are too narrow-minded to understand our responsibility.'

'What do you mean?'

'Well, locals look to short-term benefits. Everyone has a son or a daughter who is looking for a job. Everyone wants to take advantage of our beautiful beaches, our beautiful mountains, our landscapes, and our magnificent islets. Locals think in the short term. They all want development in their areas. They all want hotels and shops and entertainment facilities so their kids can get jobs. Locals think that everything belongs to them. They just don't understand that we have to keep this beauty for the next generation.'

'You mean you get no support from the locals?'

'Look, everything happens from Athens anyway. There is a benefit to living in the capital. All the final decisions, the final courts, everything happens here.'

'Final courts, why courts?'

'Oh, that is our strategy. If we can't talk sense to the locals, we sue the businesses that are trying to build resorts in our paradise.'

'And you always win?'

'There is no always, but we don't have to win.'

'What do you mean you don't have to win?'

'We have forestry on our side. There are of course environmental issues. We can claim that any development can cause hazards to the population. If we don't find anything, we even have the archaeological authorities on our side. One way or another we have enough obstacles to stop development.'

'Through courts?'

'No, as I said, we don't necessarily have to win. If partners in the system can't help, fortunately the courts take so long that any businessman would give up the idea.'

'But don't you have to listen to the locals?'

'As I said, the locals are too narrow-minded to understand the value of our land. Some of them have not even seen the beaches and the islets we are protecting.'

'How have you seen them?'

'Well, my father has a yacht. I have been sailing since I was a child. Fortunately, my fiancé's parents also have a yacht. Last summer we spent a week around the islets in your area. Have you even been around the islets?'

'No, I am from the other side of the peninsula.'

'Why haven't you seen it? It is not too far.'

'Well, I don't have a boat.'

'We have been very active there, I mean in Athens. They were trying to build a tourist resort there. It would destroy the area. If the locals want to find jobs, they can send their kids to Athens, to the big cities. Or they can go abroad; I don't care. Why destroy our beaches? I can't imagine that small island with hotels on it, with people walking around the island, beach umbrellas on every corner, empty beer cans on the glittering sand, and naked foreigners on our isolated, private beaches. You should go there. It is a paradise. Go there before they destroy it.'

'Is anything going to happen?'

'No, my father has been fighting them since I was in high school, about sixteen years or so. They have been in courts all these years.'

'Is your father an ecologist too?'

'No, my father does not get involved with politics. He is a businessman. He just loves that area and does not want it destroyed. But you know, he is getting old now. It is up to us now, the new generation, to fight for our country. But it is so difficult in the winter. At least in the summer I go to these little paradises, take pictures, find new places, and contemplate on our boat. In the winter I can't do much. I write. Well, I wanted to ask your boss if you want me to write some articles for you. It is a shame. Our people don't know much about our struggle. I ...'

My phone started ringing again.

'Are you going to write anything down? Will you write an article? I have never been interviewed like this.'

The phone kept ringing.

'Could you call the paper next week, please? I would like to continue this interview, maybe at my desk. I really need to go now.'

'Okay, I will go now too. Good-bye, I will call you next week.'

The phone stopped ringing.

'Don't forget to ask your boss about the articles.'

And with that she left, leaving me in the empty corridor. I could still hear all the voices from all the characters echoing in my ears. I checked my phone to make sure the last call was not from Maria and then took a long breath, involuntarily inhaling the stale tobacco smoke still floating in the air.

Chapter 6

MARIA HAD STILL not called me. It was very strange. Suddenly I remembered the estate agent. He said he had tried to call me. That was on my old phone! I stepped out in the cold, walking towards my car. I must have had a call from Maria. As I activated my old phone, the missed call messages started popping up. I had five calls, three from one number and two from another number. The estate agent said he tried to call me three times. So who was the other caller? It could be important. It could be from Elpida's school. I swapped phones again and called the number with two missed calls.

A man answered. 'Please, may I help you?'

'Hello, this is Panos. Did you call me?' I asked.

'You again! Look, I really want to talk and tell you a lot of things, but this time you come to my office. I am not coming to the paper.'

'Are you the estate agent?'

'Are we playing that game again? What is wrong with you?'

'I thought you said you called me three times. I only have two from you.'

'Do you only interview people who call you three times?'

'No, I interview everyone.'

'So why don't you come now? Do you want me to call you one more time? I can do it now if you hang up.'

'No, no, it is not necessary; I know you estate agents always exaggerate things.'

'And you journalists are as innocent and honest as Mother Teresa. What do you want to do? If you want, come now.'

'I have to make a phone call first.'

'So you have to call me three times?'

'No, I need to call first.'

'You don't need to call first. Just come, for God's sake. Just come over now.'

'No, I mean I have to call someone else first.'

'Is this another agent, the guy who advertises with you? Or are you still trying to find Maria?'

'Look, I've got to go.'

'Don't be coming here spying on my work for the other agent, right?'

'I promise, I won't.'

'You won't come?'

'No, I mean I will come, but I won't spy. Good-bye.'

I closed the phone and contemplated hard. It wasn't the agent, so who had called me three times? It must have been very important. I swapped phones again to get the number and changed back to the one I could call from. I dialled the number and waited impatiently.

'Hello,' a man answered.

'Hello, I am Panos, a journalist; you have called me three times today.'

'Oh, yes, thank you for returning my call. I called on behalf of your wife, about the problems. She thought it is best if I called you directly.'

'On behalf of my wife? Is she all right?'

'She is better now.'

'Why? What has happened?'

'She has told me that she left you. That is what I am calling about.'

'What are you, a family consultant?'

'Well, no. Actually, yes, I am a consultant, but not a therapist. I am a legal consultant.'

'A lawyer? My ... Maria has put in a lawyer?'

'Well, I know it is not traditional for a lawyer to call the other side. But she is very interested, even if for the sake of the kids, for you to have an amicable separation.'

'Separation? You mean a divorce?'

'Come on, it is not as scary as it sounds. Sometimes it is best for everyone. Can you come to my office? Maybe today?'

'How about Elpida? What happens to her?'

'I can arrange for you to see your daughter. I know Maria very well. We are distant relatives.'

'I can't come right now, I …'

'Just call me when you can, but don't leave it. Time doesn't heal.'

'Right. Right, I will be there as soon as I can, in about half hour.'

After I got his address I started rushing to my car. My wife, the mother of my children, had gone to another man seeking help to get rid of me. It was a relative, though. He would understand. He would have some mercy on us. Maybe he was going to persuade me to do something. Maybe he was going to ask me to change. Maybe he was going to give Maria a job and make life easier for all of us. The streets were still full of people walking around, little groups of demonstrators going home after the show. Some were carrying folded-up flags of various colours. I manoeuvred over the rubbish bags left next to the bins.

A young man with a big folded-up red flag shouted: 'Vasili, let's go for a coffee.'

Another young man from across the road shouted back: 'Later.'

The pharmacist saw me passing. I went in and put the hundred-euro bill in front of her. Without saying anything she pushed the note back to me. A group of municipal police on their motorbikes passed by, all holding Greek flags and blowing their horns. They were making as much noise as possible.

The lawyer's office was before the electricity company, but I could not go there begging to have Maria back with no electricity at home. That would be so undignified. Of course, Maria would not come home so quickly. This time it was serious, very serious. That meant I did have enough time to go to the electric company later.

The coffee shops were full of people, groups of youths just back from the demonstrations. Some couples were holding hands. It was good; they could still afford it. Most importantly, they could still afford to be together. Not like me and Maria! A pickup truck pulled right next to my feet. A gypsy man got off the truck and had a look at an overloaded recycling bin.

He turned around and shouted, 'Maria.' An overweight woman with colourful clothing got out of the truck and came to the bin. Together they emptied the bin of cans and all the metal they could find. As the man passed by me he noticed that I was staring at them.

He looked at me from top to bottom and asked: 'Do you have anything you want to get rid of? Old fridge, an oven, pipes, anything?'

As I was gathering myself to answer him, he left. He must have realized that I had nothing to throw away. In fact, he had more than me, much more. With his wife, he carried the last piece of metal, an old, rusty radiator, to the back of the truck. Suddenly a head popped up through the junk in the truck. A young girl around Elpida's age stood up and helped position the radiator amongst the other scrap metal. It is so dangerous to have young kids on the back of a pickup truck. I would never do that to Elpida. Young life is so precious. In fact, I would never let her out of my sight, even for a moment. Right now, she was – well, she was with her mother. I knew she was safe, even if she was dropped off at the lawyer. The lawyer was a relative. He would know how to take care of Elpida. I was going to be there in a few minutes anyway. I had better skip the electric company and go straight to Maria, that is Elpida, this the lawyer. Yes, this had got to be sorted out. There was enough time to sort out the electricity later.

An old man sitting in a cafeteria was holding on to his, I guess, grandson with one hand and swinging a worry bead with the other. 'Come here, stop pouting. I will buy you an orange-ade if you are good,' he said to the child.

Across the road a group of kids were walking. They were noisy. Their school must have closed down for the day. The pharmacist was still by the door of her pharmacy, still looking. I was frozen in time. Everything was happening around me, but it seemed as if nothing was progressing. My heart was beating faster than normal, but nothing was normal anyway. I sat down. The old man left his grandchild and came to me. He was interrupted by the pharmacist, who rushed to me. A child walking next to me abandoned her hot air balloon and came to look at me.

I knew that I would be okay. With all those people around me, I would be fine. Suddenly, it seemed that everyone was leaving everything behind to come to me. As the balloon gained height and headed for the sky, I took a deep breath, looked up in the sky, and felt blessed and cared for. I felt blessed to be Greek and live amongst those people.

'What is wrong with you? You are turning white. Is it your heart?' asked the pharmacist.

'I am fine. There is nothing wrong,' I replied.

'Nothing? Are you sure? You just bought aspirins, aspirins for your heart.'

'I must be in love' I replied.

Then I was shouted at. 'Get yourself together! No jokes. Breathe for me, breathe.'

'Hey, lady, I am fine. Don't make this a show. I will get up now.'

'You shouldn't walk. Wait, I will call an ambulance.'

'I have already been through this once today. Relax, I am fine. I just need to do some tests, that's all.'

'So, why don't you?'

A small crowd had gathered around us. The old man extended his hand to lift me up. He was struggling to keep his own balance, let alone help me. His grandson started coming towards us, near the road. The old man turned and looked at him. A young girl from a small group of demonstrators gave her flag to a man next to her and rushed to the old man's grandson, shouting: 'I have got him, it is okay.'

The pharmacist shouted at the old man: 'Come on, Michali, you stupid idiot. Don't just stand there watching. This is not a show. Grab his arms.'

That is when I realised that the old man was the same old man who had been arguing with her in the pharmacy.

'Yes, yes, okay, I am doing it,' he said, rushing to get me up. Before I knew it I was sitting on a chair inside the pharmacy, having my blood pressure checked. A few people who were in the pharmacy left, making room for me. One of them promised to be back soon.

'What tests has your doctor told you to have?' asked the pharmacist.

'I have to go to my lawyer.'

'Your lawyer?'

'Well, not exactly. My wife's lawyer.'

'Are you going to do your will? You might as well go to the undertaker on your way too,' said the pharmacist.

'I don't know what tests I need to do. I can't do them anyway. I have no insurance.'

'Do you work?'

'Yes, I work.' Then I put my hand in my pocket and pulled out the hundred-euro note. 'Here, here is the money that I owe you.'

'What? What money? Oh, the money for the aspirin? Are you crazy? I don't need that. Get yourself together. You are in danger.'

'They were German aspirin.'

'I am in no mood for jokes now. Are you self-employed?'

I put the money back in my pocket and said: 'I am not sure anymore.'

'Have you ever had an account with the social security?'

'Yes, I have.'

'Why don't you go there right now. They are on the next block.'

'I can't today.'

'Your blood pressure is fine. Do you feel dizzy?'

'No.'

'You should be fine. They are closed tomorrow. You must go now.'

An old lady walked in. The pharmacist stood up and said: 'You are lucky we got them.'

The old lady smiled. She got her medicine and said: 'I will, I really will. You know me. I will come as soon as I get the money for the last ones.'

'I know, I know. Just don't lose the receipt. Here, I will put it in your pocket. Don't worry, get well soon.'

The old lady looked at me sitting on the chair and said: 'Get well, young man, get well.'

I guess compared to her, I was a young man, even in my condition. The pharmacist came to me and gave me a tablet with a glass of water. 'Okay, are you sure you are okay?'

'Yes, I am.'

'Stand up.' I did.

'You are going straight to the social security office, right? No arguments.'

As I went to answer no, a sudden ray of pain went right across my chest. I took a long breath and answered: 'Yes, of course.'

'It is right over there. You turn right ...'

'I know, I have been there.'

'Go, you have nothing to lose. Ask them what you need. It is their job to help you.'

'Yes, it is. It is their job to help me.' I left the pharmacy forgetting to thank her. I thought I would go back again.

The social security office was not on strike. There were a lot of people waiting, but I was at a disadvantage. I did not know which officer to go to. It took me a few seconds before I realized that I wasn't the only one who didn't know where to go. There were queues everywhere. I looked around to find a chair. There were a lot of chairs, but they were all behind the desks. The closest line was to my left. The right one looked a bit longer, so I went there. There were two people in front of me. I couldn't really see who was at the desk. There was a thick column of smoke rising from the desk, obscuring my view. I could hear, though.

A man from another desk asked: 'So, why did you get in at eleven?'

The clerk at the end of my line answered: 'I had to wait to see what happens to my Goddamned son's school.'

The man from the other desk asked: 'Do you have any cigarettes? I didn't get any today; the kiosk downstairs is closed down. What happened to your son? I thought his teachers were on strike yesterday.'

The other woman threw a cigarette in the air and shouted: 'Catch. Do you have a lighter?'

'Yes, that I have got. Was there another strike by the teachers?'

'No, today the kids were on strike.'

'What do they want? They are the ones who have it easy – no worries, no salary cuts, no TROIKA.'

'The canteen at the school stopped selling cheese pies because the teachers don't announce when they go on strike, and the manager has to throw them away every time a strike materializes. So today, when the teachers were not on strike, the kids went on strike because they couldn't buy any cheese pies.'

Then she shuffled some papers on her desk and asked: 'What about your daughter, does she have school?'

'Yes, their school's principal gets up at six and goes to school to stop the kids closing the school gate.'

'It is because of stupid public-sector workers like them that we are all suffering, as if all the salary cuts aren't enough. That's all we need. Tomorrow they are going to ask us to get up at six too. I tell you, all we suffer is because of our own faults. Forget the politicians. We are the ones who let them take advantage of us.'

Then she suddenly shouted at the person in front of her: 'I told you so many times, you've got to go upstairs with this paper. Here, take it. Who is next?'

There was no one between us. I could see her now. There were about five picture frames on her desk, showing some young kids, a baby, a bride and a groom at their wedding, a kid on a bicycle, and a couple more which I could only see from the back. In front of her, there was a half-filled ashtray, a newspaper, a phone, some tens of files which looked like they had not been opened for years, a cup of coffee, an alarm clock, her packet of cigarettes, a bag of tomatoes, and a loaf of bread.

'What do you want? Tell me,' she said, hardly looking at me.

I had to get on good terms with her. I needed an opening line, something personal that would cheer her up. Suddenly I saw a small flag of a football team. So I immediately said: 'That's a great team.'

'Oh, you like them too? My son did this. He brought it to the office. Did you watch the match last night? He was up watching, very disappointed. They didn't do well.'

'Sorry, I didn't see it. Did they play last night?'

She looked back at her desk and asked, 'What is it you want?'

'Well, I am – I want to know if I have an insurance. I mean, a current one.'

'Have you been paying?'

'I don't know, maybe through my work.'

'If you don't know, you go upstairs. This is for people who have insurance.'

'Well, maybe I have.'

'Maybe you don't. Just go upstairs. They will help you.'

I struggled my way up the stairs, fighting the crowds. The cigarette smoke rose up with me as I climbed. The second floor was empty. This was a great break for me, an oxygen break! I took a long breath and tried to carry it with me as I went up to the next floor. There were some staff but not many clients. I tried very hard to keep my smile, almost choking from the smoke whilst approaching a lady with piles of files on her desk, but there was no use. When I got to her I could not talk!

The lady finally gave up on me talking, pointed her finger at what was to be my next destination, and said: 'You haven't made any payments, right? Go there.'

'What payments? I am employed.'

'You must make your payments yourself; you have to go to that man to make arrangements.'

Focused on my target I approached an old man at a small desk. Wait a second! Was I seeing double? This old man had not one but two lit cigarettes in his ashtray.

'Wait,' he said, 'My colleague is in the toilet. He will be with you in a minute.'

Next to his double-loaded ashtray there was a religious frame, an abandoned worry bead, and some souvenirs from different islands.

The coffee cup was still untouched. As I waited in the corner, a well-dressed man approached from behind, asking for his documents.

'Wait here. By the time you finish a cigarette your papers will be ready,' said the old man at the desk. What an ingenious way to measure time! Unfortunately, the suggestion was taken literally, and the well-dressed man promptly lit a cigarette, using the same overloaded ashtray under my nose. I had felt much better and safer on the road. I was still not feeling well, so I leaned against the wall. Desperate to sit down somewhere, I looked around. A door opened, and the person I was waiting for came in and went straight to his desk. But before I had a chance to approach him, he left again. That must be the toilet, I guessed. Maybe I could go and freshen up a bit. Then I might feel better. As I approached the door, it felt that the entire office shouted at me, but it was only one lady representing them all:

'That's the staff's private toilet. Yours is on the top floor.'

I went back to my spot in the corner against the wall and froze. She then walked towards an old lady who was standing next to a window.

'Are you cold?' she asked the old lady. Before the old lady had a chance to answer, she said: 'If not, let's get some air in here.'

She opened the window all the way. The old lady was within the range of the opening window. She did not have to move much. As she opened the window a gentle breeze gushed in. It was soft, bearable, and most certainly a necessary breeze. As the old lady positioned herself between the window and the wall the window came back around. The old lady raised her arm and stopped the window crashing into her. The clerk was halfway to her desk.

The wind got stronger. It almost pushed the old lady off balance. It was vicious. It was stubborn. It came gushing in. It reached the clerk's desk with an almighty gust. It blew into the dusty files on the desk. The files fell off, into the air. There were files and papers flying all over the place. Two leaves touched each other, and the dropping chestnut impacted them right where they met. The chestnut descended rapidly. Out of control, intoxicated with the joy of speed, it nosedived towards the bottom of the forest. With no thoughts, no preparations of landing, it crash landed onto the forest ground. When it hit the ground there was little noise, a non-event, a waste of a nut. The lower weak leaves of the chestnut tree did not move. They did not notice. The higher branches were even more proud. Nothing! It was on the peak that something happened. A falcon, an alert falcon, heard the nut's crash. She opened her wings like a pilot doing his last check. They were good for the flight. She threw herself into the wind, trusting what nature would bring. She was not flying; she was gliding. She did not look back at the chestnut tree, her unstable temporary home. Focused at the bottom of the mountain, she flew over the apple groves, coming down closer and closer to the blue sea. Trees even taller than the one she had been perching on were way below her wingspan. She flew over the tallest one, taking a second too long riding on the wind, just to show she was in charge. Focused on The Monk, the large rock right off the beach next to my green hill, the falcon zoomed in, flying straight towards the rock. As the bird glided down, she could hear the crushing waves against the rocks, but the waves were no deterrent. Skilfully and with confidence, she landed on the tip of the rock, still facing the mountain.

I knew, I just knew all this happened next to my land by the sea, even though I was in the big city, stuck in the national health office, hundreds of kilometres away. Back in the office another old man approached the desk, but he came to my corner and started coughing. I looked at him and asked if it was the smoke. Whilst still coughing he mumbled and said: 'No, it must be the scrambled eggs I had this morning. Of course it is the smoke, the smoke outside from the chimneys and the smoke inside from the workers.'

'Why don't you complain?' I asked. Then he started laughing and coughing at the same time.

'You must be kidding. You think you are ever going to get out of here if you complain about anything? This is their house. We can't tell them what to do. They're the boss here. They tell us what to do.'

'Do you owe money too?' I asked cautiously.

'No, I just come here once a week to see what new photographs from their families they have put on their desks. Of course I owe them money. Who doesn't? It is with the money they get from us that they can afford to buy all these chairs, can't you see?' he said, pointing at empty space sarcastically.

Then he continued: 'The supermarket near my house has wheelchairs for their clients, and this is supposed to be a national health insurance centre. With friends like these, who needs health insurance?'

I looked around the room. All the desks were stacked up with files. Some of the computers were not on yet. A lady walked in and went straight to a desk with no one at it.

'She has court today,' shouted one of the workers from across the room.

'I just saw her in the corridor coming up with a shopping bag,' said the lady.

The old man next to me carried on talking: 'Sometimes, I wish I was a journalist, completely independent from them. If only I didn't need them, you know what I would write about them?' Then he looked away, not expecting an answer.

'Aren't the lawyers on strike today?' asked another worker from the desk next to me.

'Only us idiots are working today,' said another worker.

'What do you want?' asked a woman passing me.

'I am here to sort out what money I owe to get my insurance.'

Pointing her finger at the other side of the room, she showed me an empty desk and said: 'You need to go to that desk, but only in the morning.'

'In the morning?'

'Yes, eight to twelve. He deals during only those hours.' Then she moved towards the other staff.

I looked at my watch and said desperately: 'But it is only eleven thirty now.'

She continued talking with her colleagues. She then turned to me and said with a condescending tone: 'Mornings from Monday to

Thursday, not Fridays. Can't you see there is no one here? If he were here the room would be full. You couldn't even get in. Everyone has the same problem that you have. They leave everything to the last minute and then all come here at once. What do you expect us to do?'

'All I want to do is to pay some money. Don't you want it? I need to arrange an instalment plan. Isn't it here that you do it?'

There was a big silence. They all turned and looked at me.

'You go and wait outside till it is your turn, okay?' shouted one of the workers at me.

'Come here, come, let me see what you want. I don't believe this day. I don't believe it. Every day we have to deal with this. Come on here,' shouted one worker at me. As I got close to him he started walking away. I assumed he wanted me to follow him, so I followed.

Halfway through the room he stopped, turned around, and shouted, 'Let me have your papers. What do you have on you?'

'Oh, nothing. I came here unexpectedly. I need to do a health check, and I don't have insurance. I think I don't have insurance."

I am leaving now, ciao,' shouted the lady I had spoken to.

The man, who still had his arm extended for my papers, looked away for a second and said: 'Have a good weekend, Erini.'

Then he turned to me, pulled back his hand, and said: 'Go home. Get your papers and come back tomorrow.'

'Tomorrow? Tomorrow you are closed. I need to start paying my instalments. Can I pay something today? Something to start the ball rolling?'

'What is the big rush? You haven't paid your insurance for so long. Now you want to pay on a Friday?'

'I have to have my heart checked. I may immediately need an operation.'

'Are you sick?'

'Yes, I am. That's what I have been telling you all along!'

'What is it? Your heart?'

'Yes.'

'That's nasty. I lost my father last year. You've got to be careful.'

'Thanks.'

'Is it your arteries?'

'I don't know what it is yet. It could be anything.'

'You should have some tests done. It is important that you know.'

'I know.'

'You must find out now.'

'I know.'

'Why have you not made your insurance payments?'

'I don't know.'

'You shouldn't smoke or go to smoky places.'

'I know.'

'Do you think you have had a heart attack?'

'I don't know.'

'You can't have one here, not in my office, not on a Friday.'

'I know.'

'We shouldn't joke about these things. This is serious.'

'I know.'

'When did you make your last insurance payment?'

'I don't know.'

'Will you be on medication?'

'I don't know.'

'You don't know anything!'

'I know.'

'Follow me. If you are going to pay, I need a signature from Ereni. I must call her before she gets too far away. Do you know your tax number?'

'Yes, yes, how can I forget?'

'Go find a seat. Just wait.'

Then he went to make a phone call. I went and stood by the window. Before I knew it, the shouting lady was back. She came up the stairs and came straight up to me. I was getting scared.

'Are you all right?' she asked.

'Thanks, I am fine right now.'

'Let me see what we can do. Do you have any money to make a payment today so we can get it started?'

'Yes, I have one hundred euros.'

'Oh, you've got to be careful. They might put you on the Lagarde list.'

'What list?'

'The list of the great tax evaders in Greece, the Lagarde list.'

'Oh, the Lagarde list. It must be a great feeling to be on that list.'

'Well, I don't know about that. Come, come to my desk. I guess if you were on that list, you wouldn't have to come here. You would pay for your own operation.'

'That's why I think it would be a great feeling.' She pulled out a sheet from her drawer, asked for my ID card, and started filling in a form. 'This is your request form. As a government worker I am not really allowed to fill it in for you, but never mind. It is a bit complicated.'

When she finished filling the form, she handed me a pen and said, 'Here, put your tax number over here, and then sign here.'

She then put a stamp on the form, picked up the phone, and said: 'Maria, give me a request number. No, just give me a number. I will send you the name later. No, I didn't go. I have too much work to do. It is turning out to be like yesterday. No, nothing – another sick person. I will see.'

She hung up, wrote a number on the form, signed it again, and gave me the paper.

'Go to Costa and tell him Ereni wants a pay form for this.'

'Sorry, who is Costa?'

'The man over there. He is the one who called me back. You are lucky I answered the phone.'

'Oh, fine, thanks a lot.'

'Hurry up so you get it done today, and take care.'

I rushed to Costa, who asked for my tax number again. He entered it in the computer and said: 'Wow, you are in a bad shape. Can you pay €86.73 today, and more in the following weeks?'

'Yes, yes,' I said excitedly and put the hundred-euro bill on his desk.

'Boy, everyone is driving me crazy today. What am I, the bank? You don't pay me. How many people should I say this to every day?

do I have to write it down and stick it to my forehead so you all understand?' Then he waited a moment and said: 'Sorry, I am tired. It has been hectic today. Go get that paper, Maria. Give him the E37 form.'

'Do I go to the cashier next?'

'No, I told you, we don't receive money anymore. You have to go to a bank. Get this and I will tell you. Go on before I close for the day. I have had enough.'

I was almost outside the office when I heard my name shouted out. I went quickly back in, happy. Maybe he was going to make some arrangement for me to make the payment right there. Hopeful but exhausted, I approached his desk again, waiting for the verdict.

'Look, I did this for you today so you can get things going now. To make an instalment payment plan we need a tax clearance from the tax office. If you get time today, go to the tax office. Bring it to me next week.'

'Tax office? What does this have to do with them?'

'Welcome to Greece. Everything here has to do with the tax office. How do I know you don't owe them money?'

'So what if I owe them money? Are they going to just let me die?'

'No. If you die, you definitely can't pay taxes anymore, and dying is the only thing you don't need a tax clearance for. Look, don't argue with me. I am just trying to help you.'

After collecting three signatures and four stamps and filling two more forms, I found myself in the street again. This time I was armed with my voucher for €86.73 cents payable to my own social security office, fully stamped and signed. It was my gateway to my national health insurance.

I rushed to get to the first bank I had passed on my way to work. Curious to see if my non-striking colleague was still there, I found the front door to the office still open. As I got into the corridor, I heard laughter. My boss, Pavlos, the union leader, and the call girl were coming down the stairs in a cheerful mood. As soon as my boss saw me he asked: 'Not again, what do you want? I already paid you once today. Did you spend it all?'

The call girl laughed and said: 'The way he keeps his money in his pocket, no wonder he runs out.'

Without thinking I quickly announced: 'I still have the hundred euros.'

Pavlos said: 'Well, I tell you, a hundred euros isn't going to get you far with this sexy lady.'

The escort hit Pavlos gently with her fist and burst into laughter. Then she looked at him and said: 'You are terrible. How do you know how much I charge? You can't afford it anyway. A hundred won't even pay for ...' She said something in the union leader's ear, and then they all burst into laughter.

'You see, Panos, you can't afford it. She won't take your money. You are safe,' said Pavlos. Then he turned to the girl and said: 'We are going to the Bouzoukia tonight. You are free, right? If you come, it will be fun.'

'Well, I might join you tonight, but I am not free.'

'I am celebrating something tonight. I want you to come as my gift to myself. You will come?'

'I can be whatever you want, even a gift. But you should know, just because I am available does not mean I am free,' said the girl, and then they all laughed again.

'What do you want, Panos?' asked my boss.

'I wanted to go and write an article. It is important.'

'You don't even have a desk, Panos,' said my boss.

Then Pavlos looked at me with some sympathy and said slowly and clearly: 'Look, first of all you can't work because we are on strike today.'

'We?' I interrupted him, but he continued.

'Yes, you are still working here. Right, boss?'

He looked at my boss to get his confirmation and then carried on:

'Secondly, you don't even have a desk. And most importantly, you already have a hundred-euro bill in your pocket. What do you need to work for? Come on, we are going to lunch. I will buy you a beer.'

He looked at my boss and then the call girl and asked: 'He can come with us, right?'

'No, I don't want to come with you. I want to write. I am really angry now. I want to complain. This is the right moment.'

Impatiently, my boss pushed his way through us, went towards the door, and said: 'Well, be angry on your own time. Go home and write, break a couple of windows, throw a chair at your wife – I don't care. I am hungry. We are going to eat. Come on, Pavlos. Come on, lady. We don't have time for this.'

Then he pulled the hand of the call girl, and they walked out. I was left with Pavlos looking at me like I was a lost child. He took a step closer to me and said: 'You want to complain? Now? Today? What is wrong with you? You remind me of Socrates. You are going to end up like him, too.'

'Who is Socrates?'

'Socrates, our classmate, the guy with all those ideas, with all those complaints, with all the philosophy – don't you remember? At the end, he became nothing. He drives a taxi, that's all.'

'I don't remember a Socrates from our school.'

My boss opened the door and asked: 'Pavlos, are you coming? I want to go. We are hungry.'

'Just a minute, we are coming out,' said Pavlos, walking towards the door.

'How can you not remember Socrates? What was his real name? Oh yeah, Stavros. Do you remember? His father wanted to call him Socrates, and his mum wanted a religious name for him. He must have told that story in class a hundred times.'

'Oh yeah, and his mum's family won because she was the one with the dowry,' I said.

'We called him Socrates to tease him, and in the end he took it seriously. Everything turned into a philosophical argument with him.' We were both in the street now. I was so excited to hear about my old classmate, to remember his nickname.

'Do you have his number? For some reason I have been thinking about him a lot these days. I want to find him. Somehow, I think he knows what has happened,' I explained.

'No, why? As I said, you two suit each other very well. You can play Plato. He used to call you that, right? Imagine Socrates and Plato getting into arguments about the recession, having a good old dialogue. Then you can go back to writing your articles for a hundred euros per month, and he can carry on driving his taxi. In a perfect world, who wants you two involved with the nation's life? You are better off as philosophers. One good thing about the job is that you will never be made unemployed. You can think as much as you want, and at the end you let us, the professionals who know about real life, have seen a factory or two, and have seen the working masses, handle the real world.'

'I will find him.'

'Yeah, well, tell him from me, just as a piece of advice, to turn off his taxi meter when he is lecturing. He should pay people to listen to him, not charge them.'

'Is he really a taxi driver?'

'Yes. I ran into someone who knows him. I don't remember who. We've got to go now before your boss fires me too.'

My boss popped his head in again, raised his eyebrows, and said: 'What's going on?'

'Right, boss? You will fire me too if I keep talking shit with Panos?'

'I will never fire you. If it wasn't for you, with these articles Panos writes, we would have closed down years ago.'

'Wait, I don't have your number. Give me your number,' I shouted.

'I will call you. I will get your number from your boss.'

'That number doesn't work,' I shouted back.

'Does your boss know that?'

'I was going to tell him today.'

'Tell him tonight. I think we are going to the Bouzoukia – the regular place, you know.'

'I don't know anything. I am not coming anyway,' I shouted. Then they all disappeared into the street. I was still standing on the pavement in front of the office. I felt optimistic about finding Stavros again. Socrates Papadopoulos was probably what he called himself.

I would find him; I knew I would find him. The bank, the bank! I must get to a bank before they made me do all the paperwork again.

I stopped at the first bank in sight, only to find out after half an hour standing in the queues that I had to deposit the money in my own account first before it could be paid to my national insurance office. So I rushed to another bank in which I had an account, only to stand in another long queue.

'Are you here for your insurance payment?' asked a young man behind me.

'Yes, how do you know?'

'The paper, it is a dead giveaway. Mine has two stamps. Why is yours like this?' he asked.

'I don't know. I think the guy at the office was just doing me a favour. Maybe he felt sorry for me and skipped the second stamp. What I don't understand is why they didn't accept the money themselves. They have cashiers, guards, counting machines, and safes. Why do they send us to the banks to pay?'

'Would you carry on working if you could send your work out to someone else?'

That made me think for a second, and then I said: 'But they have to pay a percentage to the banks.'

'Who cares? It is not their money.'

'No, it is ours.' I said loudly with obvious anger.

'No, it is theirs.'

'It is not theirs, it is the public's money'

'Since they work for the public sector, that makes it their money.'

'So you agree.'

He put his hand on my shoulder, pushed me gently towards the counter, and said: 'No, I just want my insurance. I don't care who does the work. You are next. Go on, happy paying.'

The lady at the counter recognized me and said: 'Look, if I owed so much money to the bank I wouldn't make as much noise as you do.'

'I was quiet. I didn't say anything.'

'How can I help?'

I pushed the paper from the social security office under her window slot. She took a moment to look at it and then seemed completely horrified.

'Have you gone mad?' she asked.

'I have to pay them. I need to have health insurance. What do you suggest?'

She looked at the paper again and said: 'The money has to go through your account. As soon as it touches your account the bank is going to take it.'

Suddenly, my chin required some support from my right hand; I put my elbow on her counter and rested my head for a moment.

'Do you have another account somewhere else?'

'Yes, I do, but I think I owe money there too.'

'Are you sure?'

'Here is a hundred euros. Do something with it.'

'I can't, I am sorry.'

'Okay, fine. I will go and pay my electricity bill with it then.'

'It is your money. I am just trying to help. Do whatever you want with it.'

'Why did they do that? This is supposed to be the government's money. I owe them too. They are doing the banks a favour with these stupid rules.'

'I only work here. I'm trying to help. Do you want me to deposit it?'

'No thanks.'

I left the bank and was on my way to my next destination, the tax office. I would figure out some way of paying the national insurance but without the tax complication. Nothing was going to work anyway. I had to rush. Most departments in the tax office only worked half days on Fridays. There was no use taking my car; I wanted to make the best use of my parking spot, my only achievement of the day so far. As I got closer to the tax office, the five-storey building appeared from afar. When I finally got to the entrance of the building, I felt small and insignificant. There were no boards or a sign anywhere indicating what was on which floor. I saw a few people gathering by the lift and decided to go and ask them, only to hear that they themselves were lost. The one man who knew where he was going explained that he had asked the kiosk at the corner. He joked that the kiosk owners know more about the way the tax office worked than anyone. They needed the knowledge; it helped them sell a pack of chewing gum or a pack of cigarettes.

The lift opened, and everyone got in. As the door was closing, a woman with a big file rushed to get in, and I held the lift's door for her. I decided to go to the fifth floor and try my luck from the top. It would be easier to walk down from the top and find the relevant office. The women with the file asked me to push the button for the fourth floor. She seemed to know where she was going too. There was a girl around Elpida's age in the lift with her mother.

The woman with the file looked at the girl and said: 'What a sweetie. What is your name?'

Before the girl had a chance to answer, her mother asked the lady if she knew where the payments were due for car licences. The lady immediately answered, 'Third floor.'

The mother asked: 'Do you know how much more time we have to make the payment?'

'I don't know. I work in a different department,' she answered.

'What is on the fourth floor?'

The lady answered, 'It is income tax instalment payments.'

The mother asked: 'Do you know if last week's applications are ready? Her name is Fotini. She is seven years old. She goes to school. She is a very good girl. Do you have any children?'

Another man interrupted and asked the lady: 'What time do you close on Fridays?'

The lift stopped at the second floor. A person got in and asked if we were going down. I said: 'No, we are going up.'

He then saw the woman with the file and seemed to recognise her. He said: 'Oh, I am going up too.' He then shoved his body in the lift.

The mother asked: 'If I come in on Monday, early morning, you think I will get it done?'

Before she had a chance to answer, another lady started asking questions. The lift stopped at the third floor. Everybody was looking at the lady, and nobody got out. The mother kept smiling at her, trying to bring back the momentary human connection which by now had been lost. The lady gathered herself and pushed her body closer to the lift's door. She had made the ultimate mistake of opening up personally to the callers, and now she had to pay for it. The air was getting heavy. We reached the fourth floor. The lady got out, and with her the entire lift emptied. Everyone was following her from behind, asking questions. I got to the fifth floor. There were lines of people everywhere. I saw nobody to ask for directions, and in fact I did not even know what to ask if I found someone. Then I had a brilliant idea. I would rush down to the fourth floor and try to find the lady from the lift. If I was lucky enough she would still be out of her office, vulnerable in the corridors. I started running downstairs, pushing people around to get through. Deep at the end of the main corridor of the fourth floor I saw her walking towards a door. There were still three people following her from behind. I ran and ran. As I got closer, I saw the people around her dispersing one by one. There were queues of people waiting at the windows of offices on both sides of me. Some queues on each side were longer than the others, making me have to zigzag all along. By now she had no one around her, but she was dangerously close to her office door. I ran faster. She opened the door and went in. The door started closing, and at the last second I shoved my hand in. The heavy door almost crushed my wrist, but the pain was worth it.

She heard my yell, turned around, and asked: 'What is it?'

'I also have a daughter around that age' is the only thing that came to my mind to say.

'God give her a long life. What do you want me to do about it?'

'I opened the lift door for you' is the second thing that came out of my mouth.

She looked at me closely. Surely by this time she thought I was crazy. I continued: 'I don't know how much I owe, but I am sure it is more than a hundred euros. Do you think I can make an instalment payment today?'

'I have to check your documents first. Go to the end of the queue outside the office and ask at the window.'

'But can I make an instalment payment from here?'

'No, if you want to pay by instalment you must ask your accountant to make an application. You can't do it; you wouldn't know what to do.'

'Do I have to pay the accountant?'

'I don't know. Do you work for free?'

'Well, kind of?'

'Then what are you doing here? This is the income tax department.'

'I don't know. You asked me to come here. You have told me that I have an income because I have a house and a car.'

'I asked you?'

'Well, the tax office.'

'How do you have a house and a car, if you don't have an income?'

'I got those years ago.'

'Look, go to the politicians who make the laws. I am only a tax officer; I am not here to answer your questions. It has nothing to do with me.'

'Nothing?'

'No, I just work here. They have cut my salary too and increased my workload. If anyone pushes me any more, I am going to burst.'

Chapter 7

It was at the government-owned state electricity company that I found out there was really no light at the end of the tunnel for me. After an hour of standing in the queue and begging in vain to get a copy of my statements for the year, I was given a long sheet that did not mean anything to me. In the corridor on my way up to the instalment plan manager's office, I tried one last time to make sense of all the numbers on the sheets by stopping a worker and asking if he knew what all the numbers meant.

'Why do you need to look at the numbers?' he asked.

'Look, as a child I used to be scared of the dark. But now with these bills you send me, I am beginning to be scared of the light.'

He laughed and seemed to try to be helpful; maybe he just took pity on me. He took a long look at my sheet and explained: 'The columns that start with 0103 are the payments you have made. The ones with 2303 are the ones that are for tax you haven't paid, but 2304 is the tax you have paid. Anything that ends with 07 is the bills that you have paid in full. Partial payments end with 17, and the totals are at the bottom and have a zero in front of them.'

'I paid a lot of money last month. Where is that?'

'Maybe that went to the property tax. We send that out straight to the tax office.'

'I didn't want to pay taxes then; I wanted to pay my electricity bill so I didn't get cut off.'

'If you don't want to pay taxes, you should go to the tax office and not pay it.'

'Can the neighbourhood baker take my money and instead of giving me bread pay my taxes?'

'Why are you arguing with me? Do whatever you want. Go somewhere else. This has nothing to do with me, anyway.'

'Where am I going to go? There is only one electric company.'

'Look, you think I want to pay property taxes? Nobody wants to. When you have a house they make you pay.'

'I don't have a house!'

'That's impossible. If you are renting the owner has to pay the tax.'

'I am renting, renting from the bank. The house is in my name, but it really belongs to the bank. They can take it whenever they wish.'

'Maybe they are just keeping it in your name so you pay the taxes for them.'

'This is so much like my national insurance. I paid for twenty years, and now that I haven't paid for one year, I am not insured.'

'What can I tell you? Maybe you should have gotten sick back then, when you were insured.'

'Shouldn't I at least, for God's sake, know what I have paid for?'

'As I said, go to the tax office.'

'Today I have no electricity. I want to sort that out. What are the numbers with three zeros before them?'

'You ask too many questions. It is not even my job to answer all these. They are estimates of what you use. We don't read your meter every month. It is too much work for the electricity company.'

'So do I owe for them or not?'

'Don't worry about that. If you pay too much it is deducted from your next bills – of course, not if your money goes to taxes.'

'So how much do I owe now? I am a journalist, and I don't understand a thing about my bill. How would a housewife understand all this?'

'Housewives are more careful than you. They know better. Are you a journalist? Really?'

'Yes.'

'Oh, how do you see things? When do you think the recession will end?'

'I don't know. It depends on when I finish paying my bills to you.'

'Do you think TROIKA is ever going to leave us alone to live our lives? How many years?'

'I am sorry, but I don't know. I really have to work out how much I owe you before I can answer questions relating to the national economy.'

'Well, you have to go in line and ask at accounts. I don't know. Take this sheet and tell them you are a reporter. They might help you more. Write an article about our pay. I am working double time, and they have halved my salary. You should write all these things; it is your job. We now work for the tax office. We have become tax collectors and have to do more work. Instead of thanking me, they take half my salary away too. They should pay us double.'

'Do you think the instalment officer can help me?'

'You mean the instalment plan manager? No, he only does instalments. He is very busy.'

The instalment plan officer – I mean, manager – was very busy but very kind. He took his time to explain to me that he did not know anything about the sheet. What he knew was that I owed much more money than the hundred euros that I had to put towards the first payment. Of course, there were reconnection fees to consider as well.

'What happens if you just accept the hundred euros and put the extra charges on my bill for next month?' I asked the manager.

He took a long puff from his cigarette and said: 'I will then have to do that for everyone, and I just can't.' This was my final answer before I left the building with the hundred-euro note still in the corner of my pocket.

Everything had gone wrong for me in the last couple of days. Nothing was working; I had not achieved anything. The only thing that brought a smile to my face was rescuing the dog for her owner. I only wished someone could rescue me too. Walking down a busy street in Athens with the ever-present Acropolis looking over my every action, I stopped momentarily and wondered if the falcon was perching again far away on my rock in the sea. I kept walking and walking. It was good for me, to lower my cholesterol. I went all the way back towards my car, passing again through the neighbourhood of my office. A large cauliflower in a vegetable shop attracted my attention. I wondered how Costa's night with his girlfriend had gone. I really had not had a chance to ask him that in the morning. As I was staring at the cauliflower thinking of Costa and his girlfriend, the shop owner shouted: 'Hey, Panos, how are you? Do you want that cauliflower?'

'No, thanks, how are you?'

'You are looking at it as if you haven't eaten for a week. Here, let me put it in a bag for you.'

Without weighing it, he put it in a paper bag and handed it over to me. Speechless and without hesitation, I took the bag and fished in my pocket to give him the hundred euros. With his right hand he squeezed my arm and held it in its place.

'Come on, I am just joking. I know you are not starving. It's just a gift. Keep it. How did your interview go with the farmer? Did you finally figure out why the vegetable prices keep going up?'

'No, let me pay you. How much is it?'

'You don't have to pay for this. I said it is a gift. Come to my shop again. That's all I ask. If you want to pay for something here, buy some tomatoes.'

'But I don't want any tomatoes. I don't even want the cauliflower.'

'These are just ripe, just in time. You have never had such good tomatoes in the winter. They are imported. Come, come and smell one. You would think it is summer.'

He forced me to smell a tomato. As my nose reached the tomato, he gave it a small squeeze.

'Do you smell? Do you smell?'

'Not really.' As I tried to bend down, he extended his arm further and accidentally crushed the tomato on my forehead. I was bleeding tomato juice but could still not smell anything.

'Here, sorry. Did you smell it?' he said, handing me a piece of paper to clean my face.

'It is okay. How do you know I went interviewing a farmer?'

'You told me last time you were here. You told me you were going to the farmer to find out how everything has gone wrong with the economy. I told you just to ask me, not to waste your time going to the farmer, remember? The farmer is stuck in the mud. He can't see in front of him. It's just like how you are stuck in your own mud, paying bills, fighting for more pay, getting the money you are owed, paying for your kids, queuing up to see a doctor, and all that. They don't let you see clearly.'

'The farmers are the producers, not you. You just run a shop selling their produce. I think they would know better what is going on. They are the ones who are feeding me. They are the ones who are feeding you.'

'You've got it all wrong. The farmers look around for subsidies. They are not feeding me. Their prices go up so much that I have to import from abroad. Would you like a couple of kilos of these tomatoes?'

'No, I don't want any of your imported tomatoes. If you have Greek tomatoes, maybe.'

'Greek tomatoes, now? You couldn't even afford it. I have some good bananas too. You can't expect me get Greek produce, unless you want Greek cucumbers.'

'What would you know about the economy?'

'Everything there is to know, ask me. I run a shop. I know how it works.'

An old man walked in, went straight to the shopkeeper, and asked: 'Today?'

'Not today. They didn't come. No one who owes me money came today. I just had my first sale today, and he is not paying me,' said the shopkeeper, pointing at me. Then he continued: 'I am doing everything. They owe me so much money I could buy the place, let alone pay you the rent. Everything I am doing is right. Everything is getting better. I am on the path to, on the path to – what do they call it, Panos?'

'Recovery?' I answered.

'Yes, that. I am on my path to recovery.'

The old man seemed bored. He calmly put his hand in his pocket, pulled out a coin, and put it in the shopkeeper's palm.

'Here, buy yourself a coffee.' Then he started to walk towards the exit door. He stopped on the door step, turned around, and said to the shopkeeper: 'At least try to say something new. You keep saying the same things over and over again in the same order. What are you, the government or something?'

He walked out. A few seconds later he popped his head in again and said angrily: 'I am coming one more time next week, next Wednesday. If you don't have the rent, I will show you. I will show you what recovery means.'

I waited for him to go before asking the shopkeeper: 'How are you going to do it?'

'I don't know. I am just buying time. I don't know what to do.'

'Do people really owe you so much money?'

'They owe me, but not that much. I don't know what they owe me. It's my own fault. I am not that good with numbers. Who knows? I owe so much in taxes, too.'

'Do you know if you really owe that much in taxes?'

'It doesn't matter if I know or not. The government tells me how much I owe, not on what I owe, but on what they want to get. I can't do what they do.'

'Do what?'

'Charge my next client for the mistakes. I will just lose them.'

'Charge your next client?'

'Yes. I can't charge more for the tomatoes because I didn't collect the money from the last client for last month's tomatoes.' Then he stopped talking and looked at the ceiling, contemplating. He then looked at me again and continued: 'You know, now I get it. That's what they are doing to us. They raise the taxes to make up for all their mistakes. They closed their eyes on all the tax cheats who are now on their yachts thousands of kilometres away from Greece, and now they are making me pay their bills. It is their fault.'

'Look, I've got to go now. I have so much to do. I have so many of my own problems. I can't stand here chatting with you all day.'

'I thought you were interviewing people to find out what is going on.'

'Yes, but they are organised interviews, based on some kind of scientific approach. I ask the questions. I just don't stand and let people moan.'

'Moan? You know, I can't charge more, but at least I can do one thing that the government is doing with TROIKA.'

'That's good for you, but that's not the answer. You still have to pay the rent.'

'Yes, but if I blame everything on my clients, the landlord gives me more time. I can say it is not my fault.'

'How does that work?'

'I just did it. I told him people owe me money so I can't pay him. That's the same thing the government is telling TROIKA. They charge us taxes they know we can't pay and then show the numbers to TROIKA and tell them that they are doing their job.'

'What I am trying to find out is how it all started. I know, but I need ordinary people like you to tell me, when I interview them properly, not like this.'

'Well, mine started ...'

'Your what?'

'My problems. My problems started because of that bitch, the pharmacist you were at this morning. What was going on? Why were so many people around?'

'That bitch? She is a kind lady. She helped me a lot today.'

'I don't care what she did for you. She has ruined our life.'

'How?'

'Is this an interview now? With an ordinary thing? Person?'

'Tell me, what has she done to you? She doesn't shop here?'

'No, she shops here.'

'She is one of them, the ones who owe you money?'

'No, she doesn't owe me. She is nice.'

'You are now screwing with my brain.'

'She has screwed our life without knowing it. You know my son?'

'No.'

'He is a pharmacist. We put all our money into making him a pharmacist. He passed the exams and entered the university.'

'I am sure I have also paid taxes for him to be able to become a pharmacist.'

'Whatever.'

'Where is his pharmacy?'

'That's the problem. He can't become a pharmacist because his father and his grandfather rent a fruit shop. If we sold medicine instead of tomatoes, we could pay the rent now.'

'So what? That can't stop him. We don't have a caste system in this country; it is not India of fifty years ago.'

'We wanted to turn the fruit shop into a pharmacy. The pharmacists' association rejected it. They already have their member with a pharmacy in the area.'

'Why do you need two pharmacies in the same street?'

'Why are there three fruit shops in this street?'

'I don't know. As I said, I am interested in the problems of the nation, not yours and your son's.'

'Didn't you just say you paid taxes for his education too? So your money is also wasted. He might not be your son, but he is a young Greek man, our hope.'

'But how does having two pharmacies in the same area give us hope?'

'Maybe he wanted to work for less money and let the people decide how many pharmacies and fruit shops they need, not the pharmacists themselves. If I had a pharmacy instead of a fruit shop, he would become a pharmacist because of the shop, not because of his university.'

'He couldn't charge less even if he had a pharmacy. The association sets the prices.'

'I told you, she has screwed up our lives; her son can become a pharmacist and charge a lot, like in India, as you say.'

'India isn't like that, not anymore.'

'I don't know. You are the journalist; you know these things. I am sure you write it all.'

'Where is he now, your son?'

'He saved up his pocket money, got a cheap flight to London, and found a job.'

'As a pharmacist?'

'No, he is a waiter,' he said with a sad voice, looking at the floor of his shop.

'Look, don't get so emotional on me. You are hurt because he is your son, all your hope. But that is not the problem of our nation in general. This is just one case.'

'I don't know about the problems of the nation, but maybe my son is just an example. I know about fruits and pharmacies. My son's destiny is determined by the pharmacists' association. We have no choice, but I am not letting the farmer decide my destiny.'

'What do you have against the farmers? At least they are producing something. What do you do? You just move your prices up and down artificially to suit yourself, and then you feed us imported cheap tomatoes, all for your benefit. The farmer is planting trees right now, as we speak. I am going to him again tomorrow, to interview him again. I cherish his determination. I am going to see him and thank him on behalf of all my country, on behalf of my children who will be eating, literally, the fruit of his labour. There is hope in this mess. You will see. I've got to go now.'

Suddenly, I heard a man shout from across the road. He then started crossing the road, almost getting run over by a pick-up truck. It was him, the old man who had lost his dog. He rushed into the shop.

'What is it? Did you find your dog?' I asked.

Looking distressed he walked towards me and said: 'No, I must have gone to the wrong place. They haven't had any German shepherds for a while. I rushed back to get you. Are you sure it is the right place?'

'Of course it is. How many dog shelters do you think we have?'

'Please come with me. Maybe they will remember something. They have so many dogs.'

'I am sorry, but I can't come. I ... I have to go to a doctor, to the hospital. It may be an emergency.'

'An emergency? With your cauliflower?'

'He just gave it to me, the shopkeeper; he just gave it to me. I don't know why.'

'My dog, I don't know where she is.'

'Let me call them. They will know who I am.'

'Here, use my phone. I have their number here. Let's see if it is the right place.'

'How much are your onions today?' asked a customer as I was dialling.

The phone rang and rang. I ended the call. The man kept begging me to call again. I called. The shop keeper made a sale. Someone picked up the phone.

'Yes, who is it?'

'Hello, it is me. Remember, I brought the dog?'

'Which dog? Who are –'

'I came to you with a German shepherd. Do you remember, you said the owner would surely come? You said it was a good dog.'

'Oh, yes, the German shepherd. You know, it wasn't really a pure-bred.'

'It doesn't matter. Where is it?'

'It – it was stolen. We had a break-in recently, at night. It was stolen.'

'Stolen? People steal guard dogs?'

'You asked me that before. Yes, they are very popular nowadays.'

The old man was looking straight into my eyes, waiting to hear some good news. Finally he burst into tears and shouted hysterically: 'They have sold her, they have sold my Timmy!'

Rushing out of the shop, he almost hit a large woman who was walking in. I tried to call him, to give him some hope. Maybe the dog rescue centre could help. Maybe if I gave them the money they would get the dog back. I got my phone out, and as I was holding it, it rang.

'Hi, is this Panos?'

It wasn't the bank; they would use my full name. Maybe it was good news, maybe something from Maria.

'Yes, it is Panos. How can I help you?'

'You said you would call me back. Your wife wants to know where she and her daughter are going to sleep tonight.'

'Who are you?'

'Your wife's lawyer. There is no use playing this game. She wants to know if you are out of the flat. She needs it. She is raising a family.'

'What do you think I am doing? I am at work trying to make a living, for the family. I am in the middle of an interview.'

The fruit man looked at me and smiled. I continued: 'If she is my wife, she already knows where she is sleeping tonight.'

'That's cute, but not helpful. Your ex-wife wants you out of the house so she can move in with your daughter.'

'Is she already my ex-wife?'

'That's why I need you to come to my office, so we can make things go smoothly and amicably, with no hard feelings.'

'Smoothly? No hard feelings?'

'Of course it will be hard. But the sooner you deal with it, the sooner you will get over it.'

'Is this all you want? For me to get out? Then you will help us?'

'I am your wife's lawyer.'

'I have rights.'

'Do you have a lawyer?'

'No, but I have rights. Yes, I do.'

'What? Rights or a lawyer?'

'Both. The second one I haven't got yet.'

'Which one is the second one? You mean you have rights but not a lawyer?'

'Yes, and my lawyer says that I can't come to you if there is no Elpida.'

'I thought you don't have a lawyer. And what Elpida are you expecting?'

'Elpida is the name of my daughter. I thought you were a family friend.'

'If I arrange for your daughter to be here, will you come?'

'Yes, just tell me when.'

'Will you be accompanied by your lawyer?'

'I told you, I haven't selected a lawyer yet. Right now I am talking to someone. Maybe I will appoint him.'

A client walked in, and before he had a chance to talk the shopkeeper said: 'Sir, you need to make an appointment with my secretary first.'

The client walked out in shock, and I said with full confidence: 'You call me and tell me when Elpida is dropped off at your office, and I will come, with or without my lawyer.'

Then I closed the phone. With the phone in one hand and the cauliflower in the other, I turned to the shopkeeper and said: 'Thanks for that. I guess you owed me one anyway.'

'Owed you for what?'

'For smashing the tomato on my forehead.'

'I told you, I am Greek. I do things because they feel right, not because I owe anyone anything. You know, I don't keep good records anyway.'

'Thanks for that anyway.'

'I deal with life as it comes.'

The cauliflower and I found ourselves in the street again, walking aimlessly in the crowd. I had nowhere else to go, and the most sensible thing to do seemed to walk towards my old car. For the last time today, perhaps, I passed by the pharmacy. The pharmacist was busy with clients. For some reason I didn't like her anymore. I rushed by her store as fast as I could. As I passed by the crowds, I felt that I had no purpose; I did not play any role for anyone. Nobody needed me, not because I was incapable of giving but because I was sort of irrelevant to all that was happening around me. I felt disturbingly invisible. I was in the middle of an ocean, looking for a piece of wood to hold on to before the big storm started. I had to lift myself up to see better above the big waves. Unfortunately, although I was aimless, although I was becoming numb, I was fully awake.

I was close to the hospital when my phone rang again. I knew no phone call at that moment would offer me anything. Nothing substantial could happen. Without control, the hand that was not holding the cauliflower answered the phone.

'Can you hear me? I just talked to your wife. She wants to deal with these matters as soon as possible.'

'Oh, you are the lawyer? Yes, fine. Well, I want to deal with it as soon as possible too.'

'She said she can bring your daughter too, okay?'

'Fine!'

'But we can't talk about anything in front of her. I will have to stop the meeting if you tell her anything.'

'Maria? Is she coming too? She is coming, right?'

'No. I am sorry, but she thinks it is best if we deal with this professionally.'

'What does that mean? Is it professional when you get paid and not professional if we talk to each other and you don't get paid?'

'Look, you must come this evening. It is all arranged.'

'This evening? No, I can't.'

'Do you have something more important arranged?'

'No, I am at the hospital now.'

'Hospital? I thought you were at your lawyer's now.'

'I am a journalist. I get around a lot.'

'Are you all right?'

'Yes, I am. Actually, no, I am a bit tired. I had a long day. I don't want Elpida to see me like this, not today. Maybe tomorrow morning.'

'All you have to do is not to talk in front of her.'

'She is smart; she will know. Arrange it for tomorrow, anytime you want. Just send me an SMS. I have to go now.'

'I really want to help you, but I think it is best, at this point, that you move out. That's the first thing. Sort things out now; don't leave it. Don't you have anywhere you could go and stay for a few days?'

'What are you going to do for us if I move out? It is finished then, right?'

'Come tomorrow and tell me you are out. I will see what I can do.'
'Send me an SMS. Tell me when.' I closed the phone.

I finally got to my car, removed the parking ticket, got in, threw the cauliflower in the back, and tried to start the car. No luck! After a couple of half-hearted attempts I gave up. It was as if I wanted to fail in everything that day. I wanted to victimize myself even more. There was a strange sense of relief in my self-pity. Indifferent and exhausted, I turned and looked at the bag of cauliflower in the back. Then I got out of the car. For the second time that day, I put the parking ticket back on the windscreen. Then I got back in, grabbed the cauliflower, and took a big bite of it. As I was chewing the raw cauliflower, a message came through my phone: 'Tomorrow at eleven. Elpida will be here too.' This was followed with the lawyer's address. I took another bite of the cauliflower and put the rest on the passenger's seat. Completely oblivious to my environment, I closed my eyes and fell asleep.

Chapter 8

It was almost dark when I woke up in my car. There were still a lot of people walking around in the street. Thinking of all that I still had to do woke me up even more. Bursting with real or maybe fake enthusiasm, I turned the switch to start the car. It wasn't until the car started that I remembered the problem with the starter. It is amazing how even the machines take you more seriously when you appear confident. Here I was with a running car and a bit of gas in the tank, completely alert and focused on my destination. I came out of the parking spot not having the faintest idea of where I was actually going. Since all government offices were closed, the most sensible thing to do was to go home, to my empty home without electricity, because it was cut off, without my son, because we had no Internet, without my wife, because … I really didn't know why. If she left because I did not arrange a candlelit dinner for Valentine's Day, well, so be it. If she came back now, that would be all she got, not because there was any romance left for us but because we had no fucking electricity. And my son left; my son sold his father for stupid Internet. Here I was, sick and helpless and my own son left in search of an Internet connection. He was so selfish, always thinking about himself. It was all about what he wanted. Had he ever asked me about myself? I was just there for him to provide, so he would get his things. Had he ever listened to my pain for one minute? It was enough for me to open my mouth and say something that did not directly concern him. He would jump down my throat immediately. He would not let me finish a sentence without saying the exact opposite of what I want to say. And so I was left with only one child. The only one who cared at least a bit about me was the one who couldn't make her own decisions. Poor Elpida had no choice. She had been taken away from her own house. Now it was my turn. Just to see my children again, I had to move out of my own house. Even my country had turned her back on me. I had no insurance, no future, no money – nothing. It was like everyone was looking at me, trying to see how long I could stand this.

I wondered what Stavros, or Socrates, whatever the fuck he wanted to call himself, would say if he saw me like this now. I had to find the asshole; I just had to find him. Somehow I thought he will tell me something that would calm me down. Maybe he could help me to look at things from his stupid, retarded point of view and make me laugh instead of wanting to scream. In the end, it worked out that he was right all along. He was right about all the things he made fun of. I was left with nothing, nothing at all. Everything I cared about, all that I respected, had come back and bitten me. I had been betrayed by everyone and everything. From the archaeologists to my own wife, the tax office, my health insurance, my son, my heart, and the system, my whole country has abandoned me, at the worst time in my life.

Yes, that was what I would do. I would go home and find him. Now I knew his made-up name, Socrates Papadopoulos. My pointless drive home gained a new meaning, now that I had something to do. I stepped on the pedal and drove faster. I knew I would find him, Internet or no Internet. Even the electricity company couldn't stop me. I would do what Costa said; I would go to my mum. She got Wi-Fi on her balcony from the neighbours. I could go home, pick up the laptop, and go straight to my mum. On the way out I would make sure I showed my middle finger to the electricity meter. I couldn't tamper with it, but nobody said I couldn't tell it to go and fuck itself. And I wouldn't let my boss bully me again. He could take it, like the electricity box; he could go and get electrocuted. I would do my job and let him do what he wanted. I would show everyone, just like the farmer who was still planting trees, showing all the bastards that he was still alive. I would go to the farmer's the next day, first thing in the morning. I would write a long article and show everyone – the Europeans, Troika, the Germans –what we Greeks are made of. And as for the house? Let her have it. I didn't start a family for the house. We had a family and got the house for the family. Now she didn't want the family. Fine. The house wasn't mine; it belonged to the fucking bank. Let her fight with the bank. I would move out tonight. I would go to the Bouzoukia tonight. I had money. I even had taken my nap in the car, so I could stay up late. I would go, find Pavlos, and accept his invitation this time. I would tell him I needed to stay away from my house for a couple of days.

I was relieved to get to the house because I started feeling a bit weird talking to myself in the car. I made my visit as brief as possible. As soon as I got the laptop I was out in a flash, forgetting completely to show my finger to the electricity box. The car started again, and the way to my mum's was even faster, the best part being that I found a parking spot as soon as I got close to her house. It looked like my luck was changing. It is all about attitude. If you are determined and confident, not only will the car start but you will also find parking, even if it is a bit of a walk to your destination. It was now completely dark. Zigzagging through the tree branches on the pavement, I almost hit a young guy with long hair. He seemed to be in his own world, not paying any attention to his surroundings; in fact he almost hit a tree. I turned and looked at him, expecting to hear an apology.

He finally noticed me and said: 'Dad?'

'Costa? Is that you? I didn't recognize you. Your hair is on your face. Where are you going?'

'I am going to Grandma's.'

'Grandma's house is that way,' I said, pointing my finger to my mum's house.

'Not that grandma, my other grandma.'

'Why? Does she also have Internet?'

'No, I am going there for dinner. Mum is waiting for me. She is at her mum's.'

'I know. How about Internet? Where will you get it?'

'What Internet? What do you care about Internet? That's why I went to your mum's. I couldn't stay any longer. She was force feeding me again. Do you have any money, or will you take me?'

'I don't have any change.'

'Yes, sure. You probably have a big bill, and you don't want to change it,' he said sarcastically. There was no point answering him. I reluctantly turned around and started walking with him to the car. I was already struggling with the starter again when he got in the car. As soon as the car started, he pulled the half-eaten and by now flattened cauliflower from under his bum and held it the air, trying to identify it. Then he turned around and said:

'I see you are using a lot of cauliflowers these days. Do you really think cauliflowers can save our nation?'

'I didn't buy it. It was a gift.'

'What?'

I said more loudly: 'I didn't buy it. It was a gift.'

'Women give cauliflowers on Valentine's Day too? I thought it was your invention. Who ate it?'

'I was hungry.'

'Oh yes, I forgot. You don't have any change, just big bills. Why didn't you go to your mum's?'

Desperate to change the mood, I said: 'Your hair actually looks nice.'

'I am growing it so you can't see my tattoo and complain.'

I tried again: 'Did you find your girlfriend?'

'Did you find your wife?'

There was an uncomfortable silence. Then I said: 'It doesn't matter. I met a girl you may like. She is really nice.'

'Dad, you know we have different tastes in woman, you should have kept her for yourself.'

Obviously that backfired as well, so I asked, 'Have you heard any new jokes?' I was desperately trying to re-live the good moments we had in the car the last day.

'Oh yes.'

'Not the stupid ones. Anything political?'

'Dad, you don't understand the political ones, I have a good one about the hospital.'

'Oh no, I don't want to hear about hospitals today.'

'Okay, I will tell you a political one. In a fast food shop, a man asks for a souvlaki without tomatoes. The shop keeper says, "We don't have any tomatoes. Is there anything else I can not put on it for you?"'

I forced myself to grin, but that was the best I could do. Then I asked: 'What is political about this?'

'Didn't I say you don't understand the political jokes? Who does the souvlaki shop remind you of?'

'I don't know, the system? They have run out of tomatoes?'

'No, the political parties who are running for election. They have nothing to offer, and they are competing with each other to see who can offer more of nothing.'

'I think I will have to hear your hospital one. That one was stupid.'

'Stupid? Why don't you tell me a joke.'

'Ommeh.'

'A short one, Dad, not a lecture.'

'Lecture? When do I give you lectures?'

'Go on.'

'Well, let's see. A political one, right?'

'Time out. You are not funny.'

'Okay, okay, wait. Ask me which party I will vote for in the next election.'

'Oh, that's old. I have heard that one.'

'Okay then.'

'Tell me anyways. You screw up good jokes really well.'

'If you know it, what's the point?'

'Come on, Dad, make my day. Which political party are you going to vote for in the next election?'

'I am going to vote for Ali Baba.'

'Ali Baba, really? Why, Dad?'

'I don't really know. The only thing I know is that he only has forty thieves, but our political parties have hundreds who are supposed to be representing me in the parliament. I prefer him to all of them.'

I didn't hear any laughter, so I went on: 'How can you make a small business in Greece in today's economic climate?'

'I don't know, Dad. If I knew I would have made one now.'

'Easy: You buy a big business and wait.'

This time I heard laughter. It was controlled, but it was laughter.

'Okay, Costa, tell me your hospital joke.'

'A woman gets a call from the hospital, and the caller says … wait a minute, you know the hospitals are putting their departments together?'

'You mean they are downsizing and amalgamating to save money?'

'Yes, that. Do you know about it?'

'Yes, I know. I write about these things.'

'Anyway, the caller says. "Your husband came to the hospital for a test." "Yes," says the woman. "Do you want to talk to him?" "No, no," says the caller from the hospital. "We have amalgamated and need your help." "Why do you want to talk to me? Is it bad news?" asks the woman. "Well, we need your help," says the caller. "Send your husband out to buy something. If he comes back, don't have sex with him." The woman gets confused and asks, "How does that help anything?" "Well," says the caller, "on the day that your husband came here, we had two tests with two results. We don't know which one is your husband's. One of the two men has a venereal disease, and the other one has Alzheimer's."'

Costa did not waste any time before asking me if I got the joke. I did laugh. Maybe it was an exaggerated laugh, but it was good enough for him to accept that I got it. Then he touched his hair and started looking out the window.

Trying to make sure that he did not want to tell another joke, I waited a few seconds and then asked: 'Costa, it was a funny joke, but do you know why I didn't want to hear a hospital joke?' Without waiting for him to answer I continued: 'I had an incident this morning. There is something wrong with my heart, and I went to the hospital.'

He turned and looked at me. Then he turned again and looked outside the window. Obviously he was saddened by the news.

'There is nothing to worry about. It could just be a little bit of pressure from all that is happening right now. You know, with the economy, my job, Mum, all that.'

I waited another few seconds to see if he wanted to say something but he was deep in thought. So I continued: 'All my life I have been trying so hard to be good – a good father, a good husband, a good citizen, a good friend, a good journalist. I have worked hard for our dream, to have the hotel built on our land, in one of the most beautiful parts of our country. After all these years, I just see everything fading away. My job not only does not give me any satisfaction, it doesn't even give me enough money to pay the mortgage on our little house, let alone build a five-star hotel.'

Obviously Costa was very much taken by my words. From past experience, by this stage of the conversation he would say something disturbing to stop me talking. He would ask an irrelevant question or criticize me for my way of doing things and turn the blame completely on me. His favourite quote always was, 'Dad, it is your own fault.' But this time he was listening. It was as if he could see through my heart and feel my pain. Tonight, I had hoped for a connection as good as the one we had yesterday in the car, but this was getting even better.

I loved it, so I continued: 'All of a sudden, I have nothing – I mean, except you. I didn't even have a father when I was growing up, so I tried even harder for you. It was as if I wanted to take my own revenge against the world by being there for you all the time. I did not want you to grow up like me, without the warmth of a man, a father. I don't know what I would do if I didn't even have you. Everything else I have believed in is now rejecting me: my work, my society, my country that I believed in and trusted so much, and now even my own family, my own wife. What happened? Did she wait for me to be weak and helpless? Does she think I am finished? How come when we had our dreams of building the hotel, she was next to me? How come when all my articles were published and I was getting good pay, she was next to me? You know, it is not just us who are having problems. Many families are having problems, and for a real man, it is in his nature to try to keep his family safe. We have to provide no matter what. You will grow up and see what I mean. You have to know. Why don't you take something to your grandmother? I have some potatoes in the back.'

I gently stopped the car, opened the potato sack, and put a few potatoes in the cauliflower bag. Costa turned and looked at me. I was shocked that he did not dispute the idea.

'Costa, if there is one piece of advice I can give you now, now that you are listening, it is that there is always hope. In the darkest moments, there is hope. Tomorrow I am going to be interviewing a desperate farmer who is still planting trees. I am going to do my best. I can't give up writing either. You know, it is not just my articles; people are not buying the paper anymore. They don't advertise. They have nothing to sell. And writing has become so difficult. You can't write what you see; people don't like it. I have to write what they want to hear. I am not so good at that. At least I still have a job. The most important thing is that this is not the end. I am a man, I am Greek, and this is a country with a big history. We will show them. I will show you and your mum that we can do it. We have survived so long, and now that we are maybe coming out of the recession, your mum is throwing in the towel? And where is she going to go? Is she going to start a new life from the beginning? Is she going to immigrate to another country? And who is going to rebuild our nation? Aren't we answerable to our great ancestors? With or without philosophy, our greatest strength is the family. The Greek family is known all over the world. People come here from all over to get married on our islands. This is the country of romance, of selflessness, philanthropy, and love. We have to be good examples for the world, not the other way around.'

Costa was still quiet and contemplating. I had so much more to say but was happy and content to have said what I had said. It was like a big load off my shoulders. I was content, and the fact that there was not much traffic on the road made the rest of the trip to his grandma's so much more pleasant. Costa started getting ready to get out of the car by removing his seat belt before I got to the front door. It was as if he couldn't wait to get out of the car. Maybe I had gone too far.

Maybe I had shared too much; maybe I had put too much of my own pain on my son's soul. I stopped in front of the gate.

As he was getting out of the car he turned around and said: 'Okay, Dad, thanks. Are you not coming in?'

'Coming in? Where?'

'What? Are you not coming in?' he shouted.

I looked him in the eyes and said: 'Are you crazy? You think this is the way to fix things up? What if she doesn't want to see me?'

Then Costa came a bit closer, looked me back in the eye, and with his right hand pushed the hair off his face. With the same hand he removed a headphone from his ear and asked: 'I was listening to music. I didn't hear you. What did you say?'

I kept looking at him until he repeated his question: 'Dad, what did you say? Are you coming in or not?'

I froze for a second and then replied: 'No, Costa, I am not. I have to go somewhere.'

'Okay, thanks.' He put the headphone in his ear again, shut the door, and left.

Chapter 9

I DID NOT want to get to my mother's too late. I rushed back as soon as I could but had to spend a long time driving around and wasting gas to find a parking spot. As I went to pick up the laptop, I noticed the bag of potatoes I had prepared for Costa. That was really a long shot. If he had heard me he would never have agreed to take the potatoes. I thought of taking them to my mum, but that would start a whole new saga with her that I didn't need now. I could just hear her voice in my ear telling me that I should buy the hard ones, or the green ones, or the ones from Naxos. Why are they in a plastic bag? They should be in a paper bag. Why did you buy them? Take them home. I already have some. Do you also want some of mine? They are better.

Carefully I placed the bag behind my seat. Armed with the laptop, I went to my mum's house, the battlefield!

'Panayoti, what are you doing here? Is everything all right?' she said as soon as she opened the door.

'Yes, Mum, everything is okay. I am just here because I am looking for a friend.'

'A friend?'

'Yes, I need to go to your balcony.'

'Why? Is your friend on my balcony?'

'I need to use the Internet. You don't know what that is.'

'Yes, I do. Costa was just here. He went to the balcony too. Wait, you can't go upstairs like that. Take your shoes off. Here, I will get you a pair of slippers.'

'Since when aren't shoes allowed upstairs, Mum?'

'Since always. You don't remember because you haven't been up there for years.'

'Okay, I'll take them off. I don't need slippers.'

'You can't go on the balcony without slippers. It is cold and wet. Your socks will get wet. You are still like a small kid,' she said as she put a pair of slippers in front of me. I had no choice but to wear them.

'Do you want anything to eat?' she asked.

'No, Mum, this won't take long.'

'Is Maria waiting for you for dinner?'

'Yes, Mum.'

'How is she?'

'Fine, still nagging.'

'Shall I give you something to take home? I have made boiled broccoli with potatoes from Naxos. It is nice with some lemon and olive oil.'

'No thanks, Mum. I don't like broccoli.'

'Take some. Maria likes it.'

'No, Mum, I am fine.'

'Wait a minute. I also have some fresh cauliflower. It will take me five minutes. Shall I make you some?' I decided it would be best to just ignore her and go up to the balcony.

Then she shouted: 'I am making you some coffee. Go on, I will bring it up.' I ran to the balcony to finish the mission before she had a chance to make me anything.

'Make sure the neighbour doesn't see you using his thing,' she said in a loud whisper.

The laptop still had some power left in it, good enough for a few e-mails. I turned it on and waited.

Hooray, I was connected. Without wasting any time, I went to a search engine and typed 'Socrates Papadopoulos'. Slowly but surely, I found a page full of people with that name. Some had emails; some did not. A few were abroad. I had to narrow down my search. I typed the name again and added 'taxi driver'. A bunch of irrelevant pages came up. So I went back to my original search and selected all the ones who had an e-mail. As I was struggling to find a solid lead on the pages, from the corner of my eye I saw the neighbour coming to his balcony and looking straight at me. I knew I had little time left, so I copied and pasted as many e-mail addresses as I could into a blank email. I don't know how many I managed, but as soon as he went inside his house I stopped adding more addresses and quickly wrote in the text box:

Socrates,

This is me, Panos, your old classmate that you used to make fun of all the time. You used to call me Platoli, little Plato, because of that olive tree. I really want to find you. I need to talk to you. Write to me.

Panos (Plato)

That was good enough. I didn't have much time, so I clicked the 'send' button and waited. The text was still in front of me. Then in a flash it disappeared, followed by a loud crashing sound which made the whole balcony tremble. My Internet connection stopped. I looked around. The noise continued. It was like something was descending step by step, hitting the ground at each stage. No, it was not coming from my laptop. It was coming from inside the house. I rushed back in and saw a fallen coffee table at the bottom of the stairs. I ran down the stairs, and as I reached the table one of my slippers got loose. I tripped and almost came crashing on the table. Semi-airborne and completely out of control, at the very last second before putting my foot on the table to find balance, I noticed some grey hair extending out from under the wreckage. I balanced with one foot on the stair and with my other foot pushed the table away. I fell on the floor of the narrow corridor, side by side with my motionless mother. As I was facing the wall with my mother squeezed between me and the opposite wall, not knowing if I could move at all, I screamed: 'Mum.'

She answered calmly, as if nothing had happened: 'Yes, Panayoti?'

'Are you all right, Mum?'

'I don't know.'

'Can you get up?'

'I don't know.'

I slowly turned my head towards her. She was conscious and looking at me.

'Are you fine, Panayoti?'

'Yes, I am fine.'

'Okay, nothing happened. It was an old table anyway. It wasn't broken until you kicked it.'

'What were you doing, Mum? What was the table for?'

'For your coffee.'

'What coffee?'

'I was going to make you one.'

'Who told you to make me coffee?'

As she was still lying on the floor, with our noses just a few centimetres away from each other, she stated: 'You are my son. All the things I do for you, you think somebody tells me to do them? Do I have to ask permission from someone to make you coffee? Does somebody have to tell me how to be a mother? Now get up. You are making me cross-eyed.'

'I don't drink coffee. I have high blood pressure. It is not good for me.'

'You do? Are you all right? Since when? That's what happens when you don't come here often enough. You just come and drop off Elpida and go like someone is chasing you. How bad is it? Now get up, I want to get you something.'

'What?'

'I made some tzatziki. You should have some.'

'Why would I want tzatziki like this on the floor?'

'It has garlic in it. It is good for your blood pressure. It brings it down. Get up. I can't get up if you don't.'

'You can't get up if I don't?'

'No. I have to turn, and you are in the way.'

'Mum?'

'Yes.'

'I wanted to ask you something.'

'What?'

I knew I wanted to ask her something, but nothing was coming to mind. It was as if I was just enjoying the moment. She looked straight in my eyes, perhaps for the very first time in years, and said: 'Panayoti, my eyes are getting crossed. Hurry up. Ask your question.'

'How do you know that garlic brings your blood pressure down? Do you have high blood pressure?'

'Maria is waiting for you. Get up.'

'Tell me, Mum.'

'Your father had high blood pressure; I took care of him as long as I could. Do I have to worry about you too now?'

'You never told me where you met or how you fell in love.'

She took her eyes away from me, contemplated a bit, and said: 'You have never asked me that before. Why are you asking now, in this ridiculous position?'

'I have never asked you, Mum, because you are always busy doing something.'

'Will you get up if I tell you?'

'If it is the truth.'

She turned her head towards the corner of the ceiling, staring at the altar with an icon of the Virgin Mary. I had never noticed that altar. She took a deep breath and said: 'We met on your land, on top of the hill, where you want to make your hotel.'

'My land? What were you doing up there? Collecting olives?'

'No, that was where youth met back then.'

'A quiet spot in the woods?'

'No, there were other people too, away from our parents. I remember how beautiful it was. We could see the entire Aegean Sea from there. The reflection of the big rock in the blue sea was so romantic. It was like it was yesterday. Your father was so handsome. He had come with a mule, just to make me laugh.'

'What did you tell Grandpa? Where did you tell them you were?'

'I said I was looking for dolphins. If there is a dolphin in the Aegean, you can it from up there. Granddad used to think I was a dolphin fan.'

She stopped for a moment and then turned around and asked: 'Where did you meet Maria?'

'Tell me your story. When did you decide to get married?'

'No, tell me your story.'

'I don't want to now, Mum. I just don't feel like it.'

'You are so lucky to have Maria. You are not alone. She is a good mum. She hasn't come here for a while. Is she okay?'

'Yes, Mum, she is fine. Don't ask things. Just talk to me, tell me.'

'Tell you what?'

'Talk to me. Talk to me about the past, not now.'

'The past? When?'

'Talk to me about something, about when I was a kid.'

'Back then there was no Internet.'

'I know, Mum.'

'What is it? What do they do with it?'

'That's where everything is – all your friends, all the information, games, pictures, everything.'

'It must be awful.'

'Awful? Why, Mum?'

'A friend that you find on the computer can switch off easily, like the computer itself. It must be awful to have to go to a box to talk to your friends. I used to nag at your dad when he went to the village coffee shop by the bridge.'

'It is actually not a bad thing; I even talk to Costa on it.'

'You talk to your own son on a box?'

'Mum, usually when I talk to him he doesn't listen. He has got other things.'

'So you go to the Internet?'

'Well, if I want to ask something I send him an e-mail. He always answers his e-mails, as soon as I send them.'

'And then he talks to you?'

'He usually says "I can't now, Dad." Or if I tell him something he says he doesn't care or he is busy – something like that. I know it is not much, but it is at least a response, It is a connection.'

'When you were a kid, we used to talk a lot.'

'I know, Mum.'

'Back then you used to still look at me and listen to me when I talked to you. Do you remember?'

I turned to her, looked in her eyes, and answered: 'Yes.'

'We used to play a game when you were a little boy, a game about our mountain and the sea. Do you remember? I continued playing it with you when we came to Athens. I didn't want you to forget your birthplace. I didn't want you to forget our village, our home, our mountain.'

'But you wanted me to forget everything else, Mum.'

'I only wanted to protect you. I wanted you to keep smiling, to keep playing, to keep being a kid.'

'And then I grew up.'

'You want to play the game, Panayoti?'

'You are the only person who calls me by my full name.'

'I don't like to abbreviate the names of people I love, just to make it easier for myself.'

'Mum, you don't love people any less just because you abbreviate their names.'

'Panayoti, it is not enough to feel love. You have to show it. Your generation is too lazy to even show love. Soon you will be putting numbers on people. That is the easiest, isn't it? Hey, number one, do you want to play?

'Number one?'

'What number do you want me to give you? You are my only child.'

'Is that the game when you described a place and I had to name it, mother?'

'Yes.'

'Mum, why did they call our village "Nosun"? For the tourists? Tourists want the sun.'

'Are we playing the game?'

'No, I just wanted to know.'

'What tourists? We didn't think of tourists back then. The village is tucked away under the chestnut forest, and the mountain does not allow it to get enough sun. It is cool even during a hot summer.'

'All the villages are on that side of the mountain. Why did they call our village "Nosun"?'

'They used to say our village got less sunlight than any other village in the mountain. Your father was from the opposite village. They get a lot more sun than us. When he came with his parents to ask for my hand he kept joking, saying that if I went to live with them he would have to buy me sunglasses, and if he came and lived in our village he would have to buy a flashlight. He was a funny man. My parents thought he was serious at first.'

'Shall we play, Mum?'

'Yes. Tell me which beach has fine marble gravel on it. No, wait, there are a few of them. Near which beach is there a small sea cave with a sandy beach at the bottom of the cave? You can't walk to it; you must swim.'

'Eh, I know that one. Easy! I haven't been there for so many years. Remember the one you always forced me to go to when the sea was rough?'

'I wouldn't let you go near the sea when it was rough, Panayoti.'

'Except this one. It was completely safe, a natural coral reef gulf. There could be a heavy storm in the open sea, but the reef protected the entire beach, making it look like a colourful swimming pool. I want to go there now.'

'I don't remember.'

'Do you remember, once you thought I had drowned because you couldn't see me in the water? I had gone inside the rock holes on the reef?'

'Oh yes, now I remember.'

'Those holes were like whirlpools when waves hit the surface of the rock. I have spent hours in them. Your turn, Mum. Ask me something.'

'Okay, how many islands are near our mountain village?'

'That's easy, Mum. I am not five years old.'

'What is the name of the big rock in the sea in front of your land?'

'The Monk. Stop asking easy ones.'

'Okay, where was the cave everyone thought had a centaur skeleton?'

'That was a lie. There are no centaur skeletons. The cave, you told me, was closed by a big rock. There are so many unexplored caves in the forest; there must be so many stories about them.'

'There were still people who believed there was a skeleton in that cave. Some claimed they had seen it. Why don't you ask me something for a change?'

'Okay, Mum, how far away is the winter ski resort from our village?'

'I don't know. It was after my time. I guess it was on top of the mountain? When was the last time you went skiing there?'

'Oh, a long time ago. I miss it so much. You know, Mum, as you ski down you can see the Mediterranean on both sides of the peninsula.'

'Didn't you go there last year? With some archaeologists?'

'That was in the summer, when there is swimming. Archaeologists don't travel in the winter.'

'What did they say? What happened to your hotel?'

'I don't know, Mum. I am still waiting for the paperwork.'

'You mean from the archaeology authorities?'

'Yes.'

'I thought you got your permit.'

'That was a long time ago. A lot has happened since then. Don't you know?'

'How would I know? You never tell me anything.'

'They stopped me after I got my permit.'

'Why? Have they found something?'

'No.'

'Why don't they let you dig and see if there is anything there?'

'I don't know, Mum.'

'Why did they give you a permit if they weren't going to let you build?'

'They are different people.'

'Different people? The Turks? The Germans?'

'No, Mum, the people who gave me the permit are different from the people who took it away from me.'

'Where do they come from?'

'Mum, remember, I am supposed to be a child, and you are asking me play questions. Don't interrogate me.'

'Fine. Panayoti, I wanted to ask you. I want to do something with the house. Maybe we can put it in your name before I die. Isn't that better for you? Less taxes?'

'Don't even think about it, Mum. I can't even pay my own taxes, let alone pay for yours.'

'I don't want you to pay my taxes. I thought it would be easier for you.'

'No, Mum. Half of the house is built illegally; it is more trouble for me than it is worth.'

'What are you saying, Panayoti? This is the only thing your father and I have got left. We worked years for it, and now you don't want it?'

'My father?'

'Yes, it is from both of us. We both worked for it. He worked all his life, and I continued. Don't you want it?'

'If it is in my name, my taxes will go up, and we will have to pay for all the illegalities.'

'You are the one who wanted a bathroom in the house. I was happy to use the one in the garden. It is not my fault.'

'It is not about whose fault it is, Mum. It just doesn't work like that now. I don't know how to tell you, but now it is better not to have anything in one's name.'

'What are you saying? You don't want it?'

'Well, it is better if – it is better afterward. I mean, if I inherit it.'

'After what? After what, Panayoti? I must die first?'

'I didn't say that.'

'The world has changed so much. My parents did everything for us. They lived through the war, but before they died they made sure they left something for us – a roof over our head, a bit of land to grow things. You should be doing the same thing for your children. You only have two children.'

'Things have changed now, Mum. I can't even afford the children I have now. We almost had only one child.'

'What do you mean?'

'Elpida, she was a mistake. We couldn't afford another child. Have you not noticed the age difference between Costa and Elpida?'

'A mistake?'

'Yes, Mum.'

'How do you choose which one was a mistake?'

'I – well, the one that has come ... I don't know what you mean.'

'How do you choose, Panayoti? How do you choose which one is a mistake? How can someone whose name means "hope" be a mistake? What is wrong with her? Why can't you afford her? She hardly eats anything.'

'It is not the food, Mum. It is all the expenses – private school. Without it you can't go to the university, and without the university you are nothing. Actually, nowadays even with a university degree you are nothing.'

'My generation tried hard to make things simple and provide our children with a life that was easier than our lives. Your generation took the simple life we gave you and tried to make it fancy. You screwed everything up for the next generation. We had the basics and nothing fancy. Now you have all the fancy and no basics.'

'It is not my fault, Mum. We have a recession now.'

'And whose fault is that?'

'You know, we have too few people working and so many people on pension. Older people are living longer, and there are fewer young people working to care for the old.'

'So whose fault is it then? My fault for living longer? I am so sorry!'

'No, it is not your fault, Mum. Actually, a bit of it is.'

'My fault? What have I done?'

'You kept feeding me to take revenge for your own starvation.'

'Get up. My back is hurting me.'

'You brought us up too proud.'

'Who is us?'

'I mean all of you.'

'Who is all of you?'

'All you mothers.'

'Get up. My back hurts.'

'You didn't tell us about reality. You brought us up in a dream land, from the beginning.'

'What beginning?'

'You lied to me.'

'I lied to you?'

'Remember that Easter that I ate so much that I threw up?'

'No, which Easter?'

'You told me it was me who cooked the lamb. It wasn't me. In order to reward me for a lie, you made me take all the food in front of me.'

'Panayoti, seriously, there is something wrong with you. What are you talking about? Which mother doesn't enjoy her son eating good food?'

'Mum, it is …'

'Get up, I said. What kind of a father are you? You had a child and call it a mistake. You had a child and can't even afford to bring her up. Who is a better parent? My back is hurting me,' she shouted.

'You told us about a different world, a fantasy land.'

'I won't feed you anymore. You don't deserve it. You know, it is not your fault either. You were brought up without a father. If he wasn't killed under the mud, if he hadn't gone to work that day, he would have brought you up like a man. You have got nothing from him, nothing.'

'Yes, I have.'

'What? You don't even remember him.'

'You think just because we left the village after they were killed, I forgot everything? All my life, everything I write about, everywhere I go, anything I say is influenced by the fact that my father died at work. He was a poor labourer, unprotected and underpaid, and his life, together with the lives of his colleagues, was put at risk because of neglect.'

'Because of what?'

'Because of neglect, from his boss. Back then, Mum, the workers had no rights, none whatsoever. This is what took my father away, and because of that I am a different man. Do you know who is one of my best friends, Mum? He is a union leader. Do you know what that means, Mum? His job is to protect people so what happened to my father does not happen to any other worker.'

'Is this the friend you were looking for on my balcony?'

'No, it is someone else. The union leader was at my office this morning. I respect him a lot and see him often.'

'So who is the guy you have lost?'

'That is someone else, some guy I didn't like very much. He used to make fun of everything I said.'

'So why are you looking for him? He might still make fun of you.'

'It doesn't matter, Mum. What is important is that I haven't forgotten my father, nor how he died. He died because his employer forced him to risk his life.'

'Which employer?'

'I don't know – some rich guy, the town hall, a big-shot contractor. I don't care who. I want to make sure it doesn't happen again.'

'Panayoti, your father was not working that day. That wasn't his job. He was just helping out.'

'Helping out? For what?'

'Helping, Panayoti.'

'Helping who? All five of them were not working?'

'No, four of them were working, but they wanted to finish the work quickly.'

'Finish the work? They called my dad?'

'No, they were having a drink at the village coffee shop the night before. Your father offered to help.'

'Why have you kept this from me all these years?'

'I haven't kept anything.'

'Why didn't you tell me my father was just helping and not working?'

'Why does it matter? Your father died that day. That's what is important. He died – helping, working, the same thing. In those days people worked together, helped each other, for the whole village.'

'For the village?'

'Yes, Panayoti, for the village. It was different times, different people. It was not like the life you have now made for yourselves. Nowadays you don't even have children if it doesn't have some kind of a benefit for you.'

'You could have at least told me, Mum. I had the right to know.'

'Nowadays you are all spoiled.'

'My father was not even at work …'

'Nowadays, you don't stop. You want everything. A bit of food, a roof above your head, a family – it is not enough for you. You want more. You want cars, you want phones, you want holidays, you want this, you want that, and you are not even thankful to anything, not even to your God.'

'What does God have to do with it, Mum? What has your God done for our nation?'

'What has God done?'

'Why do you keep going to the church lighting candles? How does that help? What is the church doing today for our unemployed, for our youth? What are they doing with their money?'

'Stop, stop. That's enough, Panayoti.'

'Can't you see? There are five huge churches just in your neighbourhood, but there is not even one clinic! During the Turkish occupation the churches were competing to be the least visible, the most simple. Now they are competing with their vast funds to be the most glamorous, the most imposing, to get the next weeding or the next baptism.'

My mother, in that tiny space, suddenly turned around and managed to get herself up. She kicked the broken coffee table aside and walked towards the kitchen. I got up with difficulty and walked towards her. She turned her face away, but I saw she was crying.

'Mum, Mum, are you all right? What is wrong?'

She whispered: 'Yes, I am all right. I am just fine.'

'Tell me. Talk to me.'

'You asked me to talk to you like you were a child; you didn't tell me you have really become one.'

'What have I done?'

'Nothing, Panayoti. You have ripped everything apart, everything I did for you. You have just told me I am extra – me who brought you up, who fed you, washed you, covered you at night, taught you how to walk and how to talk. I worked, I struggled. After your father was killed I was your mother and your father. You are sitting there telling me all I have done has no value. The house, the food I make, is no good. It has too much fat in it, and you might not fit in your ski suit any more. My grandchild is a mistake. I lied to you about your father. My house is illegal. My pension is too much. I am living too long. What have you left for me, Panayoti? You think the mothers are at fault? Us? We are at fault? You and your generation destroyed any pride left in any profession. You abandoned our farms and destroyed our farmers, our factory workers, our teachers, and our doctors. You made a whole generation of greedy leeches to suck on everyone and everything. It is not how we made this country. Now, I am left with nothing. I am just waiting to die so that you don't have to pay fines for the extra guest bathroom you forced me to build, so that you don't have to pay for my pension. My value is only in my death. This is my value. And now, now you have the guts to sit here and criticize my faith? That's all I have, Panayoti. In my world everything has changed. I am a foreigner in my own land. I am not needed any more. Now I am a burden on your perfect society because I am old. The only thing that has remained the same, the only thing I still recognize, is my God, my church.'

'Mum, please, I don't … I am not trying to criticize your faith. I am –'

'What if you are right, Panayoti? What if even my faith has let me down? What if what you say is true? Have you thought of that? You will just go home, and when you get there, there will be a light on. There will be people waiting for you. You will just leave and go to your family with your mistaken child and unemployed son and nagging wife. Where am I going to go? At least you have them. You have a family. What do I have? Go, Panayoti, go. I want to be alone now. Go back to your family. Let me be.'

I opened my mouth to say something but was completely muted. I never knew my mother was like this, with so much inside. Through all these years, the cheese pies were just a camouflage. There was so much pain hidden behind them. I waited a bit, hoping that she would break her silence, but it never happened.

'Do you need anything? Mum, do you need anything?'

She turned and went to the kitchen ignoring me completely. As if nothing had happened I asked calmly: 'Is there anything to eat? I haven't eaten all day.'

She shouted back from the kitchen: 'Go home. Eat there. I am not going to force feed you again.'

'Okay, I will. I will go home.'

I took a few steps towards the front door, turned back, and went to the fire, trying to buy some time. I played with the fire a bit. Then I stood up, turned around, and asked again: 'Is there anything you want me to get you, Mum?'

'No.'

'Anything? Anything you want, Mum?'

She paused for a second and said: 'Yes. When you get home, kiss Elpida, kiss Costa, and kiss Maria, and please don't ever let them know that any one of them was a mistake.'

Chapter 10

WHEN A GREEK is happy, he goes out eating, drinking, and dancing. He makes as much noise as possible; consequently he can hardly hear his latest favourite song. This gives him the excuse to complain about the music not being loud enough. Towards the middle of the night, which is actually around three in the morning, all of a sudden, all the songs are his favourite. He spends all his money ordering flowers and more drinks. He flirts with as many women as there are. He hits his cutlery against the plates to the threshold of breakage, and then as a form of punishment for the plate's tolerance, he picks it up and smashes it on the floor. He then stands up and announces proudly that he is gladly willing to pay for it, for the plate and for the floor. He shouts, he sings, and he cries with the music. He gets angry at the silliest things and then laughs in the face of tragedy. A Greek does all this when he is happy because he deserves it. But when he is sad he does it more, even harder, with more convection and with more passion, because it all becomes his right.

I had all the ingredients to go to the Bouzoukia. Firstly, I needed to go to meet Pavlos. I couldn't ask to stay at his house in the middle of the street. It should be somewhere appropriate, somewhere where we were both relaxed and comfortable. Secondly, I was free; I could go out of the dark, empty house and never come back. No one would notice, and no one would miss me. That is, of course, if a handle knob did not break, the toilet was not blocked again, and if we didn't need to change a lightbulb. In fact, some would even cherish my absence. I could go to the Bouzoukia and show my boss that in my eyes, he was not important enough to sadden me at all. Most importantly, I was now single. At last, I was a free single man. Who knew what could happen at the Bouzoukia? Maria might not think so, but I was still a man. Behind all this temporary cloud of gloom there was still a strong, desirable man. I couldn't wait to get to the Bouzoukia! If the pharmacist, the electric company, the social security office, and everyone else didn't want my money, fine. I had a hundred-euro bill. I would go and spend it. I would spend it on whores if I wanted to. Let them appreciate me! You want the house? Fine, have it. I will leave tomorrow. I will go to your lawyer and show him that I am leaving voluntarily. But I am not going to make it easy for you. There will be no electricity. Have the house like this, dark and empty, just how you left it for me. I am not even going to go to the house. I will sleep in the car; I will go to the Bouzoukia early.

It was a nice idea, but I couldn't get any rest in the car. I went home and dropped off the laptop. I couldn't find any candles, but I managed to get dressed. Thought of checking the freezer to make sure there was nothing important defrosting. But then again, what if there was something in there? What was I going to do with it, take it to the night club? It was probably best not to open the fridge door anyway and let the cold air out. What cold air? The room itself was freezing. The easiest thing to find that would keep me warm was the bed cover. The double bed was made as if nothing had happened. She had made it as if she were expecting us to use it again that night. I pulled the cover over my shoulder and walked towards the couch. There was no way I was going to sleep on that bed. The bed was now hers, not ours. She owned it on her own. As I walked towards the couch I had an image of Costa coming and sleeping between us all those years ago.

'Mum, can I sleep here tonight? I am scared.'

After several turns on the couch, I finally got comfortable and asked myself, how could the bed be just hers? It used to be ours!

I thought it was very late when I woke up in the double bed. I had no idea how much time had passed nor how I had got to the bedroom from the living room. Neither did I know, in my state, how I finally got to the Bouzoukia.

The Bouzoukia was empty. The doorman smiled and let me in.

'The music starts in a few minutes,' he said, leading me inside. I looked around. The place looked cold and undesirable, filled with empty chairs and the smell of stale cigarettes. There was no music and no musicians. There were some women sitting at a table by the bar. Apart from some musical instruments, the stage was empty.

A waiter walked towards me. 'Hello, sir. Welcome.'

'Thank you.'

'Where would you like to sit?'

'By the stage.'

'It is good you came early. They will be all taken shortly. I will just come to take your order.'

'Okay, fine.'

'Sir, excuse me, but you have a big twist on your belt. It must hurt.'

I looked down at my belt; it did indeed have a big twist on the side. That is what happens when you get dressed in the dark.

'Oh, yes, I got dressed in a hurry. I don't know what I was thinking of. I always rush when I am putting my clothes on.'

'Now that you are at it, you might as well close your zipper.'

'Oh, yes, thank you.'

Within minutes he reappeared with a plate of carrots, some nuts, and peeled apples. 'What would you like to drink, sir?'

'I will have a whiskey. Make it a double.'

'We only serve full bottles at the tables. If you want a glass you must go to the bar. There are stools there,' he said as he took the carrots off the table.

'I don't want to go to the bar. I am expecting people.'

'Good, then maybe you want to order a bottle.'

'Okay, fine, bring me a bottle. I am sure it won't be wasted.'

'We have Johnny Walker for 120 euros and Chivas Regal for 150 euros.'

'Why can't I just have a glass now until they come? I don't even know what they drink.'

'I am sorry, but I can't do that. Everyone then will ask for the same thing. Everyone wants to sit by the stage.'

'Everyone who? There is no one here.'

'It is early. Very soon …'

As soon as he said that a man was escorted towards our table by the bouncer who shouted: 'The usual table.'

The man came towards the table. The waiter greeted him with a big smile and said to him: 'Please, please come here, in front.'

Then he turned to me and said: 'Please, could you move to the bar? This is his usual table.'

'I didn't see any reservation signs on the table.'

The man by this time had got to our table. He looked at me and said to the waiter: 'It doesn't matter; I will sit at another table.'

The waiter, almost pulling my arm to get me up, said to him: 'No, no, the gentleman has decided to sit at the bar'

The waiter started guiding the new client through the narrow gap between the tables where I was standing. As he passed, our eyes met. I kept cool.

When our bellies were touching I whispered to him: 'Too noisy here, at the stage.'

He stopped for a second and said loudly, 'Well, maybe I will join you at the bar later then.'

The waiter looked at me for a second and shouted across the room: 'One bottle of Chivas for the doctor.'

Like a school boy under detention, I found myself on a stool at the corner of the bar and sat quietly, ordering myself a drink. Some more people walked in, but there was still no sign of Pavlos or my boss. I waited and waited, sipping on my whiskey as if it were a rare treasure. I wanted to keep enough drink in the glass to last me the night. The music started, and warm-up singers commenced their program. I started lip syncing with the singer. I was so lost in the music that I did not even notice having finished my drink. Suddenly, the waiter showed up from behind and asked: 'Another one?'

'No. Can I have some water, please, from the tap?'

He reached behind the bar, grabbed a bottle of water and a glass, put it in front of me and said: 'Don't worry, we don't charge for the water.'

I was beginning to feel more and more uncomfortable. There was no guarantee that Pavlos would show up anyway. I decided to leave. With my hundred-euro bill ready in my hand, I called the waiter.

'Yes, can I help?'

'I am leaving.'

'Why? I thought you are waiting for friends. What happened? Good thing you didn't order the bottle.'

'They didn't come. I have to leave anyway.'

'Are you sure you don't want another drink?'

'No, really, I am late for something. I've got to go now. Here is the money.'

'No, it is okay. The doctor paid for you.'

'The doctor? He paid for me? Why?'

'I don't know, maybe it is because of what you said in his ear?'

'I didn't say anything to him.'

I didn't want any doctor paying for me. This is usually an occasion when you thank people or buy them a drink back, but instead I walked all the way across to his table and said: 'Thanks for the drink, but no thanks. When I needed you this morning I couldn't find you; you were on strike. Now you want to buy me a drink?'

He looked at me with surprise and asked: 'Sorry, but are you one of my patients?'

'No, I mean you doctors, all of you. You are all the same. How can you go on strike?'

'I don't know who you were looking for, but I am a cardiologist. Are you okay? Do you need some help? What kind of a doctor were you looking for?'

'I am okay. I don't need your help.' The singer came closer to our table.

'Why were you looking for a doctor, then?'

'I am, I am a … well, a journalist. I wanted to interview a doctor, any doctor.'

'A journalist? Why don't you sit down. Why are you so angry?'

'I am not angry!' I shouted as I sat down.

'Waiter, waiter, another glass and a fork for my friend,' he shouted. Then he continued: 'A journalist? Very interesting. Then you should know why we went on strike today. If you were sick I would say you are angry for personal reasons.'

'I told you, I am not sick.'

'As I said, as a journalist you should know why we went on strike today.'

'Yes, because you are needed. Without you people die. If I go on strike, nobody gives a shit. If you go on strike, you get the attention you want, but it can kill people.'

'Calm down. It is not what you think.'

'It doesn't matter what I think. You have a responsibility. You are supposed to have a conscience. Did you not take the Hippocratic Oath? Did you not take your oath to upkeep an ethical standard? All new doctors in the world take this oath from our ancients, and our own doctors throw it in the rubbish bin?'

'The whole society has lost its conscience. Why should I keep mine? Why should I be the only one?'

'Don't sound like a politician. Did you take the oath, yes or no?'

'Politicians have their own oath'.

'They don't have people's lives in their hands.'

'I can't hear you! Come closer. The music is too loud.' I got off my chair and sat in the chair next to him, facing the stage.

I shouted in his ear: 'That is why I didn't want to sit by the stage. Can you hear me now?'

'Yes. Why do you hate me? What have I done to you?'

'It is your profession. Don't take it personally.'

As soon as I said that I felt a tap on my left shoulder. It was the waiter again, extending his arm between us with a drink.

'Excuse me, can I put your drink on the table?' he said.

'I didn't want a drink. I must go now,' I replied.

'It has been ordered, sir.'

'Fine, put it here. But this one I am paying for.'

Then I continued with the doctor: 'It is your profession, your whole approach, your colleagues – how can you reach such decisions?'

The female singer came crouching next to our table, looking at us and singing with all her might. Then two dressed-up ladies with heavy makeup came and sat opposite.

'How are you?' shouted the one sitting opposite me. Before I had a chance to answer, a young girl with several trays of cut flowers came and stood next to me, waiting for an order. The other woman put her hand on the doctor's shoulder and whispered in his ear. I waited momentarily to see the doctor's reaction first, but he was talking to the woman next to him. I slowly took out the hundred-euro bill and gave it to the girl with the flowers.

'All?' She asked.

'How much are they?' I asked.

'Five euros a tray. I only have ten trays, but I can get you more.'

'No, I only want one.'

'Just one?'

'Yes.'

'But I don't have any change; it is the beginning of the night.'

The doctor came to the rescue and ordered four trays. The girl took the money from the doctor, put my hundred-euro bill back on the table, and handed four of the trays to the doctor. So far he had paid for my drink and for the woman. I could no longer afford to be impolite to him. He took the trays, turned around, and threw the flowers of two of them at the singer and one at the woman opposite him. He gave me the other tray. I took the tray and threw the flowers on the girl in front of me. She smiled and asked me for a drink.

'I am not going to be here for long,' I said, hoping to get away from paying for an expensive 'lady's drink'. She then turned to the doctor and thanked him for the flowers.

Then I heard the doctor telling the other woman: 'Me and my friend have something to talk about. Maybe later.'

The girl in front of me said: 'You have come to the Bouzoukia to talk to each other?'

'Yes, it is important,' I said desperately.

The waiter came to get the order for the women. The doctor said no. The waiter looked at me, and I naturally said no too. Then the women sitting in front of me said to the other one loudly: 'Come on, I think these gentlemen prefer to be together.' She paused a second and stressed: 'Alone.'

The waiter looked at me and said: 'As you wish.'

As soon as the women and the waiter were gone, the doctor turned to me and said: 'This is their trick. They try to offend you, and just to prove a point you end up spending another hundred euros on their drinks, only for the privilege of them sitting at your table. That's Bouzoukia for you. They do anything to get money out of you, even if they have to insult you in the process. Sometimes they even bring you a wrong order, always more expensive than your actual order, and they have the perfect excuse: They didn't hear you because of the music.'

'How much taxes have I paid for the privilege of having you when I need you?'

'You are not letting this go, right?'

'No, I won't.'

'What?'

'No, I won't.'

'I can't hear you well here. Get up.'

'What?'

'Get up.' And he got up, took my hand, and started walking towards the bar.

'What are you doing?'

'Come, I am going to sort this out once and for all,' he said as he continued pulling me. We passed the bar and went towards the bathroom. He opened the door, let go of my hand, and invited me in with a hand gesture.

As soon as I got in he shut the door and started: 'Look, I have worked for years, getting up every morning, working all day, doing night shifts, and staying away from my family for Easter, New Year's, and Christmas.'

'So what? Everybody works.'

'Yes, but for the last three years I have not been paid, because I was stupid enough to work for the public insurance. They have no money, so they tell me to carry on and we will see what happens. Now, they are reducing my salary, the salary that they are not paying me. Do you know what that means?'

'If the government owes you money, it is your problem with the government, not mine. All this does not give you the right to kill people.'

'To kill people? To kill people?' He started walking around in a circle in the bathroom. He made two whole circles, and when he got to me, he stood up on his toes, came closer to me, and shouted:

'If I wanted to kill people, do you know what I would do?'

'Go on strike?'

'No.'

'Close the hospital and send people home?'

'No.'

'Ask for more bribes to do your job? More little envelopes?'

'No.'

'What then?'

'I would tell people to come to the hospital and would promise to take care of them, without the doctors, without the nurses, without the machinery, without tests, without the medicine, without anything, just like the government.'

'The government?'

'The politicians! They are the ones who are killing you, not me. If they are in power, they say it will all be okay. If not, they tell you, "Vote for me and then everything will be okay." No one is telling you the truth; no one is telling you how bad things really are. All you hear is "Come, come to my hospital. Come to my party, and I will fix you." Lies, lies, and more lies! You think I am the one killing you?'

'Now you really sound like the politicians, blaming others. What have you done for us as a doctor? Was your oath only to the gift envelopes from the sick or to the sick themselves?'

He stopped shouting and walked down towards the urinals. At first I thought he was going to urinate, but obviously it was just a nervous walk, totally out of frustration. Perhaps he had run out of words. He had his back to me and seemed to be staring at the floor.

I had the upper hand in the conversation. I was not going to let this moment go to waste, so I said again: 'You are the ones killing us, with your negligence.'

He then took a deep breath, turned around, and came charging towards me. To protect myself I raised both my hands. He came closer and with both hands grabbed my neck and with his thumbs put a bit of pressure on my throat. I tried to hold his hands, but in complete disbelief I had no other physical reaction and asked: 'Have you gone crazy?'

'Do you know, if I wanted to kill you, what I would do? Do you know what this is?'

'My throat! Leave me alone. You are mad.'

He very gradually applied more pressure and said: 'This is the most vital part of your body. Through this you get life, you get oxygen, you get food, you get water.'

Then he applied a bit more pressure and continued: 'If I want to kill you, I'd block this. Without it you will choke to death.'

I was beginning to get scared, so I went to reach for his throat. He got his grip on me even harder and started moving his head back. I finally managed to get hold of his neck and pulled it towards myself. His head came closer to me, and he started talking again.

'If you were the nation, this would be your highways. You have put your life in the hands of politicians. Instead of privatizing the monopoly of the utility companies and all the government offices, where thousands of their party members work, they have privatized your throat because it has less political cost for them.'

There was silence, and we kept staring at each other's eyes. He was not letting go, and neither was I. He continued: 'If I wanted to kill you, you know what else I would do? I would go through your body, bit by bit. I would see what moves and what bit has life in it, and then I would restrain it. I would make it difficult for your blood to circulate. I would numb your vital muscles. I would do exactly what the politicians are doing to our nation by putting taxes and new regulations on anything that dares to move and try to breathe.'

He stopped again, but it was a momentary break. 'You call yourself a journalist? You go and vote for them and blame me for killing you and the nation?'

Then he pulled me a bit closer to himself and said: 'Do you ...'

Suddenly the bathroom door opened, and the waiter appeared. As soon as he saw the doctor and me in the middle of the bathroom with our hands around each other's necks he said: 'Oh, I am sorry; I didn't know you were here.'

Both the doctor and I let go of each other's necks. I turned to the waiter and said, 'It is okay. Come on in. We are finished.'

The waiter, looking a bit confused, turned around to leave but ran into a man behind him who was also trying to get into the bathroom. The waiter said to him: 'I would come back later if I were you.'

The man shoved himself in the bathroom and said: 'Why? What is going on? Oh, Panos, what are you doing here?'

It was Pavlos with half his body in the bathroom, looking at the doctor and me. I quickly said: 'I thought you were not coming. I was about to leave. Is Nikos here too?'

'Don't you want to introduce me to your friend?'

'Oh, he is not my friend. We just met. He is a doctor.'

The doctor looked at Pavlos, and without any facial expressions turned to me and said: 'Don't make assumptions about people, and think before you insult them.'

And with that, he walked out of the bathroom. Pavlos got himself to the urinals and unzipped. I was still in the middle of the bathroom with nothing to do. I did not know whether to go after the doctor or stay and talk to Pavlos about my problems whilst he was urinating. Finally he broke the silence. 'I was not expecting to see you here.'

'You mean the bathroom?'

'No, at the Bouzoukia, stupid. You always threatened to come one day, but I didn't expect you would make it. A financially broke family man like you, here at the Bouzoukia?'

'Well, you invited me. I always wanted to catch up with you.'

Another man walked in. The urinal next to Pavlos was free. The man hesitated first and then asked me: 'Are you going to go?'

'No, I am fine. I am just waiting for him,' I said, pointing at Pavlos. The man gave me a strange look, unzipped, and stood at the urinal.

'Pavlos, I will come back. We will talk later.' I left the bathroom.

More people had come, and the stage front tables were almost full. My boss was sitting at the table next to the doctor with the two bar women. I could feel that the waiter was looking at my every move. I got closer to the stage and was still confused about my next course of action. I had to talk to Pavlos because I had to move out of the house, but not in front of my boss. I hadn't paid for my drink at the doctor's table, but I didn't want to go back there. On the other hand, I didn't want him to think he had won the argument. In the end, I didn't need to make a decision.

Nikos shouted from across the tables: 'Panos, Panos, we are here. Come on.'

Both women sitting at his table turned around. As soon as they recognized me, they looked at each other with disgust. The doctor noticed me too, and our eyes met without any expression from either side. I was still in the middle of the room when I heard the waiter whisper from behind.

'See, at the beginning of the night you didn't even have one table, and now you have two to choose from.'

I ignored him and had another look at the doctor's table. The doctor was still looking at me, and he smiled. It was like a victory smile. I wasn't going to have it. Instead of me getting my frustration out on him, he got all of his frustration out on me. My throat was still sore. I greeted Nikos from afar and indicated with my hand that I would go to him later. Then I walked to the doctor's table. The orchestra was quiet. They were waiting for a new singer. Without sitting down at his table I said to him quietly:

'It is easy to blame everything on politics and politicians. That is the easiest way out. But each one of us is responsible, and you can't pass on the blame forever. You are a doctor. Your responsibility is to the sick.'

He looked in my eyes, smirked again, and said: 'I now live in a nation where everything is sick, everything and everyone.'

'So you should work harder.'

'I can only do my bit. There are different doctors for each illness, and each illness requires a different treatment at each stage of its development.'

'What are you talking about? You have had too much whiskey.'

He ignored my smear and continued: 'First you need to have a proper diet. Maybe you need a dietician. You should prevent the illness by using professional advice. That was years ago. You didn't do it.'

I kept silent and continued observing the mad doctor. He had more to say.

'If you don't take care of yourself and do not prevent the illness, you come to me. I do a check-up and give you the bad news with some medicine and advice on your lifestyle.'

'Right, go on.'

'Then instead of accepting that you are sick and taking the medicine, or at least getting a second opinion, you go through a long stage of denial.'

'Do you know that I am sick?'

'Yes.'

'How?'

'Because of all the tests.'

'Which tests? You have never seen me before.'

'I am not talking about you. And then you say I have had too much whiskey?'

'Who are you talking about, then? Is this politics again?'

'I thought you were a journalist.'

'What does that have to do with it?'

'Anyway, you can't ignore all the advice, live in your dream, eat whatever you want, smoke as much as you want, drink, not exercise, even refuse to take the medicine, and then come to me and demand that I fix you.'

'What if I come to you now and ask for help, to cure me? What if I accept that I am sick and accept to take your medicine? Will you close the door on me, just to punish me?'

'No, this is not a school. Of course not.'

'What then?'

'Well, I am a cardiologist.'

'I know that. That's why I need you.'

'No, you don't need a cardiologist anymore. You need …'

Suddenly the music started, and the new singer already on the stage started singing. It happened to be one of our favourite songs. If Maria were there she would sing along. We had even danced to this song together.

'Do you hear me?' shouted the doctor.

'No, I need what?'

'I said it is too late. Now you urgently need a cardiothoracic surgeon.'

'What is that?'

'You need a surgeon now, not a doctor. It is too late. You have been in the stage of denial too long. You need to …'

'I need what?'

'You have wasted enough time in denial. You need to do something,' he screamed.

I picked up my glass and said: 'I will pay for this one, okay?' and walked away.

'It is too late,' screamed the doctor. I ignored him.

He continued shouting: 'I have already paid for it. Where are you going? To your comfortable land of denial? I thought you wanted to know why I went on strike.'

I stopped, turned back to the table, and said: 'Look, I have come here to take a break, a short break, just to forget things. I don't want to talk politics, nor to hear your unending excuses.'

'You are the one who asked.'

'Fine, thank you, good night.'

I started walking towards Nikos's table. My throat was still hurting, but what I had just heard from the doctor was even more painful. What if it was too late? What if I had spent all this time in denial? I know he was talking about the nation, but what if it was too late for me too? Did I really need an operation now? Had I left it for too long? Who was going to pay for the operation? I didn't even have insurance anymore.

'Didn't expect to see you here, Panos,' said Nikos as soon as I reached their table.

'I was invited by Pavlos.'

'As long as you have it cleared with him. So he is paying for your drinks, right?' Both women started laughing.

'Come on, sit down.'

As I went to sit at the only vacant chair, the woman who was sitting next to the chair put her hand on the seat and said: 'Sorry, but this one is taken. He just went to the bathroom.'

'Oh, I wasn't going to sit down anyway. I've got to go soon,' I explained.

'Come on, grab a chair and sit down now. You are going to get yelled at by your missus. anyways for coming here alone. You might as well make it worthwhile. Come on, grab a chair, grab a lady.'

As soon as he said that, both women simultaneously said: 'No thanks.'

Suddenly I felt a tap on my shoulder. 'Here is a chair for you,' said the waiter, standing behind me with a chair. 'Would you like a drink?'

As I was standing, I turned to him and whispered in his ear: 'Look, I left my wallet at home and only have a hundred euros. Do you think you can get me a bottle of Johnny for this table?'

'I don't think so, but I will check. Here, have a seat anyway.'

'Could you bring some food too with it? I am starving.'

'I said I will see what I can do.'

A moment later Pavlos came back. He smiled at the girls and sat at his reserved seat.

'Why aren't you sitting next to this beautiful lady, Panos? What is wrong with you?' The woman laughed and whispered something in Pavlos's ear. Then they both started laughing.

'This is my best friend. Do you know why?' he asked the woman.

'Him? Why? I don't know,' she replied.

'Because I only see him once every other year.'

Then the woman laughed, which caused everyone, including myself, to laugh. Pavlos turned to me and said in my ear: 'I am just joking, right? You don't mind a bit of a laugh?'

'I am fine, Pavlos. I am okay.'

'Are you? You seem a bit bothered.'

This was the perfect opportunity for me, the right moment to tell him what I needed. I moved a bit towards him, getting ready to talk.

But the woman next to him gave me a dirty look, took his hand and put it on her lap, and said: 'Pavlos, I think you have seen enough of your friend for this year.'

I was surprised to see Pavlos stop the woman, turn around to me, and say: 'What is it? Do you need something?'

'No, I don't need anything!'

'Do you need some money? What then?'

I wasn't sure if I should talk there or wait a bit. Fortunately, I was saved by the waiter, who arrived with the whiskey I had ordered. It looked like they had accepted to charge me less. As soon as I saw the bottle I thought it was good that I had ordered the whiskey so he knew I don't need him for money.

'Wait, I will tell you later. Let's have a drink,' I said proudly.

The waiter put the bottle on the table to show that it was sealed. It was in fact sealed and genuine, but it did not say Johnny Walker on it. It said, in silver letters, 'Chivas Regal 12 years.' They were at it again, if I had any more money I wouldn't care, but I was not going to let them play with me this way. I had to stop him before he opened the bottle or else there was no return. I bent toward the bottle to grab the waiter's hand to stop him and accidentally knocked over a full glass of water, which rolled towards the woman next to Pavlos. The glass then fell and broke on the floor next to her feet. Then the water on the table begin going towards her and started spilling on her short skirt.

'What are you doing?' shouted Pavlos. I finally got hold of the waiter's arm and stopped him. Everyone at the table turned and looked at me in surprise.

'Wait for your turn. There is enough whiskey for everyone,' said the waiter.

'I did not order this.'

'No, you didn't. I asked at the kitchen. If they have any half-bottles of the cheap one, I will bring it to you. That one is only sixty euros,' said the waiter.

'Who is this from, then?' asked Nikos.

'The table behind the column, over there,' said the waiter, pointing his finger at the other side of the hall. Nikos stood up and smiled like a child who has found a new toy. He filled his glass, lifted it up in the air, took a sip, and started walking towards the table that had ordered the bottle.

'Another big shot! I don't know him. I think he is in the parliament. I have seen him somewhere,' said Pavlos, looking at the table which had sent the complementary Chivas. With Nikos gone it was the perfect opportunity to talk with Pavlos. So I pulled my chair closer to him and moved my head towards his ear. The women kept giving me angry looks. Then Pavlos suddenly raised his hand in the air and called for the waiter. The waiter came rushing to the table and whispered in Pavlos's ear loudly: 'Would you like me to remove him?'

'No, do you know the man who ordered this?' asked Pavlos, pointing at the bottle of Chives.

'A man from that table, but this man has asked for half a bottle of Johnny,' said the waiter pointing at me.

'What are we going to do with half a bottle of Johnny? Cancel it,' said Pavlos to the waiter.

'Okay,' said the waiter and walked away.

Pavlos turned to me and said: 'Is that okay? We have enough drinks here. Don't waste your money. The way things are, you don't know for how long you will have a job.'

'I ordered a full bottle. I don't know what half bottle he was talking about.'

'We have enough whiskey here anyway. What is it you wanted to talk about?' One of the women pulled his arm and whispered something in his ear.

'Okay, okay' said Pavlos to her and turned around, looking for the waiter, who had disappeared.

'What is up?' I asked.

He turned his head towards me and said quietly: 'Nothing, the fucking bitch doesn't like whiskey. She wants her own drink. Tell me, what is it?'

'How would I know what she drinks?' I replied.

'What is it you wanted to tell me?'

'Oh, I see. Well, I am in a bit of ...'

Nikos returned and shouted to Pavlos: 'Guess who?'

'Who?' asked Pavlos.

'It is the junior minister I was talking about this morning.'

'Him? He got the Chivas?'

'Yes, he wants us to join him at his table.'

Pavlos looked excited at first and then said: 'But I thought we had to go. How about your appointment?'

'Yes, I know. I have to do something about that,' answered Nikos. The singer suddenly appeared at our table and sat on my lap. Nikos sat down too and ordered some flowers, which were thrown on the singer's head. Some ended up on my lap. Pavlos kissed the singer's hand and ordered more flowers.

As soon as she got up and went to the next table, Pavlos turned to me and said: 'Tell me what you want now. We are going to another table soon.'

'It is too loud here. Can we go somewhere we can talk?'

'Somewhere? Where?'

'To the bathroom? It is important,' I replied.

Pavlos got up, and we both started walking towards the bathroom. The walk seemed to take forever; on the way I was preparing myself to ask him and did not know where to start. I couldn't just directly ask to let me move to his house. I needed some kind of an ice breaker.

'So how are you, Pavlos?' I asked as I followed him.

'What?'

'How are you these days?'

'Fine, how are you?'

'What happened to the call girl? Didn't she want to come?'

'Oh, that whore?'

'Yes, where is she? Why didn't she come?'

He opened the bathroom door, and we both went in. Then he said: 'You know, Panos, I have a bit of respect for my penis. I don't just put it in anything that is on offer.' Suddenly we heard a toilet flush from one of the stalls. Immediately after, the waiter came out of the toilet and without looking at us rushed out of the bathroom.

Pavlos's eyes froze at the bathroom door. Then he raised both his hands, put them on his forehead, and said: 'Oh no.'

'What?'

'I ordered some snacks with the whiskey.'

'So?'

'Didn't you see? That was the waiter. He didn't even wash his hands.'

'Pavlos, the reason I wanted to ...'

He interrupted me and said: 'What was I saying? Oh, yeah, the call girl. What do I need her for? She was young, too young for me. I am getting on, you know. I have a daughter that age, and a name in the society. I am a union leader. I am supposed to be on the side of the weak and the vulnerable. She wanted to come, but I got scared. You know, girls like that love men in positions. They love strong men. You screw them once and then they fall in love with you, and you have to spend all your energy to get rid of them. I need my energy for my work. I have no time for that.'

'Remember inviting me to your house?'

'Yes, why?'

'I want to come and visit.'

'So come.'

'I might have to stay for a few days.'

'What happened?'

'Nothing, trouble with the missus. It won't be for too long. I am sure she will come to her senses.'

'What do you expect, spending nights in places like this without your wife?'

'Well, yes.'

'Does the doctor have anything to do with this?'

'No, what are you talking about?'

'Are you having an affair?'

'No, Pavlos, no affairs.'

'I guess you couldn't afford it anyway.'

'Yes, I can't.'

'What then?'

'I don't know, Pavlos, I just don't know.'

'Women, that's women for you. As soon as you run out of money they kick you out.'

'No, it's not money. It's complicated.'

'I have never heard of an easy divorce.'

'Divorce? No, Pavlos, it won't get there. She is not like that.'

'Get a good lawyer anyway.'

'We haven't got to that stage yet. Everything can be fixed. Do you have enough room for me?'

'I will see what I can do. When are you thinking of coming?'

'I will let you know. Very soon. I have promised her lawyer that I will move out.'

'I thought you hadn't got to that stage yet.'

'The lawyer is a relative. He's just helping us.'

'Your relative?'

'No, but what does it matter? Thanks for your offer. I will let you know when I am coming.'

'Don't thank me yet. I will have to check with the boss.'

'The boss? My boss?'

'No, my boss, the wife. She is not here. She is in the United States. My daughter is there. She is in her third year at university. My wife goes there a few months each year to help her out. It gives me a bit of peace and quiet, but I have to check with her.'

'What is your daughter doing in the United States?'

'Business administration. I help her out a lot. What you learn in school is one thing. Reality is another.'

'Yes, her dad knows more about business than her university professors; they must come and learn from you, to learn what the real world is like.'

'You know what, Panos? Come on over whenever you want. You can stay in the guest room.'

'Your wife? Don't you want to ask her?'

'No, it's okay. She is not even here. We will have an only-men weekend. It will be fun.'

As soon as I got back to the table, Nikos asked the women to leave. They gave me their last angry look of the evening, I hoped, and then they left. Our silence was very uncomfortable, even though we wouldn't have heard each other well even if we had spoken.

'Shame the call girl didn't come with you tonight,' I said.

'What?'

'Shame the call girl couldn't come with you.'

'The call girl? You know, she wanted five hundred euros just to come with us for a drink.'

'Five hundred?'

'Yes, she is a call girl. They charge a lot, but she wasn't even that hot.'

'Is that with sex?'

'Why? Do you have five hundred euros to spare, Panos? Give it to me. I will sleep with you.'

He burst into laughter. I looked around; luckily this time the waiter was not standing next to me listening.

'So what happened to her?'

'Nothing. As soon as we heard the price, Pavlos told her to go and fuck herself.'

'Is that with sex?'

'You are a funny man, Panos. I wish you would use some of your humour in your work.'

'But of course I have to check with you first.'

'What?'

'Never mind.'

'Listen, Panos, I need to talk to you,' he said, looking very serious. The time was set for the bad news to be finally announced. Obviously he had already told Pavlos that he was going to fire me. Maybe this was the most comfortable place for him to do it. Maybe I should have never come. Like a sacrificial lamb ready to be slaughtered, I changed my seat and sat next to him. I don't know if I didn't hear him well, it was a nervous reaction, or I was just buying time.

As soon as I sat next to him I asked: 'What?'

'Listen to me carefully.'

A new bar woman came and sat next to him. This time he almost pushed her away. He turned to me and said: 'Panos? Are you listening to me?'

'Yes.'

'Do you hear me now?'

'Not really, but go on.'

'This is very important. I need you to listen.'

'Yes.'

'Where are the women?' asked Pavlos as he got back to the table. If there was any way back to Maria, I had to keep my job. Even if it was a non-paying job temporarily, it was still something, a little window of hope.

'What is it you do, Panos, that drives all women away?' asked Pavlos.

'I sent them off. I need to talk to him. Come over here, Panos. Come and sit here next to me,' said Nikos. It was a tight squeeze. Why talk now? We couldn't hear each other anyway. I could go to the paper the next day and explain things to him a bit better. I would write him any article he wanted. I didn't care anymore; I just wanted to keep my job. Pavlos was looking at me with deep sympathy. He was really a great friend; he always understood people's pain and respected them for what they could offer.

'Come on, Panos, come over here. I haven't got the whole night,' shouted Nikos at me. I finally got up, manoeuvring between the chairs and the table.

Struggling to get through, I said: 'Tomorrow, you know, I am going there. I am going again, to the farmer. I have a good story.'

'Forget about tomorrow,' said Nikos. I sat next to him and started searching for something to say, this time not only to delay things but to stop them completely.

'Panos, tonight …'

Unexpectedly, the doctor showed up at our table. He came straight to me and said: 'Good night. I hope you feel better.'

'With doctors like you, I don't need to worry,' I said sarcastically. He seemed not to care or maybe he just didn't hear me. So I shouted louder: 'Will I be okay, doctor, or do I still need an operation and an envelope?'

He turned around, came closer to me, and said: 'You can always use shock therapy, a bit of defibrillation.'

'What is that?'

'We use it when the patient has not listened to our preventive recommendations and we have an emergency on our hands. It is an electric shock, just to wake you up, just to force you to come out of your little fairy tale world and remind you that things are not all right.'

'Don't worry, it is all shocking for me right now. I don't need you to shock me too.'

'We all need it. We Greeks need to be shocked before we take things seriously.'

'Who is this?' asked Nikos.

'He is a doctor,' answered Pavlos.

'I don't know him. I don't know him at all. We just met,' I explained.

'All right, Panos.'

I coughed, and the doctor went away. I shouted: 'Wait, wait.' But he had disappeared behind clouds of cigarette smoke.

'Don't tell me now that I need you, that you are sick.' said Nikos.

'You need me? You need me?' I asked excitedly.

'Yes, I need you to go to a casino tonight.'

'Casino? I am not going to a casino. What for?'

'I need you to write something and give it to me. I will fix it.'

'There is nothing to write about a casino. I don't know what to write.'

Nikos got up and said: 'If you guys are sitting here chatting, at least come and introduce me to the minister.'

'He is a junior minister now, but I am sure he will be up there soon. Just wait two minutes. Sit down. I will be back,' said Nikos. He got up, grabbed my arm, and started pulling me away. I tried to resist, but he seemed very determined.

'Where are we going? What is wrong with you?' I shouted.

He continued pulling me, this time with both his hands, and said: 'Come on, I need to talk to you somewhere quiet.'

With his hand still in mine he pulled me towards the bathroom, passing the probing waiter on the way. The waiter's eyes followed us all the way to the bathroom door.

'Listen, I don't really need you to write anything. Just pretend that you are taking notes. We need to have an article about a casino,' said Nikos as soon as we got in the bathroom.

'I don't understand. Are you kidding me? I am going to the farmer tomorrow. You hear? I have a good story. Don't worry, you will see. Just give me another day. What does the casino have to do with the recession?'

'The way things are, people's only hope is the casino. Where else do they have a chance to win anything, tax-free?'

'So, this is your solution for the recession?'

'Look, Panos, one of the casino shareholders is a good friend of mine. He has done me favours before. He is an important man.'

'Why don't you go?'

'I was going to. He is expecting me tonight. There will be full service, dinner, drinks, a limousine pick up – the whole show.'

'Why don't you go?'

'The man who treated us the whiskey is a junior minister. He has invited me to his table. It is a great opportunity. He needs me now for the elections. I can't turn this down.'

'Good, do you want me to come to the table too? Maybe I can help – do an interview, ask something.'

'No, Panos, this is an important man. He is going to be more important after the elections. You can't help like this.'

'Not even an interview, to publish in the paper?'

'You can't interview a simple farmer. How are you going to interview him? What are you going to ask him? You don't even have a question. No, Panos, the best way you can help is to stay away from us now.'

'But your casino guy is waiting for you.'

'No, he is not even there. As long as I send someone, anyone – I mean, anyone important, like you – you don't need to write anything, just take some notes. Try to look important.'

'I don't believe this.'

'Look, Panos, I am offering you an easy assignment. You can't possibly fuck this up. You just need to show up. What do you prefer to do? Be treated like a high-class reporter with champagne and dinner, be picked up by a chauffeur-driven limousine, or go to the farmer and smell his manure?'

'It is the farmer who is our last hope. I am going because he is planting new trees tomorrow.'

'Okay, go tomorrow. Who is stopping you? Will you be too tired? Is that your problem?'

'No, I am fine.'

'Panos, didn't you tell me this is like a war zone now? Didn't you tell me we need fervent and passionate reporters? Are you getting tired on me now?'

'I will go, but don't expect much, Nikos.'

'I am not expecting much. Just show up. On Monday, come to the office and we will talk about it.'

'Shall I go now? So I don't get there too late?'

'Now?'

'With my car.'

'No, they will come to pick me up – I mean, pick you up – with a limousine.'

'But I have a car.'

'Panos, it is best if they don't see you with that car.'

By the time we had got back to the table, Pavlos was already gone. There were peeled carrots, some cucumbers, olives, and assorted sliced cheese on the table. Nikos asked me to sit down. He put a carrot stick in his mouth. He was still standing. Then he called the waiter, who was still looking at us from afar. The waiter rushed to our table.

'Yes, sir?'

'Are these fresh, or they were in the fridge from this morning?' asked Nikos, pointing at the food.

'No, sir. They are fresh. I just peeled them with my own hands,' said the waiter. Then Nikos picked up the bottle of whiskey and poured a bit into my glass. With his other hand he took a carrot stick and forced it into my mouth.

'Eat something. I thought you were hungry,' he said.

'Bring the bottle with some fresh glasses to that table', said Nikos to the waiter, pointing his hand at the table of the junior minster. Then he bent towards me and pinched my cheek, saying: 'I am counting on you, Panos, okay? I am continuing on you. Behave yourself, and I will see you tomorrow.'

'He will be okay, sir,' shouted the waiter as Nikos left the table.

'Would you like more carrots with your whiskey?' asked the waiter. Before I had a chance to say anything he turned to leave, bumping into a new bar girl who was coming towards me. He then said something in her ear that made her turn around, and they both left.

Sitting at the table alone, I picked up my glass and took a sip from my whiskey to wash off any bacteria from the carrot. I wondered if Maria would make fun of me for accepting an assignment to go to the casino to write an article about the recession. It was probably good, I thought, that she wasn't with me.

I was beginning to get hungry. The food in front of me, prepared by the waiter, was not appealing. There was half a cauliflower in my car, I remembered. But I would probably eat at the casino. It is amazing how fast you get used to a new idea, especially if you are a bit hungry.

I had gone a bit deaf from the music. I could not hear very well, not even my favourite songs. Looking across the rising smoke from each table, I saw Nikos at the junior minister's table. He had his mobile phone against his ear in one hand, and his other hand was up in the air. A woman passed by, and for a moment I lost him. The smoke cleared a bit. He was not on the phone any more. This time he had both hands up in the air. I kept trying to look. He finally stood up and with his right hand pointed at me. His left hand moved up and down, like he was playing with a yo-yo. Was he trying to communicate with me? Yes, he was. As soon as our eyes met, he pointed at the main entrance. The yo-yo started going horizontal. He was telling me something. My ride, the limousine, must be here, I thought. I looked around to find the waiter. He was there within a minute.

'Yes, would you like a drink?'

'No, I must go. What do I owe?'

'The men paid for the drinks,' he said.

'The men? Which men?'

'The men from the bathroom.'

'Do I owe you anything or not? Just tell me that.'

'No, unless you want to pay a tip.' I took a few steps away from the table and put both my hands in my trousers pockets. Then quickly I took my hands out.

'No change, I have no change,' I said, showing the palm of my hands.

He gave me a fake smile and said: 'Never mind, next time.'

I waved good-bye to Nikos. He did not see me. He was busy talking to the junior minister. I put my hand in my pocket again to make sure my car key was still there. Then I walked out and saw my limousine parked right outside the entrance door. As I got close to the long car, the chauffeur got out and opened the back door for me. Suddenly a strong wind blew away his chauffeur hat. I rushed to the hat and held it with my foot. He was still holding the door whilst I put the hat on his head.

'Thank you, sir,' he said. As soon as I got in the car and he closed the door, I heard someone shouting. I looked out. It was the waiter again running towards the car. I rolled down the window. He seemed shocked to see me in the limousine. He took a long breath and then came closer, extending his hand towards me with a hundred-euro bill in it.

'This must have fallen from your pocket when you were trying to show me you have no money.'

I grabbed the note as fast as I could and said: 'Thank you, thank you, but maybe you should have kept it. I wouldn't have known.'

'No, I think you need it more than me.'

Chapter 11

THEY CAN INCREASE the VAT on all necessities to a level that makes purchase impossible. They can tax me to the point of obliteration. They can take back my now-useless credit card, repossess my broken car, or cut off my phone, my electricity, and even the water. They can cut my salary so I lose my house. They can make me pay for my kids' education and then tax me on top for their supposedly 'free education'. After that they can force them away from me in search of a job. They can tax me for building the national roads and then close them on me if I don't pay the tolls. With my boss, they can increase my national insurance pay so he can't afford me anymore, effectively making my work not worth the cost. They can shut the hospital door on me and close my roads. They can break up my family and leave me with nothing. But when it comes to my pride, my pride as a man, as a Greek, as a human being ...

My mind stopped. Sitting in the comfortable seat of the limousine without anyone to talk to, I had now nothing more to say to myself.

It wasn't till I actually entered the casino that I remembered my pride again. Yes, they couldn't take away my pride – or at least they couldn't until after the weekend. All their pride-taking offices were closed now! The banks were closed. The tax office was closed. Everyone I owed money to was closed. Over here, at the casino, I needed some luck, not pride. What was I going to do with my pride now, anyway? For whom would I use it? For my wife who left me? For my boss who could fire me at any moment and probably would soon? For my son who thought I couldn't do anything right and didn't know anything? I not only had no use for my pride but also couldn't think what I was supposed to be proud of. For the articles that I wrote that nobody read? For the five-star hotel I didn't manage to build? For the negotiations I had with the forestry or the archaeology authorities? For the future I had built for Costa, for Elpida? Even if I had any pride in anything, it would not buy me a piece of bread or allow me to bet on anything at the casino. No, I didn't need pride; I needed good luck. What I needed, and what they couldn't take away from me, was hope. That was why the casino was full of people. For many, that's all they had left. Nobody could take away hope … Either that, or the casino was busy just because it was Friday night.

A four-course meal was on offer to me at arrival, but I was too excited to eat. I could always eat later. The manager, who was expecting me, ordered a complimentary glass of whiskey and invited me to have a walk around to get a sense of the place before I interviewed him at his office. At the beginning, when I arrived, I felt rich and confident. But with so many euro notes flying around, I reconsidered my position. The notes were given away as if they had no value. It felt as if they were not just changing hands but rather being wasted. Each note that I saw being given away brought graphic images of its value. A twenty-euro note was a small basket of grocery shopping, a fifty-euro note a phone bill, a hundred-euro note an electricity bill, maybe. The two-hundred- and five hundred-euro bills – well, they had no image associated to them for me any longer. It had been so long.

Surely I could afford to risk twenty euros. I had to trust my luck. After all, they hadn't managed to take away hope. I approached a table. There was a dealer standing behind a table and several people sitting on stools on the other side betting on blackjack. It looked complicated; it surely involved thinking. I had no time to learn. I had to trust my luck. All the thinking I had done all these years had not helped me at all. I moved to another table: simple roulette. A ball moved around a disk with thirty-six numbers and a zero. It would be great if you would only lose when zero came. I made up my mind: I was in. I was going to play. I chose my number, twenty-nine, Maria's birthday. The dealer threw the ball. It rolled and rolled around the disk. A man came pushing me to the side, putting on his bets. A lady standing next to me threw a fifty-euro bill on the table and said: 'Fifty euros on twenty-nine and the neighbours.'

Who were the neighbours? They were surely not me and the man who pushed me. No matter what she meant, the dealer understood her and took her money. This made me even more certain of my choice. I had to make a move, now. I put my hand in my pocket and took the hundred-euro bill out. The dealer moved her hand across the table and said: 'Last bets.'

I extended my hand with the bill towards the dealer and said: 'Twenty euros on twenty-nine.'

'On the table, on the table,' said the dealer. The ball was losing speed and taking shorter circles with every turn, getting closer to the centre. It could fall in one of the numbers at any second. I extended my hand even further towards her and repeated. 'Twenty euros on twenty-nine.'

'Put your money on the table. I can't take it from your hand.'

I threw the money on the table. She looked at the ball and without taking my money shouted: 'No more bets.'

The ball made its last circle and fell in number twenty-nine. I would have been devastated if it had stayed there, but fortunately for me it moved out, made a few jolts, and finally landed in zero. Excitedly I shouted: 'No more bets, right?' Then I pushed the next throw.

'After pay-out,' she responded. After pay-out to whom? I wondered. Then I noticed some people had actually put some chips on zero. That couldn't be anybody's birthday. To make sure the bet was on, still staring at the ball, I tried with my fingers to move the note closer to the dealer. But the hundred-euro bill was not moving. It felt as if it was stuck. I took my eyes off the ball and looked down. There was another hand on it, pressing on the money, holding it in its place. I turned to see who was stopping the note.

'You didn't learn anything, Panos. Complete waste of time.'

I first tried to drag the money back and then had a harder look at the guy. 'Giorgos? Is that you? What are you doing here?'

'What am I doing here? What are you doing here? Looking for me? How are you?'

'I … I guess I am okay, but how would I know you are here?'

'I told you yesterday on the phone.'

'I called to interview you about the money you have lost.'

'And I told you I have lost it here.'

'You lost your money in the casino? I thought you were joking.'

'What are you doing here then? All that business training that your boss paid for is gone to waste.'

'That was marketing training, not business training.'

'Well, the marketing training must have paid off for you to have money to gamble. Obviously, you have sold a lot of advertisements for the paper.'

'No, I am the paper's journalist.'

By this time I had put the money back in my pocket. Giorgos had a lot of chips and kept putting them on the numbers. Then he asked: 'What was your number? Twenty-nine? Here, I will put two euros on it for you. If it comes we will share the win. Half and half, okay?'

'Do you do business training too?'

'Yes – business, marketing, management, all that stuff. Your paper only had a grant for marketing, so I did that. I think it was for six weeks, forty-eight hours.' The ball fell in number eleven. Giorgos lost all his money.

I pushed the bill deeper in my pocket and said: 'Forty-eight hours? Six weeks? No, you must have us mixed up with another place.'

'No, it was you; I am the one who filled all the forms for the grant. I know how much it was for.'

'But we only did one week.'

'Yes, but when did you get the leaflets for the course?' he asked, feeding the table with chips.

'I don't remember.'

'Do you remember what your number was?'

'Yes, twenty-nine.' He put another two chips on twenty-nine.

'Let's see if your luck turns. We split the win on twenty-nine. Yeah, we gave you the leaflets five weeks in advance to make up the costs to get the whole grant.'

'But the training was only for a week.'

'Look, are you in advertising?'

'No.'

'Were you then?'

'No.'

'Why didn't you say anything then? You did the course, you got the bonus for forty-eight hours, and now you are asking questions. Well, if we didn't put the hours, the whole forty-eight hours, there would have been no grants, and you wouldn't have got a bonus.'

'I see. How do you calculate the hours? Where did the forty-eight come from?'

'You divide the full grant amount by the maximum euros they pay per hour – easy. Of course, if there is more money for expenses, you charge that too. Everyone wins. I get a job. Nikos gets a certificate that his staff are trained, plus his expenses …'

'What expenses?'

'He lost staff hours.'

'We came in the evenings.'

'Then he should have charged double. But there was no more money.'

'I didn't get anything.'

'You learned something; it is good for your career.'

'Advertising? Why would I need that?'

'Why did you come then?'

'If I hadn't come to get the certificate I would have lost my job.'

'Who told you that?'

'Nikos.'

'That could be the case. He knows more about grants than I do. Look, this twenty-nine of yours hasn't come all night. Are you sure you want me to play this?'

'So you give estimates based on what is available, not based on how much each project costs or what needs to be done in the first place?'

'I thought you were a journalist. You don't even know the basic things about the economy. What do you write about? Women's fashion?'

'What do you do if a project costs more than the grant?'

'What project?'

'A project to actually make something, let's say in industry. Let's say you want to build a road. Don't you have to see how much it costs first, like the actual number of hours of labour, the material ...'

'Oh, you mean to calculate the costs the other way around?'

'No, I mean to calculate how you should. Let's say you want to build a road. How do you give an estimate?'

'Finally twenty-nine, twenty-nine! I had four euros on it this time. Half of the win is yours.'

'How do you give an estimate for a road?'

The dealer gave a couple of towers of chips to Giorgos.

'Wait, wait, get your money first. Everything is about money.' He split the chips in half and gave me a portion.

'How do you give an estimate for building a road?'

'Here, this is yours.'

'But I didn't play anything,'

'Keep it. Now tell me, what is your question? Oh, the road. Well, you don't have to complete a road to get the grant for it. You get a large deposit first. Start off, and then you get more in stages.'

'You don't have to complete the road? How is that possible?'

'It happens all the time. Sometimes the contractors, the officials, and the politicians all know that there is not enough money to complete a project, say a road, before they start it. I know it is not good for the paper to write these things, but there is no excuse for you not to know this.'

'What happens when there is much more money than really needed?'

'Oh, things will then go much more smoothly. There will be no need to do much paperwork.'

'What if it is obviously too much? You do a job that looks to be worth one million euros, but you have ten million. What do you do?'

'Nobody takes rest. If there is any possibility of some kind of an inspection, then you can do overkill.'

'Overkill? What's that?'

'You make things look bigger, more expensive; you do a lot that is not needed. There are lots of options. I know a city where there was some money to make a bicycle road. There was so much money that you could build a fortress. You know what the funny thing is, Panos?'

'What?'

'They did just that. They built a separation between the road and the bicycle path that is dangerous for everyone. You can't even break it with a bulldozer. It looks like it cost a lot, enough to justify the funds.'

'Boy, you have an answer for every situation.'

'Oh, there is more, a lot more for you to learn. Oops, almost.'

'What?'

'Almost my number.'

'What else goes into this science, Giorgos? Look, at least by the end of the day people get a bicycle path.'

'Oh no, they spent a lot of money on breaking it up after a couple of years.'

'Why?'

'I told you, it was too dangerous and not useful. People use the main road for bicycling, if any one does. It is more clear, with no bins and no parked cars.'

'I see.

'They should have found out what people needed in the first place, but there is no system for that. They do whatever there is a grant for, not what people really need – like, say, a better system of collecting the rubbish.'

'Well, that is nobody's fault. Are they supposed to have a referendum for everything they spend money on?'

'No, but there are surveys. There are scientific social and economic surveys which determine what is really needed and necessary in a city. That is the way it should really be done. There is no point spending a lot of money building something that people don't use. Damn, almost there! It came right out of thirty-five and fell in three. I think you are right. We should go to another table. This table sucks. What did you say?'

'Never mind. I don't want you to play for me anymore. I have my own money.'

'Fine. So, what was your fascination to write about me losing money?'

'For you, a business consultant, to lose money in the market – it tells a lot.'

'I lost my money here, in the casino. How many times should I tell you this?'

'I understand. It must be embarrassing for you, with your job and all, to admit to losing money in business. But how does it help to lie about it and say you have lost it in the casino? That is as bad, if not worse.'

'Here is your twenty-nine again. See, it came again. Sorry, you didn't want to play. You don't win.'

'Well done.'

'Look, there is nothing embarrassing about losing in the casino. But when it comes to investment, starting a new business, the way things are, you must be really stupid to get involved.'

'And here?'

'Here, I know it is purely luck. I know the odds are against me, but at least I know what the odds are. In business today, I can invest somewhere, and then they change the odds as they wish.'

'Change the odds?'

'Yes, change the odds – the new tax laws, the new regulations. They don't even have enough courtesy to wait for the ball to land and then change the rules. They come up with new rules, new odds, after you have made your bet and whilst the ball is still turning.'

'You mean you trust these cheats more than you trust your own system?'

'I don't believe it. This is the third time eleven has come, and I don't have anything on it. The cheats? Trust? Hah, Panos, what do you think would happen if a fire started at the bar in that corner?'

'I don't know. What?'

'What do you think the management would do first?'

'I don't know. What?'

'Do you think they would come and take my money off the table and tell me the game is off because of the fire?'

'I don't know.'

'Well, I will tell you exactly what will happen. First of all, the alarms will go off. Then the sprinklers will start working. They will open all the security doors and start informing people with the loudspeakers that there is a fire, asking everybody to leave. They will of course call the fire department, the police ...'

'Are you planning on starting a fire?'

'No. Tell me now, what is it that you think they will *not* do?'

'Go on.'

'The casino management does not start denying that there is a fire. They don't come and tell you the smoke is from the cigarettes or that you are imagining it. Once people start burning, they don't blame it on the last manager. They don't come and ask you to carry on playing so you lose more. They don't take your winnings, if you ever win, telling you they need the money for the fire damage or to buy an alarm system for the future. They don't stand on top of the burnt bodies arguing about whose fault it was and who had a better idea to prevent it. Damn, I am sick of eleven.'

'Change tables.'

'The odds are the same at all the tables.'

'It's the same with the management, right?'

'Right, the same structure. I feel safe in the casino, even when I am losing.'

'So when do you think it will change?'

'What? For eleven not to come again?'

'No.'

'The dealer? She will change shortly. They don't get stuck to a table. It is not safe for the system. If they stay too long they get used to their position, make acquaintances …'

'I don't mean that.'

'And you know what is their best and most important characteristic?'

'Who?'

'The dealers. Do you know why I trust them? Do you know why I trust the whole system?'

'I was asking something else.'

'But you know, I trust the system because I decided to come here based on the understanding of how the system works and how the odds work. I knew that, rain or shine, nobody can interfere with the agreement that I have with the casino.'

'Nobody? What do you mean?'

'The staff here, the people who run this place, are the most trustworthy people you can find.'

'Do you know them personally?'

'No, Panos, I don't know them personally. But I can trust them that they themselves will treat me fairly. If I am going to lose money, I will lose it fairly. They won't be nice to the guy next to me because he is their neighbour or has helped them somewhere before. The guy next to me and I are equals here. And you know what? They can't stay at the same table more than a set amount of time. They are changed constantly so they don't get acquainted and start doing favours for anyone.'

'Okay, they keep changing them. But that is not enough to trust them completely. We change our politicians too, and that doesn't say anything.'

'Look at them, Panos. Look at their clothes. What are they wearing?'

I looked at the dealer at our table from top to bottom and did not notice anything strange. She was wearing an ordinary red, clean, ironed uniform with a name tag on the upper left part of her jacket.

'Giorgos, what is so special about their uniform? It looks like an ordinary uniform.'

'Panos, look hard. Do you see any pockets?'

'Pockets? Yes, I do. Those are pockets, aren't they?' I said, pointing at the jacket pocket of the dealer. That made her stop for a second and look at her pocket.

'No, Panos, the pockets are cosmetic. They do not open. They can't take anything out, and more importantly, they can't put anything in them. If they could, every morning when they count the money there would be cash chips missing. Do you understand?'

'It is interesting, but I still don't understand what you are getting at.'

'Panos, we need to dress our representatives in the parliament like this, with no pockets at all. But of course, you are deaf to matters you can't write in the paper. Now let's get back to work. What was your question?'

'Look, as I said, we keep changing our politicians too. What else do you expect us to do?'

'We keep changing them, but this is working against us. We change them when their pockets are full and make room for a new group of politicians with empty pockets. After several years of them filling their pockets, right when they are saturated, we go back to the last group, whose pockets are by then empty since they have not been in power, and put them in power positions again.'

I took a harder look at the pretend pockets of the dealer. She looked uncomfortable. I finally took my eyes off her and turned to Giorgos to repeat my question, but before I opened my mouth he said: 'I have lost at least two chances talking to you. My numbers keep coming, but I am distracted. Tell me, what is it that you don't get?'

'I am asking you if you see things improving. Do you see any changes, anything? Do you see an end to this? Are we coming out of the recession? When, do you think? You are a business consultant. You should know something. When will they let us out of this cage? When will it change?'

'Them? Who are them?'

'Them, the ...'

'Panos, there is no more them and us. That was when we were in high school, in the Pink Floyd era. Today, there is us and us. We are fighting with ourselves.'

'Change is change. We need a change, now.'

'Panos, do you know anything that is changing?'

'Yes, we all change, all the time. Look at you, you are now betting on eleven.'

'No, don't mix gambling with business sense. This is purely luck. Do you see any changes? Are we taking any steps towards recovery? You are a journalist.'

'I, it is difficult ... I know that we must ...'

'Can you do me a favour?'

'What?'

'Panos, can you bring me that small coffee stool, the one near that table? I don't want to lose my seat.'

'Why? You don't even drink coffee.'

'Bring it. It brings me luck.'

I looked at the stool and reluctantly started walking towards it. As I got there I turned to Giorgos. He had one eye on the roulette table and one eye on me. He then nodded his head in confirmation that I was pointing at the right stool. As I was walking back towards Giorgos, I thought it incomprehensible that an educated person like him could be so superstitious as to believe that a stool could bring him good luck. As soon as I got to him he shouted: 'Eleven, eleven! I told you, it brings me good luck.'

My eyes went on the roulette disc searching for the ball. It was in fact on eleven, and this time Giorgos had a lot of chips on the number. His excitement had not faded yet when a waitress came and asked Giorgos if he wanted a coffee. He said no. In a desperate attempt to justify having brought the coffee table, I looked at the waitress and said: 'Yes.'

'Sorry, coffee is only for people who are playing,' she said with a cold smile.

Then she asked Giorgos: 'Can I take the stool then?'

'No, he needs it,' I said.

She ignored me and asked Giorgos again: 'Sir, can I take the stool?'

'Yes, take it. I don't need it,' replied Giorgos.

'What was all that about?' I asked in front of the waitress, who was still looking at me when she took the stool.

Giorgos looked at his watch, contemplated for a moment, and said: 'Panos, I can tell you that if you start walking right now, you will get to the Parthenon in approximately half an hour. That is, if you go at the same speed and do not get tired halfway.'

'Go to the Parthenon? Why do I want to go there now?'

'Do you know how I know that?'

'I am not going to the Parthenon.'

'Do you know how I worked out how long it will take you to get to the Parthenon? You moved, and I timed your movement. If you hadn't moved, I wouldn't have had anything to measure it with. This is what is happening with our recession. Yes, I can work with numbers and calculate things and make predictions based on some figures. But when nothing moves, I can't do anything. This economy is stagnant, completely dormant. All they do is increase taxes. Have you seen one door opening for business? One new factory? One new office? One step towards anywhere?'

'Well, thanks for forcing me make a fool out of myself in front of the waitress. This is not one of your training courses. I just asked a question. You didn't have to write a theatre script for it. I would have understood you.'

'Oh yes, I forgot. You are a journalist. You understand things easily.'

'Yes I do. And do you know why nothing is moving and it is so difficult to come out of the recession? Because people like you mix up their eights with their forty-eights.'

'And people like you forget that they are in the wrong training group.'

'At least I am not cheating the system.'

'Nobody is cheating the system. The system is cheating us.'

'How is the system cheating you? By paying you for forty-eight hours' work when you only do eight?'

'I don't get the whole forty-eight hours' pay. I have to pay the chain all along the way. Even you got something out of it.'

'How does the system cheat you?'

'Panos, I am a specialist management consultant. Let's go. Let's go from this table.'

'Why? What's wrong, you don't like interviews?'

'No, I am not concentrating. I forgot to put money on thirty-five, and it came. Once, only once, I forgot it, and it came. You are not letting me concentrate. Let's go and sit at the bar, and I will tell you how the system is cheating me. Change your money. Give it to me. I will change it for you.'

He then took my chips, added his own, and put them in front of the dealer. He was quiet and looked very intense whilst the dealer was counting the chips. The dealer gave him some new chips, other colours.

He gave me one of the chips and said: 'This is worth fifty euros. Cash it at the cashier before you leave.'

I put the chip in my pocket and replied: 'Thanks, but I still want to know how the system cheated you.'

As soon as we sat at the bar the hotel manager came to me and asked: 'Sir, will the gentleman be joining you for dinner? I will ask for seating for two at your table.'

Pretending that I was used to this kind of treatment, I asked Giorgos: 'Would you join me for dinner?'

Giorgos looked a bit confused at first and then said: 'Yes, that would be fine. I will have some Greek Merlot with dinner.'

'Yes, I will call you as soon as the table is ready,' said the manager.

Giorgos looked around and seemed very tense at the bar. He did not say a word until we got to the dinner table. He had a sip of his wine and then started.

'The system is cheating us by not letting us use our full potential. Instead of allowing us to focus on what we are good at, instead of allowing us to be creative and innovative, they keep us busy and content with petty theft.'

Then he started eating his food. I wasn't sure where he was going with this. To be honest, I didn't care anymore. The food looked good. My glass of wine was full. I was starving, and I had nothing to say anyway. We sat quietly and ate. The conversation did not start again until our last course was served. This was a far cry from the dried-up cauliflower on the back seat of my car.

I kept eating until I was completely full. Then I asked a simple question: 'So what do you think we need in order to come out of this recession?'

'Well, Panos, so how are you?'

'Are you trying to change the subject, or is this one of your embarrassing demonstrations to prove a point? You have already asked me how I am, and I answered.'

'Panos, you are a clever man. I don't know what you are doing writing for a newspaper.'

'So you think Greece will be on its way to recovery when I stop writing for the paper?'

'No, Panos. The first thing we need, the very first thing, is to think positive. It is good for business, it is good for the people, it is good for the nation, and it is good for our souls. Do you know what you answered me when I asked how you are?'

'No, I don't remember.'

'You said, I ... I ... I ... am ... okay. What the hell is that? You're a whole grown-up man with a job, the leader of a family with children, and you were even hesitant to say you are okay.'

'What do you want me to do?'

'Answer something positive. Say something that gives you hope. Try it. It is good for you. Let's do it. Panos, how are you?'

'Well, not bad.'

'"Not" and "bad" are both negative. Start your answer with something positive. Panos, how are you?'

'I ... I am a little better than disastrous.'

'Oh, you are useless, Panos.'

'Now it's my turn. Come on, say something positive. Tell me, Giorgos, how are you?'

'I ... I ...'

'Giorgos, tell me the truth. Tell me the first thing that comes to your mind.'

He took a bite of his chocolate Kormos, took his time to chew it, and then said: 'I ... I am being wasted.'

'Why?'

'What why? You asked me to say the first thing that came to my mind. You know, Panos, my specialty is human resource management training. That's what I have studied, and that's what I am really good at.'

'So no economics then?'

'Of course, economics is the base of everything. Anything you do in industry or in services has to make sense economically.'

'So why don't you do what you are good at? Why do you do marketing and other things?' 'There is no call for management training in Greece. The managers hold the budgets. They choose what training to do. Plus, I feel I am completely discriminated against in that field.'

'Discriminated against? Why?'

'I am too young for what I am supposed to teach. Who wants management training, anyway?'

'You mean there is no need for management training here?'

'No, over here we still follow the traditional management style. There is a trend that is completely against any new blood in management. The assumption is that the people who have been in an office longest know the most.'

'You may be right when it comes to the public sector, the government, and the state utilities, but how about the private sector?'

'What private sector? There is almost nothing left. They have been eaten up by the public sector.'

'Eaten up?'

'Yes, eaten up. You want examples? We have one of the most expensive electricity services in Europe. Do you know why?'

'Why?'

'They charge factories too much for their electricity so they can afford to pay the government-employed electricity company employees. Businesses fail, but the electricity company stays in business. The end result is that Greece does not produce anything.'

'Are you telling me that there is no private sector that works?'

'In the private sector, any of it that is left, we still work like tribal communities. We make decisions on instinct, we trust our experience more than science, and we make decisions based on how we feel rather than based on statistics and facts. When it comes to getting a new manager, everybody goes straight to their son or daughter, just because they think they can trust them. Sometimes in the private sector they have a kid managing tens of staff without him having any education or experience in the field. The worst thing is, some of these kids have not worked even for one day in their lives, and all of a sudden they inherit a sensitive position.'

'I happen to be proud to be Greek and belong to a family-oriented nation.'

'Business sense also believes in the family. A company must progress, must produce, and must profit. This is good for all the families who depend on that company. Don't forget, our whole nation is a family.'

'I thought you liked new blood, Giorgos!'

'I like the young blood when they get somewhere by fighting for it, by excelling, by learning, and by competing, not when they inherit the position.'

'So the public sector is right in giving management jobs to experienced staff?'

'No, in the public sector, we need just the opposite. The owners of the public sector are the public. They are not supposed to be prejudiced. They should look at where the technology is going – the new inventions, new methods, and new accounting systems. There is so much for me to do in the public sector because everyone needs to learn modern management systems,' he said with a sigh.

'Why don't you do it?'

'I told you, they select new managers from old staff. The old staff refuse training because they are close to their retirement age, and they think they should just be left to do what they are good at instead of learning new things. Old people don't want new things. You should have seen the fuss made when things were being computerized.'

'But they finally learned, right? They can't possibly carry on working in a computerized office if they don't know computers. That's what happened in my office.'

'Panos, we are talking about the public sector. Everything is possible.'

'How?'

'The senior staff were moved up to the management positions.'

'What? Instead of being sacked, they got promoted? They went up to manage people who were using technology they did not understand?'

'Yes. For one thing, they knew they couldn't be fired because the law does not allow it. They couldn't be forced to learn. The only thing possible was to send them to training.'

'And?'

'And they registered for training because there was a salary bonus involved.'

'So they did go to the training courses, right?'

'No, I said they registered for it.'

'That's all?'

'Yes. They registered to get the benefit, but hardly any senior staff participated in the training courses.'

'Why?'

'Because they were close to retirement.'

'How many months is close?'

'Five, six years, sometimes more. You know, Panos, it is simple mathematics. An economy in which people become retired at a ripe age when they are supposed to be most experienced and therefore most productive, an economy in which the retired people feed the young and not the other way around, an economy which the combined cost of education and training of an individual, combined with his retirement and health costs, far exceeds the benefits he or she brings to the society, is simply doomed to fail.'

'Are these the things Europeans want to change?'

'Partly yes, but we don't know how to negotiate. It is our own fault. We should negotiate with them to help us rebuild our industries, but our politicians negotiate with them just to borrow more money so they can stay in power. Money finishes again, but the factories would remain.'

'Why don't the Europeans know this?'

'Europeans don't know shit. You know, economics is not just numbers. It is also people.'

'Europeans don't know shit? I thought you were for change and progress.'

'Europeans aren't worried about us; they just want their money back. Their formulas don't work here for us. They only know half of the story, and they write us wrong recipes without understanding what the real sickness is.'

'What formulas? What recipes?'

'Everything they are trying to force us to do is not good for Greece.'

'Like what?'

'Like staff evaluation. That is what they do in their countries. It works there, and then they think it works here too. I know many public sector workers, like teachers, who don't like to be evaluated, but that doesn't mean it is wrong. Workers' evaluation or any kind of appraisal does not work for us here. Any evaluation must be followed up by a Performance Improvement Plan with specific goals for the worker to meet, or else they are penalized. In the end, if they don't follow the strict recommendations, they may lose their job. In Europe they evaluate themselves for progress to cut staff time or to waste less resources. We have whole departments who are against technological updates because it makes them useless. Why would they want to be evaluated? If we manage to do a proper evaluation here, it is only because we are forced to do it. And then at the end, what do we do with the results? Nothing. Will we change anything? No. So why spend so much money and have all these political arguments on whether to evaluate or not? It is a very costly process and involves a lot of unnecessary paperwork. If we are not going to use the detailed results anyway and all we need to find out is whether someone is worth the salary they make, we can just ask them. They will give us the answer.'

'Whoa, whoa, wait a minute. Do you think anyone is going to tell you they are not worth their salary? Are you that naïve, Giorgos?'

'No, we ask indirectly. We tell them we are going to evaluate them. If they have no problems with it, that means at least they think they are valuable at their office. But if they resist and go on strike, that means they know themselves they are not worth it.'

'This is dictatorship, a capitalist dictatorship. In this day and age you can't sort things out by spreading fear. It is good thing you are being wasted! If you had a say we would all be unemployed now.'

'We are almost all unemployed now anyway. I am telling you, everything has to make economic sense. If it doesn't it dies at some stage. You can't subsidize everything. You can't subsidize life. We have to go on.'

'By your thinking, can sacking people from their livelihood be considered an income?'

'No, my way is giving value to staff who actually produce, giving value to achievers. Why do you think we have so many successful Greek scientists, artists, and businessmen abroad? Why is it that when a Greek goes to New York and opens a hole in the wall and sells hamburgers he can become a successful diner chain owner in a few years, but when he opens a big restaurant here in Greece he is forced to shut down after a few months? He is the same Greek entrepreneur.'

'You tell me why.'

'Because over there, when he succeeds they interview him, put him on the TV, and praise him for his success. He writes a book about his hamburgers, and it becomes a best-seller. He writes a book on how to open chain restaurants and puts a picture of himself, drinking aged Metaxa, on the cover. Do you know what he would be doing if he were here?'

'I don't know, what? Making tsuzokakia, musaka, instead of burgers?'

'Yes, maybe a little bit of that. But most of his time would be spent on finding loopholes in the unfair tax system. He would be worried about not forgetting to put receipts on the tables in case the authorities came to check. He would be arguing with the tax office on whether they should tax him on the number of the tables or on how many cups of coffee he sells in a day. He would be trying to hide his staff so that he wouldn't have to pay the heavy national security payments. He would be spending half of his time following up court cases against him. And you know what he would do if he made any money? He would make sure nobody found out. He would have to pretend to be devastated financially. He would have to advertise that he was not a good businessman. Otherwise, they would look at him as a criminal.'

'Look, it is easy to criticize. Tell me your solution. What is your solution, Mr Business Consultant? What should we do, follow your example? Should we all come to the casino and play number thirty-five and make sure we never forget to put a bet on it?'

He went quiet. Maybe I had insulted him, but that was fine. I could only take so much criticism for one night. He took his eyes off me and looked towards the gambling tables. He did not seem to want to talk anymore. I looked at the table that he was staring at. Suddenly a big cheer erupted from that direction. Obviously, somebody's number had come.

'Is it thirty-five?' I asked expecting some kind of a reply. But I received nothing, so I tried again. 'Why don't you go to New York and do your management training? You can then put your picture on the book you will write. A successful Greek businessman in New York! It sounds good. That can be the title of your book.'

He seemed to be deep in thought, as if he couldn't hear me anymore. He took another moment and said: 'You know, this is a cultural crisis.'

'I thought you were a business consultant, not a sociologist. Everyone I know says it is an economic crisis.'

'You think a cultural crisis means people go the museums less? This is much deeper than just the economy; it has taken over our lives.'

'People are worried about how to pay their bills. They haven't lost their culture.'

'If it were only economics, it would be solved just with money. What if our debts were paid off tomorrow? Do you think we would all be fine? If TROIKA decided to write off the Greek debt tomorrow morning, what do you think would happen? Do you think we would come out of this immediately? Okay, we would pay a few bills first, but we would all go back to the life we had gotten used to. Everything would be the same, with no change.'

'And then we would wait for the next crisis?'

'Exactly, Panos, exactly. As soon as we get comfortable we will start heading towards the next crisis.'

'How is all this a cultural crisis? So you are saying the politicians play no role? It is all in our culture?'

'Panos, our politicians have not come from another planet. They are from us, from here. They could be our lawyers, our dentists, our engineers, our neighbours.'

'They are not from another planet, but as soon as they get to the top they start stealing our money.'

'That is only half the problem. The only part that you see, because you are a journalist, is what is sensational. The reality is much worse. The real tragedy is not about what the politicians and their agents do. The real tragedy is about what they don't do.'

'Their jobs?'

'Yes. What is the first thing that came to your mind when you found out the relatives of hundreds of dead pensioners had carried on taking their full pensions for months after their death?'

'You mean years.'

'Yes, for years. And that is even after they had applied for and received social security grants for the funerals.'

'Is this a great country or what?'

'What is the first thing that came to your mind when you heard that? Stop joking. This is serious.'

'What? You asked me what was the first thing that came to my mind, and I told you: This is really a great country. Everything is possible.'

'The problem is not only the money that was stolen from the public funds or that the public itself is cheating the system. To me the bigger problem is the thousands of public sector workers who are getting paid to do a job that they don't do. They get paid to check these things. They failed, and what is the result?'

'What did you expect?'

'If the cash is short by the end of the night in a supermarket, what happens?'

'The cashier will have to pay?'

'Exactly, even if he or she pays the money from his own pocket. What happens if the mistake is continued?'

'The cashier is kicked out? What are you trying to prove, Giorgos?'

'I am saying that it is not only the politicians and it is not only the public. It is the whole rotten system.'

'As they say, the fish rots from the head.'

'But a tree rots from the roots.'

'We may both be right.'

'And the sad thing is, if we are both right, the rot has now has a double chance to get into the middle.'

'But ...'

'But what, Panos? We are in the middle of it all, and instead of solving it we are arguing about from which end the rot started.'

'What else are we going to do? Listen to the Europeans? Ask them for a solution?'

'The Europeans only want to get their money back. They don't care about our future. They may even have good intentions, but how can an English man help me here? How can a German teach me how to live, a Dutch man force me to eat what they eat, a Belgian tell me to ride a bicycle? We are different. We have different ways of dealing with pain, with our problems. We have different ways for survival.'

'Giorgos, is this going to turn into another one of your lectures?'

'An English man takes one umbrella with him on a sunny day ...'

'Oh, we are telling jokes now!'

'On a rainy day he takes two umbrellas, just in case one does not work.'

'Tell me when I am supposed to laugh.'

'I am just trying to show you that we are a different people. We don't work with standard formulas.'

'Of course we are different. We are Greek. We take life as it comes. We are not scared. We have balls.'

'Panos, the last time I checked my notes I didn't notice anyone in the history of humanity trying to stop the rain with his balls. Testicles are built for a completely different reason. But like most other things in Greece, we use them for a wrong purpose, whatever suits us at the time.'

'Okay, forget the balls; I didn't know you were so sensitive in that area. It doesn't rain here like it rains in England. Why should we have an umbrella in the first place?'

'No, Panos, it is not the rain. It is just that. We Greeks are optimistic. We have a clean, loving heart.'

'And the English don't?'

'We think everything will turn out okay at the end. The Europeans are more conservative. Have you ever been to a casino in London? You hardly ever see an English person risking his money. Almost everybody is Greek, Iranian, Lebanese, or Chinese.'

'And?'

'We are a different people.'

'That's what I have been trying to tell you, Giorgos.'

'The formulas made by the Europeans to help us do not work. They don't know. They picture themselves in our position and try to think how they would come out of a recession. All along they forget that we are Greek; we don't function like them, in happiness or in crisis. They are writing us the recipes for the food they are expecting us to cook and eat. Even in cooking, water boils at different temperatures at different altitudes. Ingredients are different in different places. We are living under the economic rules of Europe, but they simply are not working.'

'Maybe because we keep breaking them! Economics is economics anywhere.'

'We keep breaking their rules, but even that we do for the wrong reasons. We break their rules, but not because they don't fit us or because we have a better way. We keep breaking their rules for short-term gains, to trick them, not to solve anything. The politicians cheat so they can pretend that they are in control so they keep their positions.'

'So, I ask again, what is your solution? To go to the gambling table, with our Iranian and Chinese friends, and bet on thirty-five?'

He went quiet momentarily, seeming to be in deep thought, finished his glass of wine, and then said: 'Imagine that. Imagine giving hope to people by giving them chances.'

'How much Greek Merlot have you drunk tonight?'

'Austerity measures, selling all you have in order not to pay taxes, saving up your money that you don't have, taxing people more, forcing them to spend less ...'

'That is the worst thing for any economy!'

'Don't tell me; tell them. Where was I? Oh, yes, forcing people to shrink up does not work for Greece. This economy is too sick now to revive. Even if we inject a bit of money in it, which we don't have, it still goes back to its old habits. We need shock therapy; we need a solution, a path out, which takes into account the Greek character. We need something that thrives on our Greekness, not something that kills any instinct we have in us.'

'Like what?'

'A lottery! Give the people something to hope for. Imagine if they did that? If they ...'

'Giorgos, why don't you get some rest now and call me tomorrow. We will have some coffee, my treat.'

'After years of making mistakes voting for wrong politicians to lead the people, I have lost a lot of confidence, not only in them but in myself too. Maybe I am not capable of selection; maybe it is time for me to try my luck. Surely I now trust my luck more than my judgment.'

'Come on, Giorgos, are you asking me to give up my democracy, our gift to the whole world, step on my pride, and wait for my luck? Instead of believing in democracy, I should believe in lottery?'

'Panos, lottery is not that strange to democracy. In ancient Athens ...'

'Don't talk to me about the ancients; they have caused me enough trouble.'

'The ancients? You have a problem with our ancients?'

'Well, not the ancients, the archaeologists.'

'The archaeology authorities? Oh shit, you got mixed up with them!'

'I don't really want to talk about it, not tonight.'

'Now, in that battle you will really need good luck. They are powerful and arrogant. They don't understand logic.'

'Who? Which battle?'

'Your battle with the public sector army of archaeologists.'

'Tell me about the lottery. That sounds more entertaining.'

'Come on you know about lottery in ancient Athenian democracy. Lottery played a big part in our democracy. A large portion of the officials who formed the government were chosen by lottery.'

'I know, but this is not ancient Athens. Our democracy, whatever you want to call it, is ...'

'You see, Panos, we have all the formulas from our ancients, but we don't pay attention to them. The only thing we do is –'

'Pay for private ancient Greek classes.'

'Yeah.'

'And pretend to be protecting their ruins.'

'Thousands of years ago, they figured out that the most democratic way to appoint government office holders was through lottery. In this way nobody could buy their way into the government, and everybody had a fair chance.'

'So, you think if today we select our prime minister through lottery we would have a better chance? And then twenty-nine keeps coming all day?'

'No, thirty-five. The point is that lottery has a place in democracy. It has a function, and it is the most fair system.'

'Man, why don't you write a book? Write it in ancient Greek. Force all ancient Greeks to read it, apart from whoever wins the lottery. Spare him the pain.'

'We don't have to use lottery for selecting who governs ...'

'But selecting whom one marries? This is fun. Go on. Do you want more wine?'

'Remember when I told you this economy needs shock therapy?'

'Yes. I met a doctor earlier who wanted to give me an electric shock to wake me up. Is he one of your students? Are you from a political party? What do you call yourselves, shockologists? If I get two shocks will I get one for free?'

Again, he seemed completely indifferent to my mucking. He was looking up towards the ceiling this time, completely oblivious. Just to bring him back to reality I asked: 'Are you making these up as we go on, or you have thought about it before?'

'We can give the economy dosages of juice.'

'Giorgos, are you with me? What juice?'

'Juice, blood, electricity – whatever you want to call it. But the areas are allotted by the lottery.'

'What areas?'

'Look, what is the mother of all the economy?'

'The National Bank of Greece? Oh no, not them. The Bank of Greece. They are the ones who hold the money.'

'Stop playing.'

'Yes, teacher, but Panayoti is throwing things at me from the end of the classroom.'

'I mean, what is the mother of all industries? What is it that, when it works, everyone is working? What is it that all industries are somehow related to?'

'I don't know. Building?'

'Panos, see? You do actually listen. You are smart when you apply yourself.'

'Thanks. I wasn't really listening, teacher.'

'So, the idea is that we give special economic privileges to geographical pockets of the country based on allotment, not selection. Our governments have proved that they lack sufficient intellect to instigate progress through any form of selection, through any form of democratic or nondemocratic process of decision-making. It is with the power of selection that we grow corrupt. That is probably the only thing we grow well now.'

He looked at me and I guess waited for a laugh. I was actually getting bored and did not give him that pleasure. But he continued: 'Selection is not democratic. It is not fair. It favours the rich, the powerful, and the influential.'

'What if we select the left?'

'Are you going to get them from another planet?'

'No, what do you mean?'

'If they are from this planet, they will become rich, powerful and influential after we elect them. Election is the worst way to spread hope. False hope is the last thing we need in our society today. With unfair laws and allocation of power, the privileged abuse their status, and the underprivileged finally give up hope completely.'

'This is exactly what is happening with our democracy.'

'I thought you weren't listening, Panos.'

'What does the building industry have anything to do with this? Where is the shock?'

'The shock is that the system gives special privileges for a limited time to a unique area chosen by lottery.'

'What kind of privileges?'

'First of all, a fast-track reduction of any bureaucracy involved in building a house or a shop in that area.'

'You mean discriminating against the other areas?'

'Yes.'

'Well done, Giorgos.'

'I mean leave the areas the way they are.'

'We just let people build anything they want, anywhere?'

'No, listen. We need a committee which has more power than the powerful bureaucrats who are for decades sealed to their positions and run the public sector powerhouses. Everything for that allotted area will be fast-tracked, even the courts. There will be no more waiting decades for courts when you have a dispute with the authorities.'

'So you mean the archaeological authorities can't stop you?'

'Panos, if you are to be a good journalist you can't concentrate on your own problems only. Yes, the archaeologists will not be exempt from this. But there are also the planning department, the forestry department, utility companies, and others who take forever to sort out the paperwork for building. The area that wins in the lottery, I don't care how small or big it is, would be treated differently.'

'You can't force them to work faster just because some people win the lottery. They have other work, other areas to look at.'

'Panos, not even a fourth of the building applications we had before are being made now. The building permit departments have not laid off any staff, but it still takes months for your application to be processed. It still takes too long to get the utilities. What are all these public sector staff doing?'

'So Giorgos, you think if you cut the paperwork in one area everybody will rush to build?'

'Imagine what happens if they apply substantial tax cuts for building in that one area for a limited time.'

'But people have no money.'

'Money exists.'

'Money exists? Are you serious?'

'Yes, it exists. It is either hidden, has been sent abroad, or is in different forms that we can't see. When a Greek sees an opportunity that he may lose if he doesn't move, he will find the money.'

'How?'

'You can borrow. Even the banks will give you money when they see you have a chance to grow. Some people have relatives in other areas who have money. Some people have already sent their money abroad, or they have a cousin abroad who can send them money.

Some can sell part of their property, which will be more attractive for investors in these conditions, and put the money in the other part.'

'If you don't have any money or a second plot or an uncle in Australia to send you money, what then?'

'Then you sell your property at its new, increased price and move somewhere else. Whatever happens, there is movement in the economy. It will change everything: construction material, engineers, transport, furniture, appliances, design. It gives life to whole communities, even those who have not won.'

'But this is not fair. We are too civilized to favour one part of the population. We have come all this way to bring equality. Why reverse?'

'The fairest thing is to give hope to people. Hopeful people are not stagnant; they move and bring hope to whole communities. Panos, a Greek should feel privileged. He should feel special. He should feel like he is chosen by at least one of his twelve gods. If he is one of the members of the crowd, if he is doing what the law says, he does not feel privileged. He feels like a goat, and he won't do anything.'

'Wait a minute, Giorgos. I thought you had been joking all this time. Are you seriously thinking this is the solution? It won't work.'

'Why?'

'What if you are in an area which is already built up?'

'I don't know. I hadn't thought about that.'

'You see.'

'Well, I guess the same rules can apply to renovation, upgrading: no permit fees, no taxes, all fast track, additional building rights, other privileges.'

'You can't help one area and neglect the rest. Everything elsewhere is going to die. No one will move and just wait for their time. It will kill the economy.'

'What? Do you see anything alive now? One area at a time can revive the economy.'

'How about the areas outside the villages? Don't they deserve hope?'

'Every city has areas immediately outside its borders that could be used for development. We can put these areas in the lottery, and whenever they come up they would be given limited time to take advantage of the favourable conditions.'

'What if we end up with half-built houses that people can't finish because their time comes up or they run out of money?'

'I don't know. We will think of something.'

'Is this what you mean about the Greek character? Just that? We will think of something?'

'Yes, we are not scared of risk as long as we know there is no organized force against our progress. We are not moving now because different authorities and the tax system have blocked our movement. They have taken away hope.'

'Come on, Giorgos, we are not going to save the economy by just giving unfair building rights.'

'Who said it would only be for building? This can apply for any industry, right across the board. Everything can be determined by lottery, as long as they don't make decisions for us.'

A short man with a moustache approached our table. He went straight to Giorgos and said: 'How are you? Here again? Trying your chances?'

Giorgos answered: 'That's all I've got left.'

'Yes, Giorgos, I know. But do you still feel wasted?' said the man.

'Wasted? When did I tell you I feel wasted?' asked Giorgos.

'Every time I have met you in the last two years, especially when I am doing your accounts. Why didn't you feel wasted before the recession? You were doing the same job. Is it all about money, Giorgos?'

'Well, you are my accountant. You tell me, what is it all about? Sorry, I didn't introduce you. This is my friend from the newspaper, Panos. Don't ask him how he is. He will answer you, "a bit better than disastrous."'

'Don't tell me you feel wasted too,' said the accountant to me.

'Actually I do. How about you?'

Without any hesitation the accountant answered: 'Very much so, maybe even more wasted than all of you. I feel I am being used for completely the wrong reasons.'

I was so exhausted from the pointless discussions that I did not even bother asking anything more. Then the accountant said: 'You are a journalist. You probably want to know why. I will tell you. When I wanted to become an accountant, I thought part of my job would be for growth for development through aspirations, dreams, and intelligent investment. I thought I would help people in investment by doing financial surveys, profitability assessment, productivity forecasts ...'

Giorgos moved both his hands up and said: 'We surrender! Fine, fine, whatever you say.'

'And now, instead of all that, what are you doing?' I asked.

'Don't you know? Don't you have an accountant?'

'No, I don't need one. I just asked you a question.'

If you had an accountant, you would know what I mean. All we do is fight the tax laws and the system. Whenever there is a new law, and there are a lot of them these days, I spend my entire time trying to find the loopholes and help my clients pay less taxes until the next set of laws.'

'At least you have a job. The government is keeping you busy with all these new laws,' said Giorgos.

'Yes, but I don't really do anything. I go home and ask myself what have I made today. The answer is nothing.'

Giorgos looked straight at the accountant and said: 'If you don't do anything, maybe you shouldn't charge me so much.'

Then all three of us burst into laughter.

'I've got to go. I want to play a bit,' said the accountant.

'What do you play?' I asked.

'Poker, I only play poker. It has the least to do with numbers,' answered the accountant. I had to leave too. After so much food I felt very relaxed. I was in no mood to interview the casino manager. Giorgos went back to his number thirty-five, and once again I left without having achieved anything. Nothing was going to change in my life. I had done nothing. On the way back to my car, whilst I was being driven in the limousine, I put my hand in my pocket to make sure I still had the hundred-euro note. Before getting to the bill my fingers touched the casino chip. I had completely forgotten about that.

'Stop, stop, I need to go back. I still have a chip,' I shouted at the driver.

He gently stopped by the side of the road, turned to me, opened the small window behind him, and said: 'Don't worry, sir. You can use it next time you go to the casino.'

'Well, I can't use it. I don't know when I am going back. I don't know what I will get for it next time I go there.'

'Don't worry, sir, you can keep it as long as you want. Whenever you go back it will have the same value as it has today. You won't lose anything. Nothing will change.'

'Well, I don't know.'

'Is it a lot, sir?'

'I ... I don't know. I think it is fifty euros.'

'Only fifty euros? That's what people leave as a tip for the limousine. Are you not a regular client? Isn't that why you have the complimentary limousine service?'

'Well, not that regular. Kind of.' He restarted the car and continued driving.

I asked: 'Are you not going to go back to the casino?'

He took his time answering me and finally said: 'I tell you what: I will split the money with you, half and half. Give me the chip, and I will give you twenty euros.'

'Half would be twenty-five,' I said.

'So you are okay with twenty-five?'

'No, I meant your calculation was wrong. Give me thirty.'

He did not answer me and kept driving. The sun was slowly rising, and the new day starting. Before I knew it we were in front of the Bouzuokia. There were hardly any cars parked outside.

'Where is your car?' asked the driver.

'Oh, the entrance door of the Bouzuokia is fine. I will get off there.'

He stopped the car right in front of the door. I could not find the handle to open the door and remembered that it was his job to come and open the door. I waited a bit, but there was no movement from his part.

He turned around and said: 'Okay, give me the chip. Here is thirty euros. The door knob is at that corner. Can you handle it?'

'Oh yes, I can do it,' I said as I gave him the chip and took the money.

'Thanks for the tip. I appreciate it. Now, don't be going back there losing money again. Casinos are not for people like you.'

I got out of the car and waited for him to leave. Then I started walking towards my car. In the car I felt safe again. I was in my own familiar environment. It was a satisfying feeling to be there – that is, until I turned the key and nothing happened except some starter noise, which sounded like the most disturbing sound I had heard. I kept trying with momentary lapses. Nothing. I tried again. The new noise was someone knocking on my window. It was the waiter again.

I rolled down the window, and he said: 'Are you okay? What's happening? Where is your limousine?'

I didn't really know what to say so I replied: 'I lost it at the casino.'

'I see. Did you lose your hundred euros too?'

'No, I still … yes, I did.'

'Do you want me to help you? Shall I push?'

'Yes, please, if you don't mind.'

He started pushing the car. The car started rolling and gained speed. I tried again, and finally it started. As soon as he heard the car start he begin walking back. I stopped the car in the middle of the street, got out, and shouted: 'Thank you.'

'It was nothing.'

'Wait, I have a bit of money left. I didn't pay you your tip.'

He stopped. I walked towards him, handing him one of the three ten-euro notes I had got from the driver. He took the money and looked at it as if to examine whether it was genuine. He smiled, handed the ten-euro note back to me, and said: 'You had your chance to tip me when I was doing my job in the Bouzoukia. Obviously you didn't want to. Here in the middle of the street I am not your waiter, and you can't pay me for something I wanted to do myself.'

The sun was by now slightly visible. It was the beginning of a new day. Not wanting to waste any gas with the car running, I quickly went back to the car and drove off.

Chapter 12

I MUST HAVE jumped half a meter up in the air when the mobile phone next to my ear rang and woke me up. Where was I? The surroundings looked familiar, but it wasn't my bed. I had fallen asleep on the sofa again. The phone kept ringing. Who could it be this early in the morning? How early was it? Not many people had my new mobile number anyway. I cleared my throat and answered.

'Yes, who is it?'

'I have good news for you,' said a male voice on the line.

'What?'

'I found her.'

'You found her?'

'Yes, I found Maria.'

'Maria? Which Maria?'

'Maria your wife. I hope that's whom you were looking for.'

'Are you the agent again? Stop mucking about. What is it? I told you, I will interview you when I have time.'

'No, really, I thought you would be happy. I found her.'

'I had never lost her. It was just a mistake.'

'Okay, well, she called me.'

'She called you? For what?'

'She wants to sell the house.'

'Which house?'

'The house you live in. Hasn't she told you?'

'Why did she tell you?'

'I am the estate agent, remember?'

'I mean, what am I supposed to do about it?'

'She said you live in the house and you can show it to me.'

'Now?'

'No, she just called to get some ideas, but she told me I can call you if I want to see the house.'

'How did you get my number?'

'You called me on this number, remember?'

'How did you know it was me?'

'You gave me your name, remember? Listen, you don't have to give me free advertising so I sell your house. I am a good agent. Forget the interview; it's not necessary. The problem is, no one is buying now.'

'If no one is buying, why are you calling me?'

'She said you were desperate and you would sell at any price, just to get out.'

'Any price?'

'There are no guarantees. Nobody is buying. If you are home, I can come now.'

'No, not now.'

'Why? You have a guest?'

'No, no, I want to clean up a bit.'

'Look, I am an agent.'

'I know. You told me that.'

'I mean, I am not the buyer. I am just having a look to advise you. I am used to mess. If you have a guest, well, you should see what kind of situations I have walked into. I will just do my job. I keep my mouth shut. I don't care who is there now.'

'I am alone.'

'I take it she is not there. On holiday?'

'No, no, just call me another time. I am not sure I want to sell.

'Why are we going around in circles? I tell you what, call other agents to see what they put you through. The first thing they want is for you to sign an exclusivity deal. If you sign that, you are done. You can never sell the house properly.'

'It is not that.'

'Let's meet first. Let's do the interview first. We can meet at your house.'

'Okay, okay. I will call you in a couple of days.'

'It's your house! Whatever. I can't promise I can sell it anyway. The market is really bad. I will do my best. You'll have to really go down on the price. Otherwise there is no chance. I don't care. You can go to other agents too, if you want. They won't do the same service. I know you now. I know your wife. I will do my best.'

'I will call you.'

'Wait, I don't know if I told you, but we also build houses. When I sell this one for you, if the price is right, I can build a house for you myself. Tell me what you want and you will have it, with key in your hand, all completed.'

'We will talk about it later.'

'Okay, fine. I just wanted you to know, if this house is too small for you then ...'

'It is actually too big for us now. We can't afford it.'

'I have a small apartment in a really good area, maybe.'

'Sorry, got to go. Talk to you later. I will call you next week. I'm really busy now.'

With that I hung up. Maria was trying to sell our house, the house in which Elpida was born. Now, lawyers and estate agents had come between us. What next? Not even ten seconds had passed before the phone rang again. It was Maria's lawyer this time.

'You wanted to see Elpida in my office, so I arranged it. You wanted me to work on a Saturday, so I arranged it. No more excuses. Maria really wants to get this over with.'

'Get this over with? You make it sound like a sickness.'

'I don't want to get personal, but you must act now. Elpida will be here at twelve. Can you make it?'

'Yes, what time is it now?'

'You have a whole hour.'

Another day had started, a cold but sunny day in my life. I had just woken up and already had two bad phone calls, both related to Maria. I wasn't going to let her sell the house. Who did she think she was? This was a house we bought for our children. It was not just hers. I wondered if she could force me to sell it. I must ask her lawyer, I thought. But if I resisted, it would get worse. She would push me even more. She was like that. She waited till I had no power left. I shouldn't show her any weakness. Nobody was buying now, anyway. I must play it cool. I should make her think I wanted to sell too. That would shock her. Let the agent come to see the condition of the house. I would give him a high price and see what happened. He was an agent. He would see the floor and notice how rotten the window frames are. He couldn't sell it. Yes, this was a good plan. I picked up the phone and called the agent.

'Hi, it is me, Panos. When do you want to come?'

'Hi, did you talk to your wife?'

'No.'

'What changed? A minute ago you said you are not sure. You journalists are just like politicians, changing your mind all the time.'

'Look. You are an agent. Come and sell my house. You do your job and let me do my job.'

'Okay, I will come now.'

'No, I am leaving now. I have to go somewhere.'

'Okay, I will come tonight.'

'No, not at night. You won't see anything.'

'Don't you have lights? Is the house abandoned? Do you have someone in there?'

'No, come before sunset. I need to go somewhere tonight. Got to go, bye.'

How dared he ask if I had someone here? It was none of his business. These agents made life hell for everyone. They pushed and pushed and pushed. I would show him who he was dealing with this time. I would make it really difficult for him. Was the house abandoned, he asked me. No, it was not. I was still here and would hold on. The only one who had abandoned the house was the mother of the children.

I had to make a good impression with Maria's lawyer, so I went to the bedroom and reached for some clean and formal clothes. Lawyers like that. They respect you when you dress like them. Then I went to the bathroom, opened the shutters to get some light in, and looked at my face in the mirror. I was a mess. I couldn't get away with that look. So I jumped in the shower and waited for the warm water to flow. After realizing that there was no hot water, I humbly went back to the sink and washed my face in cold water.

My car was on its best behaviour that morning. It started, but as I was driving to Maria's lawyer in my three-piece suit, I wondered what it was about Maria that made her always get whatever she wanted, even in fighting, even in confrontation, not just when she was nagging. She was organized and ruthless, not losing a moment. It was like a storm. She accomplished one thing after another, as if someone were chasing her. The things she had done to me in the last two days I couldn't organize in a whole month. She thought this would be the end? We would sell the house, I would take my toothbrush, she would take hers, and that would be it? She thought I would let her do this, smoothly, as if nothing had changed? I wouldn't. I should stop her plans. Anything she wanted to do, I should resist. She wanted me to sell? I would make it impossible. She wanted me to see her lawyer? I wouldn't go, except this time. Elpida was there now. She was waiting for me. Even that she planned. I know I asked to see Elpida myself and it had backfired now, but she knew. She was even abusing our daughter to get what she wants. Once again I gave her the pleasure of shooting myself in the foot. There was no point thinking about it anymore.

Lawyers always took their time opening the door or answering a phone call. This way they pretended to be busy. This gave them more value, so they could charge more. Standing outside the lawyer's office, I pulled my jacket down with both hands to get the wrinkles out. I knocked on the door once and reminded myself that I should be cool and completely reserved. I should not look bothered. I should be alert. I should …

The door opened, much sooner than I expected. First impressions in confrontations are so vital; I should look serious and determined. I looked straight ahead, trying to see right into his eyes when he opened the door. As the door moved, I saw nobody behind it. But someone, something, must have opened the door. My eyes started moving down vertically, until, until … It was Elpida! My daughter had opened the door.

'Dad, look at my slippers.' I quickly hugged her and, completely out of control, burst into tears.

'Dad, Dad, you are squeezing me. Look, look at my slippers.'

I let her loose; she stepped back and pointed at her slippers. They were shaped like two giant fake fluffy feet sticking out of a pair of plastic slippers. Each toy slipper was bigger than her whole head.

'Put something on, Elpida. Your toes are out. You will get cold.'

'My toes are warm, Dad. They are wrapped in a small fluffy duvet. You can't see them. These are just pretend feet.'

'Why are you wearing slippers? Where are your shoes?' I asked as I walked into the office.

'These aren't mine; my shoes are upstairs with Mum.'

'Mum? Is she upstairs?'

'She is at Uncle Ioannies's house. This is where his office is. He has another office near the court. He is a lawyer.'

'I know.'

'Mum said I can come down and see you, but when Uncle Ioannies comes down I have to go up. She said I shouldn't listen to anything you and Uncle Ioannies say. Do you want me to call him? I know how. Do you want to learn? I will show you. It is on his phone on that desk. If I dial nine, it rings in his kitchen upstairs – only nine, once.'

'Did you sleep here last night?'

'No, we slept at grand-mum's.'

'Since when did Uncle Ioannies become your uncle?'

'I don't know, Mum told me yesterday. She is good friends with Stella.'

'Who is Stella?'

'She is Uncle Ioannies's wife. She is upstairs. I can call her too. Do you want me to?'

'No, come and sit down. Tell me what you did yesterday. How was your school?'

'Why?'

'Why? I am your father; I want to know how your day was. What is wrong with your dad asking you how you are?'

'I thought I did something bad and that's why you asked.'

'I always ask you how you are, okay? Sometimes I am too tired and I forget, but no, you haven't done anything bad.'

'Mum said everything will be okay and you both love me.'

'What made you think we don't?'

'Nothing. I don't know why Mum said that.'

'Hasn't Mum ever told you she loves you?'

'She has. She tells me every day, but sometimes she forgets when she is very tired.'

'So, why are you so surprised?'

'She has never said, "we both love you very much". Come on, come and see me call Uncle Ioannies. Come!'

I followed her to the lawyer's desk and silently waited for her to call him. She picked up the phone, dialled the number, and said: 'Hello, Mr Lawyer, please come. Your appointment is here.'

She waited for a few seconds before gently putting the phone down and then turning to look at me, waiting for my gratitude. Instead of saying anything I began applauding.

Don't be silly, Dad. In the office you don't clap your hands. You say, "I preciet that."'

'What?'

'I don't know, pereciet. Uncle Ioannies taught me. He said, "I pere—ciate that..." Let me call him again.'

'No, never mind, he is coming down. We will ask him when he comes.'

'He might be a long time. I will forget.'

As soon as she finished her sentence, Uncle Ioannies, the lawyer, walked into the office. He looked scruffy, as if he had just woken up. He was also in his slippers, although his were much smaller. As he came towards me to introduce himself, Elpida interrupted him and said, 'Uncle, uncle, how do you say that thing? My dad doesn't know. How do you say it after your secretary does something nice? Perceit? Aprecit?'

'"Appreciate." I appreciate that, Elpida.'

'Yes, yes, "I appreciate that." You didn't say that when I called you to say dad is here. You want to go up and I will call you again?'

'No, Elpida, you have to go. If you learn all these words, I will hire you to work for me. But now, I think you'd better go upstairs. Go and practice.' Then he turned and said to me:

'My wife is upstairs.'

'I know, so is my wife.'

'Right. So you know she is here, but for obvious reasons it is best if we meet privately, at least the first time.'

'Yes, I appreciate that.'

Then he turned to Elpida and said: 'See, your dad knows that word. You just said it wrong. That's why he didn't understand you the first time.'

'Not my fault, Uncle Ioannies! We didn't practice. You even forgot it last time. Can I stay? I won't listen. Can I? Can I, please?'

'No, Elpida, your mum wants you upstairs with her,' said the lawyer.

'I will be good, I promise. I will go to the other office. There is a TV there. I will stay there and watch TV,' said Elpida, pointing at a door.

'If that is okay with your dad, fine. Are you okay with that?' the lawyer asked me.

'Fine, I have no problems.'

Elpida screamed for joy and turned to me and said: 'I appreciate that, Dad.'

Then she ran into the other room. But after only a few seconds she came back and said: 'Uncle Ioannies, can we play that game you taught me last time? I want to play it in front of my dad. I want him to see.'

'Which game?'

'The job game.'

'Okay, but just for a minute. Who works in a factory?'

'A factory worker.'

'Who works in a hospital?'

'A doctor,' said Elpida, looking at me for approval.

'Who works in a court?'

'Lawyers and jaajes.'

'Judges. Who works in schools?'

'Teachers.'

I smiled at her and said: 'Well done, Elpida. Now, can you tell me, what are all of these places made for?'

'What? Dad, that is not how the game is played. You are supposed to ask who works there.'

'No, I know. This is another game. What do all these places do? What do they make? Why were they made?'

'Dad, that is easy. They were made so people can work there.'

'Okay, okay, Elpida, that is enough. We will play later. Now go back in the other office.'

It was now only me and the lawyer in the office. I thought Elpida had been a very good ice breaker. Now, somebody had to start the real conversation. The lawyer was taking his time, and then he finally said: 'So, how come you are dressed up so formally?'

'I … I am on my way to interview a politician. You know how politicians are.'

'Politician? I thought you said you were going to interview a farmer today.'

'Oh yes, I told you that. That changed. I have another set of clothes in the car for the farmer. How come you are not dressed at all? This is your office, right?'

'Well, it is Saturday. I am doing this only for you. This is really my study. That's why there are so many books around. My main office is near the main courthouse.'

'I know.'

'From Elpida? In two minutes she has told you everything. She is really something else.'

Suddenly, the door to the other office opened. Elpida's head popped in and she said: 'Uncle, I forgot to tell Dad that you have secretaries and that they are all in your other office. In this office you only have a cleaning lady.'

'Elpida, you are not supposed to listen to us. Go watch the TV,' said the lawyer.

'I was watching the TV, but I just remembered I had forgotten to tell Dad something.'

'Okay, you told him. Now go back inside.'

'But uncle, I forgot something else.'

'What else?'

'That your cleaning lady has gone back. I don't know where, but you were telling mum that you didn't pay the cleaning lady much.'

'Okay, Elpida. If you don't go now and watch TV, I will ask you to go upstairs.'

And with that Elpida went inside the other office and shut the door. Standing with the lawyer, still in the middle of his office, I realized that we had made no progress in commencing this difficult encounter. We were both taking our time.

'Here, please sit down,' said the lawyer. I sat down. 'So how are you?' he asked.

'I am … I am a little better than disastrous.'

'I am sorry, but you don't look well, not even better than disastrous.'

'I know. I didn't sleep much last night.'

'Yes, I understand. It must be very difficult for you now.'

'No, it is not because of Maria. I was out last night. I was working.'

'Look, Maria wants you to move out of the house. It is not right for her to be out of her house with a child and you to have the house to yourself and not even use it.'

'Who said I am not using it?'

'Did you sleep there last night?'

'She is the one who chose not to stay in her house.'

'We are not here to see who started it and whose fault it is.'

'Yes, but you can't blame me for Elpida ending up in the street. If she were a good mother, her child would be in her own house now.'

'Good mother? Who are you to judge?'

'I am the father. I am close to her. Elpida is in all my dreams.'

– 251 –

'Look, whilst you are lost up in the clouds next to your hill, daydreaming about your five-star hotel, your wife is down on earth praying to get my office cleaning job to feed her child.'

'She is looking for a cleaning job?'

'Now, you tell me, who is the better parent? Can't you see how much your dream is costing your family?'

'She is Greek. She must understand.'

'What does that have anything to do with it?'

'She is not from another country; she should know how things work in Greece. I am waiting for the courts.'

'You have used up your dowry, sold everything you had and wasted the money, borrowed money on your land, borrowed money on your house, and then remortgaged it. You have left your family with nothing. Now you are telling me you are waiting for a court? What is this court going to give you, if it ever happens?'

'Everything.'

'Everything?'

'Yes, everything, even my wife. It will give me my dream, get back my respect, give back my dignity, my future. It will give me back all the value I have lost all these years, as a man and as a human being.'

'Panos, I understand you are under pressure, but more daydreaming does not help your situation.'

'I am not dreaming. This can all be real.'

'Maybe it is only real in your mind. Panos, you have risked everything for it, all your life. Right now you don't want to accept that you have lost everything. You are at a denial stage.'

'I am so angry!' I shouted.

'Okay, you have passed the denial stage, and now you are at the anger stage. So what? The important thing is that you can't go on any longer. You can't carry on dreaming any longer. You can't go on pulling and forcing other people to believe and follow your dream. If you are mixed up with the archaeology department, your dream is already dead. Whenever it happens, in five years or in two years, you are not going to get a thing from the court.'

'You are a lawyer, you get paid to defend people, and you don't believe in courts? How do you know from now how they will judge? They are independent. They are not a part of the system.'

'Don't lecture me on courts. I know, this is my job. When the other side is the archaeology authorities, I don't believe in courts.'

'So what is the point of the court? There could be a mistake made by the archaeological authorities. Everybody makes mistakes. Isn't it the court's job to review the matter?'

'You have a choice; you don't have to go to court.'

'It is not just a choice; it is a chance, a chance to get my life back.'

'How many archaeological committees have reviewed your case?'

'Four. There were two local ones and two in central Athens.'

'What were the decisions?'

'All against me, what else?'

'With what margin?'

'All four times.'

'I mean were all the decisions unanimous?'

'Unanimous, you mean all the committee? Yes.'

'How many of them'?

'All four.'

'And you are hoping that the court goes against unanimous decisions by a public sector authority, by people who are supposed to be specialists in their fields?'

'You are a lawyer. You know how they work. The decisions are always unanimous. It doesn't mean anything. They just back each other up. Why should they stand against their own colleagues? If one, if only one person doesn't want it to happen, he or she can persuade all of them to stop everything. If one of them doesn't want something, the others all agree. They are strong when they are together, like a pack of dogs. They always vote unanimously.'

'Panos, when it comes to the archaeological authorities, the courts are just like a pacifying medicine. They give you time to digest the tragedy and don't sit waiting for justice. They all vote together so that you will have no chance. The question is, why did you follow this up for years? Who told you?'

'They did. Once they stopped me building the hotel, they told me if I moved the building spot to the other side of the hill, they would agree, as long as I wasn't too close to the tower.'

'Is there a tower there?'

'No, they say there used to be one.'

'Is the land listed as an archaeological site?'

'No.'

'I am really here to find out what you have done with all your wife's money. I don't want to get involved with your problems with the archaeological authorities. What happened to your wife's dowry?'

'We bought an additional piece of land to join the hill to make it possible to build there. Back then you could do that.'

'We?'

'Yes, we. She was with me then. She believed in our dream too.'

'What about the first loan?'

'I had to spend a lot of money to get a winter sea line clarification from the relevant ministries. It took me about two years and thousands of euros. I had to pay to get this for the whole area of the coastline, including places much further away from my land. This was the job of the authorities, but they made me pay for it. In the end the whole area benefited. Other lands benefited from the work I paid for.'

'This is before you applied for a building permit, right?'

'Yes, I couldn't apply if I didn't have this certificate.'

'All the money went there?'

'No, I had to apply for a clearance from the forestry department. That took a while too.'

'And then?'

'Well, the first part took me about three years. Then I got an architect and made an application for building a hotel.'

'And they rejected it, after you spent all that money?'

'No, it all went fine. It cost me a lot, some fifteen thousand euros and another four months of waiting, but in the end I got a building permit.'

'Then what?'

'Then I had to register my permit with all the relevant authorities, even the police.'

'So, the second loan is for the fifteen thousand euros?'

'No. Once I got the permit, I was sure I could start building, but we didn't have a proper road. I paid off all the neighbours to give a bit of their land to make the road wider.'

'And?'

'I paid deposits to the contractors for them to bring their equipment onto the land and start work.'

'More money?'

'I had to. Once the road was finished and everything was in order, about a week before we were going to start building, they sent the police to my land. That scared all the workers who were making the preparations, as if they had committed a crime. They stopped everything. I went to see the police the next day. They told me nothing, stating that I had to make an application to go and see them. They gave me a date in three months' time, after the end of the building season when the rains would be starting.'

'What happened after three months?'

'After three months they told me I had to change the spot where I wanted to build because the hotel permit was too close to the old tower. I told them the area was not even listed in their protected areas.'

'What did they say?'

'There was a guy on the committee, Mr Petridis. As soon as I got to the meeting, he threw an old book at me. He threw it across the table. It almost hit my hand. He asked me if I had read it. It was a book about some Byzantine watch towers in the area.'

'What did you tell him?'

'I told him there were no ancient residential areas in the area and that the area was not even registered in their lists. I wanted to tell him that he should have read the book himself and put the area on the forbidden list before I put all my life in that place. I begged them to reconsider.'

'What did they say?'

'He asked me what I would do if my mother was under the ground there. Would I excavate? Back then I was trying to be polite. I said no, I wouldn't dig. But now that I think about it, if I knew there was a possibility that my mother was under something, I would firstly and with whatever means necessary try to remove whatever was on her, as happened yesterday.'

'What happened yesterday?'

'Nothing, leave it now. So, instead of responding I just kept begging. But there was no point. They asked me to go to another area of the land. He even told me to go buy something else, to go somewhere else. My life was in their hands. You know, he wasn't even an archaeologist, a public sector civil engineer. Those are the types who don't have enough guts to go out in the streets and compete with other engineers to get building jobs. They get a soft, no-pressure public sector position. They get their salaries every month on time. They enjoy their power. They get to shout at people and make people beg them for mercy, and they show off to everyone, pretending that they are the ones who are protecting Greece from Greeks like me.'

'Panos, don't look at this personally. Don't make it a personal thing. It doesn't help anyone.'

'People like him, like all of them sitting in that committee, have no balls to go out and do an honest day's work out in the street. They can't function in the real world, in the market. They can make any claims they want, any mistakes they want. Nobody questions them. They play with people's lives, destroy families, and destroy hopes, all at no risk to themselves. Then at the end of the day, they get their salary and then go home to their wives and say, "Woman, I saved Greece again today. I stopped another building. I stopped another hope."'

'Wait, Panos, you are going too far now. You can't blame your family's break-up on the archaeological authorities.'

'Why not? It is possible that it is their fault. I can make any claims I want. It is my life. What are they going to do, take me to court?'

'This is of no use, Panos. I told you not to take it personally.'

'Don't take it personally? How the fuck do you want me to take it?'

'You don't need to get angry. It doesn't help. You must understand, the archaeological authorities don't look at matters the way we do.'

'How do they look at it? They see things we don't? They have stopped me. What are their plans for the land? Are they going to excavate and preserve whatever is there, or will they just leave it?'

'Well, they …'

'I even hired an archaeologist with a PhD.'

'How did that help, Panos?'

'It didn't.'

'What did he say?'

'He said it doesn't look like there is anything of great importance buried there. Most probably the watch tower was the only thing standing there, and all its stones were reused by the farmers years ago. He said that they should at least excavate.'

'Of course, he wouldn't come to say this in court, right?'

'No, he wouldn't. He was hoping one day to get a job with the authorities. Why should he come to court and stand against them?'

'I don't know about your case, Panos, and to be honest, I don't really care. It doesn't change anything with your wife and the divorce. But archaeologists have a different view, a completely different view. They are trained not to think of the moment. They don't have to go excavating tomorrow morning. They have a different timeline. They feel what is from the past should be maintained. Even if they can't excavate now, it should be preserved for the future generations. We are talking about things that have existed for thousands of years. They want to let them be, maybe even for hundreds of years to come. They are not going to change their philosophy because you want to build a hotel. You must understand, the archaeologists have their own philosophy about things.'

'A philosophy that can't be logically challenged is hypocrisy, and it is dangerous. I can take this kind of shit from a priest, when they tell me about the eternal promised future. From a priest, from a religious fanatic, I can take it. I believe in it if I want, and I don't believe in it if I don't want. An archaeologist can't force me to look at life the way they want me to. They are supposed to be scientists. They must be accountable to the public. You can't tax me and pay them a salary and then put them above me to control my life without any responsibility, without any accountability.'

'What do you want to do about it, Panos? This is how things are.'

'The first thing I am going to do is to tell you not to dare tell me not to take it personally. The second thing I am going to do is say shame on you.'

'Shame on me? What have I done?'

'What kind of lawyer are you that you don't believe in justice in this country? Why are your working? Why do you get paid? How can you follow cases when you don't even trust the system?'

'Panos, let's talk about you. Your life is in a mess, not mine. I don't need advice from you. Tell me what happened when you changed the place you were going to build.'

'I thought you were not interested. What happened? They told me to go fuck myself, that's what happened. After three months of waiting, after paying the architect again for a new plan, they told me to go fuck myself. But you know what? They didn't throw a book at me this time. They, all of them, knowing that I only had one more chance with them, told me to go find another place on my land because the new place wasn't good either.'

'Why didn't you ask them to survey the area and tell you where you could build?'

'I did. They told me it was not their job to check the area and help me find a place. They told me I should keep making applications. I should change the spot where I wanted to build, make another plan, and come back in three months.'

'What happened then?'

'I did it. I paid again. I got a new plan, and I took it to them.'

'What did they tell you then?'

'That the file would go to the central archaeological committee in Athens in three months' time. I waited again. I changed lawyers. I wrote a long letter telling them if they let me build I would preserve the whole area. I asked them to let me build somewhere on my land. I even told them that I would give the rest of the land to them. I would fence it off if they wanted. I would light it up if they wanted. I would do anything. Guess what happened after three more months and another committee? Nothing! Another unanimous decision from people who hadn't even seen the land. I begged them to let me excavate with them present, so they could see there was nothing there. I asked them to send a group of archaeologists at my cost, when we excavated. I told them I would stop if they saw anything.'

'What did they say to that?'

'They said to me, unanimously, that they don't give a shit about my life. They said unanimously to go fuck myself.'

'Panos, I told you, there is no point getting angry. Don't take it so personally.'

'And I ask you, how the hell do you want me to take it? If you can help, help me, but don't fucking patronize me. I have been treated like a piece of shit by all these people for all these years. If you can help me with these books you have on the shelves, help me. If you can't, just shut up.'

And with that I rushed up to the shelves, put my hand behind a stack of books, and pushed them off. The books fell one by one, and each one made a loud noise. I had completely lost control. I had never known myself to behave like this.

'Panos, I can now understand why Maria left you.'

The door to the next office opened, and Elpida rushed in. The lawyer was standing in the corner of his office looking at me. What angered me even more was that he was calm, completely calm, as if he had seen all this before or was somehow expecting it. Elpida was also calm.

'Dad, can I come here now? You are not talking about Mum and you. Can I stay?'

'Elpida, this is not really your place. You should go to your mother now,' said the lawyer.

'Shall I tell Mum you need her help now?' Elpida asked the lawyer.

'No, no, Elpida, I don't need your mother. Why would I need her?'

'You told her you would call her when you needed help with the office. Who is going to clean up all these books?'

'I will clean them up, Elpida. Don't worry about that,' I said.

'Uncle, what happens if the archaeologist makes a mistake? What do they do to him? Is it like in school? Every time I make a mistake, my teacher gets annoyed. One time she …'

I went up to Elpida and said: 'Please go to your mum. The books are just … my hand touched them. I was standing here.'

'You said some bad words too, Dad.'

'I … you were not supposed to be listening, Elpida.'

'Mum said I shouldn't listen when you talk about you and Mum. Can I go when you start talking about you and Mum?'

'Elpida, this is not just about Mum and me.'

'What then? Are you going to say bad words again?'

'No.' I smiled at the lawyer and bent down to start collecting the books.

'Dad, Dad, please, don't. Mum wants to do that. If you pick them up she won't get a job.'

She rushed to me to stop me picking up the books, and I pushed her away with my elbow. Elpida went backwards towards a chair and landed perfectly in the seat. The lawyer looked at me, and Elpida burst into laughter. I dropped the books and went to her.

'Are you okay?' She was still laughing.

'Dad.'

'Yes?'

'Why don't the archolgist let you build? Why do we have to keep the ruins?'

'You mean archaeologists.'

'Yes.'

Then the lawyer came closer to Elpida and said: 'Because it is important to keep our past, all the things our ancestors built: their monuments, their culture. People come from all around the world to see what our ancients did.'

Elpida went silent for a moment and just kept looking at the lawyer. And then she said: 'Why do they come to see our ancients? Don't they have their own ancients?'

'Our ancients did a lot. They are the base of Western civilization. You will learn this all at school one day,' said the lawyer.

'When they come to see our ancients, where do they sleep at night?'

'Elpida, I have a lot to talk about with your dad. When your dad leaves I will come up and we can talk.'

'Dad promised he won't do anything wrong again. He loves Mummy, I know.'

'How do you know I love Mummy? Who told you?' I asked.

'I know because you came here to take her back.'

'Elpida, tourists usually stay in hotels. Now will you go up?' said the lawyer.

There was another moment of silence. At first I thought Elpida was running out of questions and at any moment she would want to go up to her mum, but she asked: 'If tourists stay in hotels, why don't they let my dad build one so they can stay in his hotel? That way Mum can work at the hotel and they will be together.'

'Your dad wants to build his hotel in the wrong place.'

'Are there any ancients there?'

'There may be some ruins there.'

'That is good, uncle.'

'No, that is bad.'

'That is good. You told me they come to see the ancients.'

'No, that's bad because that's exactly where the ancients were.'

There was another moment of silence, and then Elpida asked again: 'Uncle?'

'Yes, Elpida?'

'Do tourists pay money to archaeologists for keeping the ruins?'

'No.'

'Why are the tourists good?'

'The tourists come and spend money.'

'And they stay in hotels?'

'Yes.'

'And pay money to my dad for the hotel when he makes it?'

'Yes.'

'Who pays the archaeologists?'

'People like your dad who have a hotel. They take the tourists' money and pay taxes to the government, and the government pays the archaeologists.'

'What are taxes, Uncle?'

'Never mind. It is money.'

'Money from my dad after he builds his hotel?'

'Yes, Elpida. I told you, your dad and I have a lot to talk about. Go up to your mum.'

'The archolgists want my dad to build so they get more money, right?'

'No, Elpida, that is not how it works.'

'Why, Uncle?'

'The archaeologists get paid the same amount of money anyway.'

'Uncle, is it their job, or do they just like doing it?'

'No, Elpida, it is not a hobby. It is their job.'

That is when I jumped in the conversation and said: 'If it was their job, and they took it seriously, they would finish fixing the Parthenon in two months, not decades.'

The lawyer looked at me and said: 'Panos, this is going to confuse the kid even more.'

Then Elpida said to the lawyer: 'If you and Mum go to the archolgist and ask them to let Dad build, do you think they will let him build?'

'No, Elpida, I told you, your dad wants to build on top of the mountain. There may be ruins there.'

'Uncle, Dad said he will build anywhere they let him, not just on top. Right, Dad?'

'Elpida, your dad can't build in the whole area.'

'They didn't tell him that.'

'I don't know, Elpida. I wasn't there. We are not here to talk about that with your dad. We have other things to talk about.'

'Uncle, please don't talk about other things.'

'Why? We have things to resolve.'

'To what?'

'To resolve, to talk about.'

'No, please. If you talk about those things I will have to go.'

'Well, we must.'

'Uncle?'

'Yes?'

'Why did the ancients build in nice places so we can't build our hotel?'

This was going on for too long, and finally it was time for me to stop the pointless babbling. So I said: 'Listen, Elpida, it is not me or your uncle who makes decisions. I know what you are doing. It is just like before you have to go to bed at home. You talk and talk, asking question after question. You think we forget it is your bedtime.'

'Dad, I can't sleep when I have a question. I am like you when you couldn't sleep asking why the archolgist did these things.'

'How do you know I couldn't sleep?'

'Every time you had a fight with Mum and went to say sorry to her, you said the something archolgist didn't let you sleep all night.'

'The something archaeologists?'

'It was some bad words. I didn't hear.'

'If you are not going up to your mum, at least go to the other office and let us finish here.'

'Do I have to sleep soon?'

'No, Elpida, why?'

'Because I have another question. I can't sleep when I have a question.'

'Keep your question till later, for after we finish.'

'I will forget!'

'Okay, ask it now and then go to that office,'

'I can't. I forgot.'

She then looked at the lawyer one more time and hesitantly walked to the other office. I had to go behind her and shut the door. Then she opened the door again and said: 'I remember, Dad.'

'Yes?'

'Where is my home now?'

'I am not going to answer you anymore, Elpida. I know what you are doing.'

'Dad, if I am staying with Mum and Costa is going to leave soon, you and Mum should have another baby before you separate, so you can have a child each.'

'Okay, Elpida. We will talk about this later.'

For the second time I forced her into the other room.

'Children! They are something else these days,' said the lawyer.

'Wives! They are the ones who are something else these days!'

'Everything is different now.'

'Do you get a lot of divorce cases now?' I asked as he started putting the books back on the shelves.

'Not that many. Not as many as you would think. People don't have enough money to even separate.'

'It is funny. What causes separation itself can prevent it from happening.'

'You seem to blame everything for your divorce, everything except yourself. Couples separate for many reasons. Yes, the recession has played its role.'

'You should know. You are the lawyer, the specialist. When do you think it will end?'

'What, your divorce case?'

'No, the recession.'

'Oh, I don't think it will end, at least not soon.'

'How can it not end? Something will happen.'

'What do you expect people to do?'

'It is not the people; it is the politicians.'

'Oh, that again. We are not at fault at all, right?'

'Look at your profession, as an example. You practice law, and you don't even believe in the way it is administered. The easiest thing to say is to say the politicians are at fault. Okay, which one? Which party do you support?'

'You are like your daughter; you keep trying to avoid reality. They are all at fault, from the top to the bottom, starting from the president.'

'From the president? You mean the prime minister, right?'

'Panos, I am a constitutional lawyer. You think I don't know the difference between the president and the prime minister?'

'I thought you were a divorce lawyer. Look, the president just has a ceremonial position. He doesn't do anything. He is an old man with some patriotic history, a veteran of war who attends national ceremonies. That's why they say he has a ceremonial power.'

'Then how come we have been screwed so unceremoniously? He doesn't do anything. That is exactly the problem.'

'What do you expect him to do? What can he do?'

Then he picked up one of the books I had thrown on the floor, opened to a marked page, and started reading.

'*Article 44,1. Under extraordinary circumstances of an urgent …*'

'Wait, why are you reading me the Greek constitution? What does that have to do with anything?'

'You asked why it is his fault. The president is like the father of a nation. What would a father do when he sees his children fighting, kicking, cheating, stealing, and lying? Doesn't he stop them, sit them at a table, and tell them that we are a family and not enemies? The political parties who are fighting each other for power have little loyalty to my country. Their loyalty is to their own mafia gangs and their own families. We need a father. We need someone with no colours to come and rescue us. Once the factories start working again and there is bread on our table, we can start playing democracy. Right now we need action.'

'You mean a dictatorship? A president does not have the right to overrule things. That is why we have a democracy.'

'Listen, Panos, this is the reason I started reading you the constitution. I don't know if you have read it as a journalist, but it is my job. I know it almost by heart. Listen.' And he started reading again:

'The President of the Republic shall by decree proclaim a referendum on crucial national matters following a resolution voted by an absolute majority of the total number of Members of Parliament, taken upon proposal of the Cabinet.

A referendum of Bills passed by Parliament regulating important social matters, with the exception of fiscal ones, shall be proclaimed by decree by the President of the Republic.'

'I don't want to read you the whole constitution, but here is another example:'

'The President of the Republic may under exceptional circumstances address messages to the People with the consent opinion of the Prime Minister. Those messages should be countersigned by the Prime Minister and published in the Government Gazette.'

'Now I ask you, Panos, when has our president even attempted to do any one of these? Do we not have an urgent need for action? Should we not all as a family sit down and form a crisis committee which has overwhelming power to attend to urgent needs? Should we all not be in the emergency room?'

'Crisis committee?'

'Yes, right now we have separate parties who all want elections to get into power. They are fighting over old ideological grounds. The patient is dying. We have no time to have another election. And our president, who is the only one who can turn on the alarm, is going to weddings and funerals, talking about the war.'

'At least we still have a democracy in which one man does not rule.'

'Democracy? What are you going to do with democracy when your life is in such a mess that you can't even feed your children?'

The door to the other office opened again, and Elpida walked in with the toy slippers in her hands.

'You are out again?' I asked.

'Dad, what is deocracy?'

'Not deocracy, it is called democracy. And why are you here again?'

'Mum said I shouldn't listen when you talk about her and you.'

'I am sure Mum didn't say that. I told you, we need to talk about a lot of things.'

'But Dad, I want to know what is docracy that is more important than you and mum that you are talking about?'

The lawyer responded: 'Look, Elpida, you will learn all these things in school one day. Democracy is when everyone decided how to live together. We all vote and agree with the rules.'

'Vote?'

'Yes, vote, Elpida. We have elections, and everyone votes.'

'Oh, I know elections. I really like democracy, uncle.'

'You do? Where did you learn about democracy, Elpida?' asked the lawyer.

'At school. All the children like it.'

I was pleasantly surprised to hear Elpida talk about democracy. So I turned to the lawyer and said: 'You see? This is our pride. This is what makes the difference. It is not only that we brought the world democracy. We have also maintained it, and we promote it. Which country do you know where they teach and make a child love democracy at this early age at school? And you want to turn it all into a one-man show.'

I turned to Elpida and said: 'Elpida, tell Uncle why you love democracy.'

'I love it, Dad.'

'I know.'

'Dad, is deocracy very difficult?'

'No, why? Some countries don't have it, but here in Greece we are lucky.'

'Why do we have deocracy on Fridays? I thought that was because it is difficult.'

'On Fridays?'

'Yes, Dad, at my school the teachers always do deocracy on Friday. They get tired, and they want the weekend.'

'You mean teacher's elections?'

'Yes, Dad. How long does it take to do deocracy?'

'What? You mean elections? I don't know. Once you make up your mind, you write your decision on a piece of paper and put it in a box.'

'How long does it take, Dad?'

'A few minutes.'

'I like deocracy in my school more. We have no school for the whole day.'

The lawyer seemed to have lost patience. He looked at the ceiling and said: 'Thank you, everybody, for the seminar. We can now conclude that everybody here likes democracy – of course, each one of us for their own particular reason.'

'Uncle, can I take these slippers home?' asked Elpida, holding the giant slippers over her head. I said quickly:

'No, Elpida, they are not yours.'

'Yes, of course you can have them,' said the lawyer.

'Elpida, I will buy a pair for you. Put those back, and I will ask Uncle where he bought them from.'

As soon as I said that, Elpida went to the corner of the room and said: 'No, I don't want them. I don't like them at all.'

'Elpida, what is the matter with you? Didn't you just say you want the slippers? Now you say you don't like them? I will buy a pair for you,' I said.

'Dad, I don't want you to buy them for me, All your money goes for the, for the something archologists.'

'Something, something what? Don't talk about people like that.'

'I didn't say a bad word.'

'You were trying to say what I said.'

'I said that before. I said something before, and you didn't say anything.'

'Well, that's because you were trying to explain what I said.'

'If I say a bad word, but I say you said it, is that okay?'

'You should never say bad things. Who told you all my money goes to the archaeologists?'

'I know you want to take the archaeologists to the police.'

'You mean to court.'

'Yes, and you need the money. I don't want the slippers. I have slippers at home.'

'Nothing is going to change if I buy you slippers, Elpida.'

'If you win the court, Mum comes back to you.'

'Who told you that?'

'You, you told uncle … I wasn't listening. I just heard. But you won't win at court.'

'Who told you that, Mum?'

'No, Uncle just told you.'

'I didn't say that. When did I say that?' said the lawyer.

'You said … I wasn't listening. Maybe you didn't say,' said Elpida.

'Elpida, if your dad lets you keep the slippers, will you go upstairs?' asked the lawyer.

Elpida threw the slippers on the floor, exactly where I had dropped the books, and said angrily: 'I hate the ancients.'

The lawyer walked towards Elpida and, pointing to the slippers, said: 'Elpida, pick those up. You are too young to get angry at these things. Also, it is not good to generalize and blame an entire group of people.'

'Generalize?' asked Elpida.

The lawyer replied: 'Yes, Elpida. Just because it is possible that some people have made a mistake or done something wrong, it doesn't mean that all of them are wrong. Do you understand?'

'Then I hate only the Greek ancients,' shouted Elpida as she ran barefoot into the other office and slammed the door.

'It's amazing what imaginative minds kids have nowadays,' said the lawyer.

'What imaginative minds? She didn't imagine anything. You are the one who said I won't win the court case. I can understand her anger.'

'Panos, with the system the way it is now, even if you win the court case, you still lose. It is difficult to explain this to a kid.'

'I don't understand either.'

'I have been involved in cases that have taken years and years. Before they were heard, both sides had either given up, run out of money, or died.'

'Does that mean we shouldn't seek justice?'

'Courts take so long that some illegal businesses have the period included in their business plan.'

'What do you mean?'

'I have clients who know they will lose a case, but all they are interested in is how long it will take, so they know whether it is worth it.'

'How does that help?'

'Well, they work out that if they stay in business for the amount of years that it takes for the other side to finalize the matter, their profit is worth the hassle. One of my clients opened a Bouzouki place, knowing that he would be closed down in five years.'

'And he stayed in business for five years and made money?'

'Yes, and so did I. I kept delaying the decision for as long as I could. It is the same thing with the archaeology department. They know that this will take years to resolve, by which time …'

'I could be dead. How about justice?'

'Courts, Panos, are not just to get justice. This is especially true if you are fighting the system. I told you, courts either pacify you or completely drain you. They drain out all your energy, all your enthusiasm, all your confidence, and all your hope. You know, they say in Greece, if you want to hurt someone psychologically and financially, without getting physical, you should gently hit them on the head.'

'I thought you said without getting physical.'

'That's why I said gently. If you are lucky, they take you to court and spend a good portion of their lives waiting for court dates, trying to arrange witnesses, paying lawyers, and so on.'

'Don't you believe in fighting for justice? You are supposed to be a lawyer.'

'Yes, I do. But what does that have to do with the legal system?'

'What is the legal system for, then?'

'The legal system is to keep order in the society, not to guarantee the citizens justice. Who gave you that idea?'

'Don't you think I deserve justice for my case?'

'It doesn't matter what I think or what a judge thinks. It is the interpretation of the law which they are concerned about at court.'

'Isn't the law about justice and equality?'

'Law is what law makers make to control, keep order, and tax the society. The judge who will read your case will look at what the law says. He or she is going to believe what government agents say. The judge will not feel sorry for you because you have lost everything in your life.'

'How can a person look at my life and not feel sorry for me?'

'Panos, the only body whose sympathy would be effective is the archaeology department, and if they had felt sorry for you, you wouldn't be where you are now.'

'Can they not see what has happened to me?'

'Panos, you are just a number to them, another one of their success stories. You don't matter. All you have lost is your dream.'

'My dream, my money, my youth, my wife and children, my ...'

'People have lost their lives because of the archaeologists. You think they feel sorry for you losing your dream?'

'People have lost their lives because of the archaeologists?'

'Of course. What do you guys report in your newspaper?'

'Give me an example.'

'The ancient aqueduct in Volos. Don't tell me you don't even know where that is.'

'Of course I know where that is.'

'How many aqueduct stone columns are there?'

'I told you I know where the city is. I didn't tell you I counted the columns.'

'I will tell you: over fifty. There are over fifty abandoned, not properly preserved, not presented, not lighted, not secure, not looked after Byzantine short stone columns which used to support an aqueduct system. They are just falling apart.'

'So what? Greece is full of such monuments. They are not killing anyone.'

'Yes they are. One of these columns was removed years ago to make room for a dirt track to the city. This dirt track was later turned into a major, but narrow, tarmac road. Two trucks don't easily fit through the two columns which are on each side of the road. The two columns on each side are now a testimony to so many lives that have been lost to accidents. They don't even look good. Many vehicles have damaged them through the years; there are broken stones visible from every angle. They have put worthless traffic warning signs on them. If you look hard you can even find car parts all around the area. People have built memorials for their dead around the aqueduct.'

'Why doesn't anyone sue the archaeology department?'

'Unfortunately for me as a lawyer, dead people can't sue anyone.'

'How about their relatives?'

'Their relatives are busy trying to save their own lives. They are trying to pay the next electricity bill. Do you know what it means to have your power cut off?'

'I can imagine.'

'Plus, what is the point of suing the archaeologists? A case like this can take five to ten years. By the time it is over, they have forgotten their dead.'

'Yes, like me. I wanted to build a hotel to work in when I was young. I wanted to leave something to my kids. I wanted to enjoy it with my wife. Even if I win the court case tomorrow, it is going to take years before they give me a clear answer about what I am allowed to do. I could be in my seventies.'

'And you want your wife to stay with you until then to see what happens, to see when you can pay your loans and how you are going to feed the children? Why are you waiting for the court?'

The door to the other office opened again, and Elpida popped her head in. But before she had a chance to talk the lawyer said: 'What, Elpida?'

'Uncle, why don't they just move one of the already broken columns to another place? They have forty-nine more anyway. What are they going to do with them?'

'I don't know, Elpida.'

'Uncle, if they took one column out before, why don't they take another one out?'

– 272 –

'I don't know, Elpida.'

'Uncle, if they took one of the columns out, why don't they let my dad build his hotel? Our land doesn't even have any columns.'

I turned to the lawyer and said: 'Okay, if the laws are not for justice, they are at least supposed to be logical. Logic is the base of our civilization. If we have forgotten democracy, at least we must have kept out logic.'

'Panos, nobody said laws have to be logical.'

'Nobody said it, but they must be.'

'And who is going to check? Are you going to bring a philosopher from your ruins on your hill to check what is logical and what is not?'

'Don't play with my pain.'

'Is it logical to charge you taxes now for something you bought ten years ago, when you had money?'

'No, you are the lawyer. It is your job to defend me.'

'I can't. This is the law. Is it logical to cut off your disability benefit for a whole month just because they cared for you one night in the hospital that month?'

'They do that?'

'Is it logical to assume that your income is more than what you have reported, just because you have inherited something?'

'Uncle, uncle, my dad has no columns. You can say that in court.'

I went to Elpida, picked her up in my arms, and gave her a big kiss. Only then did I realize that I had not kissed Elpida for a long time.

'Darling, don't worry. Daddy will find a way,' I said, whispering in her ear, making sure the lawyer heard.

'She is a smart girl, Panos. What grade is she in?' asked the lawyer.

'Eh, she is in the first grade.'

'No, Dad, I am in second grade.'

'Oh yes, that was last year,' I announced desperately. 'Daddy has a big present for you … when I see you next time.'

'Slippers? I don't want any slippers, Dad. You should buy a present for Uncle.'

'No thanks, Elpida. I don't want anything from your dad.'

'How much do you want from my mum, Uncle?'

Still holding Elpida in my arms, I quickly tried to change the subject and asked the lawyer: 'So tell me, since you know so much, why are you settling with divo … with, I mean, small cases? As a constitutional lawyer, what are you doing here? Why aren't you involved with the government?'

'Dad, Dad, Uncle has another office. He has two. The cleaning lady in the other office is still working.'

'Yes, Elpida, I know he has cleaning ladies.'

'What do you want me to do, Panos? These are the jobs I get.'

'Shouldn't you be working as a constitutional lawyer, with the government or something? Don't you feel wasted?'

'Thanks for reminding me, Panos. Yes, I do, but the government has its own lawyers.'

'You could be an adviser.'

'No, governments select their own lawyers from their supporters. I am a constitutional lawyer; I can help defend the constitution. No government wants that.'

'They serve the government? But we pay for them. It is our tax money.'

'You may pay for them, but the government uses them for themselves. And since they select them, they pay for them. Even if it is from your pocket.'

'Dad has no money. I know he is broke,' said Elpida, still in my arms.

'So the lawyers …'

The lawyer interrupted me: 'Panos, don't suffer so much. Look, the government that is already in power has enough power to do what they want. They think that since they are elected, they know best. They don't want my advice.'

'So, when big national contracts are signed, like the contracts for the privatization of the roads, don't lawyers accompany the politicians to the meetings, just to make sure they are not cheated?'

'They have lawyers, but the lawyers are there to cover their ass. Sorry, I mean the lawyers are there to protect the politicians, so they don't get blamed for anything that goes wrong. They are not there to protect you and me.'

'But the other side has lawyers too, right?'

'Yes, their lawyers have no conflict of interest; they work only for the benefit of the other side. That is why all major contracts are so much in favour of the private companies, like the roads. The private road companies can charge as many tolls as they want, and they still get huge subsidies from the government. They charge more so fewer people use the roads. That's good for them. They get their money anyway, and there is less maintenance involved. That means more money for them,'

'And then the people have to go to the side roads and get killed. What if the people rise and force a change to the contract? Is that possible?

'Look, Panos, I am here – well, today I am your wife's lawyer. If you want an interview for your paper, I am happy to do it, but anonymously. Today we have other things to do.'

'I can't. Today I can't. I have so many other things to do.'

'What is more important than your wife and your ...' He briefly looked at Elpida, turned to me, and continued. 'What is more important, Panos?'

'I am really sorry, but I have to go to the farmer. I have to talk to him. I have a great use for his big truck. I also want to see him and take a picture of him planting a tree. I have much more respect for that kind of people than pessimists who ... I've got to go.' And with that I put Elpida on the floor, kissed her for the second time that day, and left the lawyer's office.

Chapter 13

IT WAS GETTING very obvious to me that my car started with no problems whenever I was heading somewhere I did not want to go, and when I was determined and excited to go somewhere, it gave me a hassle. As if the machine heard me and wanted to prove me wrong, it started. I was excited and determined because I had finally found a purpose. There was something I could do to help the mess that had become my nation. And not only that, this was, perhaps, the only way I could show Maria that I was not the push-over she thought I was. I could show her that there was a purpose to my articles and I didn't just do what my boss told me. Wait till she heard that I played a role in blocking the roads in protest against the unjust tolls!

I could not stand it anymore. The roads, because of unjust policies, were increasingly becoming a danger to my people. Maria thought I couldn't even stand up for my own rights. Wait till she saw how I fought for our people. I might not be able to write what I wanted because I had to keep my job to put bread on the table, but I could do outside work. I was a man, a Greek man, with a big heart, filled with passion and with purpose. I was going to persuade the farmer to block the road with his giant tractor. I was going to stop any traffic on the dangerous village roads until the government came to their senses. Besides, the farmer didn't need much persuasion. Obviously he was annoyed enough with the system to be on our side. Also, he seemed to be optimistic enough, to have faith in taking action. After all, he was planting trees now. He was one of the few people I knew who was planting trees in the middle of the recession, trees which would only give fruit in years to come. All this gave me a good excuse to go to his farm and see the olive tree, the tree with many colours and with many uses. In addition to the normal obstacles in my way driving to his farm, it also started raining. A sunny day had suddenly turned grey. The rain was so heavy that I could hardly see in front of me anymore. But fortunately as soon as I got to his farm the rain stopped, and I saw the old man with a small olive tree in a plastic bag and a shovel on his shoulder walking out of his yard. I stopped the car next to the tractor, got off, had a hard look at the tractor again, and went to the farmer.

'Panos, is that you?' he shouted.

'Yes, it is. I came to see you.'

'I didn't recognize you. Why are you wearing a suit? Are you involved with the topographer?'

'What topographer? No, I came to see you.'

'Why are you wearing a suit then?'

'I had to interview a politician.'

'Did you tell him about me, about the subsidies that they have cut off?'

'Yes, yes, he said they are working on it.'

'What are they working on? It is not a tree that has to grow. All they have to do is make a decision and sign some fucking papers.'

'Don't worry. I will follow up on it. Are you planting just one tree?'

'No, I planted a few, but it started raining. I only have this one left. I want to get it over with.'

'That's good; I wanted to take a picture of you whilst planting. Where are you going to plant it?'

'Up that dirt road next to my cousin's land, up there,' he replied, pointing at the hill.

'Can I come with you?'

'You can, but you will get very muddy.'

'It doesn't matter. It is my work suit; I am doing it for work.'

'Come follow me. We will walk. It is just up the road. Did they tell you from the paper to come here and take a picture of me planting?'

'Yes, I put a good word in for you. I don't know many people who are planting trees now.'

'Tell them to take care of us. Once I am gone there is no hope for the future generations. They won't be feeding you like us. Careful, it is muddy.'

'I think I am going to get muddy anyway.'

'I am not worried about your suit. You might sink in the mud. You city boys don't know these things. Okay, here we are …'

As soon as he said that, my left foot went down in a hole full of mud. Then the old man put the tree down and with his shovel started digging a hole next to a short fence.

'Why are you planting here?' I asked as I pulled my foot out of the hole with my shoe still stuck in the mud.

'Why not? The land around here is mine.'

'But you have so much more room up there.'

'Don't worry, this tree will also get big one day and will be full of olives.'

'But you are next to the road,' I said, shaking my foot to get the mud off.

'I gave half a meter of my land on this side to help build the road. They didn't help with the road, and now they have sold the land. Who knows what they are going to do with it? There are some engineers and topographers coming around lately. I won't let them pass if they are going to build.'

'Don't you want them to build?'

'I don't care, as long as they compensate me for trimming the tree. This may one day be my only source of income.'

'What variety of olive tree are you planting now?'

'I thought you came here to take a picture. Why are you asking so many questions?'

I had to at least pretend to be interested in his resolve if I was going to ask him to use his tractor. So I took my mobile phone out and started taking pictures. He started digging, and I carried on taking pictures. 'You want to take one with me and the trees behind me?'

'Yes,' I said. I moved backward and this time put my right foot in the same hole I had fallen in before. This was not at all what I had hoped to see, but I had to stay cool and smiling in the hope of getting him to help me with the tractor. Walking back with him on the muddy road, I was waiting for an opportunity to start the conversation. But luckily he himself asked me: 'Are you going back on the old road or the toll road?'

'I will go back on the old road. Why pay tolls when you can avoid them, right?'

'Obviously.'

'But we should do something about it. It is very dangerous.'

'I know, but why pay tolls? Listen, do you need gas?'

'I think I still have some left. I had an idea about this problem with the road. I think we should all protest. Your village and other villages which are affected by this should organize. We should go and block the road one day. You can bring your tractor. You have used it for blocking roads before, right?'

'Yes.'

'You blocked the roads for the subsidies. This is even more important; people's lives are at stake here.'

'Wait you want me to bring my tractor to block the road so they don't use the old road?'

'Yes, isn't that a good idea? It may be effective.'

As soon as I finally made my suggestion, we reached his house. I was hoping that he would ask me to come into his yard to clean my shoes or offer me a drink, but to my surprise and quite abruptly he said: 'Okay then, make sure you push the politician and get my pictures in the paper.'

'Wait a minute, what do you think about my idea?'

'Which idea?'

'About organizing a protest and blocking the road with your tractor.'

'Oh, I can't come.'

'We can organize it whenever you like.'

'No, I can't come at all.'

'Why? Don't you care about people's lives?'

'No, it is not that.'

'What then?'

'Nothing, forget it.'

'No, you must tell me. If you want me to talk to the politician, you must tell me. Why don't you want to help me with the road?'

'Okay, okay, it is not a secret. Remember I told you I can always get petrol, whenever I want, strike or no strike?'

'Yes, so that means you have petrol to drive the tractor to the demonstration.'

'Yes, but I get petrol from one of my distant cousins who has a petrol station on the old road. His business is actually doing better since nobody goes through the toll roads. Leave it now. You must be tired. You want to come in for some ouzo?'

'No, thanks, I must go.'

'Come in, at least to warm up and wash your shoes.'

'No, no, I must go. I have the old wife waiting for me at home.'

'Oh, yes, why wash your shoes yourself if you have a wife to wash them for you?'

As I passed the gas station of the farmer's distant cousin, I looked at the gas meter in my car. It was low, and for once I had money in my pocket. But there was no way I was going to buy gas from that guy, a vulture who was benefiting from other people's misery; it was people like him who had brought Greece to its current state. They were simple opportunists who did everything only for their own benefit and did not consider others' needs. How could they just think of themselves? I had been wrong about the farmer. There was no point. He also only thought about himself. He would never come to help with the roads. He only wanted subsidies. And why were the roads my problem? I had enough problems myself. There was no point in starting a revolution just to impress Maria. Was she worth it? Would anything change with her? She was trying to be as horrible to me as possible, she and her lawyer. But it was not the lawyer's fault. He was just doing his job. I shouldn't have behaved that way towards him, especially in front of Elpida.

I picked up the phone and called the lawyer. 'Hello, this is Panos.'

'Hello. That was quick.'

'Sorry about having to leave like that. It was urgent.'

'That's okay.'

'I am also sorry about your books.'

'Panos, you owe me nothing. It is your wife and children you must think about.'

'What do you want me to do?'

'It is wrong that you are staying in the house and your wife is out in the street. Move out and then work on your issues.'

'Why? Just because she has a small child? Women use these things. I am left in a worse position than her now, and the house is not ours anyways. It belongs to the bank. I am just here to pay the taxes on it.'

'Forget about the house. It has no value, and it is not her child only. It is both of yours. This might be the last chance, Panos. You have to fix things with her.'

'You think it is possible?'

'That only you know. Remember, it is easy to make a family. What is difficult is to keep it.'

'How do you keep a family? By running away from it?'

'No, by making everyone else run away.'

'I am not in the mood for sarcasm. I will have to think about it.'

'Okay, think about it.'

'Actually, no, I don't have to think about it. I am showing the house tonight for sale. She arranged it.'

'I know.'

'I will leave tomorrow. She will never see me again if she doesn't want to. Tell her I didn't lose; I am only doing it for Elpida. Also tell her there is no electricity in the house.'

'I know.'

'If she wants it, that's how I am going to leave it. How do you know?'

'Never mind.'

'Fine, I must go now. I won't bother you again. Take care of my family. I am not too well.'

'I know.'

'Good-bye. Tell her I am out by tomorrow.'

'Good-bye, Panos, and good luck.'

I closed the phone and immediately dialled Pavlos. The phone rang and rang. As I was about to give up he answered: 'Hello.'

'Hello, Pavlos?'

'No, hold on.'

It was a familiar voice but not Pavlos.

'Hello.' This time it was Pavlos.

'Hi, Pavlos. It is me, Panos.'

'Oh, Panos, how are you? Long time no see, all the way from last night.'

'I know. I am calling to tell you I accept your invitation and would like to come and stay at your house for a couple of days. Only if it is okay.'

'Why didn't you tell me this last night?'

'Well, it is kind of urgent. My wife and I had an argument, and I can't stand being next to her, I need to get out a bit.'

'Fine, when?'

'Today.'

'Okay, Panos, but not till the evening. I have people around.'

'I will come in the evening. Shall I bring something?'

'No, I don't need anything. I am all right.'

'Nothing for your home? Food, drinks?'

'Nothing.'

'How about the horses? Shall I bring something for them?' I asked jokingly.

'For my horses? You remember? It's okay, really. Wait a minute. Nikos wants to speak to you.'

'Nikos? Nikos who?'

'Nikos, your boss.'

'Aren't you at home? Hello, hello.'

I couldn't hear anything, and then Nikos came on the line.

'Panos, how did it go last night?'

'Fine. So that was you on the phone before. Yes, Nikos, I went to the casino.'

'So you will have something for me on Monday?'

'No, I couldn't write anything.'

'Why not? What has happened to you, Panos? Where are you now?'

'I was just with the farmer.'

'The farmer? What was he doing in the casino?'

'No, I am coming back from the farmer's village.'

'I send you to write an article about the casino and you end up in some fucking village?'

'Look, Nikos, I am supposed to be freelance now. I can write what I want. If you want you publish it, bravo. If you don't you won't.'

'It had better be good, Panos. This is your last chance. When can you bring it to me? On Monday?'

'Bring you what?'

'The article about the fucking farmer!'

'No, I am not going to write about him.'

'Why are you screwing with me, Panos?'

'I am not screwing with you. I just need some time.'

'No, Panos, I have wasted enough time with you, freelance or not. You are not reliable enough for the paper. I have to go to the office. Come in about two hours, I need to have one last word with you. I will give you one more assignment, and then that is it. If you already think you will screw it up, don't bother coming anymore.'

'Wait, tell Pavlos to SMS me his address. Hello? Hello?' There was no answer. What could his assignment be? Maybe he was going to finally make me interview some stupid politician, maybe a mayor of a small village. It couldn't be a union leader. There were no factory workers with jobs to defend. They had gone on so many strikes that they were now all unemployed. Maybe he was going to ask me to write my own opinion. Maybe he placed some value on my experience, my years of working with people. But no, I was nothing to him, just like I was now nothing to Maria. Maybe he was going to punish me with this last assignment, just like Maria was punishing me by making me leave the house. Whatever it was that he had in mind was not going to be easy. I could sense it.

Before I knew it, I was downtown near my office. I parked the car, set my phone alarm, and fell asleep. It was exactly at the two-hour point that I walked into the office. Stella, Nikos's secretary, gave me a pitying smile. That was no shock to me at all. I was getting used to these kinds of smiles now. I had already gotten them from my wife, my son, my wife's lawyer, the pharmacist, the nurse, the tax man, the electricity guy, and so on. The only person who hadn't given me a pitying smile in the last few days was my daughter, and that was only because she was too young. In a few years she would master the art too. If I was alive by then, she might give me the biggest pitying smile of all.

The first thing that Nikos said as I walked into his office was, however, unexpected and a bit of shock to me: 'Hey Panos, where are the rotten tomatoes?'

'What? What rotten tomatoes?'

'Eggs? No eggs either?'

'Did you call me here to play games?'

'No, Panos, but you seem to be going to too many Halloween parties these days. For a guy who doesn't even have a home you do well. Bouzoukia at nights and Halloween brunch parties in the morning – no work and all play!'

'What Halloween party?'

'Are you supposed to be dressed as a politician who has been thrown mud at? Don't you think you make enough fun of the local politicians who support the paper in your articles?'

'No.'

'No?'

'I mean no, I wasn't at a party. I told you, I went to the farmer's.'

'In a suit?'

'It is a long story. Which politician did I make fun of with my articles?'

'Remember the one who sued our paper because you picked on her for not knowing a technical word?'

'It was her job to know it.'

'She was new. You should have given her a chance to learn it at her job and kept her on our side.'

'Our side? What is our side? She was elected to do that job, not to come and learn about it at my expense.'

'At your expense? You mean the taxes which you are not paying because you can't make any money?'

'Not because I don't make any money; because I don't get paid.'

'Wow, what has happened to you, Panos? You have gone crazy in the last few days. Who are you to tell an elected politician what to do? Do you have the education, the knowledge, the experience?'

'I am a citizen.'

'You are a citizen outside this office. When you are here, you are a journalist working for me. I tell you what to do. I don't pay you to advise professionals on how to do their job?'

'When did you pay me?'

'By the sound of it, never again.'

'I advise people?'

'Yes, and all on my time and with the name of the paper. You have become a big liability for us.'

'When?'

'You have even advised the municipality police.'

'When?'

Then he shouted: 'Stella, Stella, bring Panos's file.'

All of a sudden I felt really important. I actually had a file, a whole file, in my name. Stella, the secretary, came in with a small batch of papers and a few pages of old newspapers. Nikos gave me a page of a newspaper. 'Go on, read it.'

It was an old article of mine. 'Go on, read it!' he shouted again.

So I started reading aloud: 'In order to avoid embarrassment the municipality police should not bring their spouse and associates to their street demonstrations against possible redundancies. This creates a false image that they are already too many for the city, and it increases the public's expectations from them, consequently resulting in the public favouring the scheduled redundancies of the excessive staff.'

'Panos, do you know how many people who read and advertise in our paper have a friend or a relative in the municipal police? How do you think they will feel when they read your article?'

Then he gave me another article and shouted: 'Read it.'

I started reading the second piece: 'At least during the summer tourist season, in case of rubbish collectors' strike we should ask the mandatory military service men to help collect the rubbish.'

'What is wrong with that?' I asked.

'Panos, besides the fact that it is in bad Greek, it is grammatically crap and not understandable, what makes you think you have the right to advise people what to do with their sons and daughters in the army?'

'So, at least you understood it.'

'Who do you think you are? Do you know how many people called and complained about this to me? People send their children to defend the nation, not to clear the rubbish in the street.'

'Defend the nation from what? Our enemy, today, is poverty, unemployment, and streets full of rubbish. Our enemy is inside. It is here ...'

'Listen, I didn't ask you to lecture me. Your case is clear to me. You are doing things without asking me. You went to a government office and wrote an article blaming them for smoking in their offices illegally, as if you were the only one who noticed.'

'I am a reporter.'

'Yes, and what did you change? You should stop mixing your personal life with the paper. The paper has another interest. Go to that government office and shout at them as much as you want, but on your own time.'

'It was on my own time.'

'Use your own name. Don't use the paper; we need these people.'

'But, Nikos …'

'But what? Who is the boss here? Who determines what goes in the paper? I have to write things that people want to read. You can write your things for your mum. I have to write for our readers so I can pay your salary.'

'I refuse to write misleading information.'

'Then write for your mum.'

'What makes you think my mum would like what I write?'

'There you go. She agrees with me then.'

'I do some work that is useful.'

'What is that, Panos? You mean your report on the factory's court case?'

'I reported the court's decision.'

'Who told you to?'

'You told me to cover the case extensively, including all the union's claims and accusations, didn't you? Didn't you, Nikos? Would you complain about my report if the court's decision had been in favour of the unions?'

'The court decision is not important. I told you to report the case. That's what people want to read, the gossip. Who cares about a court's decision? Who cares about a yes or no answer from a fucking judge? You should write what people like to read. Who wants to read that a filthy rich factory owner won a court case against the workers?'

'Would you say that if the factory owner were one of your Bouzoukia buddies? I am supposed to report …'

He got up from his seat, came close to me, and started shouting: 'Just shut up and listen to me. I don't know what has gotten into you, but I can't take it anymore. Panos, you really need to see someone. I can't afford to keep you here like this.'

'See someone? Who? Whom do you want me to see? A politician?'

'See a therapist. Take a few months off and get yourself together.'

'What is wrong with me?'

'Panos, you wear jeans when I send you to interview a parliamentarian, and you wear a suit to go and see a farmer. Do you think you are okay?'

'What is the assignment?'

'Do you think you can handle it?'

'Okay, I will wear a suit to see your politician, but can I keep the mud on?'

'If you only knew how close you are.'

'Close?'

'Yes, close to busting my balls completely.'

'Completely? I didn't know I had partially succeeded. Which one?'

He went back to his desk and sat down looking at the ceiling. Then he turned to me and said: 'Panos, I am going to give you something easy, a simple survey. I want to see if you can handle it.'

'Tell me.'

'I want you to conduct a poll.'

'A poll?'

'Yes. I will let you use my phone here at the office, and I will only pay you if I like the result.'

'The result of the poll?'

'No, the result of your job. I want you to write an article based on your findings.'

'What is it?'

'I want you to do a survey asking people which one of the last two mayors of the city they approve of more.'

'Neither.'

'You are already fucking with me again.'

'No, if you want people to answer you should ask which one is worst, not which one is better.'

'Okay, do it your way. But I won't pay you again, not even a cent, if I don't like your work.'

'You won't pay? When did you pay me last?'

'Didn't I just give you a hundred euros the other day? You really think you deserved it?'

'You owe me more than that.'

'And I ask again, do you think you are worth it?'

I couldn't stand this anymore and immediately got my wallet, took the hundred-euro bill out, walked towards him, gently put the money on his desk, and said: 'Here is your money. Take it; you probably need it more than me.'

'No, what are you doing?'

'I don't want it. I don't need it.'

'Wait a minute, you still have the hundred euros? I thought you were desperate.'

'I was desperate, but for my own money, money that I deserved. This money that you regret giving me has no value to me. I can't even spend it. Believe me, I have tried. Keep it for yourself.'

'Come, take it.'

'I owe money to everyone. My whole country owes money. I don't want to owe to you too.'

He stayed on his seat, speechless, with his eyes following me as I walked out of the office. Then he shouted: 'Are you still doing the survey, or shouldn't I bother waiting for you?'

'I will do your poll. Make sure you won't pay me if you don't like it,' I shouted from the corridor. As soon as I got out in the street I checked my wallet again to make sure that I still had my winnings from the casino to get gas for the car. More than half a day was gone, and I had achieved nothing. Nothing was getting any better, just worse. Every day, every hour, and every minute I was closer to the cliff. This, however, was not going to bring me down. I knew better. I had learned that much from my life, a life of hoping, dreaming, and fighting. I shouldn't give up, ever. Everything could be looked at from a different but positive, productive angle, even this day. Okay, the farmer was a mirage; I shouldn't have trusted him from the start. Now I knew better. I wouldn't waste my time on people like that anymore. I would concentrate on what brought hope. Maybe this job was my way forward. I should use this chance to show Nikos what I could do. I would make as many phone calls as needed. I would do a perfect poll with a professional analysis. I wanted to prove that he couldn't do without me.

The lawyer showed me the way forward: I must move out of the house so I would have no more obligations to Maria. Let her be free and not blame me for stopping her from living her own life. Let her know that I was a good person, with a good heart. They said if you loved somebody you must let them go. The way things were at the moment, she did not love me, and I didn't love her either. How could I love someone like that? Love or no love, I must move out. I would go home, mess up the place a little more, and call the estate agent to come and see the unsalable house.

With this new mission in mind I drove off towards my house, maybe for one of the last times in my life. My plans were working; the house was already smelling of rotten fish. The last meal Maria had cooked for me was doing a good job of making the house even more undesirable. First things first: I desperately needed a coffee to be able to stay up. Not even the electricity company could stop me from making myself a cup of coffee because we had a special gas burner for making Greek coffee.

After putting the coffee on I went to call the agent, but the phone rang before I reached it. 'Hello.'

'Hello, it is me, the agent. How are you?'

'I am a little bit better than horrible.'

'That doesn't make sense. Are you sure you are okay?'

'I was just going to call you. As the proverb says, you will live long. I am just on my way to the house. I should be there soon.'

'Are you not home yet? You said I should come before dark. How far are you.'

'About ten minutes away. Can you come then?'

'Well, I am already at the house. I will just wait for you here.'

'At the house? Where?'

'Outside, in front of the building. I wait till you come.'

'You are outside? Just come up – I mean, go up. The flat is on the third floor. Wait there.'

'Third floor? Your wife said you were on the second floor. I will just wait outside, and we can go up together.'

'Are you sure? It is cold outside.'

'No, I am fine.'

'But how am I going to recognize you?'

'I came to your office the other day.'

'Yes, you are right. See you soon.'

What the hell was he doing already downstairs? How was I going to now just get home when I already was home? I should show no signs of suspicious behaviour. The information would immediately go to Maria, and she would think I was intentionally making it difficult to sell the house so that I could keep her from leaving me. But what was I going to do? I rushed to Costas's room to get a glimpse of the agent by the door. That was the only room in the apartment from which I could see the front door to the building. I looked out but could not see the agent. Then I put my left hand on Costas's helmet in order to gain some height. There he was, standing right by the door. I had to find a way to get out and come back again without him seeing me. I did not have much time, either. I took my hand off the helmet, and as I lost altitude I found the answer. It is amazing how often, as soon as you change your prospective and look at things from a different angle, you find the solution right in front of you. I put on the helmet and looked at myself in the mirror on the closet. It was good enough; he wouldn't be able to recognize me like that. Then I took the fish out of the oven to smell up the place even more. It worked! How had the fish in the matter of a couple of days managed to stink so much? Maybe it was bad to begin with; maybe she was trying to poison me. Why would she hate me so much? How could she be so paranoid? I was on her side; I was fighting the same war with her, in the same army against the same enemy. I wished she would change her perspective and see reality.

I reached at the bottom of the stairs, quickly opened the door, and passed by the agent, looking away to make sure he did not see my face at all. From the corner of my eyes I noticed that he did not turn to look at me at all. I was safe. I walked far enough to make sure he did not see me. Now all I had to do was to get rid of the helmet somehow. I ran to the car and put the helmet inside. The evening air was cold, and a gentle breeze was starting. Halfway back to the house, I tried to close my jacket's buttons to keep warm. From that distance, I could see the agent still standing in front of the building. As I got closer to him it came to me that he might recognize the jacket, so I went back and left the jacket in the car.

As I approached the building, he greeted me from afar. Everything had worked out. 'Hello, Panos. Sorry to rush you like this.'

'No rush. I told you I would be here, and here I am. Let's see the house. I told you, it is not much but still saleable – of course, if you don't find anything wrong. Maybe there is something wrong. I don't know.'

'I know houses like I know the palm of my hand. I will only take a few minutes of your time.'

'Come, come up. Sorry about the state of the house. I haven't been home for a while.'

'I know, you must be really busy with all these political stuff happening.'

'Yes, I am out interviewing all the time.'

We got to the front door of the apartment, and I suddenly remembered that I had left the gas burner on in the kitchen. 'Do you travel far for your interviews too?'

'Could you wait outside for a minute? I want to check to make sure the house is decent.'

I ran into the kitchen. The kettle was boiling, and it had steamed the kitchen windows. I turned off the gas, opened the windows, and shouted: 'Just a minute. I will be there in a second. Do you want some coffee? I will put the kettle on. I will make you some coffee, some Greek coffee.'

Then I poured all the hot coffee into the sink, added some cold water to the kettle, and put it back on the burner. A lot of steam was rising from the sink. There was still no reply from him.

'I am making you some coffee. Wait, it won't take long. I will be out there in a second,' I shouted again.

'I don't want any coffee,' he finally replied softly from right behind me.

'You are here?' I said as I turned my head.

He was standing right behind me. 'Yes, but I still don't want any coffee.'

'Why not?'

'It will take too long. I will just look at the house and go. Actually, I think it is okay. I saw it. I must go now,' he said, looking very confused.

'What is the matter? Don't you like the house? Is it the fish? Maria forgot it there. I will throw it away now.'

'What is the matter with me? What is the matter with you? I think I am going to just retire after this. I am over seventy years old. It is enough. I can't take it anymore.'

'What have I done wrong?'

'You are freaking me out, man. I am getting scared of you. First you called me because you knew your wife was going to call me. Then you said it was a mistake. Then you want to interview me. Then you didn't. Then I told you your wife called me, and you acted surprised. Afterwards you said you knew she wanted to sell already, and you wanted to sell too. Then you told me you didn't want to sell the house. After that you were not sure. A few minutes later you were sure. Then you had no time to show the house. Then you wanted to show it immediately. Then you said you were not home. Then you wanted to send me to the third floor, when the house is on the second floor. After that you came out of the very house that you were not supposed to be in, dressed up in your muddy wedding suit, with a helmet. You walked on the pedestrian path with the helmet on, got rid of it, and then crossed the street. On the way back, you got cold, so what did you do? You took off your jacket. Then you stopped me at the door before coming in so that you could throw away the already-made hot coffee, and then you asked me if I wanted any coffee. When you heard no answer, you decided to make me coffee. After all that, when you saw me look surprised, you asked me if I want you to throw away your fish. And now you want to know what is wrong with me?'

I needed a few seconds before I could respond to all this and finally said: 'All I asked was if you want any coffee.'

'I don't want any coffee.'

'Fine, you don't have to get upset about it.'

'And I am supposed to look to you to tell me what is happening in our parliament? To tell me what my government is doing? To tell me when the recession is over?'

'You agents are all the same. You just talk so much. You go on and on just to confuse people so they don't know what they are getting into.'

'What have I done wrong?'

'There are many people with the same suit, and I don't even have a motorbike. Why would I wear a helmet? You are seeing things.'

'Just tell me one thing.'

'What? You want me to tell you when the recession is going to finish? I thought you don't trust my judgment anymore.'

'No, all I want from you is to tell me, are you selling or not?'

'See what I mean? Here I am in the house, showing it to you, and you are still asking me if I am selling. What do you want me to do? Can't you see the house? You are the one who is lying to yourself.'

'What am I lying about? I am not like you reporters. I sell real things. I don't sell lies. I don't sell fake hope. I don't sell fake pride. I sell products: brick and mortar, the final version, the completed version, with no bullshit and no hidden corners.'

'Except the parts that you hide!'

'That's not lying, and in your case it is going to be to your benefit. There is a lot I need to hide here if I am going to sell. And let me tell you one thing: It is not going to be the fish.'

'The fish was a joke. Forget it. I am going to eat it now, as soon as you leave.'

'It stinks.'

'I didn't ask you to have any. It is my food! What is it to you?'

'I tell you what: You sit and have your dinner. I will go and see the house myself.'

'Tell me if you want anything.'

'I don't need anything. Just tell me again, why are you selling? I need to know.'

'I told you, it is not a good house. We don't need the money, but we want to go somewhere better. Who wants to live here?'

'Somewhere bigger?'

'No, somewhere better. We don't need the space. The kids have grown up and left. What am I going to do in this big house with the old lady on our own? Do you know how much the taxes are?'

'It is not that big. How many bedrooms do you have?'

'Too many. My son hasn't used his bedroom for almost a year now. He doesn't even come here anymore. It is just me and my wife now. We need to go to a more cosy place, somewhere smaller with less cleaning to do.'

'She said you have a daughter too. How old is she?'

'Is this an investigation, or you are supposed to be trying to sell my house?'

I was waiting for him to back off a bit and do his job. But right before he was leaving the kitchen to go and look at the bedrooms, the last thing I needed happened. From behind the shadows of the agent as he was approaching the kitchen door to get out, I saw pyjama patterns. Somebody was walking into the kitchen. If he were going any faster, he would have crashed into the agent. The figure walked in, and as it was exposed to the little light still coming in from the kitchen window I recognized Costa. He stood in the middle of the kitchen, stretching one arm and wiping his eye with the other hand.

'Costa, what are you doing here?' I asked frantically.

'Why shouldn't I be here?'

'No, I mean, where did you come from? It has been so long.'

'Where does it look like I came from, Dad? I came from my bed. I was here yesterday.'

'Were you sleeping in there? In your bed?'

'No, Dad. I was drawing on the ceiling, but my arms didn't reach, so I came here to ask you for help.'

Then he turned to the estate agent and said: 'Sorry, all this must have affected him.'

'Why are you in your pyjamas?' I asked.

'I told you, I just came out of bed. Why are you wearing a suit? Were you at a funeral? Did they ask you to bury the body too?'

'No, I was ... why would they?'

'So you were.'

'No. Why?'

'You are covered in mud. Look at the floor. Mum is going to kill you – that is, if she ever comes back.'

'Since when do you care about the kitchen floor?'

'Who is going to clean it if Mum doesn't come back?'

'Costa, this gentleman is an estate agent. He is looking at the house. You know that Mum and I have decided to sell it, right?'

As usual Costa did not pay any attention to me, and he went straight to the fridge. Then he moaned: 'Oh, no, didn't you sort out the electricity yet?'

'No, Costa, I am still waiting for the electrician to come and have a look. The wires are all old. Do you want to have some breakfast?'

'I thought we got cut off for non-payment.'

'Let me make you some breakfast.'

'Since when do you make me breakfast?'

'You don't look well, Costa. Are you all right?'

'Yes, I am. I just didn't sleep well. I had nightmares all night.'

'Oh, fine, go back to bed. We won't disturb you. Go, go on.'

'I even saw you in my nightmare.'

The agent smiled and said: 'Do you think I am having a nightmare too, with your dad in it?'

Then Costa said: 'It is really weird. You had a big fight with Mum, and then you wore my helmet and were walking around the room with it.'

Costa sat on a chair and put his head between his hands with his elbows resting on the table. The agent had frozen in his place.

'I thought you were going to see the house now. Why don't you start with Costa's room so he can then go and get some rest, without nightmares this time, hopefully.'

The agent was still at his frozen state. Suddenly he looked into my eyes and said: 'As I said before, then they expect us to look to you to tell us what is happening in our parliament.'

This was obviously getting to be too much to handle. He had no right to come to my house and criticize me, even if it was not going to be my house any more. So I asked: 'And what do you know about our parliament? Do you know more than me? Have you ever been there? Do you know how it looks?'

'No, I don't need to get in it to know what is going on. I know everything about the parliament because I spend my life out here in the street. I see the result.'

Costa got up and walked towards the kitchen door, saying: 'Come and look at my room if you want now. I am going to bed again. I have heard enough shouting for this week. I don't need any more.'

I looked at the agent, and he looked at me. I was expecting him to just leave, but he was standing in the middle of the kitchen, motionless. Costa had not gone for more than a minute before he came back in the kitchen and asked: 'Dad, do you know where my helmet is? It was on my desk by the window.'

'What do you need a helmet for, Costa? You don't even have a bike anymore.'

'I'd better go now,' said the agent.

'Aren't you going to look at my room?' Costa asked the agent.

He replied: 'No, it is okay. I don't think I can find a buyer for your house.'

'Are you sure?' asked Costa.

I was shocked to hear that and asked Costa: 'That's interesting. So you do care. As much as you put on that you don't give a shit about anyone else except yourself, inside you do care.'

'Dad, you have even sold my helmet. I don't care about the house. I want to know if he is coming to my room or not so I can lock my door.'

'I will go now. I have another appointment,' said the agent.

'No, I won't let you go, now that you think you know everything about politics. Stay! Come here and sit down.'

I grabbed him by his arm, pulled him towards the table, and sat him down. Then I did the same thing with Costas. He did not resist, perhaps because he was too tired. 'Now, tell us, Mr Agent ...'

Costa interrupted me, shouting: 'If you are going to force me to sit here, at least get this smelly fish away from me.'

I got up, put the fish in the sink, returned to the table, and continued: 'Tell us, Mr Agent who knows better than me, the journalist, whose job is to report everything, what is the source of our problems?'

Costa looked very confused. The agent was scratching his head, buying time. He seemed to be waiting for an opportunity to run out the door. I kept my eyes on him, pulled out a chair, and sat next to him, still looking at him.

Then he said: 'I didn't say I knew everything.'

'No, tell us.'

'Tell you what?'

'Where is the problem? Why have we got to this stage?'

'Look, I know why we have problems. But I wouldn't be able to explain a father stealing a helmet from his son. Most fathers I know buy helmets for their sons and force them to wear them.'

'Look, he doesn't even have a bike,' I said.

'So it is okay to steal his helmet?' asked the agent.

'I am asking questions now,' I said angrily. Costa put his head between his hands again, with his head this time hanging closer to the table.

'We are waiting,' I said.

'Okay, I will tell you. It is all your fault. You journalists, you don't tell us what we need to know.'

'What do you want me to report? That it is your fault? That it is the people's fault? Who is going to read it?'

'You should do your job correctly, even if no body reads it.'

'Good, the lying estate agent has now become the moral authority of the society and is telling everyone how to be ethical.'

'I learned to lie from you.'

'From me, the journalist?'

'No, from all of you. If you don't lie in this society, you can't survive; they know you lie, so they lie to you. We all live in a lying society.'

'Who are they?'

'They, I, you, he, she, it, us, they, them.'

'Very good, at least you speak Greek really well. You know your conjugation. Who is it who lies?'

'The government! They tell the biggest lies.'

'So you don't play a role?'

'I have to play my part too. Otherwise the whole thing will collapse. If a public sector employee does not accept bribes, he doesn't have money to share with the boss, and he becomes very unpopular.'

'The public sector employees do not all take bribes. I am talking about you, you as an agent. You are the ones who all lie.'

'When everyone lies the truth does not matter anymore. The lie becomes the truth, and everyone believes it.'

'Now you have lost me.'

'I haven't been to your parliament, but have you ever been to a property sale contract signing?'

'Yes, but I am hoping that you will take me to the next one, for the sale of my own house.'

'What was your name? Your first name?'

'Panos.'

'Panos, how many people lie about a contract?'

'I don't know, how many? How many are there?'

'Usually about seven.'

'So you want to tell me all seven lie?' I asked.

'No, it is eight. The government is lying too. You have the buyer, his lawyer, the seller, his lawyer, the notary, his secretary, and me, the agent. We all declare a lower price for the contract so it brings down the taxes. Otherwise the contract would not happen.'

'When does the government lie?'

'The government? The government doesn't really lie. It just forces unfair high taxes with the justification that everyone lies anyway. If they increased the fines on cheating and lowered the taxes to a realistic level, people would not lie anymore. But I guess nobody wants that.'

'Why not?'

'People like to think they are ahead of the game. They want to feel smart. Without cheating the system, they don't feel satisfied. If they follow the rules, even accidentally, they feel stupid. They feel like they are the ones who are being cheated. That's because the system cheats them.'

'How does the system cheat you?'

'In my industry, well, it doesn't do anything, anything at all. I don't feel good paying even one euro in taxes. What do they do for me?'

'What do you want them to do for you?'

'To promote me, to promote my business, to promote Greece. But they just take turns seizing power and promoting their own people and their own agents.'

'Estate agents?'

'No, their agents in every industry. Their own people. Nobody cares about the country as a whole. And all the money that is spent goes to waste.'

'What money?'

'Do you know how many hotels I have for sale?'

'So? We have a recession. Of course people are selling their hotels. There are fewer tourists.'

'We don't have problems with tourism. Fortunately, we live in one of the most beautiful countries in the world; we have tourists all the time.'

'So why are people selling their hotels?'

'Panos, these are hotels that are brand new. They haven't worked even for one day. This is all the money from the grants. People get grants to renovate old buildings with only one condition. The condition is that they have to run it as a hotel for five years.'

'So there is some obligation, right?'

'No, there is no obligation. Before they give the money they should make sure it is the right people who are applying for it. That means hotel owners with some history in the industry.'

'So who gets the grants?' 'Businessmen, their own people, and people who get tips whenever there is a grant. They apply for it in time and all of a sudden have all the qualifications. That is how you get businessmen who are hoteliers one day and then agriculturists the next. Then they start a factory, and then all of a sudden they are into recycling, the environment, solar energy, dog pounds – you name it and they are in.'

'Tell me about your industry. Tell me about the hotels. What happens after these businessmen receive the grants?'

'Okay, they get the money. They renovate a traditional building, turn it to a private villa, invite their friends over, and show off. Then after five years they sell it and send the money abroad.'

'At least they fix up an old ruin.'

'Nothing is fixed to be fixed and become useful. It is fixed if there is money in it, and then after it is fixed, it is abandoned or left in the shop window for show.'

'Shop window? What do you mean?'

'Sometimes I think our whole country has been turned into one of those Hollywood Western movie sets. Do you know the sets I am talking about? From the front you have a wall that shows saloons, bars, barber shops, stores, houses, and so on, but on the back there is nothing. We have made a whole nation which is as thick as those sets. Nothing functions. It is all for show, and even that we have built with borrowed money. In the end, now that we can't milk it anymore, we have abandoned it. It is the wild, wild West in Eastern Europe.'

'And to think that for all these years we were being played with.'

'Panos, we were not just being played with. We were also the players ourselves.'

'There is a main city theatre building near my land …'

'Do you have land for sale?'

'No, I am keeping that to build a hotel.'

'Are there any grants now?'

'No. Anyway, the theatre was built to last a century. Only a couple of decades later it is falling apart and needs to be replaced. They had spent so much money on it.'

'You mean they stole so much money from it.'

'Whatever. We were going there all these years to see a show, and now we know that the show was really on us. Maybe it is good that there are no more grants anymore.'

'How is that good? The damage is done. The money, our money that they took as taxes or from Europe, to promote the country and advance us, the money they took to use locally to bring in more tourists for my son and your son to have jobs, is used to make someone else rich.'

Costa moved his head a bit, looked at us, and again moved his head down towards the table and seemed to be going to sleep. 'Costa. Costa, wake up. Participate! Do something. This is about your country too. Listen.'

Costa moved his head a bit, looked around again, and went back to sleep on the table. Then the agent said: 'Leave him, leave him, let him sleep. With this country that we have left for them, they are better off being asleep and not knowing what we have done to them.'

'Why are you complaining? Legally or illegally, you are surviving. You are surely better off than me. At least you still have your house, your family,' I said before I was interrupted.

'How do you know what I have? I have lost a lot of time. I am too busy trying to survive, trying to keep afloat, trying to pay less taxes if I can, trying to avoid paying my workers' national security, my own national security, and pay less on gas.'

'Everyone is in the same position.'

'I have lost all my energy, all my time, and all my enthusiasm. With all the knowledge I have about my business, I should be involved in promoting real estate. I should be involved with tourism or something to help. But instead, I am being wasted.'

'If you know so much, why don't you do something, anything, even voluntarily?' I asked.

'Look, I don't know if you are being sarcastic now or not, and I am not saying that I can help to change anything. But for my part, I have something to offer, and I don't have a place to offer it. They don't let me. They don't let you. We are just stock.'

'Who are they?'

'I don't know. It is everybody. They don't want change. Nobody wants anything to change. As soon as there is an idea, a little hope, everyone tries to kill it. Panos, sometimes I feel like everybody keeps moaning about everything, but inside, in their hearts, they want it to stay like this. They think that they have the upper hand and that if things change they will come out of it worse than before.'

'How can it be worse?'

'I don't know. Everyone has got something they think they have won by cheating and lying. Everyone feels they are the smart one. They think if it changes, they will lose the possessions they have cheated out of the system, and if the possessions go, so goes their pride. They can't boast anymore about how smart they were.'

'What do you mean by possessions? You mean houses?'

'No, anything. It doesn't have to be an object. It doesn't have to be gold or silver or an expensive car. It could be just a job, a position, an influential power.'

'Like the public sector?'

'Yes, all you need in this society to feel privileged is to be in the public sector or have someone in it. You tell me now, who in their right mind, if they feel privileged, would want anything to change? And so they don't let anything happen. I had foreign investors who wanted to invest millions of euros in a marine park, a park that could bring a lot of cash to the country and provide tens of jobs. I put three months of my life trying to help them. We found the right place. They even paid from their own pockets to get all the preliminary paperwork. All they wanted before the contract was to make sure they would get the permit to get a business license if they made the investment.'

'Don't tell me, they didn't give them the license.'

'License? What license? They didn't even get an answer.'

'How?'

'Panos, after spending a day in the queues they were told that in order to get an answer they had to buy the whole hundred thousand square meters and then fill out the relevant forms.'

'There were queues for this kind of investment in Greece?'

'Yes, there were a lot of people in the queues but for a different kind of an investment.'

'Like what?'

'The lady in the queue in front of us wanted to convert her goat shed to a kiosk.'

'Did she get the license?'

'I don't know. Who cares? That's why you are not a good reporter, Panos. You always look at irrelevant facts.'

'I know what I am asking. Don't worry. You are just giving me the worst examples here. I have seen work being done, buildings going up. It is not all for waste.'

'I had another situation where the municipality spent a lot of money renovating one of their own unused buildings in a village, and …'

'What is wrong with that? What were they going to do with it, build a hotel?'

'Yes, how do you know?'

'I told you, I am a reporter. I know how to ask questions to get to the point. So what is wrong with that?'

'Nothing. The ruin is in a big peninsula with breathtaking views, all the way from the beginning to the very end. You have views of the sea from the top of the mountain all the way down to the sea at every level.'

'That is good.'

'Except that this particular ruin is probably the only house in the remote village without a sea view because there is a hill in front of it. Needless to say, the hotel has not rented even one room since it opened, and needless to say, it has since closed down.'

'Whose is it?'

'I told you, it belongs to the municipality.'

'Well, at least they got work for a few months for some of the local builders.'

'No, they didn't. They could get more money from another grant for additional expenses not directly related to the building. They brought workers from another area so they could charge for their transport and accommodation.'

'Where did they stay?'

'In a hotel belonging to one of the relatives of the officials. Please don't ask if it had a sea view. I won't answer.'

'You are getting me depressed. Aren't you going to see the house?'

'You know, Panos, I think this is a part of a big strategy. They just don't want Greece to grow because they will end up losing their own power. In the same peninsula, there are some of the most beautiful beaches in the Mediterranean. Instead of giving proper building permits to make worthy resorts, do you know what they do?'

'What?'

'You know, in the past people didn't like living near the beach. Salt is no good for agriculture. There were also pirates.'

'I don't want to hear about pirates.'

'Are you scared of them, from childhood?'

'Never mind.'

'Anyway, there were no villages, or as they call it, residential areas, near the beach. Now, instead of giving proper planned permits to people to create resorts for the world to come and admire us and spend money, do you know what they do?'

'Is this going to be a long story?'

'No. Do you know what they do? They say because it is not a residential area you have no permit to build. And do you know what people do?'

'What?'

'They build illegally. And do you know what happens when you build illegally?'

'Look, you are not selling me a house. Just get on with your story. Stop asking me questions.'

'Fine. When people have no building permit, they build clandestinely and with cheap material, because they are not sure if the building will ever be legal and will last. And then, do you know what they do? Oh, sorry, you don't like questions. The authorities tell people with illegal buildings to come and legalize their ugly sheds and pay a fine. This is Greece today. This is what we are worth. The nation works on fines, fines that the generations to come will pay forever. The end result is that they destroy our beautiful land so that the authorities can get fines and use the fines to pay their salaries. And our beaches, the most beautiful in the world, end up being like the slums of the third world: a group of sheds, without town planning, without proper roads or an electric network. Instead of a world-class resort we end up with …'

'Shit, and we have made it with our own hands.'

'I thought you didn't like to answer!'

'I don't want to fall asleep like Costa.'

'Anyway, with our own hands, with our own feet, by using excuses like protecting the environment, and by collecting fines or bribes, we give license, indirectly, to turn our best beaches into slums. This will happen for as long as the authorities, who are on fixed salaries, come tourists or not, have full control. Think about it. If they give the go-ahead to major work involving international organizations which come with plans with targets, with visions to build and develop, what power would the little paper pushers in the ministries have?'

'Yeah, you are right.'

'Another time, there was this big plan to make a five-star hotel with a marina and a golf course.'

'Okay, make this the last story.' Costa opened his eyes, looked at us, and went to sleep again.

'They stopped it.'

'Why?'

'The place used to be a rubbish dump before. It was at the beginning of a forested peninsula.'

'Let me guess, the forestry department stopped it.'

'No, the forested area was already divided up by the government between public sector workers at the time. The area where they wanted to build the hotel, the rubbish dump, is without a tree. It's completely dry and without any plants.'

'So why did they want to build a hotel there?'

'Once cleaned up it is a beautiful spot, right by the sea looking into the sunset. Do you know who stopped it?'

'The archaeology department?'

'No, you were right the first time. It was the forestry department.'

'Why did you say no first?'

'Why should we be the only ones who have to guess what you are trying to tell us in your newspapers?'

I started laughing loudly, maybe just to make enough noise to get Costa up. Maybe I needed some relief from all these depressing stories, or maybe it was just funny. The result of my laughter, however, was good. Costa woke up again. He rubbed his eyes and asked: 'Are we telling jokes?'

'No, there is nothing funny about any of this. This is the tragedy of our lives,' said the agent.

'What are you trying to tell me, that we are all cheats? That there is no Greek who cares? There is nobody who works with honesty and dignity?' I asked.

'Oh, there are many Greeks who want to work with honesty and dignity, but they don't fit here. They have been kicked out of the workforce altogether. You can find them either working abroad or waiting in the unemployment benefit queues here.'

'No one else?'

'Today, it seems that the only ones who care, who really want change, are the extreme right.'

'And the youth, our children – they don't care? Aren't they fighting?'

'Well, your child is half asleep right in front of you. The smart ones, as I said, have already left the country looking for jobs abroad, and the revolutionary ones are out in the streets painting over traffic signs in protest, causing more death and misery.'

'And the right-wing party, what are they doing?'

'I am not a sympathizer. I am just telling you why people get to a stage that they don't believe in anything anymore and want to uproot everything.'

'So you agree with them, with them blaming everything on the foreigners?'

'Yes, I do. In my business I see a lot. I think we should do something really radical, just like the ultra-right says: kick all the foreigners out. The only difference I have with the ultra-right is my definition of a foreigner.'

'What is your definition of a foreigner?'

'It is anyone whose existence and actions do not contribute anything to the country. It is certainly not the Albanians. They have worked with me, building houses. Even if they don't want to pay taxes, they can't avoid it; it is required of them so they can stay here. I know some who paid their social security fees out of their own pockets when they were out of work, just so they could stay in the country. But when there was work, they were always working. They worked so much and so hard that they changed our language. Up to a few years ago instead of saying "do" or "make", as in, "make a stick to put next to that tree", people used to say, "get an Albanian to put a stick next to that tree".'

'I am a bit lost. So who are the real foreigners to you?'

'All the people who abused the social security money, abused the subsidies, made false claims for disability, and wasted their time instead of working whilst getting paid. All those families who claimed money for funeral expenses but did not report the death in order to carry on getting the pensions, and all those who were getting paid to check all this but were out for coffee during their work time and let all these atrocities continue. They were all dead people at work who were paying the dead.'

'What?'

'To me whoever does not do his job right is dead to the society.'

'You are exaggerating now.'

'Exaggerating? Do you know we are the only country in the world that has registered blind taxi drivers who are on disability benefit? These are the foreigners, the blind taxi drivers who looted our country, not the ones who came here to work.'

'At least we can send back all the Albanians to Albania. Where are we going to send the looters?' I commented.

Costa opened his eyes again and said: 'Lootestan.'

The agent smiled and asked Costa: 'So what do you think is the problem? What is your name?'

Costa, still rubbing his eyes, said: 'Costa. I don't know. I think we talk too much. We don't do anything. We know so much that we just talk. It is always easier to talk than do anything.'

'You mean we philosophize too much?' I asked Costa, trying to encourage him to talk, but he went quiet again. I continued: 'All developed, intelligent people think and philosophize, and the world learned it from us.'

My attempt was still unsuccessful. Costa was not sleeping anymore but stayed quiet. He looked like he was daydreaming. I asked again: 'What happened to your girlfriend?'

Costa did not answer. The agent was sitting looking at us, seeming to enjoy my struggle to get a word out of Costa. I tried again: 'Why don't you tell us a joke? You are good at that. Make it a political one.'

This time he did not hesitate and asked quickly: 'Can I make it a philosophical one?'

'Yes, whatever you want. Just sit up properly. This is no time to sleep for a young person like you. You must have been asleep all day.'

Then he started talking: 'A group of Greek university students take their tent and go camping with a foreign student from their class. After they cook on an open fire and eat, they all go to sleep. In the middle of the night the foreign student wakes up and says: "Oh no, I can see stars." All the Greek students wake up, complaining about how he woke them up. So the foreign student asks them what seeing the stars meant to everyone. One Greek guy says, "This tells me that Greece has the most beautiful and clear sky in the world." The other one says, "This tells me we may be the most intelligent beings in the universe, but we are not alone." Another one says, "This means to me that there must be a creator who has made all of this." The foreign student stays quiet, and then one of the Greek guys says, "You are the one who woke us up for this. What do you see when you look at the stars?" The foreign student says: "Somebody has stolen our tent.'"

Both the agent and myself were in deep thought. We were not laughing.

Costa asked: 'Do you see me well, or is it too dark?'

'It is too dark. I can't see you well,' I replied.

'That means I should leave. I am going to Grandma's. You guys stay here and talk a bit more. Maybe you will get somewhere.' And with that he got up and left, leaving me and the agent in the dark.

Chapter 14

THE STRONG RAYS of sunshine woke me up. It was Sunday, and I was all alone in the house. The first thing I did was to try to turn on the light to see if there was any electricity. With my fingertip, I pressed the switch half-heartedly. The act was so gentle and effortless that halfway through I had time to mock my own endeavour. Having no electricity, having no family, and having no one to talk to is not like a wound; it does not heal by itself. This was not a kind of darkness in which one could hide or find comfort.

What was I doing in that house, anyway? Why was I still there? Why was I somewhere that nobody needed me and, worse than that, where I was not even wanted? Every second in the house was a punishment to me. A punishment for what, I did not know. My presence there was pushing me away from the very people to whom I was trying to stay close. I had no choice. I could stay a bit longer and play my cards, in the hope that I would get lucky and something would change. Life is truly like a poker game; it seems that you can always bluff your way through. You can bluff with money or even without money, but what you can't do is bluff without any cards. I had no cards left to play. It was time to go.

From the moment I made the decision to leave, I was even more uncomfortable in my own house. As soon as I confirmed with Pavlos that he was still expecting me and got directions to his house, I was on the road. I needed to be with someone positive, someone who dared to fight for his rights, someone who had hope. As a union leader, Pavlos was the perfect partner, a man of action, daring, and hope.

I should have really bought a gift for him, but my last money, the money that I had won in the casino, went into filling the car with gas.

I had never been to that part of the city. The neighbourhoods started looking a bit better. There were more trees, more parking spaces, and more parks. On the side of the pavement, half-filled big black rubbish bags caught my attention. I slowed down a bit. There was a bag every twenty meters. They seemed to have been left on the side of the road to be picked up later, maybe the next day, on Monday. Then I saw some people cutting the grass and filling up the bags. It was not rubbish after all; it was grass. I reached the next crossroad. While waiting for the green light I had a thought, a brilliant thought. What was mentioned as a joke to Pavlos could save all embarrassment for me. Now I could go to his house with at least something valuable for him: food for his horses! I did not wait for the light to change. There were no cars behind me, so I backed into an alley, turned around, and went back to the park, stopping at the first half-filled bag, which by now had some workers around it.

'Good morning,' I said as I got out of the car. I received a cold reply. They seemed not to be happy to be working. So I went closer and asked: 'Excuse me, do you need these? Are they grass?'

'What are you going to do with them? Make soup for your kids?' asked one worker, and then they all started laughing.

I forced myself to fake a smile and said: 'No, for horses. They eat this, right?'

The same person answered: 'I don't know, they are your horses. Horses eat anything if they are hungry.'

'Can I take as many as I want?'

I heard no clear answer, so I went to pick up a bag. It was a strong, thick plastic bag, but as I had noticed before, it was only half filled.

'Shall I wait till you fill it up?'

'No, we won't fill those up any more'.

'Why not?'

'It is against the union laws.'

'Union laws? What do you mean?'

'It is bad for our backs. They shouldn't be too heavy.'

'But these aren't heavy at all.'

'Look, if you don't want them, don't take them. The truck will come soon and pick them up.'

'The truck comes today? How come you are working today?'

I heard no answer, so I started picking up the bags one by one, managing about four at a time. I opened my boot and started throwing the bags in the back. As I was getting further from the car, I noticed in the distance a truck stopping and some other people getting off. They were collecting the bags, four or five at a time, and throwing them in the truck. The truck driver came out of the truck, stood on a corner, and lit a cigarette. I couldn't go to Pavlos with only a dozen of the half-filled bags. That would hardly be enough to make an impression and probably not be enough for his horses. So I started running towards the men picking up the bags. The driver looked at me as he puffed on his cigarette.

I got closer to him and asked: 'Can I take the bags? I have horses.'

He nodded at me and shouted at the men picking the bags: 'Stop, kids, stop. Leave them.'

'I hope you don't mind.'

'Why should we mind? We don't get paid by the number of the bags. Take as many as you want. It is easier for us,' he said with a smile.

'Why are these bags so thick?'

'They are the expensive industrial ones, for branches. Otherwise they would rip.'

'But you are cutting grass now!'

'That's the last thing we need to have, several kinds of bags to have to choose from every morning depending on what they send us to slave away at.'

'How come you are working today, anyways? It is Sunday.'

'You see me working?'

'Well, you are here.'

'I am the driver. The kids do all the work.'

'So you sit and wait till they finish?'

'Well, somebody has to take them to the next park. I can't go home.'

'No, I mean, you don't help them?'

'I told you, I am the driver. I couldn't even help them if I wanted to. They would kick me out of the union.'

'How come your union lets you work on Sunday? Nobody works on Sundays.'

'Everybody works on Sundays when the money is good.'

'Oh I see, so you don't have a day off?'

'No, I did. I have been sitting on my ass all week. There was no work at all.'

'But the grass was … never mind.'

'Look, if you want I can tell the kids to take the bags to your car. Just give them a few euros, and they will be happy.'

'No, thanks. I just need a few more, and I will be gone.'

'Fine, as you wish. We are here to help.'

This time, being threatened with having to pay, I managed to collect not four but six bags on my shoulder and walked to the car. After that, I picked up another few. By then my car was full, perhaps with more plastic than grass, but the gesture was alive. I was going to Pavlos with something to offer.

Pavlos's villa was less impressive than I had thought. For one thing, it wasn't even finished. It was halfway up a hill on a big piece of land, and the view – well, I couldn't see the view from the mirror as I was going up the hill. My view to the back was completely blocked by the giant plastic bags. I knew I had entered the grounds to the right house, but I was having difficulty finding the entrance door. I drove all the way to the end of the house. There seemed to be an entrance, but that could not possibly be the main entrance. It seemed small and abandoned. I reversed and drove back to the start. At the beginning of the house, right at the entrance, facing a neighbour's house, there was a bigger gate with a proper arch. Obviously that was where the entrance would be. One problem was solved. But where would I put the grass? I looked around for the horses, but there were no horses in sight. I didn't want to make a big deal out of the grass. That would be too cheap. I just wanted to get rid of the bags in a corner out of the way. So I started looking around for a place to put all the bags, somewhere where it wouldn't rain on them. What better place than the little space at the other end, I thought. It would be tucked away and out of sight. Who, with such a villa, wants so much ugly plastic visible to his visitors? I drove up again and put all the bags in the little gap between the walls. The bags covered the hole completely.

After I finished shoving the bags in their place, I decided to leave the car up there and walk to the main entrance. I looked around. The garden was big. There seemed to be a stable in one corner, a big hole near the house, and some construction material spread around. I entered the big archway and was looking for a doorbell. The archway was all in marble, and I expected to see an impressive, giant gate to enter the house. Instead, there was a wall made with cement blocks. The marble archway and the cement wall reminded me of the dream that I had the other night about the structure made with half mud and straw and half shiny marble.

I begin looking for a doorbell without paying any attention to the fact that there was no door. Just then I heard someone shouting. The noise was coming from the other side of the house. It was Pavlos shouting, but the voice was muffled. As I got out of the archway, I could hear Pavlos a bit better. He was shouting and cursing, but where was the voice coming from? I started running towards the car where I had hid the grass bags. By the time I got to the other end I could hear him much more clearly. The voice was coming from behind the bags. Some of the bags on the top were moving. Finally, one bag fell on the ground in front of me, and Pavlos's head popped out from in between the bags.

He looked at me in disbelief and shouted: 'What on earth are you doing? What is all this shit? Why are you blocking my door?'

'I brought you some horse food.'

'Why have you blocked my entrance?'

'Where are your horses?'

'Why have you blocked my entrance?'

'Your entrance is down there. What are you doing here in this hole?'

'This is my temporary entrance now. What are you, from the planning department?'

'Where are the horses?'

'I don't have any horses now. Have you become an investigator, Panos? What is wrong with you? Come and help me out of here. Take these bags away.'

'I brought them some food. I asked you before.'

'I don't see any food.'

'You don't have any horses anyway,' I said as I helped him remove the bags.

'So because I have no horses you brought me these plastic bags?' he said, pushing the bags away as he got out.

'Why is your entrance here? It is much better down there. That's where the archway is.'

'Didn't you notice the cement wall?'

'Was the cement wall there before you built the archway?'

'No, why would I build an archway around a cement wall?'

'I don't know. You are the one who did the building.'

'You don't understand. I am waiting till I get my permanent electricity. Then I will open it up.'

'You don't have any electricity either?'

'I have temporary electricity. Stop asking questions.'

'Why?'

'Panos, were you born yesterday? I couldn't get a permit to have my entrance at the other end, but that's where I want it. I have my entrance here now till I finalize the building and get my final electricity confirmed. Then I will close this one and open the other one. Is this so hard to understand? What I want to know is why you have brought all these bags to my house. If you wanted to bring me horse food ...'

'It is your fault.'

'How on earth is this my fault?'

'You are a union leader, right? You forced through laws that workers should not lift up filled bags.'

'You don't understand. What is wrong with that? We should protect the workers. What if one of them is sick or has a backache? Should we not consider him or her? A kind society should always look after its weakest members.'

'Pavlos, what is the point of sending a guy with a back problem to the weight lifting competitions in the Olympics and then begging them to give him lighter weights. Send the guy with the back pain to another sport.'

'What? What sport?'

'I don't know – shooting or chess. Something that doesn't involve his back.'

'Listen, my dear Panos. From experience I can advise that there are significant and sensitive particularities in each working circumstance that must be carefully considered. Any consequential decisions resulting from these considerations must be in the spirit of the protection of the most precious and valuable, but also most vulnerable, members of society, the working class.'

'I know, you have told me all this before. Tell me something new. You still can't win the Olympics with these slogans.'

'A minute ago you didn't even know how a house was built in Greece. Now you are lecturing me on how to do my job as a unionist? All of a sudden you have become a labour consultant? It is not the Olympics here. People's health is at risk in the factories. Nobody is even trying to win. Nobody wins.'

'Except you, who wins by hurting the nation. Can you not see the waste right in front of you?'

'Look, Panos, when I pushed for the law the workers were in favour of it. That is why they voted for me. It sounded good. I didn't know that years later an idiot would gather the bags up and stack them up in front of my home.'

'Your home is first of all your country. It is Greece, not this temporary hole.'

'What has happened to you, Panos? You have changed so much. What makes you think you know what is best for the country? Your job is just to write articles that people may like to read in order to sell advertising. How dare you speak to me like that? I am the one who is the union leader, not you.'

'What has changed in me? Nothing has changed.'

'Are you sure? Maybe it is the missus. Maybe she is the one who is busting your balls. That is women for you; it is all their fault.'

'I am all right. It is not the missus. I don't care about her anymore.'

'Then what is the matter?'

'I don't know. I am impatient now, about everything. Maybe you are right. Maybe I used to write to sell advertising but, but now ...'

'But now you are going to lose that too. You are going to lose your job, Panos. If you go on like this you will. You have to find out what is causing it.'

'What is causing it? Do you live in another country? Can't you see what is happening to our nation?'

'Oh, give me a break, Panos. Can't you see what is happening to our country?' He repeated the question, imitating my voice, and then he continued: 'There are certain things you don't understand. A successful society is a society that takes best care of its weakest members. A minority, a disadvantaged group, should not feel disadvantaged. This applies to the laws we pass for rubbish collectors and gardeners. Everyone in the society must feel they can do that job. Then they have a choice of doing it or not, but the state should provide the result.'

'The result is the clean street and the manicured garden, not the provision of jobs.'

'There are certain things you don't understand. A chain is as strong as its weakest link; you should concentrate on your weakest link so the whole chain does not break.'

'A chain has to be only as strong as it needs to be for the job it is intended to do. When you make every chain as strong as you can, it becomes bulky and useless. If someone can't do their job we should bring in the more capable and give them a chance.'

'Why are you so worried about the people outside, Panos?'

'People outside?'

'The unemployed. It is the people who are working who are the union members; it is them whom we need to protect. It is them who need us so that their life gets better. The unemployed have nothing to lose. They don't listen to us as much. They betray us in the end because they are hungry. They have no loyalty to our causes. Hunger makes you selfish. I don't trust the unemployed.'

'The unemployed and the youth are Greek too. Who thinks of them? Who thinks of all the Greeks instead of just the people who may vote for you?'

'You don't understand, Panos. Greece does not vote for me. The next generations don't vote for me. Because of our negative population growth, the majority of the country is old. They are the ones who are getting benefits. They are the ones who are collecting a pension. I have to take care of them before I worry about the youth and the next generations. I have to make sure their pockets are full. That's the only way I can stay in power and fight for the cause of the workers and the nation as a whole.'

'And the future of our country?'

'You don't understand, Panos. When Greece is doing well and investing in the future, that means the Greeks, today, aren't doing well. When Greeks are getting paid and have long holidays and their table is full, they are happy. That is when the Greeks are doing well.'

'All this for you to have power and position?'

'Panos, you don't understand. Our country has always been like this. You just didn't know. Why weren't you like this a year ago? I am telling you, it is the wife. Tell me what else has changed. Okay, you have less money now. So what?'

'It is not just the money, Pavlos.'

'It is the wife, Panos.'

'You know, Pavlos, it is like the plastic bags.'

'My fault again? Are we back to that conversation now?'

'No, no, Pavlos. There is no conversation. All the problems of my country were annoying and hurting me all along but they were there, in the distance. I lived with them when they were out there. And now they have come home to me. They have all gathered around my neck. All that plastic that we created ourselves is around our necks, and it is choking us.'

'Take it easy, Panos. Come on, come on, let's get inside. Come and have a drink. For God's sake, come. You need a drink. I need a drink.'

'Are you sure you want me to come in?'

'Why not? You came in to stay, right? Come on, let's have a drink; I will forgive you for the plastic bags if you forgive the nation for all its faults. Is that a deal?' he asked as he pulled my arm and walked me through the plastic bags to his house.

The living room was big; it looked like it had been designed to host big parties. It had a bar at one end about twice the size of our kitchen. There were three sofa sets spread around the room and a large patio with tropical plants in between them. The house was cold, and the round, open fireplace in the middle of the room had no wood in it. From one end of the hall you could see the entire city, giving you a sense of power and control.

'This is big,' I said.

'Yes, I had to make it big.'

'You had to? Because of your wife?'

'No, why do you blame everything on women?'

'Me?'

'I have to always be aware of my position and image. In the political circles, I must be an accommodator, sort of a host that everyone feels comfortable with. I can't be too harsh to politicians but must look powerful, in control, and effective. After all, it is me who is representing the interests of the most valuable and vulnerable members of the society. They have to see that I am in a position of influence. That is when they trust me with their future.'

'Trust you? For their future?'

'You don't understand how sensitive my position is. I have to always be alert in defending people's rights, not just when it is necessary and not just when it becomes urgent. You see, Panos, rights are rights. They should always be defended, even if we at times feel we don't need them.'

'All that for the size of the living room?'

'Well, I just wanted you to know that it is not my wife's fault that the living room is so big. I am planning on having conferences and seminars here.'

'With the workers or the politicians?'

'What do I have to say to the workers? They already know I am on their side. They have selected me. Anyway, enough with politics. I am at home now, not at work. Let's have a drink.'

'At this time of the day?'

'I work at odd hours and party when I want. Didn't you see me at three o'clock in the morning at the Bouzoukia?'

'Which one was that?'

'The name of the place?'

'No, I mean, was the Bouzoukia work or party?'

'Panos, you are a smart man. I think you know the answer to that. What would I be doing having a party with your boss?'

'I thought you were friends.'

'Tell, me what is your drink? What do you want?'

'Without ice.'

'What?'

'Without ice, whatever. Do you want me to get you some wood?'

'Is it going to be like the horse food, does it come in bags? No, thanks. I've got some wood in the garage in the back of the house, if you want to help go get it. The garage is in the back. I have to hide it for a while.'

'No, really, I can get you some wood. I have a big piece of land in the forest. I get so much wood, I don't know what to do with it.'

'Okay, fine. How long are you staying?'

'What, you want me to go now?'

'Don't be silly. Of course not. You bring the wood. I will supply the whiskey and the bed.'

'Thanks. Is that fine with your wife?'

'Panos, you naughty boy, don't tell me you want me to supply the women too.'

'No, really, is it okay with your wife if I stay here?'

'Who gives a shit? She is not even here.'

'Did she leave you too?'

'No, stupid, I sent her away to get some breathing space. Here is your whiskey without ice.'

'Where is she?'

'I usually hide her from men who have lost theirs.'

'I haven't lost my wife; she has gone to her mum's for a few days.'

'I thought you had an argument.'

'Oh, yes, that too.'

'My wife is in Massachusetts. You know where that is? That is where the best universities are in America. She has gone to help my daughter settle in her new apartment. The last one was too small for her.'

'Why? Is she going to have conferences too? Why is your daughter in America?'

'She is in a university, doing her degree in business administration.'

'Yes, my son is doing that.'

'Your son? He is in the States?'

'No. I mean, he is not in the United States, but he is preparing for it.'

'How do you prepare for going to a university in the United States?'

'I don't know. It is very difficult. We don't have a big living room.'

'We all have to do what we can for our children, everyone at their own capacity. Why don't you send him to learn a useful skill? Maybe he will find a job in a factory.'

'You must know some factories.'

'Of course. That is my job. I know them all, but they have mostly closed down now.'

'It must be difficult for you too.'

'Oh no, I still get paid. Nobody can take my position as a union leader away from me. But yes, I do have a lot of free time. I can't wait till my daughter starts her classes so I can help her.'

'Help her in what? Are you an academic too?'

'What academics, Panos? Let's be serious now. What they learn in the universities is all theory. We are talking about real life, here on planet Earth. Do you know how many years I have sweated in the factories, dealing with business, payments, workers' rights, courts – you name it. If there is anything worth knowing in business, I know it.'

'So you are going to help your daughter with her degree?'

'Of course I am. I am the one who knows how to keep things running and keep the workers happy. I am not going to waste all this knowledge and retire completely, just because of the fucking economy.'

'What do you think your daughter will do when she finishes her education?'

'Well, the way things are now in Greece, I think she will just stay and get her master's too.'

'Master's? That's great. And after that do you think she will come and work in Greece? Or you think she will get a doctorate too?'

'I don't know. You are now talking about years away. You know, if things were a bit better in Greece, maybe she would come and work here, but I don't see it. There is no business left in this country. They have even moved all the factories out of this country. Where is she going to work? You know, Panos, hopefully by then she will be married. If she wants she can find a job there.'

'Where?'

'In America, where else? Between you and me, I think we will go there too. My wife is looking into it already. Have some whiskey. Stop asking questions. You are not at work now.'

I had a sip of the whiskey and said: 'I am not used to drinking at this time of the morning.'

'Who said it is morning? Look, Panos, one thing you have to understand is that everything depends on you. If you are rich and powerful, everything is in your hands. It can be morning or night as you wish, but first you must get there.'

And with that he drank his entire glass in one go and continued: 'You like the whiskey? This is not the urine they serve you at the Bouzoukia. This is eighteen years old. It is a gift, you know from whom?'

'Who?'

'Oh, never mind. Someone important, a politician. Drink it! Drink it before I physically force you.'

As soon as I finished the drink he filled up my glass again. I didn't know if I could have any more alcohol, aged or not aged. A mobile phone started ringing. Not knowing if it was mine or his, I put my hand in my pocket to get my phone.

'Don't worry, Panos, it is mine. You see what I mean? They don't leave me alone. And you think I have a lot of free time on my hands!'

'Hello, hello. Of course, sure. I will arrange it. Of course, I won't forget. Yes, I will. Please thank him for the nice gesture. Tell him we must have a drink soon.'

He closed the phone, looked at me, and smiled. His phone rang again. He looked at the number and said: 'I have to take this in my office. Come on, drink it!'

I drank a bit more. He asked the caller to hold, refilled my glass again, and went to another room. I waited for a while. He did not come back. I went to the garden, collected all the grass bags, and put them back in my car to take away.

When I came back, the coffee table had half dozen small plates of food on it. There was some dried bread, olives, a couple of tomatoes, and more drinks. Pavlos was sitting on the coach still talking on the phone. As I walked in the room he invited me to sit next to him with a hand gesture. Without hesitation I sat next to him and started eating. We ate and drank for hours, being interrupted only by his mobile phone, which was ringing every few minutes. I had started feeling a bit drunk. Pavlos did not look much better than me, and I don't know how he kept answering the calls. I could not understand what he was talking about anymore. When he finished with one of the calls I asked him: 'So where are your horses Pavlos? Was that a show-off? A lie? You said you had horses.'

'What? Show-off? Do you want to see their stable? Come, let's go out. I will show you.'

He then grabbed my hand and started pulling me off the couch. I felt dizzy as I got up and said: 'No, Pavlos, it is cold. I believe you.' I sat down again.

'Why should I have any horses?'

'You told me you have.'

'Yes, I did, but they stopped the grants. What am I, stupid, to keep feeding them? Do you know how much they eat?'

'Grants? What grants?'

'Look, I like horses. I have always liked to have horses – okay, maybe not so much the Thessaliki skinny red ones they used to give money for. But with no money at all, it is not possible.'

'What grants?'

'They used to pay a grant for the preservation of local breeds. The money was not enough, but I used to claim for more horses than I had, so it was okay.'

'How many did you have?'

'Two.'

'How many did you claim for?'

'It doesn't matter. What is up? Are you investigating me again?'

'No, just wondering. What happened then?'

'Nothing. The fucking authorities changed. I didn't know the new guys. They were from the other party. I might get some horses later. There might be new funding. I will find out about it.'

'I see.'

'These new guys who are running the show with these grants are completely useless. Watch it now. If they have any of their relatives working in a factory somewhere and need something, then they will come running to me and alert me of any new grants. You see, that is people for you. They only come to you when they need you.'

'I see.'

'Is that it?'

'What?'

'Any more questions, or are you done for the day?' he said sarcastically.

I didn't answer. So he asked, sounding as if he were getting drunker by the minute: 'Panos, Panos, are you all right? You look drunk. I asked you if you have any more questions.'

'No, I am fine. Wait, yes.'

'What?'

'You are a union, right?'

'I am, yes. No, I am not a union. I am a union leader. You don't know what you are talking about.'

'I mean, you are a union leader, right?'

'Yes, I am now. But I will become a politician after I become a government inspector.'

'Okay, so, let me get this right. You are supposed to be … I mean, you are left, right?'

'Right, I am left.'

'So how come you are with the conservative party now?'

'What?'

'What party are you with, Pavlos?'

'Panos, there is only one party.'

'Which one is that?'

'Pavlos.'

'What?'

'Pavlos.'

'I know who you are … Oh, I see.'

'There is only one party, and that is my own party. I have to take care of myself and my family first and then worry about ideology. Panos, Panos.'

'What? I hear you.'

'There is no right and left anymore anyways. It is all the same shit. We are all Europeans, and since we owe them money we have to see what they want. See what party they are with.'

'So why do we have elections?'

'To make sure we are democratic.'

'Just that?'

'That and also to make sure my party, the Pavlos party, can get a position with influence so I don't end up in the street like you.'

His phone rang again, but he did not answer it this time.

'What is wrong, Pavlos? I thought you were getting important calls today. Why don't you answer?'

'I have to sound serious on the phone. Am I sounding serious now? Why don't you get any phone calls? We are having an election soon. You are supposed to be a fucking reporter. Why do you get a day off and I don't?'

'Because I am free. You know, I am not like you. I don't have to answer if I don't want to. I am a freelance journalist now. Do you know what that means?'

'Oh, he played that game with you too?'

'Who?'

'Nikos, your boss.'

'I asked for it. I said enough is enough. I am my own boss now. I could be very busy if I wanted to be. I have turned my phone off because it is Sunday and I am at a friend's house now. You see?'

His phone rang again. Finally he answered. This was a short call; someone had called to ask him for someone else's phone number. He said to the caller: 'Okay, okay, I must go now. I am very busy. You know how it is before elections. My workload doubles. Everyone is trying to find me. Make sure you tell him I gave you his number, okay? Talk to you soon. Call me back next week and tell me how it went. I need something from you too. Okay, don't forget. Bye, bye, good-bye.'

He closed the phone, poured some more whiskey in my glass, and said: 'I hate this. They forget you for years, and then right before elections they remember you exist. I tell you, these politicians are such bastards, all of them.'

'A politician? That was a politician? Which one?'

'Well, not yet. He wants to be a politician.'

'When he grows up?' I asked, laughing.

'No, he is thinking of running. That's why he needs me. So, Panos, you are now a freelance journalist and still don't get any phone calls, even before elections.'

'I told you, I, I get so many that I, I … close my phone. I really have. I changed my phone, I mean the SIM card. If I put my original SIM card in, you will hear so many messages. I get a lot.'

'Why don't you? Maybe there is someone important looking for you. For God's sake, Panos, you are supposed to be a reporter. At least act like one. If you can't milk the politicians-to-be now, when can you? They need you now. It is the only time a politician listens, before the elections.'

Without answering I considered his suggestion, but not because I was hoping to get a call from a politician. They wouldn't call me anyway. The phone was now completely useless; I carried it around just like little girls carry around a lady's purse which is full of nothing, just to pretend that they have something valuable in it. Nobody important was going to call me on that phone, not even my wife or kids. As I hesitantly changed the SIM card to prove a point, I considered how embarrassing it would be if I had no missed calls or messages. There must be something from some bank, a law firm, or the phone company.

Pavlos asked: 'When was the last time you checked your messages? Why don't you have two phones?'

'I don't want to carry around two phones. Two SIM cards are enough. I am just changing the card. You will see now.'

I moved as slowly as possible, trying to buy myself some time. Maybe his phone would ring, and then he would forget about the entire thing. The whiskey had not helped. Maybe it had gotten me drunk, but it had not given me enough courage to make a fool of myself.

'I need to go to the toilet first,' I said desperately.

'Well, change the card first. It takes time for all the messages to come through if you have many.'

It was as if he were playing with me, as if he knew already there would be no messages. Like a football player whose team is ahead and in the last minutes of the game keeps falling down, I was trying to find any excuse to waste more time. So I said: 'Okay, I will do it now, but at least give me more whiskey. Oh yes, can you get me some ice?'

'I thought you don't take ice. What happened? It is on the table. Help yourself. Are you waiting for me to give you whiskey? I opened the bottle for you. Go for it.'

'Do you want me to go and get more ice, or is there enough in there?' I asked.

He was looking straight at me. He was either suspicious of me or more drunk than I had thought. I finally changed the SIM card. He moved his head closer to my phone, but there was complete silence.

'I just checked my phone an hour ago. Maybe that's why,' I said, still staring at my phone, hoping for a miracle.

'Anything, Panos?'

'Wait, I am looking.' And then the miracle happened: my phone started ringing. It wasn't messages; it was a full ring. Someone was calling me, a real person, on a Sunday.

'See, I told you! Now it is going to be ringing all day,' I said and then answered the call: 'Hello, yes, good evening.'

'Hello, could I speak to Mr Panayiotis?'

Oh no, it was the bank. Only they would use my name so formally. Pavlos was still staring at me, so I kept my smile on and said: 'Oh, hi, I have been waiting for your phone call. Where have you been?'

'We have been trying to get in touch with you for days. Don't you answer your phone calls?'

'Yes, I got all your messages.'

'Which messages? We don't leave messages.'

'I know. I am so glad you called now. You know how it is with the elections coming up. I am so busy at work.'

'Could you please confirm your tax number?'

'Yes, my wife and kids are fine. Are you going to run for office?'

'Sir, do you hear me?' It was getting to the crunch; I had to do something.

'Sir, do you hear me?'

'No, I can't hear you. It must be a bad line.' And with that I closed the phone. The uncomfortable silence in the room did not last for long. My phone rang again, and I had to answer.

'Hello.'

'Hello, is this Mr Pan ...'

'Yes, yes, it is me. What happened, your phone or mine?'

'I am calling on behalf of your bank ...'

'Yes, I know. Tell me what's new.'

'There has been nothing new, no new payments.' And the second miracle happened. This time Pavlos's phone rang. He answered his phone and went towards the kitchen in order not to be disturbed by my conversation.

'Hello, sir, hello. Are you still there?'

'Yes, it is Panos. I am here. Where are you?'

'I said you have made no payments.'

'Oh, yes, I know. How did you find out?'

'I am calling on behalf of the bank. That's how I know.'

'Well, since it is me who did not make any payments, obviously I know too – unless I sleep-walked, but wait, that doesn't work. Banks are closed at night. So there have been no payments. If I know and you know, then why are you calling?'

'Sir, your account is well past due. There could be serious consequences.'

'Is it serious now, or do I have time?'

'No, it is not serious now, but you must make payments. First I must establish that you are the person I am talking to.'

'If you are talking to me, then it must be me you are talking to. Who else would you be talking to if not me?'

'Please, just give me your tax number.'

'Oh no, I owe them money too? How do you know?'

'I don't care if you owe money to the tax office.'

'You don't care that I owe them and they don't care that I owe you, so why are you getting them into this?'

'I just need the number.'

'It is in my loan application.'

'I know. I have it in front of me. Could you tell me the name of your father?'

'I thought you said it is not serious yet.'

'No, it is not.'

'Then why are you getting my father involved?'

'I need to have his name.'

'I have given it to you so many times.'

'I know. I need to know that you know the name of your father.'

'It is my father! Do you think I would forget his name? And I tell you something: If you are hoping to get the money from my father, he is already dead.'

'We don't involve family members in your debt.'

'Yes, you do. When you gave me the loan and I said it was too much, you said I could spend it on my family, on my wife. You said I could take her on a dream holiday.'

'It wasn't me who told you that.'

'I thought you were calling on behalf of the bank.'

'I am in the debt reclaim department; you must have spoken to other people.'

'Why don't you ask them to call me? They know me better than you. I asked for one thousand euros. They gave me five, and now it has become ten. Ask them to call me. I don't want to upset you.'

'How would that help, sir?'

'I want to tell them that I spent the money on a holiday with my wife but she still left me.'

'I am really sorry to hear that, sir. We all have personal problems, but you must meet your financial obligations.'

'So what are your problems?'

'This is not a personal call, sir. I am only calling in regard to your account with the bank. If you have any questions in that regard, I am happy to help.'

'Yes, I have a question.'

'Please, ask me.'

'What is the name of your father?'

'Now you are teasing me, sir. I must remind you that this call is being recorded.'

'Oh good, can I have a copy?'

'You must make an official application through a lawyer, I think. Why do you want a copy? I have not done anything illegal.'

'I just want to know how I sound when I am half drunk.'

'Well, sir, if this is not a good time I can call you at another convenient time. When would be a good time?'

'Call me after the recession is over.'

'Sir, I need to close this call now. We are not getting anywhere with this.'

'It took you so long to find me! You shouldn't really let me go so easily. Plus, I still have some questions.'

'Anything that is related to your account?'

'How come you are calling on a Sunday?'

'Because this is a large account, so it has gone to a different category.'

'How big should it get before you start calling me, say, on a Sunday after midnight?'

'I don't know, sir. We don't work that way. I must really go now.'

'Is your shift over, or you are going to call someone else? I tell you, you will have no results. Most people are drunk by this time on a Sunday.'

'Well, I will just have to take a chance. It is my job.'

'It is really good that you have a job. I don't.'

'Well, sir, if you get your unemployment certificate and take it to the bank, they might …'

'What, give me another loan? No, I don't need another loan. I told you, my wife left me.'

'Okay, sir. I will call you tomorrow.'

'Wait, I have another question. When do you think our country will come out of this mess?'

'I told you, sir, I can only answer questions relating to your account.'

'If the recession is not related to my account, then what is? If you can't tell me on the phone because it is being recorded, can we do it another time?'

'What do you mean, sir?'

'Can I interview you? In private? You see, I am a reporter.'

'You have declared that you are unemployed.'

'Yes, and you didn't believe me and kept putting interest on my bill. Look, if you let me do my job and interview you, I might get paid. Then I can pay you. By the way, what happens if everybody owes and no one can pay? Don't tell me this is not related to my account either.'

'Hello, hello, sir. I can't hear you. What? I can't hear you. Sir ... *beeeeeeep.*'

It was a good feeling to have them, for a change, pretend to not hear me and hang up. Pavlos, now walking disturbingly sloppily, walked into the living room still holding his empty glass. By now, he could hardly walk at all, and his talking abilities were not that much better. He came towards me and said – well, he actually did not say anything. As soon as he got close to me he turned around, went to the other couch, and carefully sat down, in slow motion. Then he asked: 'So was that a politician?'

'No, it wasn't, just a bank I owe money to. How about you?'

'Me too. That's why I went to the other room. I didn't want you to hea – hear me talking to the bank.'

'So tell me, Pavlos. I have been always proud of you ... to have a friend like you, who cares about the working class, someone who cares so selflessly about the weak.'

He poured more drinks for both of us, took a sip, and said: 'Yes.'

'Yes.'

'So, Panos, what is your ... question? Have a drink.'

'My question is, do you feel proud of yourself too? When you look in the mirror, are you proud of your achievements, for the people and for the nation?'

'You don't understand. Yes, yes I do. Listen, my dear Panos, from experience I, uh, can advise that there are significant and sensitive, uh, particularities in each working circumstance … that must be carefully considered. Any consequential, uh …'

'Okay, stop. You have told me all this.'

'Good, Panos. Good, my dear Panos. I didn't remember the rest anyway. It is … it is … good that you stopped me.'

'Pavlos, do you think you gained a lot for the workers?'

'Yes, I did. They had so many rights before the recession that they didn't, uh, know what to do with. If it wasn't because of us, uh, they would be like slaves.'

'They had more than they needed? Is that what you mean?'

'Sometimes, it was funny. Actually it was sad. They used to ask me what else they needed. They asked for more holidays, and I got it for them. They wanted an office. They wanted more insurance, breaks, and early retirement. They, uh, wanted so much.'

'And?'

'And I got it for them! Before we had the union elections, they used to come to me and ask me what else I could get for them. I then had to think hard, uh, and come up with the most ridiculous demands for them. All of a sudden my demand would become the most important necessity for them, uh …'

'Why did you make up demands?'

'So they would vote for me to become the union leader! They won't vote for you if you demand basic things. Anyone can do that. And you know what is even funnier? Before the election, uh, it used to be just promises. But all I needed was a couple of calls to a few bodies, and I would get what I had, uh, promised.'

'Bodies?'

'Yeah. You like the whiskey?'

'Yes, Pavlos, it is fine.'

'Those were the good days. I used to demand outrageous things, thinking I won't get them, just to get elected. Then because there was money, I would get them. Magic! The politicians would give me anything, all of it, even more.'

'Why?'

'So that they would get elected too.'

'Pavlos, I think I have had enough whiskey. Tell me, who are these bodies?'

'The people who gave me the whiskey you are drinking, the politicians – who else?'

'What about the factories?'

'You don't understand. I wasn't the factory owner. I was the union leader. Who cares – hea – about the factory? My job was to take care of the, uh, workers.'

'I am sure your …' I had started finding it difficult to talk too.

'Panos, uh, finish your question.'

'I, I am sure your demands dried up when the recession started and the factories started closing down.'

'Yes, but no. I had other demands.'

'Like what?'

'When they were laying off the workers and paying them compensation, uh, it was so busy.'

'I see.'

'And not that, not just that! They were making skilled people do other jobs, threatening them with red – redundancy, if they didn't agree.'

'How?'

'I had a professional forklift driver who had a boy moving the plastic from the loads before he used his forklift. They fired the poor boy because there was no work.'

'Did you do anything for him?'

'For who?'

'For the boy.'

'No, he wasn't in the union. He had nothing to do with me. And then, and then you know what happened?'

'What?'

'They were expecting the professional driver to get off his forklift and move the plastic himself; otherwise they would reduce his working hours because they didn't have enough loads to keep him for seven hours.'

'What happened?'

'Nothing, what did you expect me to do? I said no. I told him to go on strike and, uh, he did. We can't have a professional skilled worker doing labour.'

'Did you ask him?'

'It is not up to him. He didn't know politics; he wasn't the union leader I was.'

'What happened at the end?'

'Uh, uh … they didn't reduce his hours, and they didn't make him get off his forklift. Then I don't know what happened. I think the factory closed down at the end. It was going that way anyway. But I am telling you, Panos, I could do anything I wanted. I have helped so many workers and their families, I, I have lost count.'

'Is there anything … anything you did not achieve all these years?'

'What do you mean?'

'Any ridiculous demands that did not materialize?'

'You don't understand. Yes, Panos, factories are private businesses. You can't get anything you want. I always envied the public sector. That was good. I would have liked to have been in their unions. They get anything they want. There is no boss around to check the demands. If you think my demands were off limits, you should hear, uh, some of theirs.'

'Like?'

'Anything! Just close your eyes and imagine something. It was possible in the public sector. They even got bonuses for being on time to work.'

'You should get a reduction for being late, not a bonus for being on time.'

'There you go! Even you understand that. There were all sorts of bonuses in the public sector. I used to get ideas from them for the unions, but it is hard out there in the real world. You know, I had a cleaning lady who used do work in the public sector as a cleaner. She photocopied her daughter's English-language certificate and handed it to her boss and started getting a bonus every month.'

'How would knowing a foreign language help you as a cleaner? Does she still work for you?'

'No, she stopped, uh, as soon as she started getting the bonus, and some other bonuses they had back then. She told me it was not worth her time anymore.'

Pavlos's phone rang again, and he immediately answered: 'Hello, hi, Nikos. What's happening? No. Why not? Oh yes, he finally came. He is here. Because he is an idiot! He says he turns his phone off because he gets too many calls from the politicians before the elections. I don't know, that's what he says. Do you want to talk to him?'

He handed me his mobile phone and said: 'It is your boss. He has been looking for you.'

I grabbed the phone and answered: 'Hello, Nikos.'

'Hi, Panos. Where are you?' He sounded tense and in a rush.

'You know where I am. I am at Pavlos's house.'

'Are you drunk?'

'No, I am not. Well, a little bit. I had a drink with Pavlos.'

'When were you at the farmer? When did you get back? Did you see anything?'

'Yes, he was planting a tree, one tree on the road. It was an olive tree. He said it was good for the road. To make the road bigger ... no, smaller. I think I got a picture. Maybe not. I don't remember now. I got back yesterday. Why?'

'Panos, there has been a terrible and tragic accident on the road near the farmer.'

'What happened?

'Three young kids – two girls, sisters, and a boy – crashed into a fruit truck last night.'

'Where are they?'

'Unfortunately, they are all dead.'

'I am really sorry to hear that. It is terrible.'

'Here is what I want you to do today. It is actually good you have a good relationship with the farmer. These farm villages are very small. He could be an uncle or a neighbour. The kids are from the nearby villages. Panos, I want you to call the farmer, give him our condolences, and arrange to meet him as soon as possible. Get as many details as possible, and come to the office first thing in the morning.'

'What? You want me ...'

He interrupted me. 'Panos, it is too fresh. He might be a close relative. You must be sensitive. We don't want to upset them anymore.'

'I am not going to call the farmer, Nikos.'

'Panos, I am sure you will find a way to talk to him. First find out if he knew them ...'

'I don't want to call the farmer, Nikos.'

'Why? Do you think it is better if you go there in person?'

'No, I don't want to see him either.'

'Why not? When I told you not to go to him, you insisted on going there. Now that I am asking you to go, you say you won't. What is the matter with you?'

'It is also his fault, Nikos.'

'It is also his fault? What is his fault?'

'The accident.'

'You call yourself a reporter, and you didn't know the accident happened. Now you even know whose fault it is?'

'I am not going to the farmer, Nikos. I can't really talk now. I am not feeling well.' And with that I closed the phone.

Chapter 15

MARIA HADN'T CALLED me in two weeks. Why would she? She had got what she wanted; I was out of the house. There was nothing else she needed from me now. And in these two weeks, at Pavlos's house, I had done nothing. I had achieved nothing! Sometimes I felt that there was now nothing to be achieved anymore anyway. But at other times I felt that all this, all this suffering, was happening for a reason. Ironically, once in a while I felt that I was walking on an invisible path, going to an invisible but warm and safe destination. It might be a place in the distance or a place just next to me. I could not focus on the place properly, but I could feel it strongly. There I did not owe anything to anyone. I was noticed for who I was and not what I could give. In that place, I would not be asked questions, and I would not care if I did not get any answers. I was not expected to go anywhere, do anything, or become anyone. Maria would be next to me but would not recognize that I had got nowhere in life. She would not notice that none of my dreams ever materialized. It would be a place above it all, above all the meaningless moments of nothingness. Paradoxically, in this dream, unlike all my other more possible dreams where Maria was absent, this time she was there. She was next to me watching my every move, judging my every action. She was silent and stationary, comfortably mum, a bit hazy, only almost real. She seemed passive and ineffective, completely withdrawn but also somehow a steady, powerful living force. She could hibernate momentarily, but eventually I knew she would explode. She could wake up and judge me again, criticize me, and belittle me. Worst of all, after doing her damage, she could withdraw again and ignore me altogether, for an unknown period.

I, on the other hand, could not reach the point of carelessness. I could not reach a state of not wondering, not trying, and not asking. I always had too many unanswered questions, the most important of which was, how could a man be so obsessed with someone whom he did not love anymore?

In her presence, with her naked expectations, with her loud and explicit impatience, and with her constant drilling of my soul, she always managed to reveal my weakest and most vulnerable disposition. Now, incredibly, she was doing exactly the same thing with her absence. With her presence she exposed my weaknesses, and with her absence she magnified them.

Outside my head and down on earth, in the real world, all I had done was to please everyone else. I had pleased her by moving out of the house. I had pleased Nikos by moving out of the office and not asking for money anymore. I was pleasing Pavlos by listening to the stories of his heroic battles in the union for the rights of mankind. I was perhaps pleasing the nation by not writing boring and pointless articles.

Pavlos's wife was still in America, and she was not going to come back for a couple of months. I had offered to pay something for rent, not because I had any money but maybe out of politeness. Or maybe it was just a bluff I had learned from my one night in the casino. Apart from the one time that Pavlos, half-jokingly, asked me to bring firewood from my land as a contribution to the household, he refused to even entertain the idea of me paying any rent. Once when I brought up the subject he got mad at me and told me that no matter how much the Europeans forced us to be like them, we were still Greek.

'We don't charge a friend rent,' he told me proudly one night.

I praised god that for once at least, TROIKA and the Europeans had not affected my life.

Pavlos had let me use his land line telephone and his daughter's PC, but Nikos's survey to find out who was the better and more popular mayor out of the last two was going nowhere. At first I had started recording the calls, but then when I noticed all the answers were the same, I stopped. As suggested by Nikos, I asked people which mayor was their favourite. The answer, short of a couple of occasions, was always the same: 'Neither.' I therefore changed my question to: 'Which mayor was the worst?' Unfortunately for me the answer was, a part from a couple of exceptions, again the same: 'They are both bad, neither is worse. Each one is worse than the other.'

During the last couple of weeks, I had visited the office a couple of times, just to show that I was still somehow associated to my job. Nikos was always cold and seemed to be just tolerating me. The atmosphere in the office was not pleasant at all, and I did not feel comfortable being there anymore. It is hard to have to ask permission from everyone around just to sit at your own desk, but in general I was gradually getting used to going places where I was no longer wanted.

I hadn't seen my mother since the night that she asked me to leave her house. Costa called me once to ask for something, and that felt good. I was still needed, I thought. I missed Elpida but strangely did not want to see her. I knew I had nothing to tell her. She was probably waiting for me to give her some good news about something, anything positive. As much as I told myself that children do not think that way and their expectations are more simple and achievable, I could not bring myself to witness her, a being to whom I helped give life, living and growing in an environment that had no future for her. I had given up on my children's lives. I had let them down. All these years, I had thought I was working to secure their future. In fact I had brought them to the middle of a wilderness and then waited for the storm to start before abandoning them. Their silent cries for help were ignored, not because they were not loud enough but because I, as a father, had nothing to offer. Not only could I not give hope for the future but also I had no spirit-lifting examples from the past to use for them. I had nothing to say. Their father was economically, idealistically, and spiritually bankrupt, just like the nation into which they were born.

Pavlos's big garden had become my new refuge. Sometimes when I was completely drained from too much thinking, I would somehow find the energy to walk to the big garden. The part of the garden which was visible from the house around the entrance, and also around the back windows, was beautifully manicured. The grass was cut short, and there were well-designed and cared-for rose gardens separated by carefully trimmed green hedges. All the trees in this part of the garden were evergreen, giving the garden an all-season charm. The ground was clean, and you could not find even one dead leaf on the grass. A few steps away from this man-made paradise, right after a half-built swimming pool full of branches and dead leaves, there was a wasteland with many leafless trees and broken branches. Somehow, this part of the garden was my favourite. After fighting the thick brownish grassland by stamping my feet on the dead branches, I used to make my way in between the sleeping trees. This is where I felt in the middle of the naked and real nature. Everything was completely free, with no pretence and no glorification. No flower was better than the others. There were no heroes. From this spot I could not be seen from the house. Everything was wet and cold.

One evening, there was some snow on the trees. I found out the hard way. I had gently leaned against a tree, causing the soft snow to fall off the branches. Instead of first shedding the snow from the top of my head, I grabbed one of the branches above me to punish it. The icy and cold branch, which only a few seconds before was purposelessly hanging in the air and seemed dead, had a different feel about it in my palm. The warmth of my hand quickly melted the icy surface of the wood and made the sleeping buds visible. It was indeed alive but patiently waiting. I could feel its non-existent pulse so clearly. All of a sudden in the midst of a quiet and frozen landscape, with dead branches hanging all around me, I felt that I was surrounded by life. The life could not be seen; it could only be felt. Looking harder at the almost-hidden buds, I imagined the trees in the spring. The branch gained my respect, and I finally let it go. It bounced back in the air and, after a few orchestrated sways, re-established its original perfect position. Its motions seemed planed and pre-rehearsed. The branch seemed full of purpose and determination, consciously waiting.

Going to that spot became a daily ritual. I would brave the cold and walk to the branch every morning, gently pull it down, wipe the frost from its surface, look carefully at the buds, and let go again. From day to day, there was no visible change. But knowing that it was still alive, still waiting in its spot, used to give me courage to face the new day. Then I would walk back to the house, go to the phone and the computer Pavlos had lent me, and start my newspaper assignment, which could be my last one.

It was proving to be a harsh winter, and I had come to the challenge armed with only a thin jacket. I was without my wife and without my children. What I had hoped to get from my high school class bully, Stavros, or my union leader friend, Pavlos, I was now getting from a naked and frosty tree branch.

Somehow, I knew that this assignment for the newspaper was my make-or-break job. But the people I surveyed, the same people that I had worked with for so many years, were not making any sense to me anymore. I could not even conduct a survey; I could not even get a simple yes or no answer. My survey was gradually turning into a full-fledged interview. With each answer, I was getting more confused. The interview seemed as if it were being conducted in different languages and at different time spans.

I would start the call by explaining that I was calling from a newspaper and then would ask which mayor out of the last two was favoured more by the respondent. Instead of answering, often, they would ask me if I was calling from a political party. My answer was obviously no. 'I am calling from a newspaper', I would say repeatedly. Then they would ask me which newspaper. This should not have affected their answers, but I would answer anyway. At this stage I usually got a response; however, it was not a response to my question. Often it wasn't even in words. It was more like a reaction, a noise, something like, 'Hmmm', 'Ahhh', or 'Vaaaa', followed by a long silence. Instead of comparing the mayors in their head, they were judging me and the newspaper. Then after I insisted on getting an answer, they would say, 'Neither. They are both bad'.

After this I always asked the follow-up question: 'Which one is worse?' And then I often got the same answer: 'Each one is worse than the other'. There was never a serious reply to my third question, 'Which one?' Some respondents ventured a bit beyond these clichés and meaningless answers by making clichéd and meaningless statements like: 'You are a reporter. If you don't know yourself, you are not good for the job.' My efforts by then would usually terminate. At this stage people were too exhausted by thinking and answering and would not be able to follow up. Before closing some asked me not to use their name in the newspaper. On several occasions I wanted to say: 'Besides the fact that I did not ask for your name, you haven't really said anything worth publishing.' But I always stopped myself because I knew I was working for the paper on borrowed time.

Sometimes when I got too frustrated and had no more will to carry on with the survey, I would go online and search for things that would cheer me up. I would look for romantic vacation destinations in the sun. Quiet and remote resorts in the mountains and beaches were my favourite. I wanted vistas; I wanted to see long mountain ranges or the open sea, with little islets in the distance. I wanted to be above it all and have some altitude in order to look down. I did not want to miss anything, not even a small bird flying between the trees. My favourite destinations were the ones that were advertised for honeymooners. They seemed to give me exactly what I wanted. The colours were fascinating: deep blue with white emphases decorated with fresh green. When I looked at the pictures, the glorious sea, the happy village houses, and the lively trees were being embossed on my soul. Somehow, the thought of sharing them with someone magnified their power. And no matter where the advertising was from, I used to pretend to be looking at my own resort in the mountain. Somehow it fit perfectly and helped me make my final decision about our holiday destination. For us, it was perfect.

Sometimes I felt ashamed looking through the holiday sites promoting romantic holidays for young lovers. Not only could I not afford a romantic holiday but also I did not have anyone to be romantic with. Those days were well beyond me. I found it embarrassing to even dream about it. The fact that I, myself, had at one point hoped to build a holiday resort in possibly one of the most romantic spots in Greece, in a country that was itself one of the most romantic destinations for holiday makers, made me feel lonelier and even more like a failure.

Like an incarcerated prisoner looking for an escape route, I looked out the window for my branch. There was no use; it was behind all the fancy trees. It was raining again. I did not want to go out again. Not even an hour had passed since I had last gone to see the branch. I sat back at the computer and for the third time looked at the depressing headline news of the day. Then I picked up the land line phone to call someone for the survey, but before dialling I put the phone down. I looked at my mobile phone, maybe hoping for it to ring. Any call would have been welcomed, even if it was from a bank asking me for money. Giving up on the phone ringing, for the fifth time in the day, I opened my e-mails to see if I had any mail. Yes, there was an e-mail in my inbox. It was from someone I did not know. It had no attachments, Maybe it was a marketing e-mail trying to sell me something. I opened it. It said:

'Hi Plato, how are you? Did you ever get married to that olive tree? Why are you looking for me after all these years? Do you need someone to make fun of you again? This is my e-mail. If you want you can write to me and tell me your news. Socrates.'

I had done it; I had made contact with an old friend. Without hesitation I replied:

'Dear Socrates, thanks for your response. This is great. I am so excited; send me your phone number quickly so we can meet. I am still in Athens. I think I saw you a couple of weeks ago standing next to your tinted glass taxi. It will be great to catch up soon. Panos (Plato).'

Like a little boy longing for his birthday present, I sat and stared at the computer for the next half hour, waiting for Stavros to reply. But there was no answer. Maybe he had sent me the e-mail right before going to work. Taxi drivers don't really have regular hours. Although I was disappointed that he did not respond immediately, inside me I had a warm feeling. I desperately needed someone to help me re-examine my life and my nation's life. I wanted to re-evaluate everything from the beginning, everything that I had stood for and everything that I had believed in. I needed to see things from a different angle. My childhood heroes, people I had admired all my life – the pillars of strength, the determined soldiers of resistance, the casual and professional fighters for the rights of the workers and the farmers, the proud nationalists, the political party hooligans, the bureaucrats, the paper pushers, the politicians, everyone and everything around me – were now drowning. I was surrounded by idealistic and opportunistic wage earners who called themselves philosophers and were all, without knowing, drowning in the ocean of confusion, taking me down with them. I desperately needed someone outside the unfortunate sinking ship called Greece to acknowledge our tragic demise and wake us up. I was now craving my old classmate's company. I wanted him to come and ridicule me again. I wanted him to force me to make better sense of it all, even if his commencing words were going to be, 'I told you so.'

I may have found him, the one person who did not understand me as a proud young student back then, the one who was not my hero at the time, the joker who was not even funny. I may have found him, after all these years, I may have found Stavros – or Socrates; it didn't matter what he called himself now. He was within my reach, and I wanted to share this news so badly. If Maria had cared for me at all, I would probably even call her and tell her. I got off the computer and rushed to the living room. Pavlos was sitting motionlessly watching the news.

I shouted: 'I found him, I found him, Pavlos.'

He raised his right arm in the air and opened his palm at me to stop me talking. I patiently waited and when he finally turned towards me repeated: 'I found Stavros, our classmate. I found him.'

'I thought you were working, Panos.'

'I am. I am working, but I am allowed a break, am I not?'

'It is not for me to decide. It is your life. So where is he? How is the taxi business?'

'I don't know. I haven't talked to him yet. He is going to e-mail me and give me his number.'

'Why are you so excited about finding him? What is he going to do for you? Help you keep your job? Get you your wife back? You didn't even like him. What do you want from him after all these years?'

'Why are you so excited about the elections? Why are you watching the news? You don't even like it. Why should it matter to you? There is no right or wrong left for you. You are just a part of a sinking ship looking for a piece of wood to save yourself.'

'Hey, hey, Panos, slow down. Where has all this come from all of a sudden? First of all, I am not the one who goes to the bottom of the garden in the freezing cold to stare at a piece of wood for hours. I am not lost. I am not sinking. I am not looking for a piece of wood; you are! Secondly, there are some things you don't understand. I have to know where the society is going. I have to know where our strengths and weaknesses are so I can develop my next strategy and work out our next move.'

'Our next move? Whose? You and the workers? The proletariat? Pavlos, there are no factories left. There are no workers left. Everyone is now unemployed.'

'Here we go again, Panos, with you telling me what is right and what is wrong. Panos, what have you done with your life? Nothing, and now you are telling me how to live mine?'

'Pavlos, I am not telling you how to live. I am telling you that you need to stick to your principles, not just go where the wind takes you. There is always a right and a wrong. Your decisions in life have to have a base, a foundation, something.'

'Panos, just because you got me drunk the other night and I loosened up a bit and talked to you doesn't mean you have the upper hand now.'

'I got you drunk? What upper hand?'

'Whatever. Panos, you have to understand, something is true if you believe in it, not because it is true. It is all relative. What you really believe in is what you make yourself believe in. When the time is right, everything is believable. At the end we have to create our own world, even if it is fake and even if we know it is fake, because that is the only world that is moving. That is the only world that you are a part of, the one that you have helped to create.'

'What are you talking about?'

'You won't understand. How can I explain it to you? I will give you an example. You see, in most places it is the complicated things people don't understand. In factories with the workers and the labourers, it is the simple things they don't understand. If you tell a worker that his factory produce is not competitive in the market and he might lose his job, he won't understand. He doesn't want to understand.'

'So what do you do? You lie to him?'

'It is easier and generates more action if they believe in some kind of a mystery that you make them feel they have solved themselves.'

'A mystery?'

'A mystery, some big secret, a conspiracy – call it what you want.'

'Like what?'

'Like that some big world power is promoting another country's products to starve the Greek industry. Hearing that gives hope to the unions; they relate to it. They feel that they can do something about it. Just the mere assumption empowers the workers. And that is when they need us, their leaders, even more. Without us they would not have the confidence to keep fighting. We have to feed them back what they already believe in so they keep coming back, so they keep being empowered and fighting for their rights. The result and the final consequence is the same, no matter what they believe in. If I tell them they are wrong, they lose confidence. They feel stupid. They won't vote for me again. They won't come to their union meetings anymore, and then the whole nation will fall apart. That is why I say, you have to make your own reality based on the targets that you want to reach.'

'As an influential person, don't you have to take responsibility and act in the interest of the nation first?'

'No, you don't. If you want to keep your influential position so that you can stay there and help in whatever way you want and whatever way you can, first of all you have to fight for your own name. You have to protect the number one. All you have to do is make people believe that you are doing your best for the interest of the nation.'

'To make them believe?'

'Yes, that is what I have done and I will do when I become a politician.'

'Pretend? Lie?'

'No, Panos, you don't have to lie. You just manage the truth. It is all about managing reality and right timing. That is what politics is all about. The mayor who inaugurated the bridge which was not completed on her last day in office before she quit did not lie; she just managed the facts in her own favour.'

'She opened a bridge that was not complete just to gain credit for herself?'

'You see, Panos, you still don't understand. I did not say "open"; I said "inaugurate". There is a difference. Mature politicians know it; common people like you don't. Listen, they were building the bridge for years whilst she was in office. Would it be fair for the bridge to be inaugurated by the next mayor just a few months after she was voted out of office?'

'What did they do? They brought a priest to bless an unfinished bridge, and then they brought him back after a few months to bless it again when it actually opened?'

'So the priest got paid twice. What is your problem?'

'What is my problem? The bridge was not built for her to get credit and the priest to get paid. It was built for people to drive on and get to the other side of the motorway.'

'Panos, in Greece nothing is built just for the people and its functionality. Things are built because there is money in them and as a tribute to the officials involved.'

'What if it goes wrong?'

'There are so many things that you can blame it on – unnamed officials, the weather, lack of funds, changes to the initial plans, unexpected difficulties, you name it. But if you are lucky, by the time the problems become obvious and the public finds out, you are already retired.'

'I can't live like that, Pavlos.'

'That is why you are not a politician, and you will never make a good one. There is our difference. Didn't you now want to be in my position, where I am actually doing something for the people? In a couple of years I will be an official industrial inspector, and then I can help the system more without even needing anyone to vote for me. Panos, whilst you went following a rainbow leading you to your unrealistic dream, your holiday resort, I looked where the society was going. I looked to see what people wanted to believe in and supported them. I am a humanist, and you are a dreamer. That is why I am still here. That's why I am still needed, with factories or without factories.'

'How about your principles? Where are they? Where do they fit, Pavlos? What do you tell people now?'

'People don't know. People are waiting for me and for people who are even more successful than me, the politicians, to tell them what reality is.'

'People don't know?'

'Panos, go and ask people if they want higher inflation. See what they tell you.'

'Nobody wants inflation. Why would you want the prices to go up?'

'Okay, go and ask them if they want less taxation. I am sure you know the answer to this one too.'

'Look, this is child's play, Pavlos. I conduct scientific surveys. I don't chase after answers that I know.'

'Panos, just answer the question. Do people want less taxes?'

'Yes. I don't need to conduct a survey to learn if people want to pay less tax.'

'Good, so you understand. If you reduce taxes, you increase inflation.'

'What?'

'If you reduce taxes, you increase inflation. But if I tell them that, they get confused and give up hope in me. You know what I tell them? I tell them I will try to reduce taxes and control the inflation.'

'So? So what, Pavlos? What are you trying to prove?'

'So the point is that people have no fucking idea what they want, and that is where I come in the picture. I read the society and excel with it. Ideology I have, but my ideology is worth nothing if I am going against the flow.'

'What is the flow?'

'You see, you don't understand. Society was rich. Money was being thrown around, and you know where it was going?'

'You tell me. Obviously I don't understand. I don't understand anything.'

'The society had money. When people are rich and their stomachs are full, they think more about their rights. They want more, and they want it all to stay that way and get better. They become idealistic. An idealistic society which is becoming selfish does not need tourists, Panos. Its citizens need strong representatives to get more rights for them, and they pay the representatives good money. I was there. I heard them and took the money, and you were up on your hill looking for the tail of your rainbow, to bring in tourists.

'I still prefer where I am.'

'Panos, I am glad you are content. Live your life the way you want to, but don't criticize me. I built my rainbow from the ground up. I am okay now. I have a big house, a wife, and a family that I can afford to care for, no matter what happens to Greece. You, you on the other hand, only have a big rainbow. Your rainbow is up in the sky, and you are now waiting for a taxi to come so you can grab the rainbow's tail. Rainbows are an illusion, Panos. They really have no tails. Even if your friend is the best taxi driver in the world, you still won't find it.'

Chapter 16

'HELLO PLATO, WHERE do u want to meet? Shall we meet at ur olive tree? Have u found any more plants to love, or r u married to an actual human being with feelings? If u want, we can first meet in a chat room. I have to find out if u r still as ridiculous as u were back then. If not then I won't be able to make fun of u. Then it is not worth meeting.'

'Hello, Socrates.'

He hasn't changed at all. He is as arrogant and rude as he was back then. But who knows? Maybe it is still a good thing to meet him. After all, I am the one who needs someone making fun of me in the first place. Maybe he will. Being made fun of is a connection. When somebody makes fun of you, at least you know that you still exist, even if they don't care about you. But I was not going to make it easy for him this time. I was going to make him work for it. I decided to respond immediately:

'Hi Socrates, how come u have to know about my life first before I know about urs? I know u r a taxi driver. Most taxi drivers r philosophers too. So in a way u r in the right place. Do u ridicule ur passengers too? I am a journalist & write for a newspaper. I have a wife & two children. She is not a plant, but not much different either. Life is not very good right now but at least I know everyone is in the same boat. U know what I mean? How about u? R u married? Plato.'

Only minutes after sending the e-mail I got a response with an Internet address inviting me to chat with him. I wasted no time and made contact:

'Hi, Stavros, how r u?'

'I thought u were going 2 call me Socrates from now.'

'Only if u call me Plato.'

'Deal.'

Plato: 'I never 4got u. especially when things r wrong, I see ur face, always giggling. After all these years u somehow still manage 2 get in my head.'

Socrates: 'Maybe that's because u deserve it.'

P: 'Shall we meet 4 a beer?'

S: 'R u going 2 bribe me 2 make fun of u? Tell me first, how r u?'

P: 'I am a little better than terrible.'

S: 'That means u r a little bit better than the last time I saw u.'

P: 'No, I think I am much worse than the last time.'

S: 'What is new? What has changed in ur life?'

P: 'Remember I told u about my father? Remember he died at work? He was not actually working. He was just helping.'

S: 'I asked u what is new in ur life. U still haven't told me about the people in yr life who r actually alive, ur children, ur wife, nothing. U r first telling me about ur father who died so many years ago? He is dead anyway. What does it matter if he was working or playing?'

P: 'He was not playing; he was helping, just helping, not expecting anything. He was there because he wanted 2. He didn't have 2.'

S: '& ur wife & children?'

P: 'My wife & children r fine.'

S: 'Where r they?'

P: 'I am staying with a friend; I am doing a project 4 my work. I have 2 be away 4 a while. R u married?'

S: 'No I am divorced. She was a bitch.'

P: 'Then u understand.'

S: 'Yes, that is women 4 u. They r all the same. Did she kick u out?'

P: 'No, we r still on friendly basis. I am staying with Pavlos, remember him? He became a union leader. I will tell him that I found u.'

S: 'How about ur children? Do u see them or doesn't the bitch let u?'

P: 'I haven't seen them 4 a couple of weeks.'

S: 'Have u tried 2 see them?'

P: 'Yes. What do u think about the economy? When do u think the recession will end?'

S: 'What do u write about, Greek cuisine?'

P: 'No, why?'

S: 'U r the reporter and u r asking me?

P: 'U r the one who is the real know-all. I thought since u made fun of everything & everyone, maybe u know better.'

S: 'R u just having an intellectual depression? & ur thoughts just crash landed? R u completely lost?

P: 'No, not completely. I am beginning 2 see what is going on, but I am not lost.'

S: 'Beginning?'

P: 'Yes.'

S: 'Why now, what changed?'

P: 'I don't know, maybe because it all hit me so personally this time, I used 2 write what they told me 2 write. I only did it because it was my job.'

S: 'So now that u understand, u must be writing better, no?'

P: 'No, now I can't write at all. There is nothing 2 write about.'

S: 'Do u use the internet 4 ur job? 4 the articles u write?'

P: 'Yes, but I am beginning 2 think, what I am looking 4 is not out there. It is not 2 be found in Google. I think it is inside me. When I find myself I won't need a search engine. But now, I am still at the stage of seeing if the glass is half full or half empty.'

S: 'Maybe instead of spending so much time on that, u should spend some time 2 see who stole the glass.'

P: 'U r right, I haven't even seen the glass 4 a while.'

S: 'Did u lose ur job too?'

P: 'Not yet, I still have another assignment. I am doing my best 2 do a good job. Maybe they will keep me.'

S: 'U either write well or u don't. U can't try 2 write well.'

P: 'Why not?'

S: 'Writing is like loving, it has 2 come from inside u. U have 2 believe in it first. Otherwise everything is just pretend, not the real thing. What is the assignment about?'

P: 'Which of the last 2 mayors was better? Sounds easy, right?'

S: 'Yes, but I am sure u will find a way 2 screw it up.'

P: 'Not me, the people. They all say they were both bad. How am I going 2 analyse that? What am I going 2 write?'

S: 'U can either write ur own analysis or nothing at all.'

P: 'I can't. I have 2 write what the paper wants. I have 2 write something that people like 2 read. Who cares about my analysis?'

S: 'That's why u r a bad journalist.'

P: 'What can I do?'

S: 'Start with urself. Why do u think people answer that way?'

P: 'They answer that way because they r unable 2 make a decision.'

S: '& what else?'

P: 'People don't have enough guts 2 make decisions.'

S: '& what else?'

P: 'People r too lazy 2 even use their brain 2 really compare.'

S: '& what else?'

P: 'The only thing they have learned from democracy is 2 make stupid choices & then start nagging about their own choice, completely ignoring that they themselves made the choice in the 1st place. Not only do they not want 2 take responsibility 4 their own choices but also they don't even want 2 bother thinking about it. It is just easier 2 say everything is bad, and they think that is democracy. They vote & then go home. U know, democracy is like a plant. U have 2 take care of it all the time. U can't neglect it & then one day wake up & see it dying & keep watering it 2 make up 4 the past. It doesn't work that way.'

S: '& what else?'

P: 'R u still there or u have put the, "what else" button on automatic replay?'

S: 'I am still here, Panos.'

P: 'I think it is the first time u called me with my real name. Maybe it is the first time u r not making fun of me. Or is it going 2 all come 2gether as a big laugh at the end?'

S: 'Lol … Plato, it is the first time I hear u being honest with urself. Not 4cing urself 2 believe something else.'

P: 'Isn't it ironic how we r chatting with fake names & in reality neither of us is Socrates or Plato?'

S: 'Ironic?'

P: 'Yes, the word is from ancient Greek. We made it, so I guess we must be good at it. Irony has become a part of our lives.'

S: 'Plato, it is not just us doing this. We r both Greek. This is the dilemma that all the Greeks have inside. We all feel like Plato & Socrates. We aspire 2 be them. All our lives, every time we think, we pretend 2 be our ancients. We even pose like the statues of our philosophers we see in the museums. We r all philosophical people. We don't take things at the surface. We always have 2 look deeper inside. It is in our genes.'

P: 'Is that a curse or a blessing?'

S: 'If this leads u 2 a better understanding, it is a blessing. If it makes u get even more lost, then it is definitely a curse.'

P: 'The only thing left 4 us, the only thing we kept from all their glory and wisdom, is an empty pride, an unproductive notion. We took advantage of and abused their philosophy and their ways, & now even their ruins r suffocating us and stopping us from going 4ward. They didn't enlighten us with their knowledge; they left us here like orphans in a big graveyard of statues, stadiums, and temples.'

S: 'We abuse things, everything. Nothing is used 4 the purpose it was meant 4.'

P: 'Yes, everything – our jobs, our ideology, our relations, our money, our power. We even abuse our own kids. We use them 2 take revenge on the world, 2 make up 4 our own unfulfilled dreams & our complexes. In the end, they lose their way and become nothing, & then we suffer even more & add 2 our complexes. It is a vicious cycle.'

S: 'U must be a good father.'

P: 'That's not what my wife thinks.'

S: 'It is what the kids think, not the wife.'

P: 'They probably agree with their mum.'

S: 'U miss her don't u? U must still love her.'

P: 'I love her a lot more than the relationship I ended up having with her.'

S: 'Relationships can be managed. It is in ur own hands.'

P: 'It needs 2 people 2 work on it, as partners.'

S: 'But u have more important things 2 take care of 1st. Stop thinking about her. Think of getting urself out of the mess. If u really think u r nothing, then really u can't expect 2 be a part of anything.'

P: 'Can we meet sometime?'

S: 'Why?'

P: 'Actually, I don't want 2 anymore.'

S: 'What happened?'

P: 'I don't know. It is okay like this. Let's just chat online 4 now.'

S: 'Tell me why.'

P: 'Socrates, u scare me. U make me confront myself. U r my worst nightmare.'

S: '& u like it? Plato, I make u face reality not urself.'

P: 'I must go now. I have something 2 do. Don't worry, it is not another tree.'

S: 'Plato, u can't run away.'

And with that I closed the chat room icon. I sat at the desk looking at the computer screen. It was as if I was expecting it to do something. I studied the entire desk from top to bottom, pretending to myself that I was doing something. Time was passing; I could hear birds singing outside. They seemed to be inviting me to the garden. The sound was so pleasing that I wanted more and felt silly when my hand, unconsciously, went to raise the volume on the computer. When I realized my gaffe I froze my hand in the air, looked outside the window, turned my head towards the computer, and clicked on the phone icon for the survey. A resident of the city was randomly called, and there was an answer.

A man with a husky voice said: 'Hello.'

'Hello, sir. I am calling from a newspaper conducting a phone survey to ask which one of the last mayor's policies you approve of more.'

'Mayors? I don't like them. They have both been bad. Which newspaper are you calling from?'

'With all due respect, that should be irrelevant to my question.'

'If I don't know which newspaper you are calling from, then how do I know what you are expecting me to answer? But anyway, I don't like either of them.'

'Has any one of them done anything that you liked?'

'They are politicians. They are good before they get in an office, and when they get there they only help themselves, not us.'

'Yes, but one of them should have done something right.'

'You can't force me to like politicians. Just write that they are both bad. They have done nothing for the city.'

'I can't. I have a box in front of each name. I have to click one, the one that you like more.'

'I told you, no. What boxes? Why should I answer you? If I let you go on like this and force me to give an answer you want, you will finally put me in a box too. Look, we live in a democracy. I answer you if I want to.'

'Don't blame me, and don't blame the question. I am a professional journalist, and there is nothing wrong with the question. The reason you don't want to answer is either because you don't care or have no guts to make a decision. If you want to participate in the survey, you have to choose one.'

'What are you, a dictator?'

'A dictator?'

'Don't pretend that you didn't hear me. I said you are a dictator, forcing people to say what you want. We have been enslaved by the Turks. We have gone through wars and starvation. And now I have you on top of me, calling me at my house, waking me up, and telling me what I can do and what I can't do?'

'You don't have to participate in the survey. I will just write that you refused to answer.'

'Do you have a box for that so that you can reach the answer you want?'

'What is the answer I want? I don't want any answer. I just ...'

'If you don't want an answer, then why are you asking a question?'

'I mean ...'

'Do you think I was born yesterday? Who are you to tell me how to live my life? This is a democracy; my fathers didn't fight for this nation for the politicians and their dogs to have it the way they want.'

'What dogs? What are you talking about?'

'Listen, you can't force me to like anyone, not even over my dead body. If I don't like them, I don't like them. It is because of people like you that the country is in this mess, little dictators. You either write they are both bad or nothing at all. Good-bye.' And he ended the call.

The birds were still singing, but I had to resist. I was determined not to go outside. Without hesitation, but still unconsciously, I clicked on the chat room icon.

Socrates was still there. It was as if he knew I was going to come back – or maybe he was talking to other people too.

P: 'Hi, it is me again, Plato.'

S: 'Hi. Where have u been?'

P: 'I just needed 2 get some fresh air. I have been working too hard. This survey is impossible. People don't want 2 bother 2 think. It is like they say it is their democratic right 2 be stupid.'

S: 'Plato, what do u consider urself? Smart?'

P: 'Well, at least I think.'

S: 'On ur own?'

P: 'What do u mean?'

S: 'Do u think u r smart on ur own?'

P: 'No, in a group. What do u expect? On my own.'

S: 'Did u used 2 talk 2 ur wife about politics?'

P: 'My wife was not political. All she thought about was the kids & when 2 pay the bills & what 2 cook 4 dinner, things like that.'

S: '& because of that u talked 2 urself?'

P: 'Talked 2 myself?'

S: 'Did u do a lot of things by urself? Tell jokes 2 urself, play with urself?'

P: 'Here u start again. This is the Stavros I remember. U have not changed at all.'

S: 'So how can u do a survey if people don't answer u? This is ur last chance. U should do something worthwhile.'

P: 'U don't need 2 tell me. I am a professional. This is my job. I am sure I will find a way.'

S: 'I am just a taxi driver. Maybe I can help.'

P: 'I will just make up some numbers & give it 2 him with a careful analysis. I have done it b4.'

S: 'What is the use of that?'

P: 'I will keep my job.'

S: 'U have been doing this, making up stories 2 keep ur job, 4 yrs & it hasn't worked. Why should it now?'

P: 'What do u expect me 2 do?'

S: 'B a man about it. If the answer is neither, it is neither.'

P: 'But there r 2 boxes, not3, not as many as I want.'

S: 'I thought u r managing the entire survey urself. What boxes?'

P: 'The boxes, the boxes in front of the names of the mayors.'

S: 'Who gave u these boxes?'

P: 'No 1.'

S: 'These boxes don't exist. U made them.'

P: 'I made them?'

S: 'Yes, u made them, & now u don't know how 2 get rid of them.'

P: 'I have 2 write my report on the survey 2night. It has 2 be in shortly. I have no time 4 bullshit, & as usual u r talking 2 me philosophically, from another planet.'

S: 'The reason u don't understand me is not because I am from another planet. It is because I am talking 2 u from inside ur head.'

P: 'I have enough problems myself; I don't need u 2 confuse me even more.'

S: 'Is that why u tried so hard 2 find me?'

P: 'I thought u would work with me in the direction that I want 2 go, not stand in front of me blocking me.'

S: 'Going the way u want 2, u can do urself. U don't need me.'

P: 'Why can't u just be a friend? Is it too much 2 ask?'

S: 'This is the only kind of friend I know how 2 be. This is the only kind of friend u need. All ur other friends, all ur life, have led u 2 here, & that is what u don't like. Why do u want 2 continue?'

P: 'What do u want me 2 do?'

S: 'B urself.'

P: 'B myself?'

S: 'Sit down & think about the survey. This survey is the story of ur life. It is a small sample. B honest with urself. B honest with the newspaper. B honest with ur family & friends. Don't worry if it is not pleasing. The truth is beautiful on its own, whatever it is. Even if it hurts it is better than a good lie because the truth will stay with u 4ever. If u don't acknowledge it, if u don't respect it, it will become harsher, & it will hurt even more. Once u accept reality, that is when u live here, amongst us. That is when u r respected. That is when u r taken seriously. That is when people listen 2 u. That is when u can be loved again.'

S: 'R u still there, Plato?'

P: 'Yes, I am. This is turning out 2 be like the dialogue, the real one between Socrates & Plato.'

S: '& this is when we Greeks go all wrong, every time. As soon as we think we r making a bit of sense we start comparing ourselves with our ancients. We have no patience. U know, I know, that we r both using fake names.'

P: 'Our names may be fake, but what we r saying is not. The difference is that instead of being on the hills of ancient Athens, next 2 the Parthenon, we r in a chat room.'

S: 'The truth is the truth no matter where u r.'

P: 'What is this with the truth, Stavros? That's all u talk about. Give it a break. Who is lying?'

S: 'We all r.'

P: 'Okay, I will write the truth about the survey, fine. But if I am kicked out of my job, will u help me?'

S: 'Whenever u need a taxi, I promise. Okay, I have 2 go 2 work now.'

P: 'Good luck.'

S: 'Panos, u r the one who needs good luck not me. U need 2 write 2 keep ur job & at the same time keep ur audience. In my taxi, people r already in. They can't go anywhere. They r in 4 the ride, not because of any prejudice 4 or against what I say or my ideology. In a way I have more freedom than u 2 say what I truly believe, without self-censorship. I can tell them what I want. As long as I don't have an accident, all is fine.'

P: '& my job here is 2 make them understand that they already have had an accident.'

S: 'If u believe it, u must say it.'

P: 'I have 2 go. Watch the roads.'

S: 'What r u going 2 do?'

P: 'I am going 2 look 4 the truth.'

S: 'Let's talk 2morrow.'

P: 'Yes, we will.'

Stavros was good at theory, but he was all talk – nice talk, but all talk. It was amazing that he always knew what to say, just to show points of weakness, without saying anything concrete. 'Be yourself,' he said. How was that going to help? If I was nothing, as my wife, my son, my boss, and everyone around me thought, how exactly was it going to help me to try harder to be myself? Stavros had grown up, though. At least instead of just making fun he talked. It was obvious that he cared. Maybe I should open up to him, just a little more. I had nothing to lose, and somehow, this time, I felt like I could trust him. Things couldn't get any worse, anyway. It couldn't go downhill anymore. For me, there was no more downhill. The worst-case scenario could be that he would have a good laugh for free at my expense. I had nothing to lose. Maybe this time I would laugh too, with him. But I would never allow him to shake my foundations, my pride and roots. Never. I had grown too. I wouldn't be subject to his laughter; I would laugh with him at everything that was wrong.

With these thoughts, I went to close the computer, but at the last second I noticed a pop-up. 'Socrates has entered the chat room', read the message.

P: 'U r back? I thought u r going 2 work.'

S: 'It was cancelled.'

P: 'Did u 4get something?'

S: 'Yes, about ur work.'

P: 'I said, I want u 2 help me if I get kicked out of my work.'

S: 'I want 2 help u so that it doesn't matter if u r fired.'

P: 'How?'

S: 'What is the most important thing in ur life?'

P: 'My family and my work. Why?'

S: 'Ur job?'

P: 'Of course. Without my job, I can't have anything.'

S: 'Panos, u don't have anything right now either. Ur job did not help u keep them.'

P: 'If I get my job back, if I become good at what I do, if I get paid, it might all come back 2 me.'

S: 'How r u going 2 get better? With what?'

P: 'Stavros, I am not like u. I have principles. I have foundations. I stick 2 my beliefs.'

S: 'What r these foundations? What r u standing on?'

P: 'Unlike u, I am proud of my past. I believe in this nation. I believe in the principles that r established, that r in our blood.'

S: 'Established by whom?'

P: 'The principles that were established by our ancients. They r a part of me, & they will help me. I think we should follow them, do everything they said.'

S: 'What do u produce?'

P: 'What do u mean?'

S: 'What do u make? Just pride? What have u learned from ur ancients that helps u produce anything? Or do u only eat pride?'

P: 'No, I do my job & I eat what our farmers produce. Everyone has a task.'

S: '2day ur farmer is paid more in compensation when his crops go wrong than when he actually produces anything. Is this what they learnd from ur ancients? R u really proud of this?'

P: 'This has nothing 2 do with my beliefs.'

S: 'Panos, everything has 2 do with ur beliefs. U have grown old.'

P: 'I thought u had changed, Stavros, but u r the same old lost soul, the same hallucinating, arrogant being.'

S: 'Panos, u r old. U have always looked 2 the past 2 find solutions. Ur pride 4 the past has blinded ur current vision & killed any hope 4 ur future.'

P: 'I am old?'

S: 'One becomes old & infirm when he thinks & talks more about the past than the future. It is a very visible threshold. Try 2 see it. U became old long time ago. U put ur bundle of hopes in the plastic bag of pride borrowed from ur ancestors. The pride was not urs; it was theirs. The only thing u brought in with u was the plastic bag. U attached urself 2 their pride without even asking them, without even trying 2 learn how they attained it. Lacking any substance & only 2 boost ur own ego, u dared 2 go around with ur overloaded plastic bag only 2 claim ur worth, only 2 show off. All that because u urself knew it was a lie. U were not worthy of the gifts in the bag, & that is what hurts u most ...'

S: 'R u still there Plato?'

P: 'How do u know me so well?'

S: 'Panos, I am a taxi driver. I know people, & now I have 2 go. I have a call.'

P: 'No, wait.'

S: 'What?'

P: 'I want 2 ask u something.'

S: 'What?'

P: 'Let me think. Wait, don't go.'

S: 'Fine, I will stay.'

P: 'What do u want me 2 do?'

S: 'I don't want u 2 do anything. It is ur life. U must decide.'

P: 'Where do I start?'

S: 'From urself?'

P: 'How does that help my people?'

S: 'U r trying 2 keep a whole nation 2gether when u can't even keep a small family 2gether? U r expecting too much from urself. Once u learn 2 help urself then u can think big ...'

S: 'What r u going 2 do 2night?'

P: 'Do u want 2 meet?'

S: 'No, u have work 2 do. Sit at home & write ur survey. U need time.'

P: 'It is just a bunch of numbers.'

S: 'Panos, it is much more than that & u know it.'

P: 'What is this, u r giving me homework?'

S: 'Yes, & if u don't have it ready by 2morrow u can 4get about this chat room. Don't 4get, it has 2 come from inside. U have 2 feel it. Good-bye.'

P: 'Good-bye.'

As soon as I closed the chat room I ran outside, forgetting to even put on a jacket. It was bitterly cold and was getting dark. More than any other time I wanted to sit and write about my findings on the survey. The block that I had experienced summing up the survey in an article was still there, but there was a strange breath of fresh air about. I slowly walked to the bottom of the garden, had a look at my sleeping tree, and rushed back inside. Pavlos was standing by the balcony window observing me patiently. I went back to my room, and after a few minutes he walked in and asked: 'Do you want me to fill up the pool, Panos? Maybe you want to have a swim?'

'No, I didn't bring my swimming suit. Maybe next time.'

'You didn't bring your skis either, but you seem to be sliding on the ice with no problem.'

'I have many talents that you don't know about.'

'Panos, I will be out tonight, all night. Are you okay on your own, or should I worry?'

'Why would you be worried? I am fine.'

'Yes, why should I be worried? You are quite fine, very normal.'

'You don't have to be sarcastic. Don't worry about me. I just wanted to get some fresh air. Where are you going, business or pleasure?'

'It is supposed to be pleasure, but whatever you have to do for work ends up not giving you any pleasure.'

'I will be okay. I have a lot of work to do. I need to finish off the survey soon.'

'Is that one of your talents or a job you are forced to do, Panos?'

'You will see.'

I got back on the computer. Trying to get comfortable, I looked at the screen and placed my fingers on the keyboard. I kept looking at the screen as if I were expecting a show to start. I kept looking, but then I felt thirsty. Walking back from the kitchen after having some water, I felt hungry. I grabbed a piece of stale bread and went back to the computer. I sat down. The screen was dusty. It was disturbing me. I had to clean it before I could start work. I went back to the kitchen and got a cloth. After cleaning the computer screen I thought I would clean the desk too. I gathered all the dried-up coffee cups, walked back to the kitchen, and put them in the sink. Back at the clean desk I felt uneasy and restless, again. Where was my phone? Where had I left it? I got up and started looking. The house was cold. How could I work in this cold?

I finally found my phone on the kitchen table. I lifted it up like a rediscovered lost treasure and looked at the short list of contact numbers. Elpida did not have a phone, but I found myself looking for her name. I was missing Elpida, I was missing Costa, and in a strange way, I was missing Maria. I wanted to call her and tell her about the new excitement in my life, my old new friend, Socrates. She would probably laugh at me for getting so excited about finding an old friend. She would ridicule me. In a way they were so similar. In a unique and unproductive way, each one reminded me of my failures. I saw her name and dialled the number without reflecting. The phone rang and rang. There was no answer. I called again. Finally after another few rings she answered: 'Hello.'

'Hello, Maria. It is me, Panos.

'Yes, hi.'

'I called to see how Elpida is.'

'Elpida is fine. She is not here now. She is playing somewhere.'

'How is Costa?'

'Costa is okay – the same, you know. If you want to see Elpida we can arrange something.'

'How are you?'

'I ... I am fine, just okay. And you?'

'I am okay, very busy at work. I have to do a survey.'

'Right.'

'Maria, how can I see Elpida? When?'

'Whenever you want. I can drop her off at your mum's.'

'Oh no, don't drop her off at my mum's. She is very tired these days.'

'I know.'

'You know? Do you see her?'

'Of course, I have no problems with her. She wants to see Elpida too. I am going there in a couple of days, unless you want to see Elpida sooner.'

'No, it is best to wait a bit. I have so much to work out.

'Fine, you have my number.'

'Maria, you didn't tell me how you are.'

'I did. I said I am fine.'

'Do you have electricity?'

'Yes.'

'That's good. Do you want to know where I live?'

'No. Yes, where do you live?'

'It doesn't matter.'

'Fine.'

'I have to go now. Kiss Elpida for me, and say hi to Costa.'

'Fine.'

'Bye.'

'Bye.'

I kept the phone open with the receiver on my ear until it beeped. This had to be the coldest conversation I had had with Maria in years, but at least it wasn't a fight. At least she wasn't shouting at me. Maybe that was why I didn't want it to finish. I could always call her again if I wanted to. She would answer. I shouldn't have said I was busy at work. Now she thought I was doing well. What was I going to tell her if I was kicked out tomorrow? Then she would blame me for the whole thing. She would think I hadn't done a good job with the survey. This stupid survey was becoming such a big deal. I had to do well or else everything would end for me. The problem was that Stavros, instead of helping me with the survey by encouraging me somehow, had confused me even more. He had forced me to push myself into a corner. I was not even good at pretending to know where I was going with my articles, let alone having the confidence to just write and see what happened.

Maria did not care to know where I was living, but would probably not like the fact that I was at Pavlos's. She did not like him at all and thought he was a bad influence on me. Even Pavlos was waiting to see what happened with the survey. Somehow, I was sure he would find a way to use my agony with the survey to confirm his own ideology and defend his own way of life. What was I going to write? How was I going to get out of this corner? I had to chat with Socrates again.

I went back online again and entered the private chat room. Socrates was still there.

P: 'Hi, r u here?'

There was no answer. I waited and waited. He must have left his computer on and gone somewhere. I wished I had his phone number. The momentary desires to chat with him were getting closer and closer. Frighteningly, hour by hour, they were becoming more of a need. And suddenly:

S: 'Don't u have a life?'

P: 'I wanted 2 tell u something. How about u, don't u have a life? Ur taxi? I guess people have no money now 4 a taxi.'

S: 'Not only that, people now don't have anywhere 2 go. Tell me, what is it?'

P: 'I can't write. I have nothing 2 write. B4 I could at least pretend that I knew something. Now, I don't know anything.'

S: 'U write what u see.'

P: 'It needs talent.'

S: 'U need more talent 2 write something u don't see.'

P: 'So, what is it that I do see?'

S: 'U have a mental block on this survey. Maybe because it is the first time u r trying 2 be urself. U r not used 2 that. Think of something else. Ask urself more general questions.'

P: 'Like what?'

S: 'Why r we like this? Why did we not grow as a nation? Tell me the first thing that comes 2 ur mind.'

P: 'The politicians.'

S: 'Well done. U r good. Now try, try hard not 2 tell me the first thing that comes 2 ur mind. This is what u have been doing all ur life, coming up with the easiest answer. Try again.'

P: 'The foreigners.'

S: 'Well done, u screwed up again. U came up with the second-easiest answer. Even if the foreigners are 2 be blamed, good for them. That is their job 2 work for the benefit of their own nations, not ours. What have we done? U can't be Plato before u become a good, true Panos. Try again, Panos. Who screwed ur life?'

P: 'Archaeological authorities.'

S: 'Why did they do that? Now 4get Panos & think about the nation. What is going on?'

P: 'The planning department, the 4estry, the courts, the bureaucracy, the political parties, the ecologists ...'

S: 'Why do they do that?'

P: 'Because they have the power.'

S: 'Who gave them the power?'

P: 'We did.'

S: 'Why?'

P: 'Because we have 2 have a system. We don't want anarchy; we want organization, fairness ...'

S: 'Do they hold u back? R u scared of them?'

P: 'Yes, I am.'

S: 'Why?'

P: 'I have 2 think. I am sure u want an educated answer.'

S: 'No, I want ur answer. The value of Plato's dialogue with Socrates is that it was not pre-rehearsed. It was not staged. It was genuine. It came from their hearts.'

P: '& that Socrates was a genius.'

S: 'No, he was an ordinary, simple man but honest with his feelings. He was not scared even of making fun of himself when he thought he was wrong. Panos, why r u scared of them?'

P: 'Because I am weak.'

S: 'Why r u weak? Why do they have so much power over u? Is there anything wrong with u? Have u done anything wrong?'

P: 'Yes, loads of things. If they look in2 my life they can put me in jail.'

S: 'How?'

P: 'I am sure I owe taxes or have made false declarations. Somewhere I have cheated. I have done loads of things, like everyone I know around me.'

S: 'Why did u do it?'

P: 'They have created a system in which u can't be honest & carry on like a normal citizen. U have 2 join everyone & find ways 2 challenge the unworkable & unfair laws. They themselves know that everyone is cheating. But in an ironic way this gives them more power 2 control. They love the grey areas in law. Ambiguity gives them more power 2 interfere & do favours 4 their own & solidify their own position. It helps them 4 me 2 be illegal & fearful & constantly ask 4 4giveness. That keeps me on my toes. That keeps me quiet, angry but quiet.'

S: 'What do u do with ur anger?'

P: 'I go & vote 4 another party.'

S: 'What happens 2 them, 2 the permanently powerful bureaucrats?'

P: 'They keep their positions & keep Greece the way they want; grey.'

S: 'How long does a system like this last?'

P: '4 as long as there is money, 4 as long as the money is coming from somewhere. Once the money stops coming, everything collapses. That is why we keep begging 4 money. And they tell us we have 2 carry on begging so that with the money we can continue 2 keep our national pride.'

S: 'That is ironic.'

P: 'One can be proud or one can beg, but no one can proudly beg.'

S: 'How do they still manage 2 keep us quiet?'

P: 'By giving us hope 4 the next election. As soon as the pockets of the politicians from the current government fill up, we go & vote 4 the next group 2 come & fill up.'

S: '4 how long?'

P: 'The system is working based on fear & hope. In dictatorships they r scared of losing their heads & over here we r scared of losing everything we have & not being allowed 2 go 4ward at all.'

S: 'What r ur hopes & aspirations?'

P: '2 learn 2 cheat the system better, 2 have good connections with the dictators who r ruling our lives so they have mercy on us ...'

S: 'On us? On all of us?'

P: 'On me & my family, not all of us.'

S: 'What keeps u content? How can u go on?'

P: 'The fact that we r democratic, whatever happens? & my pride is that democracy was born here.'

S: 'This democracy?'

P: 'No, I am sure it was different.'

S: 'Perfect?'

P: 'I think so. Well, it is surely better than this. A philosophy's value is in its practice. It is not an art piece 2 put on the wall. If u don't use it properly it rusts, like an engine.'

S: 'Plato, u tell me, why do u think this happened 2 us?'

P: 'This is what happens when a civilization has a proper dialogue only once every several thousand years.'

S: 'Don't flatter us so much just because I called u Plato. U have a long way 2 go.'

P: 'But I have changed so much, in a few weeks. I am a different person.'

S: 'All Greeks r different 2day. The recession …'

P: 'I know the recession has hit all of us, but only now I understand it.'

S: 'Why?'

P: 'It has hit me personally.'

S: 'U mean ur wife?'

P: 'Not just that. She is of course a cornerstone.'

S: 'That important?'

P: 'Well, she is the mother of my children.'

S: '& she is ur wife.'

P: 'Yes, but not anymore.'

S: 'Is it all over?'

P: 'Yes. What chance does she have now after what has happened?'

S: 'What chance do u have?'

P: 'I don't really want 2 talk about her.'

S: 'Does it hurt?'

P: 'No, she is not worth it.'

S: 'Why does it hurt then?'

P: 'I don't want 2 talk about it. I said the pain has hit me personally, not just her leaving. I mean the pain 4 me is not general like it is 4 everyone.'

S: 'Pain is pain. All pain is personal.'

P: 'But 4 me, it came 2 my home. It came so close. It went in2 my head, my bones, & now it has taken over all my life. This was my job. I was supposed 2 know the recession so well – dealing with people, interviewing, thinking, writing. But all this time I was looking in the wrong place. Now, the puzzle is finally being solved. Un4tunately, I don't have enough time 2 save my job.'

S: 'Just like u think u don't have enough time 2 save ur family.'

P: 'Maybe.'

S: 'Panos.'

P: 'I am Panos again?'

S: 'Ur salvation comes from where u r not expecting. It can't be any other way. If it comes from where u r expecting it 2 appear, it can't become ur salvation because u have already contaminated it with ur presumptions. U can't help but give it too much value. U can't help but 2 expect miracles from it, & this itself causes its demise. This is the misuse of ur opportunities in life. It is not optimism. It is dreaming, & it is only a desperate attempt 4 a quick way out of ur misery. But it is not real. This is how a blessing becomes a curse.'

P: '& the only way 2 shelter from the curse is 2 change.'

S: 'Or in any way progress. Go 4ward. Don't let it catch up with u.'

P: 'Progress comes only from daring 2 change, not just being content with going 4ward. Going 4ward can be an illusion. Change cannot be an illusion. It hurts. U feel it.'

S: 'Do u feel it?'

P: 'Yes. But I won't be able to change anything. I would just lose my job.'

S: 'U r worried about your job? How dare u call urself Plato?'

P: 'I didn't. You did.'

S: 'Plato went 2 jail 4 his work that he believed in. Panos, u can't hide 2 protect yourself 4 ever. U have already started changing everything around u because u have brought the change 2 urself. U r now a different person, & no 1 can take that back from u.'

P: 'A minute ago u were saying that I am incapable of changing, & now u r telling me that I have changed & am changing everything around me. How do u know what is around me? How long do these changes take?'

S: 'About a minute, if u believe in them.'

P: '& I am changing everything around me? Do u believe that? Do u know what is around me? I suppose u know a lot, and it is u who has brought this change in me. Am I supposed 2 thank u now?'

S: 'Panos, u were ready & ripe 4 this now. It is not me who brought it 2 u.'

P: 'But I guess u helped me.'

S: 'U come across people like me every day. But it was not new people u needed 2 meet. It was ur perception that needed changing. U r learning 2 look deeper, but u r still far away.'

P: 'Now I am getting more inspiration from a branch of a tree in the backyard than the glorious Plato tree.'

S: 'That is good.'

P: 'What do I do now?'

S: 'Now u r on ur own. U looked hard 2 find me.'

P: 'Yes.'

S: 'What u learn from me has no value. It is what u learn urself.'

P: 'I tried hard 2 find u. Now that I found u there must be something u can give me.'

S:'I don't know anything, & I promise if u think u know anything now, by the time u finish with me u will know nothing too.'

P: 'Then what is the point of chatting?'

S: 'The point is that u re-examine urself. U ask urself questions from the gift of confusion that I will give u.'

P: 'What is the point of being confused?'

S: 'An unexamined life leads 2 wrong knowledge, the only thing which is worse than confusion.'

P: 'Where did this come from?'

S: '4 if we don't think, we r no more than animals, simply eating, sleeping, working, & procreating.'

P: 'I have heard these b4. Where r u getting them from?'

S: 'I Googled Socrates. It is all there. If I am him I might as well use his words.'

P: 'But u r cheating. This is not urs.'

S: 'At least I used it where it helped. U knew it all along. What had u done with it so far? What had u learnt from them? Just pride?'

P: 'This is getting too philosophical 4 me. I think I will go 2 bed now.'

S: 'U can't run away. U r not free.'

P: 'R u going 2 4ce me 2 chat with u?'

S: 'No, u can't run away from philosophy, because u r Greek. U were born 2 think, examine, & re-examine.'

P: 'It is a curse from our ancients.'

S: 'U were more convincing when u blamed everything on the 4eigners.'

P: 'If the ancients knew so much, why didn't they tell us that their philosophy has a double edge? It can turn back & cut us.'

S: 'They don't owe u anything. They did everything 4 themselves, not 4 us. Curse or a blessing, it is up 2 us 2 decide. It has many edges, & it doesn't belong 2 anyone, It doesn't belong 2 the Greeks. It doesn't belong 2 others. It belongs 2 whoever can use it. The only thing that is urs is what u understand from the ancients. That is urs. Philosophy is like a knife. All u need 2 know is that it is sharp. U can use it 2 cut a melon. If u abuse it u cut ur hand or kill someone.'

P: 'Just like democracy, just like love. It needs cherishing. It needs care. It needs respect. U need 2 check it every day 2 make sure it is alive & growing. Once u take it 4 granted, once u expect it 2 be there when u need it, without preparing 4 it, it either gradually rusts without u noticing it or it vanishes all 2gether, leaving u completely stranded.'

S: 'I thought u r done with ur wife & u don't think of her anymore.'

P: 'I was talking more about democracy. It is an interesting comparison.'

S: 'Maybe she wouldn't leave u if u had 2ld her all this.'

P: 'I told u, she wasn't very politically minded. As I have said b4, democracy is like a plant. U can't let it dry out & then all of a sudden flood it. Eventually it will die. U can't water it 4 all the lost times.'

S: 'Yes, but if u have money u can go & buy a lot of fresh flowers, a lot 2 make up 4 all the times u did not, & offer them 2 her.'

P:'U can't buy the flowers u didn't give her in the past. Those flowers r dead now. They gave their life 2 other loves. They were offered 2 other people 2 keep their own loves alive. Those loves may be alive now, but the flowers r dead, & nothing can replace them.'

S: 'What does all this have 2 do with politics? U have started sounding like a woman. U have gone all soft & romantic on me.'

P: 'U r the one who turns the conversation soft and mushy. U r the one who talks like a woman.'

S: 'Don't worry about me sounding like a woman. Worry about yourself not sounding like a man.'

P: 'I am. I didn't talk romantically? Can't u see? Look at our governments all these years. They didn't pay attention 2 the tax evaders & all those who sent money abroad, the money that was supposed 2 help build Greece. All these years they let people cheat the system in any creative way they wanted, & now all of a sudden they r trying 2 make up 4 the lost time. Now they r trying 2 tax everyone. Taxes must be based on income, which is based on production. If it is anything else it brings more regression. U can't tax people on something they already have. U should help them grow & then tax them on their surplus, on their profits. U can't fish from a dried-up lake. U can't make someone pay u tax 4 their house, something they built in the past. It is like expecting someone 2 love you because of past 4gotten memories, 4 what u used 2 be not what u r 2day and what u can be 2day.'

S: 'Is that why u don't call ur wife? U think u have nothing 2 give her 2day? U think u would be only pressing her 2 love u 4 what u used 2 be?'

P: 'No, I didn't used 2 be anything b4 either.'

S: 'She must have loved something in you 2 have married u. But don't try 2 find out what it was. Obviously you don't have it now.'

P: 'U know, as I said, u haven't changed much. I thought u had matured a bit, but no. U used 2 make fun of me because of the tree and my feelings 4 my country, and now u r making fun of me because of my failed relationship with my wife. U haven't done much better either. Why r u making fun of me?'

S: 'Okay, let's stick 2 politics. I am sure I will find something there 2 make fun of u.'

P: 'I thought u liked what u were hearing.'

S: 'I also said u have a long way 2 go.'

P: 'Ask. I will do my best.'

S: 'Do u think things will improve after the election? Maybe people will trust the next government more.'

P: 'U have 2 trust the system first. If you don't trust the system, trusting the government is meaningless.'

S: 'Why do you think we can't trust the system?'

P: 'Because of the Turks.'

S: '4igners again?'

P: 'Turks weren't just 4eigners. They ruled us 4 four hundred years.'

S: 'So we can blame them 4 all our faults?'

P: 'No, just one. That is enough.'

S: 'Which one?'

P: 'They couldn't change our religion. They couldn't change our language or our culture. But they changed a fundamental thing in us: They made us 4ever feel occupied.'

S: '4ever?'

P: 'Well, we still have not changed. We still think systems, authority, laws, & regulations r bad. We feel that they r designed 2 be against us. We believe whatever comes from the top is not good 4 the society. We think someone, some authority, made it 4 their own benefit. That is why when a new law comes about, in most cultures in the world everyone tries 2 get their head around how 2 obey it and make it work. In Greece we all think of ways 2 break it, regardless of if disobeying & breaking the system helps us in any way. We also have no concept of the community. We have become so individualistic that apart from our national sport teams we only think about ourselves, our families, & our own people. The community means little. That is why when we get our hands on any sort of public funds we take as much as possible 4 ourselves, not even thinking about the community's needs 4 2morrow.'

S: 'We steal 4 ourselves. Why do you say "take"?'

P: 'It sounds better. Un4tunately, 2day is the day we did not think of, & that is why we r here. We didn't expect this day 2 come now, during our lifetime. We took whatever there was, just 4 the sake of it, even if we had 2 waste it. We took it all as if it belongs 2 someone else, just as if we were still occupied.'

S: 'U have learned a lot.'

P: 'I learned a lot from my separation. I learned how unstable everything is. I learned how every little effort we make in life makes a difference, everything we do affects something, & sooner or later u will have 2 face the consequences. I have learned that u can't hide from reality. U can't ignore pain. I have learned that politics, economics, the whole society is not like a body's wound; it does not heal by itself. If u leave it, it gets worse, every day.'

S: 'U have become a philosopher.'

P: 'Am I supposed 2 thank u?'

S: 'No, go change ur pants.'

P: 'What?'

S: 'People who instead of acting do everything only in their head usually end up finishing in their pants.'

P: 'U r the one who is supposed 2 be the philosopher. Why don't u philosophise anymore instead of just making jokes?'

S: 'The heroes in successful societies r the real big achievers who helped the society progress. The heroes in failed societies r the comics who made everyone at least laugh at their own misery & maybe question their ways.'

P: 'So u r the hero?'

S: 'Panos, u can't be the hero. U keep all this in ur head. Why don't u write these things that u say?'

P: 'My job is 2 write what people want 2 read. I have explained all this.'

S: 'Then you r the one who turns things comical, not me. U r the real comedian.'

P: 'I wasn't even that a few months ago. At least I have brought change 2 myself.'

S: 'U didn't bring it. It was 4ced upon u, & now it is time 2 help bring it 2 ur people, 2 ur society. Use the change. Don't just sit on it.'

P: 'The country is not ready 4 real change. Everyone talks about it. They may even like it a bit, only on the surface. But anything deeper is opposed fiercely. People don't want 2 go 2 the unknown.'

S: 'Unless they r also 4ced. Maybe things should get worse.'

P: 'No. Don't wish that on us.'

S: 'I don't wish it. I am Greek too. But all u r offering is a dead end. What is the solution? U can at least do ur part, as small and as insignificant as it may seem.'

P: 'I will think about it, I promise. I will use the change. I will do anything, I will talk, write, and do whatever necessary.'

S: 'How?'

P: 'Step by step. 4 now I have an article 2 write, about the survey.'

S: 'What r u going 2 write?'

P: 'U will read it in the paper. I want 2 go now. I want 2 start writing.'

S: 'Okay, Plato. Don't 4get, b honest with the people & even more importantly, with urself. Good luck.'

Chapter 17

THE SQUAWKING SOUND of the bedroom door opening made me jump. I had still not opened my eyes properly when I noticed the rushed presence of another person in the bedroom. My early-morning reward for not being able to sleep all night was to wake up to the excited and troubled image of Pavlos standing less than half a meter from my bed.

'What have you done, Panos? What have you done?'

'Nothing, what is wrong?'

'Why did you call the police?'

'How do you know?'

'Why did you call them?'

'I couldn't work; there was so much noise from the bar further up the hill.'

'It is not a bar. It is a sports club.'

'Sports club? What kind of a sports club?'

'It is a mini-golf club. Say it is a whorehouse – what is it to you?'

'They weren't playing golf at three o'clock in the morning. I was trying to work; I had to finish my article. Why is there a golf club here? Who plays golf?'

'Why don't you mind your own business?'

'It is my business; they have no right to play music so loudly at that time of the morning.'

'You shouldn't have called the police. Their whole establishment is illegal.'

'So what? If they are illegal they should be even more considerate and careful.'

'And who is now going to stop them from calling the authorities on me?'

'You own the house; you have the right to be able to sleep at nights.'

'If it is my house, I choose which rights I want to defend.'

'Who was it who said the other day: Rights are rights and they should always be defended, even if we, at times, may feel we don't need them?'

'Didn't you hear me, Panos? Don't you understand? Who is going to stop them now calling the authorities over all the illegal things I have here?'

'What illegal things?'

'What illegal things? Are you completely mad? My entrance, the balconies, the swimming pool without the permit, my garage in the back of the house, and this fucking extra room that you are sleeping in, which is not even on my housing permit plans. If they come, I am screwed.'

'So fighting for one's rights is all relative? It depends?'

'What are you talking about?'

'It all depends! Pavlos, you can stop a whole revolution with that. I like it.'

'Don't screw with me. It is too early in the morning.'

'Why are you so illegal? Why?'

'What is it to you? The important thing is that if they get into serious problems I will also get into serious problems. Do you understand?'

'You can just call the police and apologise for having called last night. Say you don't care about the noise anymore. Tell them the noise only bothers you sometimes, when you are fully legal.'

'You are crazy, not just stupid. How can I tell them I changed my mind?'

'Okay, tell them a guest had called and it won't happen again. Tell them you kicked me out.'

'That is not a bad idea, Panos, kicking you out.'

'How come as a union leader you always fight for rights, no matter what, without thinking about any consequences, and now you are so shy? Why are you scared here, in your own house? You know why? Over here, you are vulnerable because you are illegal. So are your neighbours, in their own houses, but at work …'

'Panos, it is enough.'

'At work you are the boss. You are the hero. You are not vulnerable. Nobody can kick you out. Nobody can tell you which rights to fight for.'

'Panos –'

'Nobody can remind you to think about principles, your rights, workers' rights, the proletariat, the –'

'Panos, just get out.'

'How can you defend the workers when no one is working, Pavlos? Which one of the closed factories are you going to inspect? Which unemployed worker are you going to give extra holidays to? What –'

'I will kick you out right now if you don't stop talking.'

I stopped talking and stood up. Pavlos went to the window and looked outside. Then he went to the corner of the room, pulled up a chair, and sat down. He looked like he wanted to talk but seemed uncomfortable. I waited. He stood up again and started talking: 'I have spent years trying to have good relations with my neighbours. I won't let you screw it in a month. This is my home.'

'You have not done it to have good relations. Whatever you have done has been to cover up your own ass, so they don't tell on you. You have done the same thing to your primary home, your nation.'

'You can't even manage your own life. How are you going to help the nation?'

'Can't you see, Pavlos? This is what we have done to this country. We have made a system in which one can't be straight, one can't be honest, and one can't be a good citizen. It just doesn't work. That is why we are so vulnerable. That is why we don't protest. That is why our democracy doesn't work. That is why we don't want things to change. We all live our lives like criminals on the run.'

'What are you talking about?'

I continued: 'We have no sense of a society. Instead of seeing the cause of our misery we wake up every day and feel proud and lucky for not having been caught. Every day we feel lucky, every day we feel smart, and every day we feel that we have successfully taken advantage of a weak and unjust system. And if anyone questions us on the virtue of our behaviour we claim self-assuredly that we commit all of this nonsensical crime for the sake of our children's future, and that washes off any guilt.'

'You must be on drugs. Have you memorized all this? Are you reading this off something?'

'Yes, I memorized it! I wrote it myself, for the paper.'

'It won't be published. You are wasting your time. Your survey is about democracy, not this shit.'

'I will leave. I will leave tomorrow. Let me just finish the survey. Let me send it off to Nikos. I need your computer; you can give me that much, can't you?'

'What do you think will change in your life if you write or don't write your article?'

'It is my responsibility to write it, my obligation to my job. My due to my society is not relative anymore. The truth is the truth at all times.'

'Responsibilities? Obligations? What do you know about responsibilities? You have left a whole family in the air and have come to my house under my roof; you can't even fulfil your obligations to me, to this household, let alone to your nation. What is the one thing I asked you to do for the house, the small society that you live in? I gave you the responsibility of getting some wood for the fireplace.'

'From my land?'

'I don't give a shit from where! Go and cut the trees in the forest if you have no money, like everyone else, but fulfil your own obligations before you talk big. I even told you that there is some wood in the garage. At least go and get that.'

'You mean your illegal garage.'

'You don't understand. You are lost in your own world.'

'I still trust my world more because I question. I try, I fight, inside me. In my world I am more vulnerable but more real, more human, more Greek.'

'No, you were lost as a schoolboy back then, and you are lost as an adult today. Nothing has changed.'

'I was lost as a child because I had lost my father; today I am lost because I have lost my nation. And my nation is lost because it doesn't have a father. It has no one to care for it.'

'It doesn't matter why you are lost. What matters is that you are lost, and you have taken your whole family with you …'

'Me and my family may be up in the air, but …'

'But nothing, Panos. You live on land. You have to come down to earth.'

'I see the land much better from there. When the time comes, it doesn't matter if I crash down or land safely; at least I have experienced the real thing. An unexamined life is not worth living.'

'Panos, I don't care if you finish your worthless assignment or not. I want you out by tomorrow morning.'

Pavlos left the room with the same vigour that he had entered it and abandoned me alone sitting on the bed. With my eyes focused on the shut door, my brain replayed the shutting scene several times. It was not exactly in slow motion, but each time it took a while longer. Each time there was a louder and more exaggerated shutting noise. Unconsciously, I continued to keep my eyes on the door. Now there was one fewer person in my life, one fewer person to talk to, one fewer person with whom to share the search, one fewer person to jointly examine existence. The last time Pavlos had left me in the dining room, I had felt cheated out of a conversation. I was left on the sofa, as Maria had left me, feeling that I had not been given enough chance to say everything I had to say. Today I felt abandoned again, but this time, I had said too much. I said so much without making a difference. With every word I said to Pavlos, I successfully managed to distance my thoughts from being valued.

Socrates, after all, was the only one who understood me, even at times when I was not certain about my words. Suddenly, the chat room was becoming more and more attractive. There was nothing like the triumph of a virtual world over your entire existence to show how empty your life really was.

I lay back on the bed and closed my eyes, trying to sleep again. There was too much light and too much happening around me. As if more pressure would result in my falling asleep, I shoved my fists into my eyes. I wanted to fall asleep and dream again. Maybe it would be a repeat of my last dream on the sofa in my house, with my children around, with my wife in the kitchen. The more I tried to dream, the more awake I became. Not achieving breaks you. Not having ambitions destroys you. But the worst feeling is when you realize that you can't even dream anymore because you have no more dreams.

I felt a sudden chill. My mouth was dry. I sat up again. The room was cold and lifeless. I looked out the window, trying to find my branch among all the dead wood in the garden. I stood up to see better, but the view did not change. When you lose your perspective, even going up does not help. I sat back on the edge of the bed again but did not lie down. Maybe sometimes you can't dream because you don't need to anymore.

I looked out the window again, focusing on the woods. I sensed myself moving up the hill, slowly but steadily. I was climbing up through my olive grove again, my olive grove by the sea. This time I wasn't dreaming. I was alone but not lonely. I was timid but not scared. I was out of options, but there were so many possibilities. Many possibilities were out of my control, but somehow I knew I could influence at least a few. Which ones, I didn't know, and that itself was so exciting, so beautiful. How boring it must be to be able to dictate the course of all future possibilities. I was the child in my dream again, flying over the hill and seeing everything from above, like the hawk.

When you are up there, you can't see any strings that tie you to anything. You are way above all the traps that strap you down. You are not forced to smile, because you don't see anyone face to face. You don't see eyes. No one can hear you, so you are not expected to win any argument. And if you see or sense something you don't like, you just fly away and not look back, just like in the chat room. It is all there. You see what you want. It doesn't matter if it is real or not, and if you don't like it, you just switch off.

Maybe that was why I could get along so well with Stavros. Maybe it was a good idea not to see him at all, ever. I did not owe him anything, and he did not owe me anything. It would be great to keep it that way. Reality can be painful, but it is unrealistic expectations that kill any hope of connection between two human beings.

Before I knew it, I was sitting in front of the computer again. I turned it on. It was ten thirty in the morning on a Wednesday in the middle of the winter of 2013. The weather forecast for the day was grim: a cold, cloudy day with strong possibilities of snow or showers in the late evening. I looked out the window, this time to look at the sky. It was clear and blue with no sign of any clouds. I moved the mouse to open the chat room, but at the last moment my finger froze. I did not want to chat with Stavros. What if he asked me to see the article about the survey? I had not managed to finish it, and I didn't even know what I had written the previous night. My God, Stavros was already making demands on me. He was coming out of the chat room. The chat room, suddenly, was no longer safe for me. I didn't like it. Maybe I was still not as independent as I would have liked to be. I went to check on what I had written to see if it was worth sharing with anyone. Instead of a survey I found a bunch of notes, one following the other. It read:

Nobody approves of either of the two mayors who were elected by the same people I surveyed. Everyone I asked repeatedly told me that they are both the worst mayors they have seen. A few who slightly preferred one of the mayors admitted later that they had some kind of a connection with the mayor in question or that the mayor had specifically done something for them.

A citizen should not vote for a mayor in order to get the dirt road in front of his house asphalted. Voting is a form of participation in the democratic process; it is a civil duty and a civil responsibility for the good of the society. It should not be done for payback or because of family or social connections. Democracy is not about tribalism.

My survey leads me to the understanding that we as a nation have a very limited and narrow understanding of democracy. We have concentrated so much on whom to vote for that we have lost any perception of why we vote. That is why our selection is determined by selfish and non-democratic values.

Democracy is not food; you can't eat it. It is a recipe. When we practice it, we are entering a social contract, a contract that imposes direct obligations on all of us.

Democracy is not to vote for someone to do you favours, and your obligation to your society does not end after you vote. Voting for favours strips the rightful and necessary powers of the citizen; it makes the citizen ineffective and silent in the face of injustice and turns the entire nation vulnerable to corruption and abuse. It leaves the politicians with a free hand to take advantage of a naive and weak society for their own benefits, and all this without any accountability. In this way the process of selection, the very pillar of a healthy democracy, becomes its own hurdle. Voting without due understanding also creates the false notion that one lives in a democratic society, which dampens the citizen's freedom- and justice-seeking instincts.

Democracy is not the right to complain; it is the right to make changes. Democracy is about choosing the best path for the long-term interest of the society, not using the easiest and most popular path for the elected.

Democracy is like a barrel of honey in which every citizen has the right to make a hole. If people start making big holes or multiple holes for themselves, all the honey spills on the ground, and no-one gets any. Regardless of how good or bad the mayor may be, it spills on the ground. Onto asphalt or dirt, it spills.

When we remember democracy only to promote our own interest and benefit, democracy becomes a tool and not a way of communal living. This is when, like a sharp knife that can either cut our fruit or our finger, democracy becomes a dangerous tool with which we support and maintain all the hidden dictatorial and regressive tendencies of the society.

Our parents' generation was scared of dictatorship; now we and our children should be scared of too much democracy.

When a society is sick, it dies. It doesn't matter how ancient it is and what solutions it has found in the past for itself and the world. No society can keep itself alive with past memories.

Democracy cannot be built from top to bottom. It can only start from the roots, which include not only ideological roots but day-to-day practices in trade, economics, and relationships. It can only survive and evolve on fair grounds, where a subgroup of the society is not favoured by the system and does not get more holidays, standard guaranteed pay, and protection. Yes, democracy is about sharing power. But that does not mean you give the power to a mass of bureaucrats who use it not for the benefit of the public but for themselves. This creates little dictators who share power only with fellow bureaucrats in the other department. This is how we have created the dictatorship of the unproductive paper pushers.

Democracy without social …

'Stavros has joined the chat room' was announced on my desktop. What was I going to do? He would know that I was online too. I had no choice but to send a message.

P: 'Hi, Socrates. I was just working.'

S: 'Great. Did u finish it?'

P: 'No, I didn't. I had some problems. I couldn't sleep. I couldn't concentrate. It went all wrong.'

S: 'Did u do anything?'

P: 'I got some notes. I just read them again. They're not related. He won't publish them.'

S: 'How bad are they?'

P: 'Bad. He wanted a survey, & I have written about democracy.'

S: 'How did u get there? Do u really think it is not related?'

P: 'It doesn't matter what I think. It is what he thinks.'

S: 'Everything is related 2 democracy. Don't worry, Panos. I have told u be4, the only person u can be that is of any value is urself. There is no point being someone else with great value because in the end, that is not u. Send it 2 him. If he publishes it, fine. If he doesn't, that means u don't belong there.'

P: 'That is like if u love something u must let it go, if it comes …'

S: 'That is bullshit. If u love something, at first u should let it go. If it takes too long 2 come back & u really want it, u must show that u care.'

P: 'Yes, that is true.'

S: 'Well, how badly do u want this job?'

P: 'If it was only 4 the job, I know what 2 write. The problem is that I am not myself anymore. I have learned too much 2 be able 2 carry on as normal.'

S: 'What do u think the problem is?'

P: 'I don't know. I feel as If I have awakened. Maybe I am allergic 2 reality.'

S: 'We all r. If we weren't we wouldn't believe in all these myths they tell us.'

P: 'Which myths?'

S: 'Never mind. Just send it 2 him. Send him the article.'

P: 'Just send it 2 him? Like this? It is just a bunch of notes.'

S: 'The truth does not have 2 be pretty. It has 2 remain genuine. If he likes it & appreciates it, he will ask u 2 put on the make-up 4 it. If not u will know from now.'

P: 'Shall I send it 2 u first, 2 have a look at?'

S: 'No, I want 2 read it in the paper.'

P: 'How can u be so sure?'

S: 'I know that whatever happens from now is going 2 be good. When we find ourselves, it is always good. Only then do we know exactly what we want from our life. Just send it. Ask him 2 have a look & tell u his thoughts. Do it right now. Don't think about it. Too much thinking makes us scared of our own targets in life. Thinking about actions is always more difficult than the acts themselves. Don't u agree?'

P: 'It doesn't matter anymore. I just sent it off.'

S: 'Well done, Plato. Now go in the garden & get some air.'

P: 'It is cold.'

S: 'I know. It is going 2 snow 2night. Let me know what happens. I will be around.'

P: 'U r crazy, Socrates.'

S: 'That is why we match. Bye.'

P: 'Maybe. Bye.'

I looked out again. There was no more blue sky. The snow had not waited for the evening, and it was gently coming down. I put my jacket on and walked out. As soon as I put my foot on the wet ground outside and felt the cold, I rushed back in to see if the e-mail had already gone. Maybe I would stop it and think about it a bit more.

It had gone. Socrates was right: too much thinking kept us from daring to be bold. Before reaching the computer I turned around and walked outside again. It was either gone or not. What did it matter now? I would find out soon. If it hadn't gone, I would send it again.

I started walking towards my branch. It was still early afternoon. Nikos would be at his desk now. His secretary always received his e-mails; she printed them out and then put them on his desk. He would probably see my name and put the page at the bottom of his pile to look at later. Nothing that came from me was urgent for him. I would probably hear from him when he came back to work in the evening.

With the snow coming down harder and harder, I reached the bottom of the garden. The trees were covered in snow. I could not distinguish my branch anymore, but I knew it was there, waiting for an opening to prove its powers, for its patience to pay off. Maybe I should have taken my work to him personally. Maybe I should have been there when he read it so I could defend myself.

I could not stand the cold anymore. I had one more look towards the branches and rushed back in. As soon as I had dried my head with a towel, I went to the computer and opened my e-mails. There was a response from Nikos. So quickly? I wrapped the towel around my head and opened the e-mail. It read:

Dear Panos,

I would like to thank you for your cooperation with our newspaper over the last few years and wish you luck in your future endeavours. However, at this time, we no longer require your services.

He had not bothered to invite me to the office or at least call me to give me the news. I couldn't believe it. He was not even giving me a chance to talk to him about it. All these years …

My phone started ringing. I was so sure it was him that I didn't even look at the number and answered quickly.

'Hello, Panos, have you stolen any helmets recently?' It wasn't his voice.

'Hi, what helmets? Who is this?'

'It is me, the estate agent who came to your house a couple of weeks ago.'

'Hi, you? Listen, I can't now. I am expecting a call.'

'Don't worry, I am not calling you about the house.'

'Just talk to Maria. I have nothing to do with that house.'

'I told you, I am not calling about that house.'

'What then? What do you want?'

'I am calling about another house.'

'Another house? I don't have another house.'

'I am calling about your mum's house.'

'My mum's house? What do you have to do with my mum's house?'

'Maria gave me her number.'

'Maria? My wife?'

'Are we playing that game again?'

'Look, I can't talk now. I have just lost my job. I am waiting for a phone call.'

'I thought that's why you were all selling already. I mean, I don't want to get personal. It is your life.'

'Look, you know my wife. Now you know my mum. How much more personal do you want to get? You might as well move in.'

'Move in where? I thought you didn't have a house.'

'Look, why are you getting involved with my life?'

'That is my job.'

'What do you mean, it is your job? Are you a family therapist?'

'No, I am an estate agent. I sell houses.'

'Yes, I know.'

'Then why do you ask? You always freak me out, man. I know you are a bit strange in person. I saw you with that thing on your head. But on the phone you get even worse. You completely lose it.'

I quickly took the towel off my head and looked out the window to see if he was out there.

'Are you out here?'

'Out where?'

'Here, at my friend's house?'

'Why? Is he selling?'

'You tell me.'

'How do I know if your friend is selling?'

'Then why are you here? How do you know I was wearing a towel on my head?'

'What towel? I was talking about the helmet on your head last time I saw you.'

'Oh, I see. That's better.'

'What is better? Towel is better than a helmet? Look, I can't talk to you anymore; I will go to your mum tonight and ask her to sort it out herself, without your help.' And he closed the phone without saying good=bye.

'I have finally lost my job,' I typed in my chat room box and waited. Stavros started writing immediately, but the wait was unbearable. I was waiting and waiting, as if his answer was more important than what had just happened to me. What was he going to say? Was it important? Was it going to change anything? I felt like a drowning victim struggling to grab a piece of wood to save himself. The size of the piece of wood did not matter. It did not matter if it could keep me afloat or not. I was just going through the motions to convince myself that I was doing something. Really now, what was Stavros, the philosopher Socrates, going to say? After all, it was his fault that I had thrown myself into this mess. Maybe I should tell him that. I started typing again.

P: 'U have thrown me in a mess.'

S: 'U may have lost ur job, but u have found urself.'

Obviously he had send me his message before getting my second one. So I waited. He started writing again:

S: 'I thought u already were in a mess.'

P: 'U mean with my wife? My family?'

S: 'I mean with ur life. Ur problem is not about ur personal relationships. Those are just the symptoms. Ur problem is about ur beliefs. It is about ur work. U are not allowed 2 reach ur potential, & that is what is hurting u most. Sometimes it is better not 2 know than 2 know & not be able 2 say. Whilst gazing at the ceiling, u did not believe in urself. U did not believe in being able 2 fulfil ur dreams, & yet u were expecting ur whole family 2 support u.'

P: 'I didn't take her with me. Maria was never in my dreams.'

S: 'Why?'

P: 'Maybe unconsciously I was trying 2 protect her?'

S: 'Maybe u were protecting urself from an inevitable embarrassment. What if u were her dream & u ended up destroying urself in front of her?'

P: 'What am I going 2 do now? I have just lost my job, the whole country is falling apart, & u r giving me family advice?'

S: 'Panos, ur situation is very much like our country's. You have the same dreams, the same aspirations, the same mistakes, & the same pain. U r Greece.'

P: 'Anyway, I don't want 2 talk about her.'

S: 'Okay, 4get the bitch. Take a first step 4 urself. Do u believe in what u wrote?'

P: 'What does it matter now?'

S: 'If u really believe in what u wrote, u will be all right. U will find the way 4ward with everything.'

P: 'Tell that 2 Maria. See what she says, that is, if she has time 4 u. She might be too busy with the estate agent selling everything.'

S: 'Estate agent? How do u know she is selling everything?'

P: 'She has even put my mum in2 it. She has persuaded my mum 2 sell too.'

S: 'Have u spoken 2 ur mum?'

P: 'No.'

S: 'U have cut contact with everyone. Sitting at home & making assumptions, u may be wrong. U will go crazy like this.'

P: 'I spoke a couple of weeks ago with my mum. She was fine. She was content with her life.'

S: 'Did u tell her how u r?'

P: 'Yes, we talked.'

S: 'Did u tell her u r happy with ur life?'

P: 'No.'

S: 'Then how come she gave u the impression that she was happy with her life?'

P: 'The important thing now is that thanks 2 u I have lost my job. It doesn't matter what my mum or my wife or my children think of me.'

S: 'Do u really think ur boss, ur job, has so much influence in ur life, more than anything else? Including ur country?'

P: 'What does my country have 2 do with anything?'

S: 'Ur country is the place where ur children will leave the nest.'

P: 'What nest? It is destroyed. It is broken.'

S: 'Ur country is where ur children will go out of the broken nest. Don't just think of urself. It doesn't matter if the nest is broken or not. What matters is where they go from there. Don't u believe in the future? U still have that. U still have a future. No one can take that away from u. All u have 2 do is believe in it & fight 4 it.'

P: 'I know how the future will be. I live with him 2day.'

S: 'Who, Pavlos?'

P: 'Yes, he will be our next politician; he is not going 2 be any better than the other ones.'

S: 'How do u know? Maybe u can change him. Use ur wisdom. Make him understand.'

P: 'He knows what he is doing. It is all planned.'

S: 'All planned?'

P: 'Yes, he has secured everything 4 the future, but not 4 me or 4 my children, 4 his own.'

S: 'It is not wrong 2 want the best 4 ur children, if u can afford it.'

P: 'He has campaigned 4 so many years 2 ban & devalue private education in Greece, & from the money he has made from these activities he can afford 2 send his daughter 2 a private university abroad. I can even see our distant future, his daughter.'

S: 'This is all negative. Train urself 2 influence people. If it doesn't work with him, change others.'

P: 'It was him whom I admired when we were in high school, & I hated u 4 picking on me. I admired his ways, his ideals, & hated u 4 mocking people. It is amazing that after all these years, 2day, I agree with u more than I agree with him.'

S: 'We learn all along. What is amazing is how all of a sudden we all appreciate things that we took 4 granted.'

P: 'I know. Sometimes, I think maybe my wife was right. She tried so hard 2 change me, help me stop dreaming & not 2 expect so much from our society.'

S: 'U are still talking about the past; u have glued urself 2 what is already gone. If u continue u will also be wasted, without having any impact on anything. U will be like a leaf that falls from a tree in the autumn. Nobody will notice.'

P: 'What do u want me 2 do?'

S: 'Make ur boss underst & that u believe in what u wrote. That is a good start. That is one step 4ward.'

P: '& u think that way I will get my job back?'

S: 'If u do it only 4 the job, nobody trusts that u believe in it. Do u have any confidence?'

P: 'I am not sure.'

S: 'Read what u wrote again, & see what is wrong with it.'

P: 'Shall I send it 2 u?'

S: 'I will only read it if I know u have confidence in what u wrote. Don't send me anything. Show me who u really r.'

P: 'Just wait. Let me call him. If he is there I will go there right now.'

S: 'Do whatever u have 2 do, but don't do it 4 me. Do it 4 urself.'

Still keeping the chat room open, I dialled the office phone number. Nikos's secretary answered.

'Hi, Stella. It is me, Panos. Is Nikos there?'

'Yes, wait a minute. I will put you through.'

I waited, and after a few seconds she answered again.

'He is busy now. He can't talk to you.'

'He is busy? I need to talk to him about my article. I will wait.'

'I gave it to him, Panos, a while ago. He has it. Don't worry, he will call you.'

'No he won't. I am coming there now.'

'Panos, he is leaving soon.'

'I will come in the evening.'

'He won't be here.'

'Where is he going to be?'

'He is going to an election campaign party, for a junior minister, I think.'

'Which junior minster?'

'I don't know, but there aren't many junior ministers giving a campaign party tonight.'

'Okay, thanks. Don't tell him I called, please.'

'Why?'

'If he knows I am coming, he will be prepared for it, and I won't be able to have any influence on him. Real change comes from where you are not expecting.'

'Panos, be careful. You may lose your job.'

'I already have, Stella. That's why I am not scared anymore.'

'You did? I am so sorry. I won't tell him, Panos. Don't worry. Good luck.'

'Bye.'

I got back to the chat room and typed:

P: 'He is going 2b at a junior minister's campaign party tonight. I will go there & track him down. I will tell him everything I have piled up all these years.'

There was no answer. Stavros must have gone away.

I went back to my notes and read them again. I was not happy with them, but it relaxed me. After closing the computer I lay on the bed and gazed at the ceiling for a few seconds before closing my eyes. I closed my eyes because I was exhausted and needed some energy for the night, not because I wanted to dream again. I was sick and tired of dreaming and trying to dream.

Chapter 18

S: 'FIGHT UR case but do it with respect. That works better. Make sure u wear ur suit when u go 2 find Nikos at the junior minister's campaign party. U don't want 2 stand out too much,' said the message in the chat room box.

So Stavros was supporting me in this. He wanted me to go. But given that he kept telling me: 'the frame is not important; it is the words that count. The truth is the truth', why did he want me to look good and formal? Maybe he was scared for me. Maybe he was somehow hoping that I would get my job back. Stavros had changed. He kept telling me that I had to change, but all along he was the one who needed changing and was changing. Once again I had been fooled by him. I thought he cared, but he was doing all this for himself. I knew what to do. Regardless of his intention, I would listen to him. I would wear the suit, but just as it was, with the dried-up mud. As he said, I shouldn't draw too much attention to myself.

One thing he didn't understand, one thing Maria never understood either, was that under this rubble of shattered dreams, within this melting candle of hope, under the burnt ashes of this human's soul, there was still a man holding on. My only problem was, I did not know any longer what it was that I was holding on to. But that was my problem now. Stavros and Maria did not need to know. What they did not know was that I was not going to the campaign party to get my job back; I was going to the campaign party to get my country back. Yes, I would go in a suit, as was customary, but I would go with my muddy suit. I would wear my muddy shoes. I would go with mud, the same mud that they all threw on my people. It shouldn't offend them; they must be used to it.

I didn't want to be late and waste more time. I had one last glimpse of the branches from the window and begin praying that the car would start. As soon as I got ready I rushed to the car. The windshield of the car was covered with melted snow, soft enough to be pushed away with my bare hands. More determined than ever, I got in the car and turned the switch. The car started with the first go. Maybe it worked better in the cold. There was just about enough gas to get me downtown and maybe enough to get me back. I didn't care; if I had to, I would walk there. Without pushing on the pedal, in neutral gear, I started rolling down the hill, trying to use as little gas as possible.

The streets were icy and wet, but as I got closer to the centre, they improved. The Parthenon was lit, and I could glance at it from behind the buildings and the tall trees. I tried not to lose sight of it as I drove. I didn't know whether it was me trying not to lose sight of our ancient temple or the Parthenon was watching my every move.

As I got close to the function, I started looking for a parking space. After a few minutes I gave up and abandoned the car on the pavement near the function hall where the campaign was organized. A group of well-dressed people was gathered by the entrance. They were all talking; no one was listening. They did not even notice me pushing through them trying to get in.

More well-dressed people were inside. Fewer of them were talking, but still fewer were listening. A small group of men on a platform against a wall got my attention. I recognized the back of Nikos's head and quickly walked towards them. A guy in another group noticed me and had a hard look at my suit and shoes. His intense scrutiny made the other people in his group turn around and look at me. Steadily and calmly, I continued walking towards Nikos' group. As I got close I could hear a familiar voice. It was Pavlos talking to the junior minister I had seen from afar at the Bouzouki place:

'...significant and sensitive particularities in each working circumstance that must be carefully considered. Any consequential decisions resulting from these considerations must be in the spirit of the protection of the most precious and valuable, but also vulnerable, members of the society: the working class.'

I got closer. The junior minister who was facing me noticed my descent upon them. His first reaction was to smile at me. Everyone in the group turned around to look at me, the newcomer. As soon as Nikos recognized me his smile turned to horror. At first he seemed to be able to control himself well. He continued smiling. But when he noticed Pavlos's shock at seeing me there, he lost it and opened his mouth. It was, however, the junior minister who had the first word:

'Welcome! Thank you for your support. Thank you so much, to come in this weather. How are you, my dear?'

'Thank you, I am just a little bit better than horrible.' He looked confused.

Nikos finally spoke: 'What are you doing here? I mean, what happened to you? Are you okay?'

Then he turned to the junior minister and said: 'My staff are so dedicated to their work. Rain or shine, it is their motive to cover everything and inform the public. Rain or shine, they are there.'

'Rain or shine? Thanks to all of you it is always muddy out there,' I said calmly.

The junior minister gave a cold smile, gathered himself, and said: 'That is why we are here, to bring change and hope.'

'To bring change? You are in power now. Why haven't you brought change already?' I said.

'Our power is from our people. Without people we have no power, and the power we have is to use for them.'

There was a moment of silence. I could see that Nikos and Pavlos were furious. The other people in the group were still trying to figure out who I was. A lady asked Nikos: 'Is the gentleman one of your journalists?'

Nikos quickly answered: 'He is freelance; he works for other papers too. Maybe he is on a mission from another paper today because I don't have an assignment for him now.'

The junior minister looked at me and with a fake smile said: 'My friend, tell me … sorry, what was your name? Why do you think it is all mud out there? Whose fault is it?'

Suddenly he looked away and greeted some new people who also joined our group. They started talking to each other. Nikos got closer to me and with an angry look said: 'Get out of here, now.'

'Nikos, what are you going to do if I don't? Fire me?'

'Why are you here anyway? What do you want? A job? You think you will get it back like this?'

'I don't want my job back. I want to know why I lost it.'

'Panos, you say democracy without responsibility is like a flashlight without batteries. It is only good for sunny days, when you don't even notice that it is not working. This hard recession is a blessing for Greece; otherwise we would never learn this. You write this rubbish and expect me to publish it? The recession is good for Greece?'

'For something you didn't like, you have memorized it well. I wrote this?' I said proudly.

'Yes, you.'

'That is good! I like it, I like it,' I repeated.

Pavlos entered the conversation and said: 'Good? Then go home and write for your mum. What are you doing here?'

'I am not here as a journalist. I am freelance.'

'Freelance? Freelance what?' asked Pavlos.

'A freelance Greek.'

More people arrived. The junior minister was busy welcoming everyone but could not ignore the fact that there were some curious people gathered around our group. Mostly were just observing, and a few were looking at me with disgust. He finally took a step toward us and asked Nikos: 'Is there a problem? Anything I can do?'

Nikos said: 'No, no problem. This is just a guy I owe some money to for a job he did that I didn't accept. Sorry about this. Let me pay him so he leaves.'

By this time more people had joined our circle and were trying to figure out what was going on. Nikos turned to Pavlos and said loudly: 'I don't have money on me. Could you pay this guy one hundred euros so he leaves?'

Pavlos quickly reached in his pocket for a hundred-euro note, gave it to me, and said in my ear: 'Look, now you are not owed any money. Take this and leave, and I don't mean just here. Leave, leave the house tonight.'

I took the money and gently said in his ear: 'You don't owe me anything now, but I still owe you some firewood.'

The junior minister and the whole crowed were looking at me. I walked towards him, extended my hand offering the money, and said loudly: 'Here, take it. It is my contribution to our democracy.'

He smiled and kept staring at me with a fake smile, shaking his head in refusal.

'Please take it, I insist.' I said.

'No', he said, 'Any contribution has to be registered.'

I walked to him and shoved the hundred-euro bill in the front pocket of his suit.

'It doesn't matter. I trust you,' I said.

He obviously did not know how to react. He looked at the people around us, forced himself to another fake smile, and said loudly: 'Thank you, thank you for your trust. This time it is your votes that count.'

He then whispered in my ear again: 'Thank you for your trust.'

I continued talking loudly: 'I don't have a problem with you. It is the system that I don't trust, and I don't trust that you can change it because this system is working to your benefit. It benefits you and all the people around you but not Greece.'

'Okay, okay, Panos. This is an election campaign party, not a lecture hall. You can talk to the candidate later. He is available later,' said Nikos. Then he stepped towards the junior minister, putting his hand on his shoulder, and said to him: 'You have so many people to talk to. Please feel free to go to them. We are just going to have some coffee from the table.'

'Yes, please, please, help yourself. There are some drinks too. Let me know if you need anything,' said the junior minister and started walking away.

I moved aside so he could see me and shouted: 'Do you want to know what we need now or after the election?'

He first pretended not to have heard me and continued walking. Some of the people turned their heads towards him, expecting a reaction. He must have noticed it. He stopped moving and then turned around with a smile and said: 'This is what is beautiful about our democracy. People have access to their candidates; they meet them before the election and see what their candidates believe in. God save our democracy, our secular democracy with our roots in our religion.'

I took a long breath. I didn't know whether it was worth continuing talking or not. What was I going to change anyway? What was I trying to prove? Maybe it was best to just leave before they kicked me out. Pavlos made the decision for me. He came close to me, put his hand on my shoulder, and started gently pulling me away towards the exit door, saying loudly: 'Come on, my friend, come on. You must have been on that bottle again.'

The junior minister, noticing that people were looking at him, shouted: 'No, Pavlos, no. Let the man say what he wants to say. This is what democracy is all about, and once I am elected I guarantee to keep our democracy alive.'

Resisting Pavlos's pressure on my shoulder, I stopped completely, took another long breath, and said loudly and with unexpected force: 'The ideology that is capable of saving the nation cannot be the ideology that gets votes. You have all created a system in which you get elected if you lie about people's dreams rather than say the truth about their real potentials.'

Then he said: 'Every candidate has the right to promote his ideology and speak about his commitment to his ideology; this is what you vote for. Have faith in the system and stick to what you believe. Tomorrow is not too far away. Success will come.'

'What ideology? For your own benefit? We have taken the worst parts from capitalism, communism, and socialism. We have borrowed the most suitable parts of fascism that fit us, and then we call ourselves idealists? This is not idealism; this is the betrayal of ideology,' I replied loudly.

Pavlos tried again to push me away, but I continued: 'And what secular democracy are you talking about? Instead of promoting secular democracy, you have turned our politics to a religion. You have made us believe in your ideologies as if they were a religion. Instead of having politics at the service of people, with your political parties you have made our people devotees of your narrow ideologies.'

He smiled again and started walking away, saying loudly: 'Thank you, thank you, I will address all these issues in my speech.'

I continued shouting: 'You have made the state work like a religious order. Only those who believe in it and support it and vote for you go to heaven.'

He continued walking away, so I shouted more loudly: 'In this country elections are no longer about democracy. We have an election every once in a while so that the guilt that is piling up on you, the politicians, can be put back on the public's shoulder.'

Pavlos, began to put more pressure on me pushing me away. As I turned to leave I shouted: 'We have elections not for democracy anymore but to justify the wrong and corrupt system. We give new life to it every time we vote.'

The junior minister turned around again and shouted: 'Come on, come on, have faith in the system. Have faith in the future. Have faith in what we can do.'

Then, as I was being pulled by Pavlos, he rushed away. Two more men came to Pavlos's help and gently, trying not to make a scene, pulled me out of the hall. As Pavlos pushed me out the door he said: 'I want you out of the house tonight, not tomorrow. And don't bother ever again going to Nikos. You are finished.'

As I was thrown out on the pavement, I noticed a couple of flashes of lightning. It was pouring with rain, soaking me completely wet. The mud on my suit began softening and dripping down onto the ground. I walked towards the car, looking abandoned in a corner. At first I tried to shake off some of the mud from my suit before getting in the car, but eventually I gave up and got in as I was. The engine started. Hopefully I had enough gas to get home. I hadn't driven more than hundred meters before I remembered that I did not have a home. This made me drive even faster; I wanted to move out of Pavlos's house as soon as possible. The slippery roads, the rain, and the fog all came to my rescue, helping me to not think too much. Finally, I made it to Pavlos's house. I turned the car to face the gate, making sure that if I was out of gas or if for some reason it did not start again, I could at least push it out of his property. Before going in, since I was wet anyway, I decided to walk to my snow-covered branch to say good-bye to the plant that had actually helped me during those days. The trees were covered with snow, which by now had become slush. I got closer but could not see my branch. I took another step towards the tree and finally saw it. Under the weight of the slush, my branch had broken. I looked up and scanned the tree to see if it was damaged anywhere else. It was not; there were many other branches above. Maybe my branch had given its life to the higher branches in the tree. It was the whole tree that was important, not just the branch. I walked back to the house, took my shoes off, and went in. The house was cold, not just from the temperature but from being empty of people. I turned the lights on and walked towards my room, stopping in front of the dormant fireplace. If I could not bring him wood, maybe I could at least bring the firewood he had told me was in his garage! I went back to the door, put my shoes on again, and went outside in search of the garage. It was all the way in the back of the house. I opened the heavy, thick iron door. It was dark inside, and I couldn't find the light switch. I could see a bit, though, so I walked in. On one side there were some garden tools hanging on the wall, and on the other side there were a few small pieces of firewood.

I got closer to the pile. There was not even enough wood to be worth taking it in. He would just have to go without a fire.

As I was walking out, my sleeve got caught on something and ripped, forcing an object which was hanging on the wall to fall on my foot. I screamed from pain and then bent down to see what had caused the pain. It was a chainsaw, a petrol chainsaw. I picked it up, carefully put it back on its hook, and walked out. I tried to close the garage door behind me, but my hands were too greasy. I ripped a bit of the cloth that was hanging from my sleeve and wiped my hands with it. The grease must have been from the chainsaw. Maybe I had broken it. I went inside again and picked it up. The grease was from the chain. I pulled on the pull cord to make sure it still worked. It started immediately! As I stared at the chain making its rounds, an idea came to my mind. I gently turned it off and walked out of the garage, shutting the gate behind myself with much difficulty. I held the saw carefully to make sure it did not get wet.

I left the chainsaw in my car and rushed to my room to clear away my stuff, throwing everything into the bag. I felt so close to the computer that I almost went to pick it up, forgetting for a moment that it was not even mine. I owed Stavros at least a good-bye, perhaps for the last time. Turning the computer on came to me so naturally. I went straight to the chat room and typed:

P: 'Am leaving now; I don't know when I will chat with u again, maybe never.'

He started typing.

S: 'Do u know where u r going?'

P: 'Yes, 4tunately I know.'

S: '4tunately?'

P: 'Yes, when u have 2 leave, sometimes things r so desperate that just having a destination is a luxury. Good-bye.'

Before closing, I waited for a few seconds to make sure the message got through.

S: 'Where r u going, Plato?'

P: 'I have an important thing 2 do.'

S: 'What?'

S: 'I don't want 2 tell u.'

S: 'R u scared?'

P: 'No. I have nothing left 2 be scared about.'

S: 'Don't do something stupid. Think about what u can do 4 ur country. Think about what u have 2 offer. What u can really give! Have u thought about all this?'

P: 'Look, I have a lot on my mind. I don't want 2 get in2 philosophy again. I am leaving Pavlos's house. He kicked me out. So did Nikos. So did my wife.'

S: 'Whom do u blame?'

P: 'All of them & u. U pushed me 2 be someone I couldn't handle being.'

S: 'I pushed u 2b urself. From there onwards, it is not my fault.'

P: 'Whose fault is it then?'

S: 'All I have done is make u ask urself questions about ur illogical ways, and now u r on the right path. Nothing has gone wrong.'

P: 'How do u know I am on the right path?'

S: 'I saw ur picture on the TV when u were being thrown out of the campaign party. By the way, thank u 4 listening 2 me and wearing a suit. It was muddy even be4e they threw u on the ground.'

P: 'They took pictures? I thought it was lightning.'

S: 'The lightning could have been u. Look at it the way u want.'

P: 'And u r proud of me 4 getting myself so low?'

S: 'Panos, u went 2 the party 2 find Nikos. Instead u found Plato. U should be happy.'

P: 'Is that the right path? 2 be thrown out of a campaign party?'

S: 'I don't know if that is the right path or not. What I know is that what u want 2 do now is wrong.'

P: 'How do u know it is wrong?'

S: 'Because u r not telling me. That is either because u r too scared, too unsure, too embarrassed, I don't know. Whatever it is, it can't b right.'

P: 'I am going 2 the cause of our suffering & am going 2 cut it down. We 4got the philosophy but kept the tree.'

S: 'What tree?'

P: 'I am going 2 the tree that I cried 4. It is the tree, Plato's Olive Tree, that is keeping us behind. It doesn't give olives anymore; it is too old. Instead it gives us too much pride, stopping us from going & planting new olive trees.'

S: 'U don't get the philosophy back by cutting down the tree.'

P: 'I am going 2 make use of the useless tree; I am going 2 turn it 2 fire wood 4 Pavlos, my childhood hero.'

S: A real hero is not visible. It is in our minds.

P: 'So many years ago u made fun of me 4 crying 4 the tree, & now u r trying 2 stop me going 2 cut it?'

S: 'It is not ur tree; u are not really Plato when u think like this. Go & plant new trees 4 urself & ur nation. Promote ur own ideas.'

P: 'U want me 2 go & plant new trees, now, on my own?'

S: 'What we learn from suffering & losing is that sometimes, we should not use all that we end up with 4 more destruction. U should learn 2 channel ur anger 2 productive influence.'

P: 'I tried, but I couldn't. I have 2 go now.'

S: 'Wait.'

P: 'What?'

S: 'Get help.'

P: 'Nobody cares.'

S: 'Call ur wife.'

P: 'She is the last person I would call.'

S: 'Why?'

P: 'If she cared she would have not left me. She would be next 2 me.'

S: 'She doesn't know how u r now.'

P: 'She never cared. She never agreed with anything I wrote.'

S: 'I thought u said she is not politically minded.'

P: 'She thinks she is. Maybe she is. I just don't know anymore. Politics is not just about having a strong ideology & belonging 2 a party. It is not about nagging & complaining. It is not about going & voting once every few years.'

S: 'What is it then?'

P: 'It is all that I have learned now. It is about life, everyday life, the small things side by side with the big ones (1s). It is not a right. It is not a philosophy. It is not a demand. Maybe she is even more political than me. Anyway, I don't want her 2 see me like this. Why do u care so much? R u enjoying this? I told u, I've got 2 do what I've got 2 do. Don't waste my time like this.'

S: 'U don't have 2 resort 2 violence just because u think u have no talent 2 do anything better.'

P: 'One thing worse than not having talent is 2 have it but spend ur life trying 2 kill it. I am tired; I am going 2 do what I have 2 do.'

S: 'I won't let u, even if I have 2 stop u physically.'

P: 'U r the one who led me 2 this. All u can do is talk. U have no action; u r a philosopher hiding behind his taxi. How can u stop me? Good-bye, Stavros. Good-bye.'

With that I closed the chat room and then the computer. I picked up all my stuff and had a last look at the room. There was some mud on the floor in front of the computer. I bent down, wiped it up with the sleeve of my jacket, and then slowly walked to my car. As the engine started, with a reassuring smile, I looked at the chainsaw and tapped on it. Together we were now on a mission I should have completed years ago. I should have completed this mission on the day that I realized that I was a foreigner in my own nation. I should have done it when I realized that, like myself, this county does not have a father who cares for his children, when I realized that those in power and with influence are all just your uncles who care about your cousins, who belong to a syndicate, have a government job, or are bribing their way forward. I should have acted on the day that I realized that those who cheat and hide better are ahead of the honest ones, the day that they stopped me building my dream and told me I lived in a nation where the dead are more important than the living, or the day that my illiterate father died for the love of his people, for his honesty, in the name of a future for his son and for all his children.

My phone rang. I was in no mood to talk to anyone. I was on a mission. I had to get firewood for my syndicalist friend so he would not be cold when he got back from the party. The phone kept ringing. It stopped, and then it rang again. It was only a few kilometres to the olive tree. The rain had picked up. I drove faster to get there sooner but was worried that the car might run out of gas. I reduced my speed to save on gas. The rain got harder. My windscreen wipers could not move fast enough. I reduced my speed even more. Nothing should stop me. I had another look at the gas meter. I had never seen it so low. My worst nightmare finally came true. The car started stalling and becoming sluggish. Holding on to the steering wheel tightly, I could feel the palms of my hands sweating.

There was little visibility, but I could still see the road. There was a gentle uphill in front of me. The tree was only a couple of kilometres from the spot. If I could make it to the top of the slope, I could probably just roll all the way to the tree. The car was climbing up with much difficulty, stalling and shaking. As I reached the top, it was not just the car that was shaking; my entire body was having spasms. Finally, I was at the top of the road. From here onwards, with gas or without, nothing could stop me anymore. I passed the threshold of the peak. The car became steady for a second, which worried me. Then slowly but surely, as it started descending, it gained speed. Suddenly, I heard a knock. It sounded as if something had fallen onto the car floor from the backseat. The car gained more speed with more rain gathering on the windshield. Then I heard something rolling from the back of the car and coming forward. I was going even faster by now, using the momentum. I thought it was a necessary speed. I wanted the natural forces come to help, just in case the car ran out of gas completely. The slope was longer and sharper than I had anticipated. I gently pressed on the brake pad. As if it was stuck or had something under it, the brake was completely disabled. I pressed harder, but nothing happened. The car was still gaining more speed and was getting more and more out of control. In front of me, the last things I could see between the rain drops and through the steam building on the windshield were olive trees, old olive trees with thick brown bark. One of the old olive trees was getting closer to me, closer and closer, and I could not stop the car.

Chapter 19

Sadly, it was not Plato's Olive Tree that I had crashed into. Now, I had to walk to it.

The force of the crash had squeezed the driver's door of the car, and I had to go over the chainsaw to open the passenger door. Finally, armed with the saw, I was out of the car, standing in heavy rain looking around to find my direction. It was going to be all downhill from now on. I went back to the main road and started walking; diluted blood was dripping from my forehead as I began running. The dried-up mud on my suit was absorbing the rain, and the suit was getting heavier and heavier.

Images of Elpida, Costa, Maria, my mother, and the reflection of sunshine in the sea next to my land were dancing in front of my watery eyes. I did not know if I was crying or it was just bloody rain. The tree seemed to be further than I thought. At first I tried running but then felt out of breath and completely exhausted. My feet were freezing, and my fingertips were numb. I slowed down again. Determined and focused, I carried on walking. Several cars passed by, and a few slowed down to look at me, waiting to see if I needed help. I kept walking. One car came close to me and stopped. I looked inside; it was a young woman driving it:

'Do you need some help? Can I take you somewhere?' she asked.

'No, thanks, I am too muddy; I can't get in like this.'

'Don't worry, get inside. I will take you where you are going.'

I did not know how far the tree was, so with some hesitation I got in the car, and she started driving.

'Thank you, you are very kind. Now you will have to clean the seat.'

'I have more than that to clean up. Why are you bleeding from your forehead every time I see you?' she asked calmly.

I turned around. It was the nurse. For a moment I could not talk. She turned, looked at me, and smiled. Then she put her hand on her stomach as if she had pain. I was still speechless but finally asked: 'Why do you have stomach pain whenever I see you?'

'I have a reason. What is yours?'

'Are you pregnant?'

'Yes. What is the big saw for? Are you going to shave with it?'

'I know, I have been too busy to shave lately. How many months pregnant are you?'

'Oh, it is very recent. Nobody knows.'

'Nobody? Not even the father?'

'No. Well … just the grandfather.'

'Why doesn't the father know?'

'I was going to tell him, but he did something stupid. I haven't spoken to him for a while.'

'You might lose him like this'

'I don't think so. I am in touch with his mum. I get all the news. He loves me. He is just immature.'

'Does she know?'

'I told you, nobody knows. You know what? I will tell him right now. He should know.' Then she got her phone and pressed a button.

'You didn't have a driver's license, right?'

'I still don't. Are you worried that we are going to crash? How are your potatoes by the way? Did you eat them, or they are still rolling around in your car?'

'So that is what it was.'

'What?'

'Nothing.'

Then she started talking on the phone.

'Hello? Is that you? No, I am fine. Just around. Listen, I wanted to tell you that I am pregnant. Where?. I am on the road. No, I am not going to the hospital. Your mum knows. Call her. She will tell you. Yes, your mum. It is a long story. I've got to go now, bye. Okay, I will. Don't bother. It is not necessary. Your mum said you were busy. Whatever, up to you.'

Then she closed the phone. I asked: 'Was he happy?'

'He was a bit shocked. But ...'

'But what?'

'But happy, I think. How is your son? Are you still looking for a girlfriend for him, or you were just trying to flirt with me yourself?'

'I haven't spoken to him for a long time.'

'Why? Did he do something stupid to you too?'

'No, we always get into arguments.'

'Who wins?'

'He usually does. He is the younger one.'

'If you, as the older person, won, the world would be going backwards, not forward.'

Her mind was working too fast for me. I was too exhausted to follow, but I replied: 'For me, right now, everything is going backwards.'

'You are so confused and hurt right now that you don't even know what forward and backward are anymore.'

'How do you know what I am going through?'

'I don't know. Maybe from the blood, the sweat, the suit ... no, I think it is the chainsaw that gives it away. So tell me, what is new in your life? What else have you been doing besides not shaving?'

'I thought you were just going to give me a ride to help me. What is this, an inquiry? Some sort of an interrogation?'

'I was just being polite, having a conversation; I told you my secret. Why shouldn't I know yours? Okay, fine, I won't ask anymore. You ask me something if you want.'

'Okay, fine. I don't know anything about you. All I know is that you are a nurse, you don't have a driver's license, and you are pregnant.'

'What else do you want to know?'

'Well, what is your name?'

'My name is like your daughter's name.'

'Elpida?'

'Yes.'

'How do you know my daughter's name?'

'I think you told me, last time.'

'Why would I tell you my daughter's name whilst having a heart attack?'

'It wasn't a heart attack. If it had been I wouldn't have left you. Anyway, here we are. This is where you wanted to go, right?'

She slowed down, parked by the field next to Plato's Olive Tree, and got out of her car. I grabbed the chainsaw, stepped out, and asked: 'What are you doing here?'

'I didn't ask you what you are doing here. Why are you asking me? I thought we weren't going to interrogate each other.'

'How did you know where I was going? Why are you here?'

'I am waiting for someone.'

I paused for a few seconds, looked around, and said: 'Okay, thanks for the ride.' I started walking towards the tree.

Then she shouted: 'Listen, we don't need a hero. Please don't be a hero on my account. I don't need it. Just live your life to the end and let us find our own way. I want things to get worse, to come to an end so that we can have a new start.'

I turned around to see her, but I could only hear her voice from behind the car. She continued: 'We don't need another three hundred Spartans to fight this system. We need all the Greeks, all ten million of them. Do you understand? Just wait for your pension and collect what you can every month. Go to the café and drink your coffees and play backgammon. Let the youth find their way themselves. Leave the nation on its own. It has a better chance of surviving without you.'

I pretended not to pay attention and continued walking towards the tree. The rain had stopped, but a thick fog had covered the entire area. Holding tight to the chainsaw, I reached the tree. The olive tree looked majestic and mysterious. I felt as if I were meeting an important person, some kind of a holy religious figure.

I put the chainsaw on the ground and put myself in the right position to start the motor. Suddenly, there were strong rays of light cutting through the heavy fog, glittering on the wet tree. I looked behind me. A car came closer and finally stopped by the edge of the road. It was him! It was his taxi! He had come; he had come to rescue the tree that he had insulted years back. I did not expect him to show up; I thought he was only a man of words. Maybe it was the tree that he had come for, not me. Then he distorted my vision by turning on his high beams, perhaps to see me better. Finally he got out of his taxi and started walking towards me.

The figure came closer and closer. It was obvious that he was finding it difficult to walk on the mud. The combination of the thick fog and the rays of strong lights from the taxi made it impossible for me to recognize the figure, even though it was standing only a few meters from me. By now I could see that it had long hair. He took a few more steps and got yet closer to me. It was not him at all. The figure was a woman. She took another step closer. My God, it was Maria. It was her, Maria.

Now it all made sense to me. That was why he was asking me so many questions in the chat room about Maria, about my failed marriage. They knew each other, and now he didn't even have the guts to get out of his taxi to come and face me. I swallowed my saliva, still not believing that she was standing in front of me, and said: 'Maria.'

She said angrily: 'What the hell are you doing here? Why don't you answer your phone?'

'What the hell I am doing here? Why did he bring you here? How long have you known him?'

She turned around to the taxi and waved.

'Why doesn't he get out of his taxi? Isn't he man enough to get out?' I asked.

'I told him to wait till I was sure it is you. Panos, I can't believe you actually came. Have you gone crazy?'

'Where is Elpida?'

'The older one is waiting by the road for Costa. The younger one I gave to the state.'

'You gave her to the state? What do you mean?'

Stavros backed up to the road and drove off. Maria continued: 'I listened to you; you said the ancients knew everything best and we should follow their philosophy fully, so I gave Elpida to the state to bring up. Are you happy now?'

Then she came closer to me and started wiping the blood from my forehead. I pushed her hand away angrily, but she came even closer and said: 'I left Elpida at your mum's. She is fine.'

'At my mum's? Why?'

'Did you want me to bring her here? To see you like this?'

'Where did he go? Why did he leave you here?'

'Who?'

'Stavros. Why did he leave you here?'

'There is no Stavros, Panos.'

'There is no Stavros? Who was driving the taxi, then?'

'A taxi driver.'

'A taxi driver? Then how did you know I was here?'

'Socrates told me.'

'Stop playing games with me, Maria. I have had enough. What is going on? Why are you here? How did you know?'

'I told you, Plato. I told you I would stop you, even if I have to use force.'

'You?'

'Yes, it was me. I am Socrates, the woman who has no clue about life, is not politically minded, does not care about you, and does not understand you and your dreams, remember?'

'This is not right. You tricked me. Why didn't you tell me?'

'Are you disappointed that I am not Socrates?'

'I would only be disappointed if I were really Plato.'

'As it works out, Panos, you are just an ordinary Greek. Actually, I am not too sure about the ordinary part.'

'You could have at least told me.'

'Panos, I did, but you are too stupid to understand.'

'Real change only comes from where you are not expecting. Is that why you said it?'

'Yes, that is why all these years I could not get through to you. All these years we were related, but we had no relationship. And now I am not too sure if anything has changed. You don't change, Panos. See the result? Look at yourself. After all these insults in the chat room I shouldn't have even bothered.'

'Why did you come, then?'

'You need a woman to sort you out. You are wasting yourself.'

'You feel sorry for me? I am okay, woman; I will do all right by myself.'

'Panos, shall I get a camera so you can pose with your chainsaw? Do you want to see your face?'

'I just haven't shaved for a while and had a small accident.'

'In what kind of an accident do you bleed from your forehead, cry because two parts of your suit, the sleeve and your trousers on your ass, are ripped, and then go swimming in the mud?'

'Okay, I can explain all that. Actually it happened the other way around. I first went to interview a farmer and got muddy. Then I ripped my sleeve in a dark garage, and then I had to slide over the chainsaw, but it was off.'

'Okay, Panos, I really feel much, much better now that you explained what happened,' she said sarcastically and continued, 'It is okay. I didn't like this suit anyways. We will have to get you another one in case you want to go to another campaign party. Come on, let's go.' She turned around and started walking towards the nurse's car.

'You still came here, after all those insults. Why, Maria? Why?'

She stopped, turned around, came closer to me, with her index finger wiped the blood and the rain from my lips, and started kissing me. I was too shocked to be able to prevent her, and by the time I could react it was too late. I was enjoying it. Still holding me in her arms she said: 'Because you didn't just insult me, you also showed me how much you love me.'

'When did I say I loved you? I hardly even mentioned you in the chat room.'

'Okay, okay, you didn't even mention me. I am used to this, you didn't tell me you love me for years and now that you finally showed me that you love me you are taking it back. You know what? I didn't come for you. I came for Plato. Do you want to carry on playing philosophers with me, or you prefer your Socrates with a penis? Come on, let's go. We have a lot to do?'

'No. It is not as easy as you think. There are so many things that stop me.'

'What? What is in your way? Your penis? Let's relate again, as if nothing has happened. We can start from the beginning, somewhere else.' I contemplated briefly and asked:

'Isn't this a kind of an escape?'

'Panos, what we have been doing all these years has been an escape. We have been faking progress. We have been faking knowledge. We have been faking happiness. We have been faking life. All we are doing now is going back to our origins. We will let natural forces dictate the course of our lives. We are going back to a time when we could sit under a tree and touch reality, when together we could walk into a field and have a dialogue without a mobile phone interrupting our connection, when we didn't need a chat room to trust the other side without prejudice. Today, over here, we have nothing, and we are not needed.'

'This is so utopian.'

'How do you know? You haven't tried it. We will just go and grow our food. That's just what we need. It is not utopia, believe me.'

'We Greeks made the word. We smell it from afar.'

'We Greeks also invented democracy. Unfortunately, just because you invent something doesn't mean you understand it and you know how to use it.'

'Is this what our philosophers taught us? To go and grow tomatoes in a field?'

'Panos, there is no Socrates. There is no Plato. They have gone. They have abandoned us. It is now only us. Whatever we can do we will have to do ourselves. We Greeks are now philosophically orphaned. Do you understand? We will go to the mountain and start from the beginning.'

'What? What are we going to do? I don't even have a job. I don't even ...'

'Panos, shut up. I know all this.'

'You want me back? Is that what this is all about?'

'No, actually I came here to water the trees. I'm just waiting here for the rain to stop, and then I will start watering. Look, Panos, you have done so well in the last few weeks, sorting your life out. I wasn't going to let you spoil it all like this.'

'I sorted my life out?'

'Yes, Panos. I have decided that you don't have a Greek brain like our ancestors, but you have a Greek heart. I will keep you a bit longer to see what happens.'

'After all you have done, what makes you think I will agree?'

'I said you don't have their brain. I didn't say you have no brain at all.'

'Look, Maria, I am not a bus that you can get on and get off whenever it suits you.'

'Fine, don't be a bus anymore. Let's walk together.'

'Where are we going to go?'

'We won't stay in the big city. We will sell everything, take Elpida, and go somewhere far away, in the mountains, near the sea, amongst the olive groves, by the sea caves and the chestnut forests. We will make friends with our new neighbours, the centaurs.'

'You want us to go to Pelion?'

'Yes, why not? We will go to your land on top of the hill.'

'Since when do you make all the decisions for this family?'

'You have been the one who makes all the decisions so far. Nothing has changed. I am just following my husband. You have always wanted to go to Pelion. It is your mountain. It is your dream. You can't say no now.'

'What are we going to do there?'

'You can write about all the stuff you learnt.'

'Write? My articles don't even get published in a stupid newspaper. I just lost my job. Whom do you want me to write for, my mum?'

'You just do the writing and leave it at that. Whoever wants to read it will read it.'

'This is crazy.'

'Okay, I have another idea; we will just stay here and cut ancient olive trees for firewood. What have you learned all this time, Panos?'

'From whom?'

'Do you know to whom this olive grove was dedicated?'

'No.'

'Athena, the goddess of wisdom. What have you inherited from her? What have you learned that you can share? What do you have to give? What, Panos?'

'Plato.'

'Oh, sorry, Plato. This is Socrates talking to you again, the female one. Listen, they can stop you building your hotel. They can stop you building even a house there. But nobody can stop you going there and living on the land. They can stop you from making a road or having electricity. What they can't do is put taxes on your thoughts and stop you thinking.'

'Where am I going to write? In a tent?'

'It is not where you write or on what you write. It is what you write that is important. We will write together. Come on, we can talk about these things later. You are soaking wet. Come, let's go.'

'Maria, why didn't you say all this before?'

She seemed to be struggling to give me a straight answer. The fog had disappeared, giving its place to a gentle rain. As I was waiting for an answer from her, a car came stopping near the edge of the road. The passenger door opened, and a small figure got out. It looked like a kid with long hair. She then started running towards us. Maria was still speechless, looking at me.

Then she said: 'Because I was not in your dreams before.'

'And now you are?'

'Now, it is our dream, and I will make sure I will stay in it.'

The little girl got closer. It was Elpida. Maria turned around and screamed: 'What are you doing here?'

Elpida ran towards me, jumped in my arms, and shouted back: 'The agent came! Grandma was worried for you. She asked the agent to bring us here. I wanted to see Dad.'

My mum got out of the car and started walking towards us. Maria grabbed my hand and whispered in my ear: 'And I thought this was going to be a romantic reunion.'

Elpida whispered loudly in my other ear: 'I think the agent likes Grandma.'

Maria, pulling my arm harder, said: 'Never mind, I like Bollywood movies too. Let's not make the poor woman come all the way here.' She then walked me towards the road.

'You are all wet and smelly, Dad. Put me down,' said Elpida. As soon as I put her down she grabbed my other hand and started walking with us.

'Dad, you know there is another Elpida here?'

'Yes.'

'Do you know why she came?'

'No.'

'Mum called her so she would come and stop you before you did something crazy. She has a car, you know. She can drive.'

'Yes, I know.'

'Mum had to call a taxi. She didn't want to waste time.'

'I know.'

'Dad, can I say something to you?'

'Yes, Elpida, tell me.'

'I have to say it in your ear.'

'Okay, say it,' I said, bending down towards her.

'But I can't.'

'Why not, Elpida?'

'Because you are smelly and wet.'

'I know what you mean, Elpida. I will go to Grandma, so you can talk to Dad without having to smell him,' said Maria as she walked faster ahead, leaving me and Elpida behind.

'Dad, do you wash only when you are with Mum?'

'No, Elpida, I was out working today.'

'Chopping wood?'

'No, other jobs.'

'Dad, have you cried? Your eyes are red.'

'No, it is the rain.'

'You have a little blood on your head.'

'I know. What was it you wanted to tell me?'

'Look, Dad, look over there. The big Elpida is walking with Grandma, helping her walk,' she said, pointing her finger at them. Then she continued: 'Oh yes, I wanted to tell you that Mum told me she talked to you every day to make sure you are okay.'

'I know.'

'Dad.'

'What?'

'If you and Mum fight again, now you know what you should do to make her come back to you, right?'

'What should I do?'

'You know, silly. You should do something crazy.'

I stopped and looked at her and went to kiss her. She let go of my hand and ran to my mum, shouting: 'Grandma, Grandma, don't kiss Dad. He is not romantic today.'

'Hello, Mum. How are you?' I asked my mum.

'I am a little bit better than terrible.'

'Where did you learn that?'

'From the agent,' she replied.

'I am so sorry to drag you all the way here, Mum. Let's go back to the car. Why are you walking in this mud?'

'I will have to get used to the mud, Panayoti,' said my mum.

The agent came to my mother's aid and said: 'Hi, Panos, you looked much better with the helmet on. What has happened to you?'

'What is it? Have you become part of the family now? The family is not for sale,' I said to him.

'I know, but your mum's house was for sale, and I already bought it.'

I turned to my mum and asked: 'You have sold your house? Why didn't you tell me about it?'

The agent answered: 'That is why I called you, but you didn't want to talk. Perhaps you were in one of those moods of yours.'

'Why did you sell your house, Mum?' I asked.

Instead of my mum the agent answered: 'It is not finished yet. It has a lot of problems. I am the only one she could sell it to; nobody else would buy it. It is a mess. Only I can fix it.'

'Mum, where are you going to go?'

'I am going to my village, Panayoti. I am going to Anelio. I am not for here, and nobody needs me here anymore. I want to spend the rest of my life in my mountain, where I lost my husband. I want to be with him again.'

'Mum, what are you going to do there?'

'What am I going to do there? I think I will walk up to a tree and pick an apple and eat it. If not I will spend some time looking at the cherry blossoms. I will wait for the spring. It is not too far away.'

'That is why you are going to Pelion? To look at cherry blossoms?'

'Not just that, Panayoti. There are also chestnut trees. There are walnut trees. There are wild berries. Do you remember those big mulberries you used to love? I couldn't get you off the tree. When you would finally come down, you used to be completely red. I had to soak your clothes for days. Remember? It is just like it was last month. You know, Panayoti, you can come. You can come and visit me if you want.'

'No, really, Mum, what are you going to do there? Be serious. How will you get by?'

'Panayoti, what am I doing here? You have never asked me that. Why are you asking me what I will do there? At least in Anelio I can relate to some people. I will have a neighbour to talk to, grow a tomato in my back yard, walk to the sea, and listen to the birds. It is going to be difficult, I know. I am not looking forward to the pain. I will miss all of you, but at least I will live the way I want to live and die the way I want to die.'

A taxi with tinted windows stopped at the side of the road, and this time Costa got out from the passenger door. He ran to the nurse. They hugged each other and froze. She seemed to be talking into his ear. Elpida said: 'Look, Dad, they are kissing. I think Costa has done something crazy. They weren't talking before.'

As soon as Costa saw me, he let go of the nurse and walked to us, asking: 'Dad, are you okay?'

'Yes, Costa, I am fine.'

Then he turned to Maria and said: 'I told you I would find a way to come.'

Maria said: 'It took me forever. My taxi driver got lost.'

Costa put his arm around the nurse, who had joined us, and said: 'I was lucky; my taxi driver knew the area really well. He said he had been here on a few school trips.'

The taxi driver rolled his window halfway down and shouted: 'Are you okay? Shall I go now?'

I did not wait for Costa to answer and without hesitation shouted back: 'Yes, we are all okay. Thank you, thank you.' With my eyes following him the taxi driver, completely unceremoniously, drove away into the dark.

The following day, I felt liberated and relieved the second we passed through the narrow road between the stone columns of the ancient aqueduct before the port city of Volos. We were on a short trip to Pelion to check the condition of the house where I was born. Most probably we would have to rent a place for the winter and fix my mum's house in Anelio before she could travel up there in the spring. The agent had promised to help Mum with the renovation; that was, he said, 'one of his jobs'. The adult Elpida had borrowed her father's car again and was driving us from Athens to Anelio, and the little Elpida was fast asleep sitting between me and Maria in the back. Costa was in the passenger seat with his left hand on adult Elpida's belly. The sun was out in full force.

As we were reaching the foothills of the majestic mountain, Costa made his announcement: 'Elpida and I have decided to come and live in Pelion. We want our child to be born in Anelio. If she is a girl we are not going to call her Elpida. That is the only thing we are sure about at this time.'

'What? That is great,' I said excitedly.

'I want to help you with the farm, Dad. This time I want to become a farmer. And I want you to want me to be a farmer, just a farmer.'

Then adult Elpida interrupted him and asked: 'When you grow up?'

Costa answered: 'Yes, I want to become a big farmer. With my dad we will make the best farm in Greece.'

Adult Elpida grinned at him and said: 'Don't get overexcited. You men have no patience! Go step by step. Things don't have to be the best to be good and practical. You men never change.'

I jumped in the middle of the conversation and said: 'I thought you women liked Bollywood movies. What is wrong with you? First you encourage us, then you slow us down. Typical woman! How are we going to work with you?'

Costa laughed and said: 'Don't worry, Dad. Elpida is not going to help in the farm. She is going to volunteer as a nurse at the health centre in Zagora. We are going to be a big family.'

I turned to Maria and whispered with a smile: 'That just leaves your parents. When will they join us?'

Maria answered: 'Well, they can come and visit us at Easter. Do you know how to roast a whole lamb?'

'I am sure turning the skewer will be the least of our problems,' I answered.

'We won't call them problems; we will call them challenges, part of life, real life. As Elpida said, we will take everything one by one, step by step. When you restart from zero it can't be any other way. Just concentrate on turning the skewer once we get some meat on it. Can you or not?'

'I don't know. If I can't do it, I am sure I can get some help from little Elpida.'

We both turned and looked at the sleeping Elpida. With her eyes still closed, little Elpida smiled. She was not completely asleep.

We drove on a long coastal road, passing through quaint waterfront villages, and then started ascending towards Mount Pelion. This time we passed through stone villages which seemed to have been hand painted on a massive tapestry of olive and plane trees. All along, my mind was on the big rock called The Monk, in the sea in front of my hill. I couldn't wait to get there and see it standing boldly against the winter waves of the Aegean. It did not matter at all if the hawk was there or not. What mattered was that this time I was going to climb up our hill with my entire family. This time I was not alone, and I was not scared. This time I was not going up there to beg anyone to give me a building permit or justify my ambitions or be forced to swallow my dreams. Maybe all those years ago my granddad had known that this day would come for me. Maybe he had known I would finally find my strength up on that hill.

We continued driving, passing by running creeks, sleeping apple groves, and tall pine and chestnut forests. I made sure we went through the central road of my village, Anelio. As soon as we got to the spot where my father was killed under the mud in the summer of 1975, I asked Elpida to stop the car. I got out and stood in front of the tablet baring the names of all five people who sacrificed their life by building for Greece. I made sure that I read all five names before I got back in the car and continued our journey.

It was not until we arrived at my grove that I heard on the car radio that someone had chopped down and stolen Plato's Olive Tree, allegedly for firewood. I felt sad and ashamed. I shouldn't have forgotten the chainsaw there on the previous night. But there was no time for sadness; we had a lot to do. We were going to make all our olive trees on the hill Plato's Olive Trees. And if she was going to be good to me this time, maybe I would dedicate a few of the trees to Socrates. Between us, walking up the hill we promised to remain Panos and Maria for each other – just a regular Greek couple, Panos and Maria, nothing more and nothing less.

Lightning Source UK Ltd.
Milton Keynes UK
UKOW02f1445160616

276407UK00002B/98/P